A Fool and his Money

George Barr McCutcheon

Contents

A FOOL AND HIS MONEY

BY

George Barr McCutcheon

CHAPTER I

I MAKE NO EFFORT TO DEFEND MYSELF

I AM quite sure it was my Uncle Rilas who said that I was a fool. If memory serves me well he relieved himself of that conviction in the presence of my mother—whose brother he was—at a time when I was least competent to acknowledge *his* wisdom and most arrogant in asserting my own. I was a freshman in college: a fact—or condition, perhaps,—which should serve as an excuse for both of us. I possessed another uncle, incidentally, and while I am now convinced that he must have felt as Uncle Rilas did about it, he was one of those who suffer in silence. The nearest he ever got to openly resenting me as a freshman was when he admitted, as if it were a crime, that he too had been in college and knew less when he came out than when he entered. Which was a mild way of putting it, I am sure, considering the fact that he remained there for twenty-three years as a distinguished member of the faculty.

I assume, therefore, that it was Uncle Rilas who orally convicted me, an assumption justified to some extent by putting two and two together after the poor old gentleman was laid away for his long sleep. He had been very emphatic in his belief that a fool and his money are soon parted. Up to the time of his death I had been in no way qualified to dispute this ancient theory. In theory, no doubt, I was the kind of fool he referred to, but in practice I was quite an untried novice. It is very hard for even a fool to part with something he hasn't got. True, I parted with the little I had at college with noteworthy promptness about the middle of each term, but that could hardly have been called a fair test for the adage. Not until

Uncle Rilas died and left me all of his money was I able to demonstrate that only dead men and fools part with it. The distinction lies in the capacity for enjoyment while the sensation lasts. Dead men part with it because they have to, fools because they want to.

In any event, Uncle Rilas did not leave me his money until my freshman days were far behind me, wherein lies the solace that he may have outgrown an opinion while I was going through the same process. At twenty-three I confessed that *all* freshmen were insufferable, and immediately afterward took my degree and went out into the world to convince it that seniors are by no means adolescent. Having successfully passed the age of reason, I too felt myself admirably qualified to look with scorn upon all creatures employed in the business of getting an education. There were times when I wondered how on earth I could have stooped so low as to be a freshman. I still have the disquieting fear that my uncle did not modify his opinion of me until I was thoroughly over being a senior. You will note that I do not say he changed his opinion. Modify is the word.

His original estimate of me, as a freshman, of course,—was uttered when I, at the age of eighteen, picked out my walk in life, so to speak. After considering everything, I decided to be a literary man. A novelist or a playwright, I hadn't much of a choice between the two, or perhaps a journalist. Being a journalist, of course, was preliminary; a sort of makeshift. At any rate, I was going to be a writer. My Uncle Rilas, a hard-headed customer who had read Scott as a boy and the Wall Street news as a man,—without being misled by either,—was scornful. He said that I would outgrow it, there was some consolation in that. He even admitted that when he was seventeen he wanted to be an actor. There you are, said he! I declared there was a great difference between being an actor and being a writer. Only handsome men can be actors, while I—well, by nature I was doomed to be nothing more engaging than a novelist, who doesn't have to spoil an illusion by showing himself in public.

Besides, I argued, novelists make a great deal of money, and playwrights too, for that matter. He said in reply that an ordinarily vigorous washerwoman could make more money than the average novelist, and she always had a stocking without a hole to keep it in, which was more to the point.

Now that I come to think of it, it ***was*** Uncle Rilas who oracularly prejudged me, and not Uncle John, who was by way of being a sort of literary chap himself and therefore lamentably unqualified to guide me in any course whatsoever, especially as he had all he could do to keep his own wolf at bay without encouraging mine, and who, besides teaching good English, loved it wisely and too well. I think Uncle Rilas would have held Uncle John up to me as an example,—a scarecrow, you might say,—if it hadn't been for the fact that he loved him in spite of his English. He must have loved me in spite of mine.

My mother felt in her heart that I ought to be a doctor or a preacher, but she wasn't mean: she was positive I could succeed as a writer if I set my mind to it. She was also sure that I could be President of the United States or perhaps even a Bishop. We were Episcopalian.

When I was twenty-seven my first short story appeared in a magazine of considerable weight, due to its advertising pages, but my Uncle Rilas didn't read it until I had convinced him that the honorarium amounted to three hundred dollars. Even then I was obliged to promise him a glimpse of the check when I got it. Somewhat belated, it came in the course of three or four months with a rather tart letter in which I was given to understand that it wasn't quite the thing to pester a great publishing house with queries of the kind I had been so persistent in propounding. But at last Uncle Rilas saw the check and was properly impressed. He took back what he said about the washerwoman, but gave me a little further advice concerning the stocking.

In course of time my first novel appeared. It was a love story. Uncle Rilas read the first five chapters and then skipped over to the last page. Then he began it all over again and sat up nearly all night to finish it. The next day he called it trash but invited me to have luncheon with him at the Metropolitan Club, and rather noisily introduced me to a few old cronies of his, who were not sufficiently interested in me to enquire what my name was—a trifling detail he had overlooked in presenting me as his nephew—but who *did* ask me to have a drink.

A month later, he died. He left me a fortune, which was all the more staggering in view of the circumstance that had seen me named for my Uncle John and not for him.

It was not long afterward that I made a perfect fool of myself by falling in love. It turned out very badly. I can't imagine what got into me to want to commit bigamy after I had already proclaimed myself to be irrevocably wedded to my profession. Nevertheless, I deliberately coveted the experience, and would have attained to it no doubt had it not been for the young woman in the case. She would have none of me, but with considerable independence of spirit and, I must say, noteworthy acumen, elected to wed a splendid looking young fellow who clerked in a jeweller's shop in Fifth Avenue. They had been engaged for several years, it seems, and my swollen fortune failed to disturb her sense of fidelity. Perhaps you will be interested enough in a girl who could refuse to share a fortune of something like three hundred thousand dollars—(not counting me, of course)—to let me tell you briefly who and what she was. She was my typist. That is to say, she did piece-work for me as I happened to provide substance for her active fingers to work upon when she wasn't typing law briefs in the regular sort of grind. Not only was she an able typist, but she was an exceedingly wholesome, handsome and worthy young woman. I think I came to like her with genuine resolution when I discovered that she could spell correctly and had the additional knack of uniting my stray infinitives with stubborn purposefulness, as well as the ability to administer my grammar with, tact and discretion.

Unfortunately she loved the jeweller's clerk. She tried to convince me, with a sweetness I shall never forget, that she was infinitely better suited to be a jeweller's wife than to be a weight upon the neck of a genius. Moreover, when I foolishly mentioned my snug fortune as an extra inducement, she put me smartly in my place by remarking that fortunes like wine are made in a day while really excellent jeweller's clerks are something like thirty years in the making. Which, I take it, was as much as to say that there is always room for improvement in a man. I confess I was somewhat disturbed by one of her gentlest remarks. She seemed to be repeating my Uncle Rilas, although I am quite sure she had never heard of him. She argued that the fortune might take wings and fly away, and then what would be to pay! Of course, it was perfectly clear to me, stupid as I must have been, that she preferred the jeweller's clerk to a fortune.

I was loth to lose her as a typist. The exact point where I appear to have made a fool of myself was when I first took it into my head that I could make something else of her. I not only lost a competent typist, but I lost a great deal of sleep, and had to go abroad for awhile, as men do when they find out unpleasant things about themselves in just that way.

I gave her as a wedding present a very costly and magnificent dining-room set, fondly hoping that the jeweller's clerk would experience a great deal of trouble in living up to it. At first I had thought of a Marie Antoinette bedroom set, but gave it up when I contemplated the cost.

If you will pardon me, I shall not go any further into this lamentable love affair. I submit, in extenuation, that people do not care to be regaled with the heartaches of past affairs; they are only interested in those which appear to be in the process of active development or retrogression. Suffice to say, I was terribly cut up over the way my first serious affair of the heart turned out, and tried my best to hate myself for letting it worry me. Somehow I was able to attribute the fiasco to an inborn sense of shyness that has always made me faint-hearted, dilatory and un-aggressive No doubt if I had gone about it roughshod and fiery I could have played hob with the excellent jeweller's peace of mind, to say the least, but alas! I succeeded only in approaching at a time when there was nothing left for me to do but to start him off in life with a mild handicap in the shape of a dining-room set that would not go with anything else he had in the apartment.

Still, some men, no matter how shy and procrastinating they may be—or reluctant, for that matter—are doomed to have love affairs thrust upon them, as you will perceive if you follow the course of this narrative to the bitter end.

In order that you may know me when you see me struggling through these pages, as one might struggle through a morass on a dark night, I shall take the liberty of describing myself in the best light possible under the circumstances.

I am a tallish sort of person, moderately homely, and not quite thirty-five. I am strong but not athletic. Whatever physical development I possess was acquired through the ancient and honourable game of golf and in swimming. In both of these sports I am quite proficient. My nose is rather long and inquisitive, and my chin is considered to be singularly firm for one who has no ambition to become a hero. My thatch is abundant and quite black. I understand that my eyes are green when I affect a green tie, light blue when I put on one of that delicate hue, and curiously yellow when I wear brown about my neck. Not that I really need them, but I wear nose glasses when reading: to save my eyes, of course. I sometimes wear them in public, with a very fetching and imposing black band draping across my expanse of shirt front. I find this to be most effective when sitting in a box at the theatre. My tailor is a good one. I shave myself clean with an old-fashioned razor and find it to be quite safe and tractable. My habits are considered rather good, and I sang bass in the glee club. So there you are. Not quite what you would call a lady killer, or even a lady's man, I fancy you'll say.

You will be surprised to learn, however, that secretly I am of a rather romantic, imaginative turn of mind. Since earliest childhood I have consorted with princesses and ladies of high degree,—mentally, of course,—and my bosom companions have been knights of valour and longevity. Nothing could have suited me better than to have been born in a feudal castle a few centuries ago, from which I should have sallied forth in full armour on the slightest provocation and returned in glory when there was no one left in the neighbourhood to provoke me.

Even now, as I make this astounding statement, I can't help thinking of that confounded jeweller's clerk.

At thirty-five I am still unattached and, so far as I can tell, unloved. What more

could a sensible, experienced bachelor expect than that? Unless, of course, he as-
pired to be a monk or a hermit, in which case he reasonably could be sure of himself
if not of others.

Last winter in London my mother went to a good bit of trouble to set my
cap for a lady who seemed in every way qualified to look after an only son as he
should be looked after from a mother's point of view, and I declare to you I had a
wretchedly close call of it. My poor mother, thinking it was quite settled, sailed for
America, leaving me entirely unprotected whereupon I succeeded in making my
escape. Heaven knows I had no desperate longing to visit Palestine at that particular
time, but I journeyed thither without a qualm of regret, and thereby avoided the
surrender without love or honour.

For the past year I have done little or no work. My books are few and far between, so few in fact that more than once I have felt the sting of dilettantism inflict-
ing my labours with more or less increasing sharpness. It is not for me to say that I
despise a fortune, but I am constrained to remark that I believe poverty would have
been a fairer friend to me. At any rate I now pamper myself to an unreasonable
extent. For one thing, I feel that I cannot work,—much less think,—when opposed
by distracting conditions such as women, tea, disputes over luggage, and things
of that sort. They subdue all the romantic tendencies I am so parsimonious about
wasting. My best work is done when the madding crowd is far from me. Hence I
seek out remote, obscure places when I feel the plot boiling, and grind away for
dear life with nothing to distract me save an unconquerable habit acquired very
early in life which urges me to eat three meals a day and to sleep nine hours out of
twenty-four.

A month ago, in Vienna, I felt the plot breaking out on me, very much as the
measles do, at a most inopportune time for everybody concerned, and my secretary,
more wide-awake than you'd imagine by looking at him, urged me to coddle the
muse while she was willing and not to put her off till an evil day, as frequently I am
in the habit of doing.

It was especially annoying, coming as it did, just as I was about to set off for a fortnight's motor-boat trip up the Danube with Elsie Hazzard and her stupid husband, the doctor. I compromised with myself by deciding to give them a week of my dreamy company, and then dash off to England where I could work off the story in a sequestered village I had had in mind for some time past.

The fourth day of our delectable excursion brought us to an ancient town whose name you would recall in an instant if I were fool enough to mention it, and where we were to put up for the night. On the crest of a stupendous crag overhanging the river, almost opposite the town, which isn't far from Krems, stood the venerable but unvenerated castle of that highhanded old robber baron, the first of the Rothoefens. He has been in his sarcophagus these six centuries, I am advised, but you wouldn't think so to look at the stronghold. At a glance you can almost convince yourself that he is still there, with battle-axe and broad-sword, and an inflamed eye at every window in the grim facade.

We picked up a little of its history while in the town, and the next morning crossed over to visit the place. Its antiquity was considerably enhanced by the presence of a caretaker who would never see eighty again, and whose wife was even older. Their two sons lived with them in the capacity of loafers and, as things go in these rapid times of ours, appeared to be even older and more sere than their parents.

It is a winding and tortuous road that leads up to the portals of this huge old pile, and I couldn't help thinking how stupid I have always been in execrating the spirit of progress that conceives the funicular and rack-and-pinion railroads which serve to commercialise grandeur instead of protecting it. Half way up the hill, we paused to rest, and I quite clearly remember growling that if the confounded thing belonged to me I'd build a funicular or install an elevator without delay. Poor Elsie was too fatigued to say what she ought to have said to me for suggesting and even insisting on the visit.

The next day, instead of continuing our delightful trip down the river, we three were scurrying to Saalsburg, urged by a sudden and stupendous whim on my part, and filled with a new interest in life.

I had made up my mind to buy the castle!

The Hazzards sat up with me nearly the whole of the night, trying to talk me out of the mad design, but all to no purpose. I was determined to be the sort of fool that Uncle Rilas referred to when he so frequently quoted the old adage. My only argument in reply to their entreaties was that I had to have a quiet, inspirational place in which to work and besides I was quite sure we could beat the impoverished owner down considerably in the price, whatever it might turn out to be. While the ancient caretaker admitted that it was for sale, he couldn't give me the faintest notion what it was expected to bring, except that it ought to bring more from an American than from any one else, and that he would be proud and happy to remain in my service, he and his wife and his prodigiously capable sons, either of whom if put to the test could break all the bones in a bullock without half trying. Moreover, for such strong men, they ate very little and seldom slept, they were so eager to slave in the interests of the master. We all agreed that they looked strong enough, but as they were sleeping with some intensity all the time we were there, and making dreadful noises in the courtyard, we could only infer that they were making up for at least a week of insomnia.

I had no difficulty whatever in striking a bargain with the abandoned wretch, who owned the Schloss. He seemed very eager to submit to my demand that he knock off a thousand pounds sterling, and we hunted up a notary and all the other officials necessary to the transfer of property. At the end of three days, I was the sole owner and proprietor of a feudal stronghold on the Danube, and the joyous Austrian was a little farther on his way to the dogs, a journey he had been negotiating with great ardour ever since coming into possession of an estate once valued at several millions. I am quite sure I have never seen a spendthrift with more energy than this fellow seems to have displayed in going through with his patrimony. He was on his uppers, so to speak, when I came to his rescue, solely because he couldn't find a purchaser or a tenant for the castle, try as he would. Afterwards I heard that he had offered the place to a syndicate of Jews for one-third the price I paid, but luckily for me the Hebraic instinct was not so keen as mine. They let a very good bargain get away from them. I have not told my most intimate friends what I paid for the castle, but they are all generous enough to admit that I could afford it, no matter what it cost me. Their generosity stops there, however. I have never had so many unkind things said to me in all my life as have been said about this purely personal matter.

Well, to make the story short, the Hazzards and I returned to Schloss Roth-hoefen in some haste, primarily for the purpose of inspecting it from dungeon to battlement. I forgot to mention that, being very tired after the climb up the steep, we got no further on our first visit than the great baronial hall, the dining-room and certain other impressive apartments customarily kept open for the inspection of visitors. An interesting concession on the part of the late owner (the gentleman hurrying to catch up with the dogs that had got a bit of a start on him),—may here be mentioned. He included all of the contents of the castle for the price paid, and the deed, or whatever you call it, specifically set forth that I, John Bellamy Smart, was the sole and undisputed owner of thing the castle held. This made the bargain all the more desirable, for I have never seen a more beautiful assortment of antique furniture and tapestry in Fourth Avenue than was to be found in Schloss Rothhoe-fen.

Our second and more critical survey of the lower floors of the castle revealed rather urgent necessity for extensive repairs and refurbishing, but I was not dismayed. With a blithesome disregard for expenses, I despatched Rudolph, the elder of the two sons to Linz with instructions to procure artisans who could be depended upon to undo the ravages of time to a certain extent and who might even suggest a remedy for leaks.

My friends, abhorring rheumatism and like complaints, refused to sleep over night in the drafty, almost paneless structure. They came over to see me on the ensuing day and begged me to return to Vienna with them. But, full of the project in hand, I would not be moved. With the house full of carpenters, blacksmiths, masons, locksmiths, thismiths, plumbers, plasterers, glaziers, joiners, scrub-women and chimney-sweeps, I felt that I couldn't go away and leave it without a controlling influence.

They promised to come and make me a nice short visit, however, after I'd got the castle primped up a bit: the mould off the walls of the bedrooms and the great fireplaces thoroughly cleared of obstructive swallows' nests, the beds aired and the larder stocked. Just as they were leaving, my secretary and my valet put in an appearance, having been summoned from Vienna the day before. I confess I was glad to see them. The thought of spending a second night in that limitless bed-chamber, with all manner of night-birds trying to get in at the windows, was rather disturbing, and I welcomed my retainers with open arms.

My first night had been spent in a huge old bed, carefully prepared for occupancy by Herr Schmick's frau; and the hours, which never were so dark, in trying to fathom the infinite space that reached above me to the vaulted ceiling. I knew there was a ceiling, for I had seen its beams during the daylight hours, but to save my soul I couldn't imagine anything so far away as it seemed to be after the candles had been taken away by the caretaker's wife, who had tucked me away in the bed with ample propriety and thoroughness combined.

Twice during that interminable night I thought I heard a baby crying. So it is not unreasonable to suppose that I was *more* than glad to see Poopendyke clambering up the path with his typewriter in one hand and his green baise bag in the other, followed close behind by Britton and the Gargantuan brothers bearing trunks, bags, boxes and my golf clubs.

"Whew!" said Poopenayke, dropping wearily upon my doorstep—which, by the way, happens to be a rough hewn slab some ten feet square surmounted by a portcullis that has every intention of falling down unexpectedly one of these days and creating an earth-quake. "Whew!" he repeated.

My secretary is a youngish man with thin, stooping shoulders and a habit of perpetually rubbing his knees together when he walks. I shudder to think of what would happen to them if he undertook to run. I could not resist a glance at them now.

"It is something of a climb, isn't it?" said I beamingly.

"In the name of heaven, Mr. Smart, what could have induced you to—" He got no farther than this, and to my certain knowledge this unfinished reproof was the nearest he ever came to openly convicting me of asininity.

"Make yourself at home, old fellow," said I in some haste. I felt sorry for him. "We are going to be very cosy here."

"Cosy?" murmured he, blinking as he looked up, not at me but at the frowning walls that seemed to penetrate the sky.

"I haven't explored those upper regions," I explained nervously, divining his thoughts. "We shall do it together, in a day or two."

"It looks as though it might fall down if we jostled it carelessly," he remarked, having recovered his breath.

"I am expecting masons at any minute," said I, contemplating the unstable stone crest of the northeast turret with some uneasiness. My face brightened suddenly. "That particular section of the castle is uninhabitable, I am told. It really doesn't matter if it collapses. Ah, Britton! Here you are, I see. Good morning."

Britton, a very exacting servant, looked me over critically.

"Your coat and trousers need pressing, sir," said he. "And where am I to get the hot water for shaving, sir?"

"Frau Schmick will supply anything you need, Britton," said I, happy on being able to give the information.

"It is not I as needs it, sir," said he, feeling of his smoothly shaven chin.

"Come in and have a look about the place," said I, with a magnificent sweep of my arm to counteract the feeling of utter insignificance I was experiencing at the moment. I could see that my faithful retinue held me in secret but polite disdain.

A day or two later the castle was swarming with workmen; the banging of hammers, the rasp of saws, the spattering of mortar, the crashing of stone and the fumes of charcoal crucibles extended to the remotest recesses; the tower of Babel was being reconstructed in the language of six or eight nations, and everybody was happy. I had no idea there were so many thismiths in the world. Every artisan in the town across the river seems to have felt it his duty to come over and help the men from Linz in the enterprise. There were so many of them that they were constantly getting in each other's way and quarrelling over matters of jurisdiction with even more spirit than we might expect to encounter among the labour unions at home.

Poopendyke, in great distress of mind, notified me on the fourth day of rehabilitation that the cost of labour as well as living had gone up appreciably since our installation. In fact it had doubled. He paid all of my bills, so I suppose he knew what he was talking about.

"You will be surprised to know, Mr. Smart," he said, consulting his sheets, "that scrub-women are getting more here than they do in New York City, and I am convinced that there are more scrub-women. To-day we had thirty new ones scrubbing the loggia on the gun-room floor, and they all seem to have apprentices working under them. The carpenters and plasterers were not so numerous to-day. I paid them of last night, you see. It may interest you to hear that their wages for three days amounted to nearly seven hundred dollars in our money, to say nothing of materials—and breakage."

"Breakage?" I exclaimed in surprise.

"Yes, sir, breakage. They break nearly as much as they mend. We'll—we'll go bankrupt, sir, if we're not careful."

I liked his pronoun. "Never mind," I said, "we'll soon be rid of them."

"They've got it in their heads, sir, that it will take at least a year to finish the—"

"You ten the foremen that n this job isn't finished to our satisfaction by the end of the month, I'll fire all of them," said I, wrathfully.

"That's less than three weeks off, Mr. Smart. They don't seem to be making much headway."

"Well, you *tell* 'em, just the same." And that is how I dismissed it. "Tell 'em *we've* got to go to work ourselves."

"By the way, old man Schmick and his family haven't been paid for nearly two years. They have put in a claim. The late owner assured them they'd get their money from the next—"

"Discharge them at once," said I.

"We can't get on without them," protested he. "They know the ropes, so to speak, and, what's more to the point, they know all the keys. Yesterday I was nearly two hours in getting to the kitchen for a conference with. Mrs. Schmick about the market-men. In the first place, I couldn't find the way, and in the second place all the doors are locked."

"Please send Herr Schmick to me in the—in the—" I couldn't recall the name of the administration chamber at the head of the grand staircase, so I was compelled to say: "I'll see him here."

"If we lose them *we* also are lost," was his sententious declaration. I believed him.

On the fifth day of our occupancy, Britton reported to me that he had devised a plan by which we could utilise the tremendous horse-power represented by the muscles of those lazy giants, Rudolph and Max. He suggested that we rig up a huge windlass at the top of the incline, with stout steel cables attached to a small car which could be hauled up the cliff by a hitherto wasted human energy, and as readily lowered. It sounded feasible and I instructed him to have the extraordinary railway built, but to be sure that the safety device clutches in the cog wheels were sound and trusty. It would prove to be an infinitely more graceful mode of ascending the peak than riding up on the donkeys I had been persuaded to buy, especially for Poopendyke and me, whose legs were so long that when we sat in the saddles our knees either touched our chins or were spread out so far that we resembled the Prussian coat-of-arms.

That evening, after the workmen had filed down the steep looking for all the world like an evacuating army,

I sought a few moments of peace and quiet in the small balcony outside my bedroom windows. My room was in the western wing of the castle, facing the river. The eastern wing mounted even higher than the one in which we were living, and was topped by the loftiest watch tower of them all. We had not attempted to do any work over in that section as yet, for the simple reason that Herr Schmick couldn't find the keys to the doors.

The sun was disappearing beyond the highlands and a cool, soft breeze swept up through the valley. I leaned back in a comfortable chair that Britton had selected for me, and puffed at my pipe, not quite sure that my serenity was real or assumed. This was all costing me a pretty penny. Was I, after all, parting with my money in the way prescribed for fools? Was all this splendid antiquity worth the—

My reflections terminated sharply at that critical instant and I don't believe I ever felt called upon after that to complete the inquiry.

I found myself staring as if stupefied at the white figure of a woman who stood in the topmost balcony of the eastern wing, fully revealed by the last glow of the sun and apparently as deep in dreams as I had been the instant before.

CHAPTER II

I DEFEND MY PROPERTY

FOR ten minutes I stood there staring up at her, completely bewildered and not a little shaken. My first thought had been of ghosts, but it was almost instantly dispelled by a significant action on the part of the suspected wraith. She turned to whistle over her shoulder, and to snap her fingers peremptorily, and then she stooped and picked up a rather lusty chow dog which promptly barked at me across the intervening space, having discovered me almost at once although I was many rods away and quite snugly ensconced among the shadows. The lady in white muzzled him with her hand and I could almost imagine I heard her reproving whispers. After a few minutes, she apparently forgot the dog and lifted her hand to adjust something in her hair. He again barked at me, quite ferociously for a chow. This time it was quite plain to her that he was not barking at the now shadowy moon. She peered over the stone balustrade and an instant later disappeared from view through the high, narrow window.

Vastly exercised, I set out in quest of Herr Schmick, martialing Poopendyke as I went along, realising that I would have to depend on his German, which was less halting than mine and therefore, more likely to dovetail with that of the Schmicks, neither of whom spoke German because they loved it but because they had to,— being Austrians. We found the four Schmicks in the vast kitchen, watching Britton while he pressed my trousers on an oak table so large that the castle must have been built around it.

Herr Schmick was weighted, down with the keys of the castle, which never left his possession day or night.

"Herr Schmick," said I, "will you be so good as to inform me who the dickens that woman is over in the east wing of the castle?"

"Woman, mein herr?" He almost dropped his keys. His big sons said something to each other that I couldn't quite catch, but it sounded very much like "der duyvil."

"A woman in a white dress,—with a dog."

"A dog?" he cried. "But, mein herr, dogs are not permitted to be in the castle."

"Who is she? How did she get there?"

"Heaven defend us, sir! It must have been the ghost of—"

"Ghost, your granny!" I cried, relapsing into English. "Please don't beat about the bush, Mr. Schmick. She's over there in the unused wing, which I haven't been allowed to penetrate in spite of the fact that it belongs to me. You say you can't find the keys to that side of the castle. Will you explain how it is that it is open to strange women and—and dogs?"

"You must be mistaken, mein herr," he whined abjectly. "She cannot be there. She—Ah, I have it! It may have been my wife. Gretel! Have you been in the east—"

"Nonsense!" I cried sharply. "This won't do, Mr. Schmick. Give me that bunch of keys. We'll investigate. I can't have strange women gallivanting about the place as if they owned it. This is no trysting place for Juliets, Herr Schmick. We'll get to the bottom of this at once. Here, you Rudolph, fetch a couple of lanterns. Max, get a sledge or two from the forge. There *is* a forge. I saw it yesterday out there back of the stables. So don't try to tell me there isn't one. If we can't unlock the doors, we'll smash 'em in. They're mine, and I'll knock 'em to smithereens if I feel like it."

The four Schmicks wrung their hands and shook their heads and, then, repairing to the scullery, growled and grumbled for fully ten minutes before deciding to obey my commands. In the meantime, I related my experience to Poopendyke and Britton.

"That reminds me, sir," said Britton, "that I found a rag-doll in the courtyard yesterday, on that side of the building, sir—I should say castle, sir."

"I am quite sure I heard a baby crying the second night we were here, Mr. Smart," said my secretary nervously.

"And there was smoke coming from one of the back chimney pots this morning," added Britton.

I was thoughtful for a moment. "What became of the rag-doll, Britton?" I enquired shrewdly.

"I turned it over to old Schmick, sir," said he. He grinned. "I thought as maybe it belonged to one of his boys."

On the aged caretaker's reappearance, I bluntly inquired what had become of the doll-baby. He was terribly confused.

"I know nothing, I know nothing," he mumbled, and I could see that he was miserably upset. His sons towered and glowered and his wife wrapped and unwrapped her hands in her apron, all the time supplicating heaven to be good to the true and the faithful.

From what I could gather, they all seemed to be more disturbed over the fact that my hallucination included a dog than by the claim that I had seen a woman.

"But, confound you, Schmick," I cried in some heat, "it barked at me."

"Gott in himmel! they all cried, and, to my surprise, the old woman burst into tears.

"It is bad to dream of a dog," she wailed. "It means evil to all of us. Evil to—"

"Come!" said I, grabbing the keys from the old man's unresisting hand. "And, Schmick, if that dog bites me, I'll hold, you personally responsible. Do you under-stand?"

Two abreast we filed through the long, vaulted halls, Rudolph carrying a gigan-tic lantern and Max a sledge. We traversed extensive corridors, mounted tortuous stairs and came at length to the sturdy oak door that separated the east wing from the west: a huge, formidable tiling strengthened by many cross-pieces and studded with rusty bolt-heads. Padlocks as large as horse-shoes, corroded by rust and ren-dered absolutely impracticable by age, confronted us.

"I have not the keys," said old Conrad Schmick sourly. "This door has not been opened in my time. It is no use."

"It is no use," repeated his grizzly sons, leaning against the mouldy walls with weary tolerance.

"Then how did the woman and her dog get into that part of the castle?" I de-manded. "Tell me that!"

They shook their heads, almost compassionately, as much as to say. "It is al-ways best to humour a mad man."

"And the baby," added Poopendyke, turning up his coat collar to protect his thin neck from the draft that smote us from the halls.

"Smash those padlocks, Max," I commanded resolutely.

Max looked stupidly at his father and the old man looked at his wife, and then all four of them looked at me, almost imploringly.

"Why destroy a perfectly good padlock, mein herr?" began Max, twirling the sledge in his hand as if it were a bamboo cane.

"Hi! look out there!" gasped Britton, in some alarm. "Don't let that tiling slip!"

"Doesn't this castle belong to me?" I demanded, considerably impressed by the ease with which he swung the sledge. A very dangerous person, I began to perceive.

"It does, mein herr," shouted all of them gladly, and touched their forelocks.

"Everything is yours," added old Conrad, with a comprehensive sweep of his hand that might have put the whole universe in my name.

"Smash that padlock, Max," I said after a second's hesitation.

"I'll bet he can't do it," said Britton, ingeniously.

Very reluctantly Max bared his great arms, spit upon his hands, and, with a pitiful look at his parents, prepared to deal the first blow upon the ancient padlock. The old couple turned their heads away, and put their fingers to their ears, cringing like things about to be whipped.

"Now, one—two—three!" cried I, affecting an enthusiasm I didn't feel.

The sledge fell upon the padlock and rebounded with almost equal force. The sound of the crash must have disturbed every bird and bat in the towers of the grim old pile. But the padlock merely shed a few scabs of rust and rattled back into its customary repose.

"See!" cried Max, triumphantly. "It cannot be broken." Rudolph, his broad face beaming, held the lantern close to the padlock and showed me that it hadn't been dented by the blow.

"It is a very fine lock," cried old Conrad, with a note of pride in his voice.

I began to feel some pride in the thing myself. "It is, indeed," I said. Try once more, Max."

It seemed to me that he struck with a great deal more confidence than before, and again they all uttered ejaculations of pleasure. I caught Dame Schmick in the act of thanking God with her fingers.

"See here," I exclaimed, facing them angrily, "what does all this mean? You are deceiving me, all of you. Now, let's have the truth—every word of it—or out you go to-morrow, the whole lot of you. I insist on knowing who that woman is, why she is here in my hou—my castle, and—everything, do you understand?"

Apparently they didn't understand, for they looked at me with all the stupidity they could command.

"You try, Mr. I Poopendyke," I said, giving it up in despair. He sought to improve on my German, but I think he made it worse. They positively refused to be intelligent.

"Give me the hammer," I said at last in desperation. Max surrendered the clumsy, old-fashioned instrument with a grin and I motioned for them all to stand back. Three successive blows with all the might I had in my body failed to shatter the lock, whereupon my choler rose to heights hitherto unknown, I being a very mild-mannered, placid person and averse to anything savouring of the tempestuous. I delivered a savage and resounding thwack upon the broad oak panel of the door, regardless of the destructiveness that might attend the effort. If any one had told me that I couldn't splinter an oak board with a sledge-hammer at a single blow I should have laughed in his face. But as it turned out in this case I not only failed to split the panel but broke off the sledge handle near the head, putting it wholly out of commission for the time being as well as stinging my hands so severely that I doubled up with pain and shouted words that Dame Schmick could not put into her prayers.

The Schmicks fairly glowed with joy! Afterwards Max informed me that the door was nearly six inches thick and often had withstood the assaults of huge battering rams, back in the dim past when occasion induced the primal baron to seek safety in the east wing, which, after all, appears to have been the real, simon pure fortress. The west wing was merely a setting for festal amenities and was by no means feudal in its aspect or appeal. Here, as I came to know, the old barons received their friends and feasted them and made merry with the flagon and the horn of plenty; here the humble tithe payer came to settle his dues with gold and silver instead of with blood; here the little barons and baronesses romped and rioted with childish glee; and here the barons grew fat and gross and soggy with laziness and prosperity, and here they died in stupid quiescence. On the other side of that grim, staunch old door they simply went to the other extreme in every particular. There they killed their captives, butchered their enemies, and sometimes died with the daggers of traitors in their shivering backs.

As we trudged back to the lower halls, defeated but none the less impressed by our failure to devastate our stronghold, I was struck by the awful barrenness of the surroundings. There suddenly came over me the shocking realisation: the "contents" of the castle, as set forth rather vaguely in the bill of sale, were not what I had been led to consider them. It had not occurred to me at the time of the transaction to insist upon an inventory, and I had been too busy since the beginning of my tenancy to take more than a passing account of my belongings. In excusing myself for this rather careless oversight, I can only say that during daylight hours the castle was so completely stuffed with workmen and their queer utensils that I couldn't do much in the way of elimination, and by night it was so horribly black and lonesome about the place and the halls were so littered with tools and mops and timber that it was extremely hazardous to go prowling about, so I preferred to remain in my own quarters, which were quite comfortable and cosy in spite of the distance between points of convenience.

Still I was vaguely certain that many articles I had seen about the halls on my first and second visits were no longer in evidence. To or three antique rugs, for instance, were missing from the main hall, and there was a lamentable suggestion of emptiness at the lower end where we had stacked a quantity of rare old furniture in order to make room for the workmen.

"Herr Schmick," said I, abruptly halting my party in the centre of the hall, "what has become of the rugs that were here last week, and where is that pile of furniture we had back youder?"

Rudolph allowed the lantern to swing behind his huge legs, intentionally I believe, and I was compelled to relieve him of it in order that we might extract ourselves from his shadow. I have never seen such a colossal shadow as the one he cast.

Old Conrad was not slow in answering.

"The gentlemen called day before yesterday, mein herr, and took much away. They will return to-morrow for the remainder."

"Gentlemen?" I gasped. "Remainder?"

"The gentlemen to whom the Herr Count sold the rugs and chairs and chests and—"

"What!" I roared. Even Poopendyke jumped at this sudden exhibition of wrath. "Do you mean to tell me that these things have been sold and carried away without my knowledge or consent? I'll have the law—"

Herr Poopendyke intervened. "They had bills of sale and orders for removal of property dated several weeks prior to your purchase, Mr. Smart. We had to let the articles go. You surely remember my speaking to you about it."

"I don't remember anything," I snapped, which was the truth. "Why—why, I bought everything that the castle contained. This is robbery! What the dickens do you mean by—"

Old Conrad held up his hands as if expecting to pacify me. I sputtered out the rest of the sentence, which really amounted to nothing.

"The Count has been selling off the lovely old pieces for the past six months, sir. Ach, what a sin! They have come here day after day, these furniture buyers, to take away the most priceless of our treasures, to sell them to the poor rich at twenty prices. I could weep over the sacrifices. I have wept, haven't I, Gretel? Eh, Rudolph? Buckets of tears have I shed, mein herr. Oceans of them. Time after time have I implored him to deny these rascally curio hunters, these blood-sucking—"

"But listen to me," I broke in. "Do you mean to say that articles have been taken away from the castle since I came into possession?"

"Many of them, sir. Always with proper credentials, believe me. Ach, what a spendthrift he is! And his poor wife! Ach, Gott, how she must suffer. Nearly an of the grand paintings, the tapestries that came from France and Italy hundreds of years ago, the wonderful old bedsteads and tables that were here when the castle was new—all gone! And for mere songs, mein herr,—the cheapest of songs! I—I—"

"Please don't weep now, Herr Schmick," I made haste to exclaim, seeing lachrymose symptoms in his blear old eyes. Then I became firm once more. This knavery must cease, or I'd know the reason why. "The next man who comes here to cart away so much as a single piece is to be kicked out. Do you understand? These things belong to me. Kick him into the river. Or, better still, notify me and I'll do it. Why, if this goes on we'll soon be deprived of anything to sit on or sleep in or eat from! Lock the doors, Conrad, and don't admit any one without first consulting me. By Jove, I'd like to wring that rascal's neck. A Count! Umph!"

"Ach, he is of the noblest family in all the land," sighed old Gretel. "His grand-father was a fine man." I contrived to subdue my rage and disappointment and somewhat loudly returned to the topic from which we were drifting.

"As for those beastly padlocks, I shall have them filed off to-morrow. I give you warning, Conrad, if the keys are not forthcoming before noon to-morrow, I'll file 'em off, so help me."

"They are yours to destroy, mein herr, God knows," said he dismally. "It is a pity to destroy fine old padlocks—"

"Well, you wait and see," said I, grimly.

His face beamed once more. Ach, I forgot to say that there are padlocks on the *other* side of the door, just as on this side. It will be of no use to destroy these. The door still could not be forced. Mein Gott! How thankful I am to have remembered it in time."

"Confound you, Schmick, I believe you actually want to keep me out of that part of the castle," I exploded.

The four of them protested manfully, even Gretel.

"I have a plan, sir," said Britton. "Why not place a tall ladder in the courtyard and crawl in through one of the windows?"

"Splendid! That's what we'll do!" I cried enthusiastically. "And now let's go to bed! We will breakfast at eight, Mrs. Schmick. The early bird catches the worm, you Know."

"Will you see the American ladies and gentlemen who are coming to-morrow to pick out the—"

"Yes, I'll see them," said I, compressing my lips. "Don't let me over-sleep, Britton."

"I shan't, sir," said he.

Sleep evaded me for hours. What with the possible proximity of an undesirable feminine neighbour, mysterious and elusive though she may prove to be, and the additional dread of dogs and babies, to say nothing of the amazing delinquencies to be laid to the late owner of the place, and the prospect of a visit from coarse and unfeeling bargain-hunters on the morrow, it is really not surprising that I tossed about in my baronial bed, counting sheep backwards and forwards over hedges and fences until the vociferous cocks in the stable yard began to send up their clarion howdy-dos to the sun. Strangely enough, with the first peep of day through the decrepit window shutters I fell into a sound sleep. Britton got nothing but grunts from me until half-past nine. At that hour he came into my room and delivered news that aroused me more effectually than all the alarm clocks or alarm cocks in the world could have done.

"Get up, sir, if you please," he repeated the third time. "The party of Americans is below, sir, rummaging about the place. They have ordered the workmen to stop work, sir, complaining of the beastly noise they make, and the dust and all that, sir. They have already selected half a dozen pieces and they have brought enough porters and carriers over in the boats to take the stuff away in—"

"Where is Poopendyke? I cried, leaping out of bed. "I don't want to be shaved, Britton, and don't bother about the tub." He had filled my twentieth century portable tub, recently acquired, and was nervously creating a lather in my shaving mug.

"You look very rough, sir."

"So much the better."

"Mr. Poopendyke is in despair, sir. He has tried to explain that nothing is for sale, but the gentlemen say they are onto his game. They go right on yanking things about and putting their own prices on them and reserving them. They are perfectly delighted, sir, to have found so many old things they really want for their new house."

"I'll—I'll put a stop to all this," I grated, seeing red for an instant.

"And the ladies, sir! There are three of them, all from New York City, and they keep on saying they are completely ravished, sir,—with joy, I take it. Your great sideboard in the dining-room is to go to Mrs. Riley-Werkheimer, and the hall-seat that the first Baron used to throw his armour on when he came in from—" Your great sideboard in the dining-room is to go to Mrs. Riley-Werkheimer, and the hall-seat that the first Baron used to throw his armour on when he came in from—"

"Great snakes!" I roared. "They haven't moved it, have they? It will fall to pieces!"

"No, sir. They are piling sconces and candelabra and andirons on it, regard-less of what Mr. Poopendyke says. You'd better hurry, sir. Here is your collar and necktie—"

"I don't want 'em. Where the dickens are my trousers?"

His face fell. "Being pressed, sir, God forgive me!"

"Get out another pair, confound you, Britton. What are we coming to?"

He began rummaging in the huge clothespress, all the while regaling me with news from the regions below.

"Mr. Poopendyke has gone up to his room, sir, with his typewriter. The young lady insisted on having it. She squealed with joy at seeing an antique typewriter and he—he had to run away with it, 'pon my soul he did, sir."

I couldn't help laughing.

"And your golf clubs, Mr. Smart. The young gentleman of the party is perfectly carried away with them. He says they're the real thing, the genuine sixteenth century article. They *are* a bit rusted, you'll remember. I left him out in the courtyard trying your brassie and mid-iron, sir, endeavouring to loft potatoes over the south wall. I succeeded, in hiding the balls, sir. Just as I started upstairs I heard one of the new window panes in the banquet hall smash, sir, so I take it he must have sliced his drive a bit."

"Who let these people in?" I demanded in smothered tones from the depths of a sweater I was getting into in order to gain time by omitting a collar.

"They came in with the plumbers, sir, at half-past eight. Old man Schmick tried to keep them out, but they said they didn't understand German and walked right by, leaving their donkeys in the roadway outside."

"Couldn't Rudolph and Max stop them?" I cried, as my head emerged.

"They were still in bed, sir. I think they're at breakfast now."

"Good lord!" I groaned, looking at my watch. "Nine-thirty! What sort of a rest cure am I conducting here?"

We hurried downstairs so fast that I lost one of my bedroom slippers. It went clattering on ahead of us, making a shameful racket on the bare stones, but Britton caught it up in time to save it from the clutches of the curio-vandals. My workmen were lolling about the place, smoking vile pipes and talking in guttural whispers. All operations appeared to have ceased in my establishment at the command of the far from idle rich. Two portly gentlemen in fedoras were standing in the middle of the great hall, discussing the merits of a dingy old spinet that had been carried out of the music room by two lusty porters from the hotel. From somewhere in the direction of the room where the porcelains and earthenware were stored came the shrill, excited voices of women. The aged Schmicks were sitting side by side on a window ledge, with the rigid reticence of wax figures.

As I came up, I heard one of the strangers say to the other:

"Well, if you don't want it, I'll take it. My wife says it can be made into a writing desk with a little—"

"I beg your pardon, gentlemen," said I confronting them. "Will you be good enough to explain this intrusion?"

They stared at me as if I were a servant asking for higher wages. The speaker, a fat man with a bristly moustache and a red necktie, drew himself up haughtily.

"Who the devil are you?" he demanded, fixing me with a glare.

I knew at once that he was the kind of an American I have come to hate with a zest that knows no moderation; the kind that makes one ashamed of the national melting pot. I glared back at him.

"I happen to be the owner of this place, and you'll oblige me by clearing out."

"What's that? Here, here, none of that sort of talk, my friend. We're here to look over your stuff, and we mean business, but you won't get anywhere by talking like—"

"There is nothing for sale here," I said shortly. "And you've got a lot of nerve to come bolting into a private house—"

"Say," said the second man, advancing with a most insulting scowl, "we'll understand each other right off the reel, my friend. All you've got to do is to answer us when we ask for prices. Now, bear that in mind, and don't try any of your high-and-mighty tactics on us."

"Just remember that you're a junk-dealer and we'll get along splendidly," said the other, in a tone meant to crush me. "What do you ask for this thing?" tapping the dusty spinet with his walking-stick.

It suddenly occurred to me that the situation was humorous.

"You will have to produce your references, gentlemen, before I can discuss anything with you," I said, after swallowing very hard. (It must have been my pride.)

They stared. "Good Lord!" gasped the bristly one, blinking his eyes. "Don't you know who this gentleman is? You—you appear to be an American. You **must** know Mr. Riley-Werkheimer of New York."

"I regret to say that I have never heard of Mr. Riley-Werkheimer. I did not know that Mrs. Riley-Werkheimer's husband was living. And may I ask who **you** are?"

"Oh, I am also a nobody," said he, with a wink at his purple-jowled companion. "I am only poor old Rocksworth, the president of the—"

"Oh, don't say anything more, Mr. Rocksworth," I cried. "I have heard of you. This fine old spinet? Well, it has been reduced in price. Ten thousand dollars, Mr. Rocksworth."

"Ten thousand nothing! I'll take it at seventy-five dollars. And now let's talk about this here hall-seat. My wife thinks it's a fake. What is its history, and what sort of guarantee can you—"

"A fake!" I cried in dismay. "My dear Mr. Rocksworth, that is the very hall-seat that Pontius Pilate sat in when waiting for an audience with the first of the great Teutonic barons. The treaty between the Romans and the Teutons was signed on that table over there,—the one you have so judiciously selected, I perceive. Of course, you know that *this* was the Saxon seat of government. Charlemagne lived here with all his court."

They tried not to look impressed, but rather over-did it.

"That's the sort of a story you fellows always put up, you skinflints from Boston. I'll bet my head you *are* from Boston," said Mr. Rocksworth shrewdly.

"I couldn't afford to have you lose your head, Mr. Rocksworth, so I shan't take you on," said I merrily.

"Don't get fresh now," said he stiffly.

Mr. Riley-Werkheimer walked past me to take a closer look at the seat, almost treading on my toes rather than to give an inch to me.

"How can you prove that it's the genuine article?" he demanded curtly.

"You have my word for it, sir," I said quietly.

"Pish tush!" said he.

Mr. Rocksworth turned in the direction of the banquet hall.

"Carrie!" he shouted. "Come here a minute, will you?"

"Don't shout like that, Orson," came back from the porcelain closet. "You almost made me drop this thing."

"Well, drop it, and come on. This is important."

I wiped the moisture from my brow and respectfully put my clenched fists into my pockets.

A minute later, three females appeared on the scene, all of them dusting their hands and curling their noses in disgust.

"I never saw such a dirty place, said the foremost, a large lady who couldn't, by any circumstance of fate, have been anybody's wife but Rocksworth's. "It's filthy! What do you want? "

"I've bought this thing here for seventy-five. You said I couldn't get it for a nickle under a thousand. And say, this man tells me the hall seat here belonged to Pontius Pilate in—"

"Pardon me," I interrupted, "I merely said that he sat in it. I am not trying to deceive you, sir."

"And the treaty was signed on this table," said Mr. Riley-Werkheimer. He addressed himself to a plump young lady with a distorted bust and a twenty-two inch waist. "Maude, what do you know about the Roman-Teutonic treaty? We'll catch you now, my friend," he went on, turning to me. "My daughter is up in ancient history. She's an authority."

Miss Maude appeared to be racking her brain. I undertook to assist her.

"I mean the second treaty, after the fall of Nuremburg," I explained.

"Oh," she said, instantly relieved. "Was it *really* signed here, right here in this hall? Oh, Father! We *must* have that table."

"You are sure there *was* a treaty, Maude?" demanded her parent accusingly.

"Certainly," she cried. "The Teutons ceded Alsace-Lorraine to—"

"Pardon me once more," I cried, and this time I plead guilty to a blush, "you are thinking of the other treaty—the one at Metz, Miss Riley-Werkheimer. This, as you will recall, ante-dates that one by—oh, several years."

"Thank you," she said, quite condescendingly. "I was confused for a moment. Of course, Father, I can't say that it was signed here or on this table as the young man says. I only know that there was a treaty. I *do* wish you'd come and see the fire-screen I've found—"

"Let's get this out of our system first," said her father. "If you can show me statistics and the proper proof that this is the genuine table, young man, I'll—"

"Pray rest easy, sir," I said. "We can take it up later on. The facts are—"

"And this Pontius Pilate seat," interrupted Rocksworth, biting off the end of a fresh cigar. "What about it? Got a match?"

"Get the gentleman a match, Britton," I said, thereby giving my valet an opportunity to do his exploding in the pantry. "I can only affirm, sir, that it is common history that Pontius Pilate spent a portion of his exile here in the sixth century. It is reasonable to assume that he sat in this seat, being an old man unused to difficult stairways. He—"

"Buy it, Orson," said his wife, with authority. "We'll take a chance on it. If it isn't the right thing, we can sell it to the second-hand dealers. What's the price?"

"A thousand dollars to you, madam," said I.

They were at once suspicious. While they were busily engaged in looking the seat over as the porters shifted it about at all angles, I stepped over and ordered my workmen to resume their operations. I was beginning to get sour and angry again, having missed my coffee. From the culinary regions there ascended a most horrific odour of fried onions. If there is one thing I really resent it is a fried onion.

I do not know why I should have felt the way I did about it on this occasion, but I am mean enough now "to confess that I hailed the triumphal entry of that pernicious odour with a meanness of spirit that leaves nothing to b explained.

"Good gracious!" gasped the aristocratic Mrs. Riley-Werkheimer, holding her nose. "Do you smell *that*?"

"Onions! My Gawd!" sniffed Maude. "How I hate 'em!"

Mr. Rocksworth forgot his dignity. "Hate 'em?" he cried, his eyes rolling. "I just love 'em!"

"Orson!" said his wife, transfixing him with a glare. "*What* will people trunk of you?"

"I like 'em too," admitted Mr. Riley-Werkheimer, perceiving at once whom she meant by "people." He putted out his chest.

At that instant the carpenters, plumbers and stone masons resumed their infernal racket, while scrubwomen, polishers and painters began to move intimately among us.

"Here!" roared Mr. Rocksworth. "Stop this beastly noise! What the deuce do you mean, sir, permitting these scoundrels to raise the dead like this? Confound 'em, I stopped them once. Here! You! Let up on that, will you?"

I moved forward apologetically. "I am afraid it is not onions you smell, ladies and gentlemen." I had taken my cue with surprising quickness. "They *are* raising the dead. The place is fairly alive with dead rats and—"

"Good Lord!" gasped Riley-Werkheimer. "We'll get the bubonic plague here."

"Oh, I know *onions*," said Rocksworth calmly. "Can't fool me on onions. They *are* onions, ain't they, Carrie?"

"They *are!*" said she. "What a pity to have this wonderful old castle actually devastated by workmen! It is an outrage—a crime. I should trunk, the owner would turn over in his grave."

"Unhappily, I am the owner, madam," said I, slyly working my foot back into an elusive slipper.

"You ought to be ashamed of yourself," she said, eyeing me coldly with a hitherto unexposed lorgnon.

"I am," said I. "You quite took me by surprise. I should have made myself more presentable if I had know—"

"Well, let's move on upstairs," said Rocksworth. Addressing the porters he said: "You fellows get this lot of stuff together and I'll take an option on it. I'll be over to-morrow to close the deal, Mr.—Mr.—Now, where is the old Florentine mirror the Count was telling us about?"

"The Count?" said I, frowning.

Yes, the *real* owner. You can't stuff me with your talk about being the proprietor here, my friend. You see, we happen to *know* the Count.

They all condescended to laugh at me. I don't know what I should have said or done if Britton had not returned with a box of matches at that instant—sulphur matches which added subtly to the growing illusion.

Almost simultaneously there appeared in the lower hall a lanky youth of eighteen. He was a loud-voiced, imperious sort of chap with at least three rolls to his trousers and a plum-coloured cap.

"Say, these clubs are the real stuff, all right, all right. They're as brittle as glass. See what I did to 'em. We can have 'em spliced and rewound and I'll hang 'em on my wall. All I want is the heads anyhow."

He held up to view a headless mid-iron and brassie, and triumphantly waved a splendid cleek. My favourite clubs! I could play better from a hanging lie with that beautiful brassie than with any club I ever owned and as for the iron, I was deadly with it.

He lit a cigarette and threw the match into a pile of shavings. Old Conrad returned to life at that instant and stamped out the incipient blaze.

"I shouldn't consider them very good clubs, Harold, if they break off like that," said his mother.

"What do you know about clubs?" he snapped, and I at once knew what class he was in at the preparatory school.

If I was ever like one of these, said I to myself, God rest the sage soul of my Uncle Rilas!

The situation was no longer humorous. I could put up with anything but the mishandling of my devoted golf clubs.

Striding up to him, I snatched the remnants from his hands.

"You infernal cub!" I roared. "Haven't you any more sense than to smash a golf club like that? For two cents I'd break this putter over your head."

"Father!" he yelled indignantly. "Who is this mucker?"

Mr. Rocksworth bounced toward me, his cane raised. I whirled upon him.

"How dare you!" he shouted. The ladies squealed.

If he expected me to cringe, he was mightily mistaken. My blood was up. I advanced.

"Paste him, Dad!" roared Harold.

But Mr. Rocksworth suddenly altered his course and put the historic treaty table between him and me. He didn't like the appearance of my rather brawny fist.

"You big stiff!" shouted Harold. Afterwards it occurred to me that this inelegant appellation may have been meant for his father, but at the time I took it to be aimed at me.

Before Harold quite knew what was happening to him, he was prancing down the long hall with my bony fingers grasping his collar. Coming to the door opening into the outer vestibule, I drew back my foot for a final aid to locomotion. Acutely recalling the fact that slippers are not designed for kicking purposes, I raised my foot, removed the slipper and laid it upon a taut section of his trousers with all of the melancholy force that I usually exert in slicing my drive off the tee. I shall never forget the exquisite spasm of pleasure his plaintive "Ouch!" gave me.

Then Harold passed swiftly out of my life.

Mr. Rocksworth, reinforced by four reluctant mercenaries in the shape of porters, was advancing upon me. Somehow I had a vague, but unerring instinct that some one had fainted, but I didn't stop to inquire. Without much ado, I wrested the cane from him and sent it scuttling after Harold.

"Now, get out!" I roared.

"You shall pay for this!" he sputtered, quite black in the face. "Grab him, you infernal cowards!"

But the four porters slunk away, and Mr. Rocksworth faced me alone. Rudolph and Max, thoroughly fed and *most* prodigious, were bearing down upon us, accounting for the night of the mercenaries.

"Get out!" I repeated. "I am the owner of this place, Mr. Rocksworth, and I am mad through and through. skip!"

"I'll have the law—"

"Law be hanged!"

"If it costs me a million, I'll get—"

"It *will* cost you a million if you don't get!" I advised him, seeing that he paused for want of breath.

I left him standing there, but had the presence of mind to wave my huge henchmen away. Mr. Riley-Werkheimer approached, but very pacifically. He was paler than he will ever be again in his life, I fear.

"This is most distressing, most distressing, Mr.—Mr.—ahem! I've never been so outraged in my life. I—but, wait!" He had caught the snap in my atavistic eye. "I am not seeking trouble. We will go, sir. I—I—I think my wife has quite recovered. Are—are you all right, my dear?"

I stood aside and let them file past me. Mrs. Riley-Werkheimer moved very nimbly for one who had just been revived by smelling-salts. As her husband went by, he half halted in front of me. A curious glitter leaped into his fishy eyes.

"I'd give a thousand dollars to be free to do what you did to that insufferable puppy, Mr.—Mr.—ahem. A cool thousand, damn him!"

I had my coffee upstairs, far removed from the onions. A racking headache set in. Never again will I go without my coffee so long. It always gives me a headache.

CHAPTER III

I CONVERSE 'WITH A MYSTERY

LATE in the afternoon, I opened my door, hoping that the banging of hammers and the buzz of industry would have ceased, but alas! the noise was even more deafening than before. I was still in a state of nerves over the events of the morning. There had been a most distressing lack of poise on my part, and I couldn't help feeling after it was all over that my sense of humour had received a shock from which it was not likely to recover in a long time. There was but little consolation in the reflection that my irritating visitors deserved something in the shape of a rebuff; I could not separate myself from the conviction that my integrity as a gentleman had suffered in a mistaken conflict with humour. My headache, I think, was due in a large measure to the sickening fear that I had made a fool of myself, notwithstanding my efforts to make fools of them. My day was spoilt. My plans were upset and awry.

Espying Britton in the gloomy corridor, I shouted to him, and he came at once.

"Britton," said I, as he closed the door, "do you think they will carry out their threat to have the law on me? Mr. Rocksworth was very angry—and put out. He is a power, as you know."

"I think you are quite safe, sir," said he. "I've been waiting outside since two o'clock to tell you some-thing, sir, but hated to disturb you. I—"

"Thank you, Britton, my head was aching dreadfully."

"Yes, sir. Quite so. Shortly before two, sir, one of the porters from the hotel came over to recover a gold purse Mrs. Riley-Werkheimer had dropped in the excitement, and he informed Mr. Poopendyke that the whole party was leaving at four for Dresden. I asked particular about the young man, sir, and he said they had the doctor in to treat his stomach, sir, immediately after they got back to the hotel."

"His stomach? But I distinctly struck him on the verso."

"I know, sir; but it seems that he swallowed Jus cigarette."

To my shame, I joined Britton in a roar of laughter. Afterwards I recalled, with something of a shock, that it was the first time I had ever heard my valet laugh aloud. He appeared to be in some distress over it himself, for he tried to turn it off into a violent fit of coughing. He is such a faithful, exemplary servant that I made haste to pound him on the back, fearing the worst. I could not get on at all without Britton. He promptly recovered.

"I beg pardon, sir," said he. "Will you have your shave and tub now, sir?"

Later on, somewhat refreshed and relieved, I made my way to the little balcony, first having issued numerous orders and directions to the still stupefied Schmicks, chief among which was an inflexible command to keep the gates locked against all comers. The sun was shining brightly over the western hills, and the sky was clear and blue. The hour was five I found on consulting my watch. Naturally my first impulse was to glance up at the still loftier balcony in the east wing. It was empty. There was nothing in the grim, formidable prospect to warrant the impression that any one dwelt behind those dismantled windows, and I experienced the vague feeling that perhaps it had been a dream after all.

Far below at the foot of the shaggy cliff ran the historic Donau, serene and muddy, all rhythmic testimonials to the contrary. With something of a shudder I computed the distance from my eerie perch to the rocks at the bottom of the cliff. Five hundred feet, at least; an impregnable wall of nature surmounted by a now rank and obsolete obstruction built by the hand of man: a fortress that defied the legions of old but to-day would afford no more than brief and even desultory target practice for a smart battery. To scale the cliff, however, would be an impossibility for the most resourceful general in the world. All about me were turrets and minarets, defeated by the ancient and implacable foe—Time. Shattered crests of towers hung above me, grey and forbidding, yet without menace save in their senile prerogative to collapse without warning. Tiny windows marked the face of my still sturdy walls, like so many pits left by the pox, and from these in the good old feudal days a hundred marksmen had thrust their thunderous blunderbusses to clear the river of vain-glorious foes. From the scalloped bastions cross-bowmen of even darker ages had shot their random bolts; while in the niches of lower walls futile pikemen waited for the impossible to happen: the scaling of the cliff!

Friend and foe alike came to the back door of Schloss Rothhoefen, and there found welcome or stubborn obstacles that laughed at time and locksmiths: monstrous gates that still were strong enough to defy a mighty force. There was my great stone-paved courtyard, flanked on all sides by disintegrating buildings once occupied by serfs and fighting men; the stables in which chargers and beasts of burden had slept side by side until called by the night's work or the day's work, as war or peace prescribed, ranged close by inc. gates that opened upon the steep, winding roadway that now dismayed all modern steeds save the conquering ass. Here too were the remains of a once noble garden, and here were the granaries and the storehouses.

Far below me were the dungeons, with dead men's bones on their dripping floors; and somewhere in the heart of the peak were secret, unknown passages, long since closed by tumbling rocks and earth, as darkly mysterious as the streets in the buried cities of Egypt.

Across the river and below me stood the walled-in town that paid tribute to the good and bad Roth-hoefens in those olden days: a red-tiled, gloomy city that stood as a monument to long-dead ambitions. A peaceful, quiet town that had survived its parlous centuries of lust and greed, and would go on living to the end of time.

So here I sat me down, almost at the top of my fancy, to wonder if it were not folly as well!

Above me soared huge white-bellied birds, cousins germain to my dreams, but alas! infinitely more sensible in that they roamed for a more sustaining nourishment than the so-called food for thought.

I looked backward to the tender years when my valiant young heart kept pace with a fertile brain in its swiftest flights, and pinched myself to make sure that this was not all imagination. Was I really living in a feudal castle with romance shadowing me at every step? Was this I, the dreamer of twenty years ago? Or was I the last of the Rothhoefens and not John Bellamy Smart, of Madison Avenue, New York?

The sun shone full upon me as I sat there in my little balcony, but I liked the dry, warm glare of it. To be perfectly frank, the castle was a bit damp. I had had a pain in the back of my neck for two whole days. The sooner I got at my novel and finished it up the better, I reflected. Then I could go off to the baths somewhere. But would I ever settle down to work? Would the plumbers ever get off the place? (They were the ones I seemed to suspect the most.)

Suddenly, as I sat there ruminating, I became acutely aware of something white on the ledge of the topmost window in the eastern tower. Even as I fixed my gaze upon it, something else transpired. A cloud of soft, wavy, luxurious brown hair eclipsed the narrow white strip and hung with spreading splendour over the casement ledge, plainly, indubitably to dry in the sun!

My neighbour had washed her hair!

And it was really a most wonderful head of hair. I can't remember ever having seen anything like it, except in the advertisements.

For a long time I sat there trying to pierce the blackness of the room beyond the window with my straining eyes, deeply sensitive to a curiosity that had as its basic force the very natural anxiety to know what disposition she had made of the rest of her person in order to obtain this rather startling effect.

Of course, I concluded, she was lying on a couch of some description, with her head in the window. That was quite clear, even to a dreamer. And perhaps she was reading a novel while the sun shone. My fancy went to the remotest ends of probability: she might even be reading one of mine!

What a glorious, appealing, sensuous thing a crown of hair—but just then Mr. Poopendyke came to my window.

"May I interrupt you for a moment, Mr. Smart?" he inquired, as he squinted at me through his ugly bone-rimmed glasses.

"Come here, Poopendyke," I commanded in low, excited tones. He hesitated. "You won't fall off," I said sharply.

Although the window is at least nine feet high, Poopendyke stooped as he came through. He always does it, no matter how tall the door. It is a life-long habit with him. Have I mentioned that my worthy secretary is six feet four, and as thin as a reed? I remember speaking of his knees. He is also a bachelor.

"It is a dreadful distance down there," he murmured, flattening himself against the wall and closing his eyes.

A pair of slim white hands at that instant indolently readjusted the thick mass of hair and quite as casually disappeared. I failed to hear Mr. Poopendyke's remark.

"I think, sir," he proceeded, "it would be a very good idea to get some of our correspondence off our hands. A great deal of it has accumulated in the past few weeks. I wish to say that I am quite ready to attend to it whenever—"

"Time enough for letters," said I, still staring.

"We ought to clean them all up before we begin on the romance, sir. That's my suggestion. We shan't feel like stopping for a lot of silly letters—By the way, sir, when do you expect to start on the romance? He usually spoke of them as romances. They were not novels to Poopendyke.

I came to my feet, the light of adventure in my eye.

"This very instant, Poopendyke," I exclaimed.

His face brightened. He loves work.

"Splendid! I will have your writing tablets ready in—"

"First of all, we *must* have a ladder. Have you seen to that?"

"A ladder?" he faltered, putting one foot back through the window in a most suggestive way.

"Oh," said I, remembering, "I haven't told you, have I? Look! Up there in that window. Do you see *that*?"

"What is it, sir? A rug?"

"Rug! Great Scott, man, don't you know a woman's hair when you see it?"

"I've never—er—never seen it—you might say—just like that. Is it **hair**?"

"It is. You **do** see it, don't you?"

"How did it get there?"

"Good! Now I know I'm not dreaming. Come! There's no time to be lost. We may be able to get up there before she hears us!"

I was through the window and half way across the room before his well-meant protest checked me.

"For heaven's sake, Mr. Smart, don't be too hasty. We can't rush in upon a woman unexpectedly like this. Who knows? She may be entirely—" He caught himself up sharply, blinked, and then rounded out his sentence in safety with the word "deshabille."

I was not to be turned aside by drivel of that sort; so, with a scornful laugh, I hurried on and was soon in the courtyard, surrounded by at least a score of persons who madly inquired where the fire was, and wanted to help me to put it out. At last we managed to get them back at their work, and I instructed old Conrad to have the tallest ladder brought to me at once.

"There is no such thing about the castle," he announced blandly, puffing away at his enormous pipe. His wife shook her head in perfect serenity. Somewhat dashed, I looked about me in quest of proof that they were lying to me. There was no sign of anything that even resembled a ladder.

"Where are your sons?" I demanded.

The old couple held up their hands in great distress.

"Herr Britton has them working their souls out, turning a windlass outside the gates—ach, that terrible invention of his!" groaned old Conrad. "My poor sons are faint with fatigue, mein herr. You should see them perspire,—and hear them pant for breath."

"It is like the blowing of the forge bellows," cried his wife. "My poor little boys!"

"Fetch them at once Conrad," said I, cudgelling my brain for a means to surmount a present difficulty, and but very slightly interested in Britton's noble contraption.

The brothers soon appeared and, as if to give the lie to their fond parents, puffed complacently at their pipes and yawned as if but recently aroused from a nap. Their sleeves were rolled up and I marvelled at the size of their arms.

"Is Britton dead?" I cried, suddenly cold with the fear that they had mutinied against this brusque English overlord.

They smiled. "He is waiting to be pulled up again, sir," said Max. "We left him at the bottom when you sent for us. It is for us to obey."

Of course, everything had to wait while my obedient vassals went forth and reeled the discomforted Britton to the top of the steep. He sputtered considerably until he saw me laughing at him. Instantly he was a valet once more, no longer a crabbed genius.

I had thought of a plan, only to discard it on measuring with my eye the distance from the ground to the lowest window in the east wing, second floor back. Even by standing on the shoulders of Rudolph, who was six feet five, I would still find myself at least ten feet short of the window ledge. Happily a new idea struck me almost at once.

In a jiffy, half a dozen carpenters were at work constructing a substantial ladder out of scantlings, while I stood over them in serene command of the situation.

The Schmicks segregated themselves and looked on, regarding the window with sly, furtive glances in which there was a distinct note of uneasiness.

At last the ladder was complete. Resolutely I mounted to the top and peered through the sashless window. It was quite black and repelling beyond. Instructing Britton and the two brothers to follow me in turn, I clambered over the wide stone sill and lowered myself gingerly to the floor.

I will not take up the time or the space to relate my experiences on this first fruitless visit to the east wing of my abiding place. Suffice to say, we got as far as the top of the stairs in the vast middle corridor after stumbling through a series of dim, damp rooms, and then found our way effectually blocked by a stout door which was not only locked and bolted, but bore a most startling admonition to would-be trespassers.

Pinned to one of the panels there was a dainty bit of white note-paper, with these satiric words written across its surface in a bold, feminine hand:

"Please keep out. This is private property."

Most property owners no doubt would have been incensed by this calm defiance on the part of a squatter, either male or female, but not I. The very impudence of the usurper appealed to me. What could be more delicious than her serene courage in dispossessing me, with the stroke of a pen, of at least two-thirds of my domicile, and what more exciting than the thought of waging war against her in the effort to regain possession of it? Really it was quite glorious! Here was a happy, enchanting bit of feudalism that stirred my romantic soul to its very depths. I was being defied by a woman—an amazon! Even my grasping imagination could not have asked for more substantial returns than this. To put her to rout! To storm the castle! To make her captive and chuck her into my dungeon! Splendid!

We returned to the courtyard and held a counsel of war. I put all of the Schmicks on the grill, but they stubbornly disclaimed all interest in or knowledge of the extraordinary occupant of the east wing.

"We can smoke her out, sir," said Britton.

I could scarcely believe my ears.

"Britton," said I severely, "you are a brute. I am surprised. You forget there is an innocent babe—maybe a collection of them—over there. And a dog. We shan't do anything heathenish, Britton. Please bear that in mind. There is but one way: we must storm the place. I will not be defied to my very nose."

I felt it to see if it was not a little out of joint. "It is a good nose."

"It is, sir," said Britton, and Poopendyke, in a perfect ecstasy of loyalty, shouted: "Long live your nose sir!"

My German vassals waved their hats, perceiving that a demonstration was required without in the least knowing what it was about.

"To-night we'll plan our campaign," said I, and then returned in some haste to my balcony. The mists of the waning day were rising from the valley below. The smell of rain was in the air. I looked in vain for the lady's tresses. They were gone. The sun was also gone. His work for the day was done. I wondered whether she was putting up her hair with her own fair hands or was there a lady's maid in her ménage.

Poopendyke and I dined in solemn grandeur in the great banquet hall, attended by the clumsy Max.

"Mr. Poopendyke," said I, after Max had passed me the fish for the second time on my right side—and both times across my shoulder;—"we must engage a butler and a footman to-morrow. Likewise a chef. This is ***too*** much.

"Might I suggest that we also engage a chambermaid? The beds are very poorly—"

I held up my hand, smiling confidently.

"We may capture a very competent chambermaid before the beds are made up again," I said, with meaning.

"She doesn't write like a chambermaid," he reminded me.

Whereupon we fell to studying the very aristocratic chirography employed by my neighbour in barring me from my own possessions.

After the very worst meal that Frau Schmick had ever cooked, and the last one that Max under any circumstance would be permitted to serve, I took myself off once more to the enchanted balcony. I was full of the fever of romance. A perfect avalanche of situations had been tumbling through my brain for hours, and, being a provident sort of chap in my own way, I decided to jot them down on a pad of paper before they quite escaped me or were submerged by others.

The night was very black and tragic, swift storm clouds having raced up to cover the moon and stars. With a radiant lanthorn in the window behind me, I sat down with my pad and my pipe and my pencil. The storm was not far away. I saw that it would soon be booming about my stronghold, and realised that my fancy would have to work faster than it had ever worked before if half that I had in mind was to be accomplished. Why I should have courted a broken evening on the exposed balcony, instead of beginning my labours in my study, remains an unrevealed mystery unless we charge it to the account of a much-abused eccentricity attributed to genius and which usually turns out to be arrant stupidity.

I have no patience with the so-called eccentricity of genius. It is merely an excuse for unkempt hair, dirty finger-nails, unpolished boots, open placquets, bad manners and a tendency to forget pecuniary obligations, to say nothing of such trifles as besottedness, vulgarity and the superior knack of knowing how to avoid making suitable provision for one's wife and children. All the shabby short-comings in the character of an author, artist or actor are blithely charged to genius, and we are content to let it go at that for fear that other people may think we don't know any better. As for myself, I may be foolish and inconsequential, but heaven will bear witness that I am not mean enough to call myself a genius.

So we will call it stupidity that put me where I might be rained upon at any moment, or permanently interrupted by a bolt of lightning. (There were low mutterings of thunder behind the hills, and faint flashes as if a monstrous giant had paused to light his pipe on the evil, wind-swept peaks of the Caucasus mountains.)

I was scribbling away in serene contempt for the physical world, when there came to my ears a sound that gave me a greater shock than any streak of lightning could have produced and yet left sufficient life in me to appreciate the sensation of being electrified.

A woman's voice, speaking to me out of the darkness and from some point quite near at hand! Indeed, I could have sworn it was almost at my elbow; she might have been peering over my shoulder to read my thoughts.

"I beg your pardon, but would you mind doing me a slight favour?"

Those were the words, uttered in a clear, sweet, perfectly confident voice, as of one who never asked for favours, but exacted them.

I looked about me, blinking, utterly bewildered. No one was to be seen. She laughed. Without really meaning to do so, I also laughed,—nervously, of course.

"Can't you see me?" she asked. I looked intently at the spot from which the sound seemed to come: a perfectly solid stone block less than three feet from my right shoulder. It must have been very amusing. She laughed again. I flushed resentfully.

"Where are you?" I cried out rather tartly.

"I can see you quite plainly, and you are very ugly when you scowl, sir. Are you scowling at me?"

"I don't know," I replied truthfully, still searching for her. "Does it seem so to you?"

"Yes."

"Then I must be looking in the right direction," I cried impolitely. "You must be—Ah!"

My straining eyes had located a small, oblong blotch in the curve of the tower not more than twenty feet from where I stood, and on a direct line with my balcony. True, I could not at first see a face, but as my eyes grew a little more accustomed to the darkness, I fancied I could distinguish a shadow that might pass for one.

"I didn't know that little window was there," I cried, puzzled.

"It isn't," she said. "It is a secret loop-hole, and it isn't here except in times of great duress. See! I can close it." The oblong blotch abruptly disappeared, only to reappear an instant later. I was beginning to understand. Of course it was in the beleaguered east wing! "I hope I didn't startle you a moment ago."

I resolved to be very stilt and formal about it. "May I enquire, madam, what you are doing in my hou—my castle?"

"You may."

"Well," said I, seeing the point, "what *are* you doing here?"

"I am living here," she answered distinctly.

"So I perceive," said I, rather too distinctly.

"And I have come down to ask a simple, tiny little favour of you, Mr. Smart," she resumed.

"You know my name?" I cried, surprised.

"I am reading your last book—Are you going?"

"Just a moment, please," I called out, struck by a splendid idea. Reaching inside the window I grasped the lanthorn and brought its rays to bear upon the—perfectly blank wall! I stared open-mouthed and unbelieving. "Good heaven! Have I been dreaming all this? I cried aloud.

My gaze fell upon two tiny holes in the wall, exposed to view by the bright light of my lamp. They appeared to be precisely in the centre of the spot so recently marked by the elusive oblong. Even as I stared at the holes, a slim object that I at once recognised as a finger protruded from one of them and wiggled at me in a merry but exceedingly irritating manner.

Sensibly I restored the lanthorn to its place inside the window and waited for the mysterious voice to resume.

"Are you so homely as all that?" I demanded when the shadowy face looked out once more. Very clever of me, I thought.

"I am considered rather good-looking," she replied, serenely. "Please don't do that again. It was very rude of you, Mr. Smart."

"Oh, I've seen something of you before this," I said. "You have long, beautiful brown hair—and a dog."

She was silent.

"I am sure you will pardon me if I very politely ask who you are?" I went on.

"That question takes me back to the favour. Will you be so very, very kind as to cease bothering me, Mr. Smart? It is dreadfully upsetting, don't you know, feeling that at any moment you may rush in and—"

"I like that. In my own castle, too!"

"There is ample room, for both of us," she said sharply. "I shan't be here for more than a month or six weeks, and I am sure we can get along very amiably under the same roof for that length of time if you'll only forget that I am here."

"I can't very well do that, madam. You see, we are making extensive repairs about the place and you are proving to be a serious obstacle. I cannot grant your request. It will grieve me enormously if I am compelled to smoke you out but I fear—"

"Smoke me out!"

"Perhaps with sulphur," I went on resolutely. "It is said to be very effective."

"Surely you will not do anything so horrid."

"Only as a last resort. First, we shall storm the east wing. Failing in that we shall rely on smoke. You will admit that you have no right to poach on my preserves."

"None whatever," she said, rather plaintively.

I can't remember having heard a sweeter voice than hers. Of course, by this time, I was thoroughly convinced that she was a lady,—a cultured, high-bred lady,—and an American. I was too densely enveloped by the fogginess of my own senses at this time, however, to take in this extraordinary feature of the case. Later on, in the seclusion of my study, the full force of it struck me and I marvelled.

That plaintive note in her voice served its purpose. My firmness seemed to dissolve, even as I sought to reinforce it by an injection of harshness into my own manner of speech.

"Then you should be willing to vacate my premises er—or"—here is where I began to show irresolute-ness—"or explain yourself."

"Won't you be generous?"

I cleared my throat nervously. How well they know the cracks in a man's armour!

"I am willing to be—amenable to reason. That's all you ought to expect." A fresh idea took root. "Can't we effect a compromise? A truce, or something of the sort? All I ask is that you explain your presence here. I will promise to be as generous as possible under the circumstances."

"Will you give me three days in which to trunk it over? "she asked, after a long pause.

"No."

"Well, two days?"

"I'll give you until to-morrow afternoon at five, when I shall expect you to receive me in person."

"That is quite impossible."

"But I demand the right to go wherever I please in my own castle. You—"

"If you knew just how circumspect I am obliged to be at present you wouldn't impose such terms, Mr. Smart."

"Oho! Circumspect! That puts a new light on the case. What have you been up to, madam?" I spoke very severely.

She very properly ignored the banality. "If I should write you a nice, agreeable letter, explaining as much as I can, won't you be satisfied?"

"I prefer to have it by word of mouth."

She seemed to be considering. "I will come to this window to-morrow night at this time and—and let you know," she said reluctantly.

"Very well," said I. "We'll let it rest till then."

And, by the way, I have something more to ask of you. Is it quite necessary to have all this pounding and hammering going on in the castle? The noise is dreadful. I don't ask it on my own account, but for the baby. You see, she's quite ill with a fever, Mr. Smart. Perhaps you've heard her crying."

"The baby?" I muttered.

"It is nothing serious, of course. The doctor was here to-day and he reassured me—"

"A—a doctor here to-day?" I gasped.

She laughed once more. Verily, it *was* a gentle, high-bred laugh.

"Will you please put a stop to the noise for a day or two?" she asked, very prettily.

"Certainly," said I too surprised to say anything else. "Is—is there anything else?"

"Nothing, thank you," she replied. Then: "Good night, Mr. Smart. You are very good."

"Don't forget to-morrow—"

But the oblong aperture disappeared with a sharp click, and I found myself staring at the blank, sphinx-like wall.

Taking up my pad, my pipe and my pencil, and leaving all of my cherished ideas out there in the cruel darkness, never to be recovered,—at least not in their original form,—I scrambled through the window, painfully scraping my knee in passing,—just in time to escape the deluge.

I am sure I should have enjoyed a terrific drenching if she had chosen to subject me to it.

CHAPTER IV

I BECOME AN ANCESTOR

TRUE to the promise she had extracted from me, I laid off my workmen the next morning. They trooped in bright and early, considerably augmented by fresh recruits who came to share the benefits of my innocuous prodigality, and if I live to be a thousand I shall never again experience such a noisome half hour as the one I spent in listening to their indignant protests against my tyrannical oppression of the poor and needy. In the end, I agreed to pay them, one and all, for a full day's work, and they went away mollified, calling me a true gentleman to my face and heaven knows what to my back.

I spoke gently to them of the sick baby. With one voice they all shouted:

"But *our* babies are sick!"

One octogenarian—a carpenter's apprentice—heatedly informed me, through Schmick, that he had a child two weeks old that would die before morning if deprived of proper food and nourishment. Somewhat impressed by this pitiful lament, I enquired how his wife was getting along. The ancient, being in a placid state of senility, courteously thanked me for my interest, and answered that she had been dead for forty-nine years, come September. I overlooked the slight discrepancy.

During the remainder of the day, I insisted on the utmost quiet in our wing of the castle. Poopendyke was obliged to take his typewriter out to the stables, where I dictated scores of letters to him. I caught Britton whistling in the kitchen about noon-time, and severely reprimanded him. We went quite to the extreme, however, when we tiptoed about our lofty halls. All of the afternoon we kept a sharp lookout for the doctor, but if he came we were none the wiser. Britton went into the town at three with the letters and a telegram to my friends in Vienna, imploring them to look up a corps of efficient servants for me and to send them on post-haste. I would have included a request for a competent nurse-maid if it hadn't been for a report from Poopendyke, who announced that he had caught a glimpse of a very nursy looking person at one of the upper windows earlier in the day.

I couldn't, however, for the life of me understand why my neighbour enjoined such rigid silence in our part of the castle and yet permitted that confounded dog of hers to yowl and bark all day. How was I to know that the beast had treed a lizard in the lower hall and couldn't dislodge it?

Britton returned with news. The ferrymen, with great joy in the telling, informed him that the season for tourists parties was just beginning and that we might expect, with them, to do a thriving and prosperous business during the next month or two. Indeed, word already had been received by the tourists company's agent in the town that a party of one hundred and sixty-nine would arrive the next day but one from Munchen, bent on visiting my ruin. In great trepidation, I had all of the gates and doors locked and reinforced by sundry beams and slabs, for I knew the overpowering nature of the collective tourist.

I may be pardoned if I digress at this time to state that the party of one hundred and sixty-nine, both, stern and opposite, besieged my castle on the next day but one, with the punctuality of locusts, and despite all of my precautions, all of my devices, all of my objections, effected an entrance and over-ran the place like a swarm of ants. The feat that could not have been accomplished by an armed force was successfully managed by a group of pedagogues from Ohio, to whom "Keep off the Grass" and "No Trespass" are signs of utter impotence on the part of him who puts them up, and ever shall be, world without end. They came, they saw, they conquered, and they tried to buy picture postcards of me.

I mention this in passing, lest you should be disappointed. More anon.

Punctually at nine o'clock, I was in the balcony, thanking my lucky stars that it was a bright, moonlit night. There was every reason to rejoice in the prospect of seeing her face clearly when she appeared at her secret little window. Naturally, I am too much of a gentleman to have projected unfair means of illuminating her face, such as the use of a pocket electric lamp or anything of that sort. I am nothing if not gallant,—when it comes to a pinch. Besides, I was reasonably certain that she would wear a thick black veil. In this I was wrong. She wore a white, filmy one, but it served the purpose. I naturally concluded that she was homely.

"Good evening," she said, on opening the window.

"Good evening," said I, contriving to conceal my disappointment. "How is the baby?"

"Very much better, thank you. It was so good of you to stop the workmen."

"Won't you take off your veil and stay awhile?"

I asked, politely facetious. "It isn't quite fair to me, you know."

Her next remark brought a blush of confusion to my cheek. A silly notion had induced me to don my full evening regalia, spike-tail coat and all. Nothing could have been more ludicrously incongruous than my appearance, I am sure, and I never felt more uncomfortable in my life.

"How very nice you look in your new suit," she said, and I was aware of a muffled quality in her ordinarily clear, musical voice. She was laughing at me. "Are you giving a dinner party?"

"I usually dress for dinner," I lied with some haughtiness. "And so does Poopendyke," I added as an afterthought. My blush deepened as I recalled the attenuated blazer in which my secretary breakfasted, lunched and dined without discrimination.

"For Gretel's benefit, I presume."

"Aha! You *do* know Gretel, then?"

"Oh, I've known her for years. Isn't she a quaint old dear?"

"I shall discharge her in the morning," said I severely. "She is a liar and her husband is a poltroon. They positively deny your existence in any shape or from."

"They won't pay any attention to you," said she, with a laugh. "They are fixtures, quite as much so as the walls themselves. You'll not be able to discharge them. My grandfather tried it fifty years ago and failed. Alter that he made it a point to dismiss Conrad every day in the year and Gretel every other day. As well try to remove the mountain, Mr. Smart. They know you can't get on without them."

"I have discharged her as a cook," I said, triumphantly. "A new one will be here by the end of the week."

"Oh," she sighed plaintively, "how glad I am. She is an atrocious cook. I don't like to complain, Mr. Smart, but really it is getting so that I can't eat *anything* she sends up. It is jolly of you to get in a new one. Now we shall be very happy."

"By Jove!" said I, completely staggered by these revelations. Unable to find suitable words to express my sustained astonishment, I repeated: "By Jove!" but in a subdued tone.

"I have thought it over, Mr. Smart," she went on in a business-like manner, "and I believe we will get along much better together if we stay apart."

Ambiguous remarks ordinarily reach my intelligence, but I was so stunned by preceding admissions that I could only gasp:

"Do you mean to say you've been subsisting all this time on *my* food?"

"Oh, dear me, no! How can you think that of me? Gretel merely cooks the food I buy. She keeps a distinct and separate account of everything, poor thing. I am sure you will not find anything wrong with your bills, Mr. Smart. But did you hear what I said a moment ago?"

"I'm not quite sure that I did."

"I prefer to let matters stand just as they are. Why should we discommode each other? We are perfectly satisfied as we—"

"I will not have my new cook giving notice, madam. You surely can't expect her—or him—to prepare meals for two separate—"

"I hadn't thought of that," she interrupted ruefully. "Perhaps if I were to pay her—or him—extra wages it would be all right," she added, quickly.

"We do not require much, you know."

I laughed rather shortly,—meanly, I fear.

"This is most extraordinary, madam!"

"I—I quite agree with you. I'm awfully sorry it had to turn out as it has. Who would have dreamed of your buying the place and coming here to upset everything?"

I resolved to be firm with her. She seemed to be taking too much for granted. "Much as I regret it, madam, I am compelled to ask you to evacuate—to get out, in fact. This sort of thing can't go on."

She was silent for so long that I experienced a slow growth of compunction. Just as I was on the point of slightly receding from my position, she gave me another shock.

"Don't you think it would be awfully convenient if you had a telephone put in, Mr. Smart?" she said. "It is such a nuisance to send Max or Rudolph over to town every whip-stitch on errands when a telephone—in your name, of course—would be so much more satisfactory."

"A telephone!" I gasped.

"Circumstances make it quite unwise for me to have a telephone in my own name, but you could have one in yours without creating the least suspicion. You are—"

"Madam," I cried, and got no farther.

"—perfectly free to have a telephone if you want one," she continued. "The doctor came this evening and it really wasn't necessary. Don't you see you could have telephoned for me and saved him the trip?"

It was due to the most stupendous exertion of self-restraint on my part that I said: "Well, I'll be—jiggered," instead of something a little less unique. Her audacity staggered me. (I was not prepared at that time to speak of it as superciliousness.)

"Madam," I exploded, "will you be good enough to listen to me? I am not to be trifled with. "To-morrow sometime I shall enter the east wing of this building if I have to knock down all the doors on the place. Do you understand, madam?"

"I do hope, Mr. Smart, you can arrange to break in about five o'clock. It will afford me a great deal of pleasure to give you some tea. May I expect you at five—or thereabouts?"

Her calmness exasperated me. I struck the stone balustrade an emphatic blow with my fist, sorely peeling the knuckles, and ground out:

"For two cents I'd do it to-night!"

"Oh, dear,—oh, dear!" she cried mockingly.

"You must be a dreadful woman," I cried out. "First, you make yourself at home in my house; then you succeed in stopping my workmen, steal my cook and men-servants, keep us all awake with a barking dog, defying me to my very face—"

"How awfully stern you are!"

"I don't believe a word you say about a sick baby,—or a doctor! It's all poppycock. To-morrow you will find yourself, bag and baggage; sitting at the bottom of this hill, waiting for—"

"Wait!" she cried. "Are you really, truly in earnest?"

"Most emphatically!"

"Then I—I shall surrender," she said, very slowly,—and seriously, I was glad to observe.

"That's more like it," I cried, enthusiastically.

"On one condition," she said. "You must agree in advance to let me stay on here for a month or two. It—it is most imperative, Mr. Smart."

"I shall be the sole judge of that, madam," I retorted, with some dignity. "By the way," I went on, knitting my brows, "how am I to get into your side of the castle? Schmick says he's lost the Keys."

A good deal depended on her answer.

"They shall be delivered to you to-morrow morning, Mr. Smart," she said, soberly. "Good night."

The little window closed with a snap and I was left alone in the smiling moonlight. I was vastly excited, even thrilled by the prospect of a sleepless night. Something told me I wouldn't sleep a wink, and yet I, who bitterly resent having my sleep curtailed in the slightest degree, held no brief against circumstances. In fact, I rather revelled in the promise of nocturnal distraction. Fearing, however, that I might drop off to sleep at three or four o'clock and thereby run the risk of over sleeping, I dashed off to the head of the stairs and shouted for Britton.

"Britton," I said. "I want to be called at seven o'clock sharp in the morning."

Noting his polite struggle to conceal his astonishment, I told him of my second encounter with the lady across the way.

"She won't be expecting you at seven, sir," he remarked. "And, as for that, she may be expecting to call on you, instead of the other way round."

"Right!" said I, considerably dashed.

"Besides, sir, would it not be safer to wait till the tourist party has come and gone?"

"No tourists enter this place to-morrow or any other day," I declared, firmly.

"Well, I'd suggest waiting just the same, sir," said he, evidently inspired.

"Confound them," I growled, somehow absorbing his presentiment.

He hesitated for a moment near the door.

"Will you put in the telephone, sir?" he asked, respectfully.

Very curiously, I was thinking of it at that instant.

"It really wouldn't be a bad idea, Britton" I said, startled into committing myself. "Save us a great deal of legging it over town and all that sort of thing, eh?"

"Yes, sir. What I was about to suggest, sir, is that while we're about it we might as well have a system of electric bells put in. That is to say, sir, in both wings of the castle. Very convenient, sir, you see, for all parties concerned."

"I see," said I, impressed. And then repeated it, a little more impressed after reflection. "I see. You are a very resourceful fellow, Britton. I am inclined to bounce all of the Schmicks. They have known about this from the start and have lied like thieves. By Jove, she must have an extraordinary power over them,—or claim,—or something equally potent. Now I think of it, she mentioned a grandfather. That would go to prove she's related in some way to some one, wouldn't it?"

"I should consider it to be more than likely, sir," said Britton, with a perfectly straight face. He must have been sorely tried in the face of my inane maunderings. "Pardon me, sir, but wouldn't it be a tip-top idea to have it out with the Schmicks to-night? Being, sir, as you anticipate a rather wakeful night, I only make so bold as to suggest it in the hopes you may 'ave some light on the subject before you close your eyes. In other words, sir, so as you won't be altogether in the dark when morning comes. See wot I mean?"

"Excellent idea, Britton. We'll have them up in my study."

He went off to summon my double-faced servitors, while I wended my way to the study. There I found. Mr. Poopendyke, sound asleep in a great arm-chair, both his mouth and his nose open and my first novel also open in his lap.

Conrad and Gretel appeared with Britton after an unconscionable lapse of time, partially dressed and grumbling.

"Where are your sons?" I demanded, at once suspicious.

Conrad shook his sparsely covered head and mumbled something about each being his brother's keeper, all of which was Greek to me until Britton explained that they were not to be found in their customary quarters,—that is to say, in bed. Of course it was quite clear to me that my excellent giants were off somewhere, serving the interests of the bothersome lady in the east wing.

"Conrad," said I, fixing the ancient with a stern, compelling gaze, "this has gone quite far enough."

"Yes, mein herr?"

"Do you serve me, or do you serve the lady in the east wing?"

"I do," said he, with a great deal more wit than I thought he possessed. For a moment I was speechless, but not for the reason you may suspect. I was trying to fix my question and his response quite clearly in my memory so that I might employ them later in, the course of a conversation between characters in my forthcoming novel.

"I have been talking with the lady this evening," said I.

"Yes, mein herr; I know," said he.

"Oh, you do, en? Well, will you be good enough to tell me what the devil is the meaning of all this two-faced, underhanded conduct on your part?"

He lowered his head, closed his thin lips and fumbled with the hem of his smock in a significantly sullen manner. It was evident that he meant to defy me. His sharp little eyes sent a warning look at Gretel, who instantly ceased her mutterings and gave over asking God to bear witness to something or other. She was always dragging in the Deity.

"Now, see here, Conrad, I want the truth from you. Who is this woman, and why are you so infernally set upon shielding her? What crime has she committed? Tell me at once, or, by the Lord Harry, out you go to-morrow, all of you."

"I am a very old man," he whined, twisting his gnarled fingers, a suggestion of tears in his voice. "My wife is old, mein herr. You would not be cruel. We have been here for sixty years. The old baron—"

"Enough!" I cried resolutely. "Out with it, man. I mean all that I say."

He was still for a long time, looking first at the floor and then at me; furtive, appealing, uncertain little glances from which he hoped to derive comfort by catching me with a twinkle in my eye. I have a stupid, weak way of letting a twinkle appear there even when I am trying to be harsh and domineering. Britton has noticed it frequently, I am sure, and I think he rather depends upon it. But now I realised, if never before, that to betray the slightest sign of gentleness would be to forever forfeit my standing as master in my own house. Conrad, saw no twinkle. He began to weaken.

"To-morrow, mein herr, to-morrow, he mumbled, in a final plea. I shook my head. "*she* will explain everything to-morrow," he went on eagerly. "I am sworn to reveal nothing, mein herr. wife, too, and my sons. We may not speak until she^ gives the word. Alas! we shall be turned out to die in our—"

"We have been faithful servants to the Rothhoefens for sixty years," sobbed his wife.

"And still are, I suspect," I cried angrily.

"Ach, mein herr, mein herr!" protested, Conrad, greatly perturbed.

"Where are the keys, you old rascal?" I demanded so sternly that even Poopendyke was startled.

Conrad almost resorted to the expediency of grovelling. "Forgive! forgive!" he groaned. "I have done only what was best."

"Produce the keys, sir!"

"But not to-night, not to-night," he pleaded. "She will be very angry. She will not like it, mein herr. Ach, Gott! She will drive us out, she will shame us all! Ach, and she who is so gentle and so unhappy and so—so kind, to all of us! I—I cannot—I cannot! No!"

Mr. Poopendyke's common sense came in very handily at this critical juncture. He counselled me to let the matter rest until the next morning, when, it was reasonable to expect, the lady herself would explain everything. Further appeal to Schmick was like butting one's head against a stone wall, he said. Moreover, Conrad's loyalty to the lady was most commendable.

Conrad and Gretel beamed on Poopendyke. They thanked him so profoundly, that I couldn't help feeling a bit sorry for myself, a tyrant without a backbone.

"Jah, jah!" Conrad cried gladly. "To-morrow she will explain. Time enough, Herr Poopendyke. Time enough, eh?"

"Well," said I, somewhat feebly, "where do I come in?"

They caught the note of surrender in. my voice and pounced upon their opportunity. Before they had finished with me, it was quite thoroughly established that I was not to come in at all until my neighbour was ready to admit me. They convinced me that I was a meek, futile suppliant and not the master of a feudal stronghold. Somehow I was made to feel that if I didn't behave myself I stood in considerable danger of being turned off the place.

However, we forced something out of Schmick before his stalwart sons came tramping up the stairs to rescue him. The old man gave us a touch of inside history concerning Schloss Rothhoefen and its erstwhile powerful barons, not to minimise in the least sense the peculiar prowess of the present Amazon who held forth to-night in the east wing and who, I had some reason to suspect, was one of the family despite the unmistakable flavour of Fifth Avenue and Newport.

About the middle of the nineteenth century the last of the real barons,—the powerful, land-owning, despotic barons,—I mean,—came to the end of his fourscore years and ten, and was laid away with great pomp and glee by the people of the town across the river. He was the last of the Rothhoefens, for he left no male heir. His two daughters had married Austrian noblemen, and neither of them produced a male descendant. The estate, already in a state of financial as well as physical disintegration, fell into the hands of women, and went from bad to worse so rapidly that long before the last quarter of the century was fairly begun the castle and the reduced holdings slipped away from the Rothhoefens altogether and into the control of the father of the Count from whom I purchased the property. The Count's father, it appears, was a distiller of great wealth in his day, and a man of action. Unfortunately he died before he had the chance to carry out his projects in connection with the rehabilitation of Schloss Rothhoefen, even then a deserted, ramshackle resort for paying tourists and a Mecca for antique and picture dealers.

The new Count—my immediate predecessor—was not long in dissipating the great fortune left by his father, the worthy distiller. He had run through with the bulk of his patrimony by the time he was twenty-five and was pretty much run down at the heel when he married in the hope of recouping his lost fortune.

The Schmicks did not like him. They did not approve of him as lord and master, nor was it possible for them to resign themselves Jo the fate that had put this young scapegrace into the shoes, so to speak, of the grim old barons Rothhoefen, who whatever else they may have been in a high-handed sort of way were men to the core. This pretender, this creature without brains or blood, this sponging reprobate, was not to their liking, if I am to quote Conrad, who became quite forceful in his harangue against the recent order of things.

He, his wife and his sons, he assured me, were full of rejoicing when they learned that the castle had passed from Count Hohendahl's hands into mine. I, at least, would pay them their wages and I might, in a pinch, be depended upon to pension them when they got too old to be of any use about the castle.

At any rate, it seems, I was a distinct improvement over the Count, who had been their master for a dozen very lean and unprofitable years. Things might be expected to look up a bit, with me at the head of the house. Was it not possible for a new and mighty race to rise and take the place of the glorious Rothhoefens? A long line of Baron Schmarts? With me as the prospective root of a thriving family tree!

At least, that is what Conrad said, and I may be pardoned for quoting him.

I am truly sorry the old rascal put it into my head.

But the gist of the whole matter was this: There are no more Rothhoefens, and soon, God willing, there would be no more Hohendahls. Long live the Schmarts! Conrad invariably pronounced my name with the extra consonants and an umlaut.

All attempts on my part to connect the lady in the east wing with the history of the extinct Rothhoefens were futile. He would not commit himself.

"Well," said I, yawning in helpless collusion with the sleepy Gretel, "we'll let it go over till morning. Call me at seven, Britton."

Conrad made haste to assure me that the lady would not receive me before eleven o'clock. He begged me to sleep till nine, and to have pleasant dreams.

I went to bed but not to sleep. It was very clear to me that my neighbour was a disturber in every sense of the word. She wouldn't let me sleep. For two hours I tried to get rid of her, but she filtered into my brain and prodded my thoughts into the most violent activity. She wouldn't stay put.

My principal thoughts had to do with her identity. Somehow I got it into my head that she was one of the female Rothhoefens, pitiable nonentities if Conrad's estimate is to be accepted. A descendant of one of those girl-bearing daughters of the last baron! It sounded very agreeable to my fancy's ear, and I cuddled the hope that my surmise was not altogether preposterous.

My original contention that she was a poor relation of old Schmick and somewhat dependent upon him for charity—to say the least—had been set aside for more reliable convictions. Instead of being dependent upon the Schmicks, she seemed to be in an exalted position that gave her a great deal more power over them than even

I possessed: they served her, not me. From time to time there occurred to me the thought that my own position in the household was rather an ignoble one, and that I was a very weak and incompetent successor to baronial privileges, to say nothing of rights. A real baron would have had her out of there before you could mention half of Jack Robinson, and there wouldn't have been any sleep lost over distracting puzzles. I deplored my lack of bad manners.

It was quite reasonable to assume that she was young, but the odds were rather against her being beautiful. Pretty women usually adjure such precautions as veils. Still, this was speculation, and my reasoning is not always sound, for which I sometimes thank heaven. She had a baby. At least, I suppose it was hers. If not, whose? This set me off on a new and apparently endless round of speculation, obviously silly and sentimental.

Now I have humbly tried to like babies. My adolescent friends and acquaintances have done their best to educate me along this particular line, with the result that I suppose I despise more babies than any man in the world. My friends, it would appear, are invariably married to each other and they all have babies for me to go into false ecstasies over. No doubt babies are very nice when they don't squawk or pull your nose or jab you in the eye, but through some strange and prevailing misfortune I have never encountered one when it was asleep. If they are asleep, the parents compel me to walk on tip-toe and speak in whispers at long range; the instant they awake and begin to yawp, I am ushered into the presence, or vice versa, and the whole world grows very small and congested and is carried about in swaddling clothes.

There is but one way for a bachelor to overcome his horror of babies, and he shouldn't wait too long.

I went to sleep about four o'clock, still oppressed by the dread of meeting a new baby.

My contact with the one hundred and sixty-nine sight-seers was brief but exceedingly convincing. They invaded the castle before I was out of bed, having—as I afterwards heard—the breweries, an art gallery and the Zoological gardens to visit before noon and therefore were required to make an early start. The cathedral, which is always open to visitors and never has any one sleeping in it, was reserved for the afternoon.

I was aroused from my belated sleep by the sound of mighty cataracts and the tread of countless elephants. Too late I realised that the tourists were upon me! Too late I remembered that the door to my room had been left unlocked! The hundred and sixty-nine were huddled outside my door, drinking in the monotonous drivel of the guide who had a shrill, penetrating voice and not the faintest notion of a conscience.

I listened in dismay for a moment, and then, actuated by something more than mere fury, leaped out of bed and prepared for a dash across the room to lock the door. On the third stride I whirled and made a flying leap into the bed, scuttling beneath the covers with the speed and accuracy of a crawfish. Just in time, too, for the heavy door swung slowly open a second later, and the shrill, explanatory voice was projected loudly into my lofty bed chamber.

"Come a little closer, please," said the morose man with the cap. "This room was occupied for centuries by the masters of Schloss Rothhoefen. It is a bed chamber. See the great baronial bed. It has not been slept in for more than two hundred years. The later barons refused to sleep in it because one of their ancestors had been assassinated between its sheets at the tender age of six. He was stabbed by a step-uncle who played him false. This room is haunted. Observe the curtains of the bed. They are of the rarest silk and have been there for three hundred years, coming from Damascus in the year 1695. Now we will pass on to the room occupied by all of the great baronesses up to the nineteenth—"

A resolute beholder spoke up: "Can't we step inside?"

"If you choose, madam. But we must waste no time."

"I do so want to see where the old barons slept."

"Please do not handle the bedspreads and curtains. They will fall to pieces—"

I heard no more, for the vanguard had pushed him aside and was swooping down upon me. A sharp-nosed lady led the way. She was within three feet of the bed and was stretching out her hand to touch the proscribed fabrics when I sat bolt upright and yelled:

"Get out!"

Afterwards I was told that the guide was the first to reach the bottom of the stairs and that he narrowly escaped death in the avalanche of horrified humanity that piled after mm, pursued by the puissant ghost of a six-year-old ancestor.

CHAPTER V

I MEET THE FOE AND FALL

TIIE post that morning, besides containing a telegram from Vienna apprising me of the immediate embarkation of four irreproachable angels in the guise of servants, brought a letter from my friends the Hazzards, inquiring when my castle would be in shape to receive and discharge house parties without subjecting them to an intermediate season of peril from drafts, leaky roofs, damp sheets and vampires.

They implored me to snatch them and one or two friends from the unbearable heat of the city, if only for a few days, appending the sad information that they were swiftly being reduced to grease spots. Dear Elsie added a postscript of unusual briefness and clarity in which she spelt grease with an e instead of an a, but managed to consign me to purgatory n I permitted her to become a spot no larger than the inky blot she naïvely deposited beside her signature, for all the world like the seal on a death warrant.

I sat down and looked about me in gloomy despair. No words can describe the scene, unless we devote a whole page to repeating the word "dismal." Devastation always appears to be more complete of a morning I have observed in my years of experience. A plasterer's scaffolding that looks fairly nobby at sunset is a grim, unsightly skeleton at breakfast-time. A couple of joiners' horses, a matrix or two, a pile of shavings and some sawed-off blocks scattered over the floor produce a matutinal conception of chaos that hangs over one like a pall until his æsthetic sense is beaten into subjection by the hammers of a, million demons in the guise of carpenters. Morning in the midst of repairs is an awful thing! I looked, despaired and then dictated a letter to the Hazzards, urging them to come at once with all their sweltering friends!

I needed some one to make me forget.

At eleven o'clock, Poopendyke brought me a note from the chatelaine of the east wing. It had been dropped into the courtyard from one of the upper windows. The reading of it transformed me into a stern, relentless demon. She very calmly announced that she had a headache and couldn't think of being disturbed that day and probably not the next.

My mind was made up in an instant. I would not be put off by a headache,— which was doubtless assumed for the occasion,—and I would be master of my castle or know the reason why, etc.

In the courtyard I found a score or more of idle artisans, banished by the on-sweeping tourists and completely forgotten by me in the excitement of the hour. Commanding them to fetch their files, saws, broad-axes and augurs, I led the way to the mighty doors that barred my entrance to the other side. Utterly ignoring the supplications of Conrad Schmick and the ominous frowns of his two sons, we set about filing off the padlocks, and chiselling through the wooden panels. I stood over my toiling minions and I venture to say that they never worked harder or faster in their lives. By twelve o'clock we had the great doors open and swept on to the next obstruction.

At two o'clock the last door in the east ante-chamber gave way before our resolute advance and I stood victorious and dusty in the little recess at the top of the last stairway. Beyond the twentieth century portières of a thirteenth century doorway lay the goal we sought. I hesitated briefly before drawing them apart and taking the final plunge. As a matter of fact, I was beginning to feel ashamed of myself. Suppose that she *really* had a headache! What an uncouth, pusillanimous brute I—

Just then, even as my hand fell upon the curtains, they were snatched aside and I found myself staring into the vivid, uptilted face of the lady who had defied me and would continue to do so if my suddenly active perceptions counted for anything.

I saw nothing but the dark, indignant, imperious eyes. They fairly withered me.

In some haste, attended by the most disheartening nervousness, I tried to find my cap to remove it in the presence of royalty. Unfortunately I was obliged to release the somewhat cumbersome crowbar I had been carrying about with me, and it dropped with a sullen thwack upon my toes. In moments of gravity I am always doing something like that. The pain was terrific, but I clutched at the forlorn hope that she might at least smile over my agony.

"I beg your pardon," I began, and then discovered that I was not wearing a cap. It was most disconcerting.

"So you *would* come," she said, very coldly and very levelly. I have a distinct recollection of shrinking. If you have ever tried to stand flatly upon a foot whose toes are crimped by an excruciating pain you may understand something of the added discomfiture that afflicted me.

"It—it was necessary, madam," I replied as best I could. "You defied me. I think you should have appreciated my position—my motives—er—my—"

She silenced me—luckily, heaven knows—with a curt exclamation.

"Your position! It is intensely Napoleonic," said she with fine irony. Her gaze swept my horde of panting, wide-eyed house-breakers. "What a noble victory!"

It was quite time for me to assert myself. Bowing very stiffly, I remarked:

"I regret exceedingly to have been forced to devastate my own property in such a trifling enterprise, madam. The physical loss is apparent,—you can see that for yourself,—but of course you have no means of estimating the mental destruction that has been going on for days and days. You have been hacking away at my poor, distracted brain so persistently that it really had to give way. In a measure, this should account for my present lapse of sanity. Weak-mindedness is not a crime, but an affliction.

She did not smile.

"Well, now that you are here, Mr. Smart, may I be so bold as to inquire what you are going to do about it?"

I reflected. "I think, if you don't mind, I'll come in and sit down. That was a deuce of a rap I got across the toes. I am sure to be a great deal more lenient and agreeable if I'm *asked* to come in and see you. Incidentally, I thought I'd step up to inquire how your headache is getting on. Better, I hope?"

She turned her face away. I suspected a smile.

"If you choose to bang your old castle to pieces, in order to satisfy a masculine curiosity, Mr. Smart, I have nothing more to say," she said, facing me again—still ominously, to my despair. Confound it all, she was such a slim, helpless little thing—and all alone against a mob of burly ruffians! I could have kicked myself but even that would have been an aimless enterprise in view of the fact that Poopendyke or any of the others could have done it more accurately than I and perhaps with greater respect. "Will you be good enough to send your—your army away, or do you prefer to have it on hand in case I should take it into my head to attack you?"

"Take 'em away, Mr. Poopendyke," I commanded hurriedly. I didn't mind Poopendyke hearing what she said, but it would be just like one of those beggars to understand English—and also to misunderstand it. "And take this beastly crowbar with you, too. It has served its purpose nobly."

Poopendyke looked his disappointment, and I was compelled to repeat the order. As they crowded down the short, narrow stairway, I remarked old Conrad and his two sons standing over against the wall, three very sinister figures. They remained motionless.

"I see, madam, that you do not dismiss **your** army," I said, blandly sarcastic.

"Oh, you dear old Conrad!" she cried, catching sight of the hitherto submerged Schmicks. The three of them bobbed and scraped and grinned from ear to ear. There could be no mistaking the intensity of their joy. "Don't look so sad, Conrad. I know you are blameless. You poor old dear!"

I have never seen any one who looked less sad than Conrad Schmick. Or could it be possible that he was crying instead of laughing? In either case I could not afford to have him doing it with such brazen discourtesy to me, so I rather peremptorily ordered him below.

"I will attend to you presently,—all of you," said I. They did not move. "Do you hear me?" I snapped angrily. They looked stolidly at the slim young lady.

She smiled, rather proudly, I thought. "You may go, Conrad. I shall not need you. Max, will you fetch up another scuttle of coal?"

They took their orders from her! It even seemed to me that Max moved swiftly, although it was doubtless a hallucination on my part, brought about by nervous excitement.

"By Jove!" I said, looking after my trusty men-servants as they descended. I like *this!* Are they my servants or yours?"

"Oh, I suppose they are yours, Mr. Smart," she said carelessly. "Will you come in now, and make yourself quite at home?"

"Perhaps I'd better wait for a day or two," said I, wavering. "Your headache, you know. I can wait just as well as—"

"Oh, no. Since you've gone to all the trouble I suppose you ought to have something for your pains."

"Pains?" I murmured, and I declare to heaven I limped as I followed her through the door into a tiny hall.

"You are a most unreasonable man," she said, throwing open a small door at the end of the hall. "I am terribly disappointed in you. You looked to be so nice and sensible and amiable."

"Oh, I'm not such a nincompoop as you might suspect, madam, said I, testily, far from complimented. I dislike being called nice, and sometimes I think it a mistake to be sensible. A sensible person never gets anything out of life because he has to avoid so much of it.

"And now, Mr. Smart, will you be kind enough to explain the incomprehensible proceeding on your part?" she said, facing me sternly.

But I was dumb. I stood just inside the door of the most remarkable apartment it has ever been my good fortune to look upon. My senses reeled. Was I awake? Was this a part of the bleak, sinister, weather-racked castle in which I was striving so hard to find a comfortable corner?

"Well?" she demanded relentlessly.

"By the Lord Harry," I began, finding my tongue only to lose it again. My bewilderment increased, and for an excellent reason.

The room was completely furnished, bedecked and rendered habitable by an hundred and one articles that were mysteriously missing from my side of the castle. Rugs, tapestries, curtains of the rarest quality; chairs, couches, and cushions; tables, cabinets and chests that would have caused the eyes of the most conservative collector of antiques to bulge with—not wonder—but greed; stands, pedestals, brasses, bronzes, porcelains—but why enumerate? On the massive oaken centre table stood the priceless silver vase we had missed on the second day of our occupancy, and it was with fresh yellow roses. I sniffed. Their fragrance filled the room.

And so complete had been the rifling of my rooms by the devoted vandals in their efforts to make this lady cosy and comfortable that they did not overlook a silver-framed photograph of my dear mother! Her sweet face met my gaze as it swept the mantel-piece, beneath which a coal fire crackled merrily. I am not quite sure, but I think I repeated "by the Lord Harry" once if not twice before I caught myself up.

I tried to smile. "How—how cosy you are here," I said.

"You couldn't expect me to live in this awful place without some of the comforts and conveniences of life, Mr. Smart," she said defiantly.

"Certainly not," I said, promptly. "I am sure that you will excuse me, however, if I gloat. I was afraid we had lost all these things. You've no idea how relieved I am to find them all safe and sound in my—in their proper place. I was beginning to distrust the Schmicks. Now I am convinced of their integrity."

"I suppose you mean to be sarcastic."

"Sarcasm at any price, madam, would be worse than useless, I am sure."

Crossing to the fireplace, I selected a lump of coal from the scuttle and examined it with great care. She watched me curiously.

"Do you recognise it?" she asked.

"I do," said I, looking up. "It has been in our family for generations. My favourite chunk, believe me. Still, I part with it cheerfully." Thereupon I tossed it into the fire. "Don't be shocked! I shan't miss it. We have coals to burn, madam!"

She looked at me soberly for a moment. There was something hurt and wistful in her dark eyes.

"Of course, Mr. Smart, I shall pay you for everything—down to the smallest trifle—when the time comes for me to leave this place. I have kept strict account of—"

She turned away, with a beaten droop of the proud little head, and again I was shamed. Never have I felt so grotesquely out of proportion with myself as at that moment. My stature seemed to increase from an even six feet to something like twelve, and my bulk became elephantine. She was so slender, so lissom, so weak, and I so gargantuan, so gorilla-like, so heavy-handed! And I had come gaily up to crush her! What a fine figure of a man I was!

She did not complete the sentence, but walked slowly toward the window. I had a faint glimpse of a dainty lace handkerchief fiercely clutched in a little hand.

By nature I am chivalrous, even gallant. You may have reason to doubt it, but it is quite true. As I've never had a chance to be chivalrous except in my dreams or my imagination, I made haste to seize this opportunity before it was too late.

"Madam," I said, with considerable feeling. "I have behaved like a downright rotter to-day. I do not know who you are, nor why you are here, but I assure you it is of no real consequence if you will but condescend to overlook my insufferable—"

She turned towards me. The wistful, appealing look still lingered in her eyes. The soft red nether lip seemed a bit tremulous.

"I *am* an intruder," she interrupted, smiling faintly. "You have every right to put me out of your—your home, Mr. Smart. I was a horrid pig to deprive you of all your nice comfortable chairs and—"

"I—I haven't missed them."

"Don't you ever sit down?"

"I will sit down if you'll let me," said I, feeling that I wouldn't appear quite so gigantic if I was sitting.

"Please do. The chairs all belong to you."

"I'm in sorry you put it in that way. They are yours as long as you choose to—to occupy a furnished apartment here."

"I have been very selfish, and cattish, and inconsiderate, Mr. Smart. You see, I'm a spoilt child. I've always had my own way in everything. You must look upon me as a very horrid, sneaking, conspiring person, and I—I really think you ought to turn me out."

She came a few steps nearer. Under the circumstances I could not sit down. So I stood towering above her, but somehow going through a process of physical and mental shrinkage the longer I remained confronting her.

Suddenly it was revealed to me that she was the loveliest woman I had ever seen in all my life! How could I have been so slow in grasping this great, bewildering truth? The prettiest woman I had ever looked upon! Of course I had known it from the first instant that I looked into her eyes, but I must have been existing in a state of stupefaction up to this illuminating moment.

I am afraid that I stared.

"Turn you out?" I cried. "Turn you out of this delightful room after you've had so much trouble getting it into shape? Never!"

"Oh, you don't know how I've imposed upon you!" she cried plaintively. "You don't know how I've robbed you, and bothered you—"

"Yes, I do," said I promptly. "I know all about it. You've been stealing my coals, my milk, my ice, my potatoes, my servants, my sleep and"—here I gave a comprehensive sweep of my hand—"everything in sight. And you've made us walk on tiptoe to keep from waking the baby, and—" I stopped suddenly. "By the way, whose baby is it? Not yours, I'm sure."

To my surprise her eyes filled with tears.

"Yes. She is my baby, Mr. Smart."

My face fell. "Oh!" said I, and got no further for a moment or two. "I—I—please don't tell me you are married!"

"What would you think of me if I were to tell you I'm not?" she cried indignantly.

"I beg your pardon," I stammered, blushing to the roots of my hair. "Stupid ass!" I muttered.

Crossing to the fireplace, she stood looking down into the coals for a long time, while I remained where I was, an awkward, gauche spectator, conscious of having put my clumsiest foot into my mouth every time I opened it and wondering whether I could now safely get it out again without further disaster.

Her back was toward me. She was dressed in a dainty, pinkish house gown—or maybe it was light blue. At any rate it was a very pretty gown and she was wonderfully graceful in it. Ordinarily in my fiction I am quite clever at describing gowns that do not exist; but when it comes to telling what a real woman is wearing, I am not only as vague as a savage, but painfully stupid about colors. Still, I think it was pink. I recall the way her soft brown hair grew above the slender neck, and the lovely white skin; the smooth, delicate contour of her half-averted cheek and the firm little chin with the trembling red lips above it; the shapely back and shoulders and the graceful curves of her hips, suggestive of a secret perfection. She was taller than I had thought at first sight, or was it that I seemed to be getting smaller myself? A hasty bit of comparison placed her height at five feet six, using my own as something to go by. She couldn't have been a day over twenty-two. But she had a baby!

Facing me once more she said: "If you will sit down, Mr. Smart, and be patient and generous with me, I shall try to explain everything. You have a right to demand it of me, and I shall feel more comfortable after it is done."

I drew up a chair beside the table and sat down. She sank gracefully into another, facing me. A delicate frown appeared on her brow.

"Doubtless you are very much puzzled by my presence in this gloomy old castle. You have been asking yourself a thousand questions about me, and you have been shocked by my outrageous impositions upon your good nature. I confess I have been shockingly impudent and—"

"Pardon me; you are the only sauce I've had for an excessively bad bargain."

"Please do not interrupt me," she said coldly. "I am here, Mr. Smart, because it is the last place in the world where my husband would be likely to look for me."

"Your husband? Look for you?"

"Yes. I shall be quite frank with you. My husband and I have separated. A provisional divorce was granted, however, just seven months ago. The final decree cannot be issued for one year."

"But why should you hide from him?"

"The—the court gave him the custody of our child during the probationary year. I—I have run away with her. They are looking for me everywhere. That is why I came here. Do you understand?"

I was stunned. "Then, I take it, the court granted *him* the divorce and not you," I said, experiencing a sudden chill about the heart. "You were deprived of the child, I see. Dear me!"

"You are mistaken," she said, a flash in her eyes. "It was an Austrian court. The Count—my husband, I should say—is an Austrian subject. His interests must be protected." She said this with a sneer on her pretty lips. "You see, my father, knowing him now for what he really is, has refused to pay over to him something like a million dollars, still due for the marriage settlement. The Count contends that it is a just and legal debt and the court supports him to this extent: the child is to be his until the debt is cleared up, or something to that effect. I really don't understand the legal complications involved. Perhaps it were better if I did."

"I see," said I, scornful in spite of myself. "One of those happy international marriages where a bride is thrown in for good measure with a couple of millions.

Won't we ever learn!"

"That's it precisely," she said, with the utmost calmness and candour. "American dollars and an American girl in exchange for a title, a lot of debts and a ruined life."

"And they always turn out just this way. What a lot of blithering fools we have in the land of the free and the home of the knave!"

"My father objected to the whole arrangement from the first, so you must not speak of him as a knave," she protested. "He doesn't like Counts and such things."

"I don't see that it helps matters. I can hardly substitute the word 'brave' for the one I used," said I, trying to conceal my disgust.

"Please don't misunderstand me, Mr. Smart," she said haughtily. "I am not asking for pity. I made my bed and I shall lie in it. The only thing I ask of you is—well, kindness."

She seemed to falter again, and once more I was at her feet, figuratively speaking.

"You are in distress, in dread of something, madam," I cried. "Consider me your friend."

She shook her head ruefully. "You poor man! You don't know what you are in for, I fear. Wait till I have told you everything. Three weeks ago, I laid myself liable to imprisonment and heaven knows what else by abducting my little girl. That is really what it comes to—abduction. The court has ordered my arrest, and all sorts of police persons are searching high and low for me. Now don't you see your peril? If they find me here, you will be in a dreadful predicament. You will be charged with criminal complicity, or whatever it is called, and—Oh, it will be frightfully unpleasant for you, Mr. Smart."

My expression must have convicted me. She couldn't help seeing the dismay in my face. So she went on, quite humbly.

"Of course you have but to act at once and all may be well for you. I—I will go if you—if you command me to—"

I struck my knee forcibly. "What do you take me for, madam? Hang the consequences! If you feel that you are safe here—that is, comparatively safe,—*stay!*"

"It will be terrible if you get into trouble with the law," she murmured in distress. "I—I really don't know what might happen to you." Still her eyes brightened. Like all the rest of her ilK, she was selfish.

I tried to laugh, but it was a dismal failure. After all, wasn't it likely to prove a most unpleasant matter?

I felt the chill moisture breaking out on my forehead.

"Pray do not consider my position at all," I managed to say, with a resolute assumption of gallantry. "I—I shall be perfectly able to look out for myself,—that is, to explain everything if it should come to the worst." I could not help adding, however: "I certainly hope, however, that they don't get on to your trail and—" I stopped in confusion.

"And find me here?" she completed gloomily.

"And take the child away from you," I made haste to explain.

A fierce light named in her eyes. "I should—kill—some one before that could happen," she cried out, clenching her hands.

"I—I beg of you, madam, don't work yourself into a—a state," I implored, in considerable trepidation. "Nothing like that can happen, believe me. I—"

"Oh, what do you know about it?" she exclaimed, with most unnecessary vehemence, I thought. "He wants the child and—and—well, you can see why he
wants her, can't you? He is making the most desperate efforts to recover her. Max
says the newspapers are full of the—the scandal. They are depicting me as a brain-
less, law-defying American without sense of love, honour or respect. I don't mind
that, however. It is to be expected. They all describe the Count as a long-suffering,
honourable, dreadfully maltreated person, and are doing what they can to help him
in the prosecution of the search. My mother, who is in Paris, is being shadowed;
my two big brothers are being watched; my lawyers in Vienna are being trailed
everywhere—oh, it is really a most dreadful thing. But—but I will not give her up!
She is mine. He doesn't love her. He doesn't love me. He doesn't love anything in
the world but himself and his cigarettes. I know, for I've paid for his cigarettes for
nearly three years. He has actually ridiculed me in court circles, lie has defamed me,
snubbed me, humiliated me, cursed me. You cannot imagine what it has been like.
Once he struck me in—"

"Struck you!" I cried.

"—in the presence of his sister and her husband. But I must not distress you
with sordid details. Suffice it to say, I turned at last like the proverbial worm. I applied for a divorce ten months ago. It was granted, provisionally as I say. He is a de-
generate. He was unfaithful to me in every sense of the word. But in spite of all that,
the court in granting me the separation, took occasion to placate national honour
by giving him the child during the year, pending the final disposition of the case.
Of course, everything depends on father's attitude in respect to the money. You see
what I mean? A month ago I heard from friends in Vienna that he was shamefully
neglecting our—my baby, so I took this awful, this perfectly bizarre way of getting
her out of his hands. Possession is nine points in the law, you see. I—"

"Alas!" interrupted I, shaking my head. "There is more than one way to look at
the law. I'm afraid you have got yourself into a serious—er—pickle."

"I don't care," she said defiantly. "It is the law's fault for not prohibiting such marriages as ours. Oh, I know I must seem awfully foolish and idiotic to you, but—but it's too late now to back out, isn't it?

I did not mean to say it, but I did,—and I said it with some conviction: "It is! You **must** be protected."

"Thank you, thank you!" she cried, clasping and unclasping her little hands. I found myself wondering if the brute had dared to strike her on that soft, pink cheek!

Suddenly a horrible thought struck me with stunning force.

"Don't tell me that your—your husband is the man who owned this castle up to a week ago," I cried. "Count James Hohendahl?"

She shook her head. "No. He is not the man." Seeing that I waited for her to go on, she resumed: "I know Count James quite well, however. He is my husband's closest friend."

"Good heaven," said I, in quick alarm. "That complicates matters, doesn't it? He may come here at any time."

"It isn't likely, Mr. Smart. To be perfectly honest with you, I waited until I heard you had bought the castle before coming here myself. We were in hiding at the house of a friend in Linz up to a week ago. I did not think it right or fair to subject them to the notoriety or the peril that was sure to follow if the officers took it into their heads to look for me there. The day you bought the castle, I decided that it was the safest place for me to stay until the danger blows over, or until father can arrange to smuggle me out of this awful country. That very night we were brought here in a motor. Dear old Conrad and Airs. Schmick took me in. They have been perfectly adorable, all of them."

"May I enquire, madam," said I stiffly, "how you came to select my abode as your hiding place?"

Oh, I have forgotten to tell you that we lived here one whole summer just after we were married. Count Hohendahl let us have the castle for our—our honeymoon. He was here a great deal of the time All sorts of horrid, nasty, snobbish people were here to help us enjoy our honeymoon. I shall never forget that dreadful summer. My only friends were the Schmicks. Every one else ignored and despised me, and they all borrowed, won or stole money from me. I was compelled to play bridge for atrociously high stakes without knowing one card from the other. But, as I say, the Schmicks loved me. You see they were in the family ages and ages before I was born."

"The family? What family?"

The Rothhoefen family. Haven't they told you that my great-grandmother was a Rothhoefen? No? Well, she was. I belong to the third generation of American-born descendants. Doesn't it simplify matters, knowing this?"

"Immensely," said I, in something of a daze.

"And so I came here, Mr. Smart, where hundreds of my ancestors spent their honeymoons, most of them perhaps as unhappily as I, and where I knew a fellow-countryman was to live for awhile in order to get a plot for a new story. You see, I thought I might be a great help to you in the shape of suggestion."

She smiled very warmly, and I thought it was a very neat way of putting it. Naturally it would be quite impossible to put her out after hearing that she had already put herself out to some extent in order to assist me.

"I can supply the villain for your story if you need one, and I can give you oceans of ideas about noblemen. I am sorry that I can't give you a nice, sweet heroine. People hate heroines after they are married and live unhappily. You—"

"The public taste is changing," I interrupted quickly. "Unhappy marriages are so common nowadays that the women who go into 'em are always heroines. People like to read, about suffering and anguish among the rich, too. Besides, you are a Countess. That puts you near the first rank among heroines. Don't you think it would be proper at this point to tell me who you are?"

She regarded me steadfastly for a moment, and then shook her head.

"I'd rather not tell you my name, Mr. Smart. It really can't matter, you know. I've thought it all out very carefully, and I've decided that it is not best for you to know. You see if you don't know who it is you are sheltering, the courts can't hold you to account. You will be quite innocent of deliberately contriving to defeat the law. No, I shall not tell you my name, nor my husband's, nor my father's. If you'd like to know, however, I will tell you my baby's name. She's two years old and I think she'll like you to call her Rosemary."

By this time I was quite hypnotised by this charming, confident trespasser upon my physical—and I was about to say my moral estate. Never have I known a more complacent violater of all the proprieties of law and order as she appeared to be. She was a revelation; more than that, she *was* an inspiration. What a courageous, independent, fascinating little buccaneer she was! Her calm tone of assurance, her overwhelming confidence in herself, despite the occasional lapse into despair, staggered me. I couldn't help being impressed. If I had any thought of ejecting her, bag and baggage, from my castle, it had been completely knocked out of my head and I was left, you might say, in a position which gave me no other alternative than to consider myself a humble instrument in the furthering of her ends, whether I would or no. It was most amazing. Superior to the feeling of scorn I naturally felt for tier and her kind,—the fools who make international beds and find them filled with thorns,—there was the delicious sensation of being able to rise above my prejudices and become a willing conspirator against that despot, Common Sense.

She was very sure of herself, that was plain; and I am positive that she was equally sure of me. It isn't altogether flattering, either, to feel that a woman is so sure of you that there isn't any doubt concerning her estimate of your offensive strength. Somehow one feels an absence of physical attractiveness.

"Rosemary," I repeated. "And what am I to call you?"

"Even my enemies call me Countess," she said coldly.

"Oh," said I, more respectfully. "I see. When am I to have the pleasure of meeting the less particular Rosemary?"

"I didn't mean to be horrid," she said plaintively. "Please overlook it, Mr. Smart. If you are very, very quiet I think you may see her now. She is asleep."

"I may frighten her if she awakes," I said in haste, remembering my antipathy to babies.

Nevertheless I was led through a couple of bare, unfurnished rooms into a sunny, perfectly adorable nursery. A nursemaid,—English, at a glance,—arose from her seat in the window and held a cautious finger to her lips. In the middle of a bed that would have accommodated an entire family, was the sleeping Rosemary—a tiny, rosy-cheeked, yellow haired atom bounded on four sides by yards of mattress.

I stood over her timorously and stared. The Countess put one knee upon the mattress and, leaning far over, kissed a little paw. I blinked, like a confounded booby.

Then we stole out of the room.

"Isn't she adorable?" asked the Countess when we were at a safe distance.

"They all are," I said grudgingly, "when they're asleep."

"You are horrid!"

"By the way," I said sternly, "how does that bedstead happen to be a yard or so lower than any other bed in this entire castle? All the rest of them are so high one has to get into them from a chair."

"Oh," she said complacently, "it was too high for Blake to manage conveniently, so I had Rudolph saw the legs off short."

One of my very finest antique bedsteads! But I didn't even groan.

"You will let me stay on, won't you, Mr. Smart?" she said, when we were at the fireplace again. "I am really so helpless, you know."

I offered her everything that the castle afforded in the way of loyalty and luxury.

"And we'll have a telephone in the main hall before the end of a week," I concluded beamingly.

Her face clouded. "Oh, I'd much rather have it in my hallway, if you don't mind. You see, I can't very well go downstairs every time I want to use the 'phone, and it will be a nuisance sending for me when I'm wanted."

This was rather high-handed, I thought.

"But if no one knows you're here, it seems to me you're not likely to be called."

"You never can tell," she said mysteriously.

I promised to put the instrument in her hall, and not to have an extension to my rooms for fear of creating suspicion. Also the electric bell system was to be put in just as she wanted it to be. And a lot of other things that do not seem to come to mind at this moment.

I left in a daze at half-past three, to send Britton up with all the late novels and magazines, and a big box of my special cigarettes.

CHAPTER VI

I DISCUSS MATRIMONY

POOPENDYKE and I tried to do a little work that evening, but neither of us seemed quite capable of concentration. We said "I beg pardon" to each other a dozen times or more, following mental lapses, and then gave it up. My ideas failed in consecutiveness, and when I did succeed in hitching two intelligent thoughts together he invariably destroyed me sequence by compelling me to repeat myself, with the result that I became irascible.

We had gone over the events of the day very thoroughly. If anything, he was more alarmed over our predicament than I. He seemed to sense the danger that attended my decision to shelter and protect this cool-headed, rather self-centred young woman at the top of my castle. To me, it was something of a lark; to him, a tragedy. He takes everything seriously, so much so in fact that he gets on my nerves. I wish he were not always looking at things through the little end of the telescope. I like a change, and it is a novelty to sometimes see things through the big end, especially peril.

"They will yank us all up for aiding and abetting," he proclaimed, trying to focus his eyes on the shorthand book he was fumbling.

"You wouldn't have me turn her over to the law, would you?" I demanded crossly. "Please don't forget that we are Americans."

"I don't," said he. "That's what worries me most of all."

"Well," said I loftily, "we'll see."

We were silent for a long time.

"It must be horribly lonely and spooky away up there where she is," I said at last, inadvertently betraying my thoughts. He sniffed.

"Have you a color?" I demanded, glaring at him.

"No," he said gloomily; "a presentiment."

"Umph!"

Another period of silence. Then: "I wonder if Max—" I stopped short.

"Yes, sir," he said, with wonderful divination. "He did."

"Any message?"

"She sent down word that the new cook is a jewel, but I think she must have been jesting. I've never cared for a man cook myself. I don't like to appear hypercritical, but what did you think of the dinner tonight, sir?"

"I've never tasted better broiled ham in my life, Mr. Poopendyke."

"Ham! That's it, Mr. Smart. But what I'd like to know is this: "What became of the grouse you ordered for dinner, sir? I happen to know that it was put over the fire at seven—"

"I sent it up to the countess, with *our* compliments," said I, peevishly. I think that remark silenced him. At any rate, he got up and left the room.

I laid awake half the night morbidly berating the American father who is so afraid of his wife that he lets her bully him into sacrificing their joint flesh and blood upon the altar of social ambition. She had said that her father was opposed to the match from the beginning. Then why, in the name of heaven, wasn't he man enough to put a stop to it? Why—But what use is there in applying whys to a man who doesn't know what God meant when He fashioned two sexes? I put him down as neutral and tried my best to forget him.

But I couldn't forget the daughter of this browbeaten American father. There was something singularly familiar about her exquisite face, a conviction on my part that is easily accounted for. Her portrait, of course, had been published far and wide at the time of the wedding; she must have been pictured from every conceivable angle, with illimitable gowns, hats, veils and parasols, and I certainly could not have missed seeing her, even with half an eye. But for the life of me, I couldn't connect her with any of the much-talked-of international marriages that came to mind as I lay there going over the meagre assortment I was able to recall. I went to sleep wondering whether Poopendyke's memory was any better than mine. He is tremendously interested in the financial doings of our country, being the possessor of a flourishing savings' account, and as he also possesses a lively sense of the ridiculous, it was not unreasonable to suspect that he might remember all the details of this particular transaction in stocks and bonds.

The next morning I set my labourers to work putting guest-rooms into shape for the coming of the Hazzards and the four friends who were to be with them for the week as my guests. They were to arrive on the next day but one, which gave me ample time to consult a furniture dealer. I would have to buy at least six new beds and everything else with which to comfortably equip as many bed-chambers, it being a foregone conclusion, that not even the husbands and wives would condescend to "double up" to oblige me. The expensiveness of this ill-timed visit had not occurred to me at the outset. Still there was some prospect of getting the wholesale price. On one point I was determined; the workmen should not be laid off for a single hour, not even if my guests went off in a huff.

At twelve I climbed the tortuous stairs leading to the Countess's apartments. She opened the door herself in response to my rapping.

"I neglected to mention yesterday that I am expecting a houseful of guests in a day or two," I said, after she had given me a very cordial greeting.

"Guests?" she cried in dismay. "Oh, dear! Can't you put them off?"

"I have hopes that they won't be able to stand the workmen banging around all day," I confessed, somewhat guiltily.

"Women in the party?"

"Two, I believe. Both married and qualified to express opinions."

"They will be sure to nose me out," she said ruefully. "Women are dreadful nosers."

"Don't worry," I said. "We'll get a lot of new padlocks for the doors downstairs and you'll be as safe as can be, if you'll only keep quiet."

"But I don't see why I should be made to mope here all day and all night like a sick cat, holding my hand over Rosemary's mouth when she wants to cry, and muzzling poor Jinko so that he—"

"My dear countess," I interrupted sternly, "you should not forget that these other guests of mine are invited here."

"But I was here first," she argued. "It is most annoying."

"I believe you said yesterday that you are in the habit of having your own way."

She nodded her head. "Well, I am afraid you'll have to come down from your high horse at least temporarily."

"Oh, I see. You—you mean to be very firm and domineering with me."

"You must try to see things from my point of—"

"Please don't say that!" she flared. "I'm so tired of hearing those words. For the last three years I've been **commanded** to see things from some one else's point of view, and I'm sick of the expression."

"For heaven's sake, don't put me in the same boat with your husband!"

She regarded me somewhat frigidly for a moment longer, and then a slow, witching smile crept into her eyes.

"I sha'n't," she promised, and laughed outright. "Do forgive me, Mr. Smart. I am such a piggy thing. I'll try to be nice and sensible, and. I will be as still as a mouse all the time they're here. But you must promise to come up every day and give me the gossip. You *can* steal up, can't you? Surreptitiously?"

"Clandestinely,' I said, gravely.

"I really ought to warn you once more about getting yourself involved," she said pointedly.

"Oh, I'm quite a safe old party," I assured her. "They couldn't make capital of me."

"The grouse was delicious," she said, deliberately changing the subject. Nice divorcees are always doing that.

We fell into a discussion of present and future needs; of ways and means for keeping my friends utterly in the dark concerning her presence in the abandoned east wing; and of what we were pleased to allude to as "separate maintenance," employing a phrase that might have been considered distasteful and even banal under ordinary conditions.

"I've been trying to recall all of the notable marriages we had in New York three years ago," said I, after she had most engagingly reduced me to a state of subjection in the matter of three or four moot questions that came up for settlement. "You don't seem to fit in with any of the international affairs I can bring to mind."

"You promised you wouldn't bother about that, Mr. Smart," she said severely.

"Of course you *were* married in New York?"

"In a very nice church just off Fifth Avenue, if that will help you any," she said. "The usual crowd inside the church, and the usual mob outside, all fighting for a glimpse of me in my wedding shroud, and for a chance to see a real Hungarian nobleman. It really was a very magnificent wedding, Mr. Smart." She seemed to be unduly proud of the spectacular sacrifice.

A knitted brow revealed the obfuscated condition of my brain. I was thinking very intently, not to say remotely.

"The whole world talked about it," she went on dreamily. "We had a real prince for the best man, and two of the ushers couldn't speak a word of English. Don't you remember that the police closed the streets in the neighbourhood of the church and wouldn't let people spoil everything by going about their business as they were in the habit of doing? Some of the shops sold window space to sight-seers, just as they do at a coronation."

"I daresay all this should let in light, but it doesn't."

"Don't you read the newspapers?" she cried impatiently. She actually resented my ignorance.

"Religiously," I said, stung to revolt. "But I make it a point never to read, the criminal news."

"Criminal news?" she gasped, a spot of red leaping to her cheek. "What do you mean?"

"It is merely my way of saying that I put marriages of that character in the category of crime."

"Oh!" she cried, staring at me with unbelieving eyes.

"Every time a sweet, lovely American girl is delivered into the hands of a foreign bounder who happens to possess a title that needs fixing, I call the transaction a crime that puts white slavery in a class with the most trifling misdemeanours. You did not love this pusillanimous Count, nor did he care a hang for you. You were too young in the ways of the world to have any feeling for him, and he was too old to have any for you. The whole hateful business therefore resolved itself into a case of give and take—and he took everything. He took you and your father's millions and now you are both back where you began. Some one deliberately committed a crime, and as it wasn't you or the Count,—who levied his legitimate toll,—it must have been the person who planned the conspiracy. I take it, of course, that the whole affair was arranged behind your back, so to speak. To make it a perfectly fashionable and up-to-date delivery it would have been entirely out of place to consult the unsophisticated girl who was thrown in to make the title good. You were not sold to this bounder. It was the other way round. By the gods, madam, he was actually paid to take you!"

Her face was quite pale. Her eyes did not leave mine during the long and crazy diatribe,—of which I was already beginning to feel heartily ashamed, and there was a dark, ominous fire in them that should have warned me.

She arose from her chair. It seemed to me she was taller than before.

"If nothing else came to me out of this transaction," she said levelly, "at least a certain amount of dignity was acquired. Pray remember that I am no longer the unsophisticated girl you so graciously describe. I am a woman, Mr. Smart."

"True," said I, senselessly dogged; "a woman with the power to think for yourself. That is my point. If the same situation arose at your present age, I fancy you'd be able to select a husband without assistance, and I venture to say you wouldn't pick up the first dissolute nobleman that came your way. No, my dear countess, you were not to blame. You thought, as your parents did, that marriage with a count would make a real countess of you. What rot! You are a simple, lovable American girl and that's all there ever can be to it. To the end of your days you will be an American. It is not within the powers of a scape-grace count to put you or any other American girl on a plane with the women who are born countesses, or duchesses, or anything of the sort. I don't say that you suffer by comparison with these noble ladies. As a matter of fact you are surpassingly finer in every way than ninety-nine per cent, of them,—poor things! Marrying an English duke doesn't make a genuine duchess out of an American girl, not by a long shot. She merely becomes a figure of speech. Your own experience should tell you that. Well, it's the same with all of them. They acquire a title, but not the homage that should go with it."

We were both standing now. She was still measuring me with somewhat incredulous eyes, rather more tolerant than resentful.

"Do you expect me to agree with you, Mr. Smart?" she asked.

"I do," said I, promptly. "You, of all people, should be able to testify that my views are absolutely right."

"They are right," she said, simply. "Still you are pretty much of a brute to insult me wren them."

"I most sincerely crave your pardon, if it isn't too late," I cried, abject once more. (I don't know what gets into me once in a while.)

"The safest way, I should say, is for neither of us to express an opinion so long as we are thrown into contact with each other. If you choose to tell the world what you think of me, all well and good. But please don't tell me."

"I can't convince the world what I think of you for the simple reason that I'd be speaking at random. I don't know who you are."

"Oh, you will know some day," she said, and her shoulders drooped a little.

"I've—I've done a most cowardly, despicable thing in hunting you—"

"Please! Please don't say anything more about it. I dare say you've done me a lot of good. Perhaps I shall see things a little more clearly. To be perfectly honest with you, I went into this marriage with my eyes wide open, but I was only one fool among many. Dozens of other girls in my set were crazy to marry him. I—haven't told you that he is extremely good-looking. And he was—was adorable in those days."

A far-away, dreamy look came into her eyes. She was staring at me, but I felt myself quite outside the range of her vision.

I ventured a shrewd conjecture, considering the obvious character of her abstraction.

"Stranger things have happened than that you should paten up your difficulties and go back to live with your husband."

She uttered a little cry of revulsion. The dreamy light died in her eyes and she transfixed me with a look of indignation.

"How dare you suggest such a thing! How dare you speak to me in that way! You—I ought to order you out of this room and never—never"

My luminous smile checked the outburst.

"Splendid!" I cried. "You convince me that it can never happen."

She smiled doubtfully, quite uncertain how to take my humour.

"Oh, dear me," she sighed, "I don't believe we shall ever get on at all well together, Mr. Smart. You are such a whimsical person."

"I'll try to do better," I cried, frankly pleased with the situation. "Give me a chance."

"You spoke of him as my husband," she said, going back to my remark. "He is *not* my husband. Please be good enough to remember that."

"It will be easy, I assure you. May I therefore venture the hope that if you ever decide to marry again you'll give some deserving American a chance to make you his queen? You'll find it better than being a countess, believe me."

"I shall never marry, Mr. Smart," she said with decision. "Never, never again will I get into a mess that is so hard to get out of. I can say this to you because I've heard you are a bachelor. You can't take offence."

"I fondly hope to die a bachelor," said I with humility.

"God bless you!" she cried, bursting into a merry laugh, and I knew that a truce had been declared for the time being at least. "And now let us talk sense. Have you carefully considered the consequences if you are found out, Mr. Smart?"

"Found out?"

"If you are caught shielding a fugitive from justice. I couldn't go to sleep for hours last night thinking of what might happen to you if—"

"Nonsense!" I cried, but for the life of me I couldn't help feeling elated. She *had* a soul above self, after all!

"You see, I am a thief and a robber and a very terrible malefactor, according to the reports Max brings over from the city. The fight for poor little Rosemary is destined to fill columns and columns in the newspapers of the two continents for months to come. You, Mr. Smart, may find yourself in the thick of it. If I were in your place, I should keep out of it."

"While I am not overjoyed by the prospect of being dragged into it, Countess, I certainly refuse to back out at this stage of the game. Moreover, you may rest assured that I shall not turn you out."

"It occurred to me last night that the safest thing for you to do, Mr. Smart, is to—to get out yourself." I stared. She went on hurriedly: "Can't you go away for a month's visit or—"

"Well, upon my soul!" I gasped. "Would you turn me out of my own house? This beats anything I've—"

"I was only thinking of your peace of mind and your—your safety," she cried unhappily. "Truly, truly I was."

"Well, I prefer to stay here and do what little I can to shield you and Rosemary," said I sullenly.

"I'll not say anything horrid again, Mr. Smart," she said quite meekly. (I take this occasion to repeat that I've never seen any one in all my life so pretty as she!) Her moist red lip trembled slightly, like a censured child's.

At that instant there came a rapping on the door. I started apprehensively.

"It is only Max with the coal," she explained, with obvious relief. "We keep a fire going in the grate all day long. You've no idea how cold it is up here even on the hottest days. Come in!"

Max came near to dropping the scuttle when he saw me. He stood as one petrified.

"Don't mind Mr. Smart, Max," said she serenely. "He won't bite your head off."

The poor clumsy fellow spilled quantities of coal over the hearth when he attempted to replenish the fire at her command, and moved with greater celerity in making his escape from the room than I had ever known him to exercise before. Somehow I began to regain a lost feeling of confidence in myself. The confounded Schmicks, big and little, were afraid of me, after all.

"By the way," she said, after we had lighted our cigarettes, "I am nearly out of these." I liked the way she held the match for me, and then nicked it snappily into the centre of a pile of cushions six feet from the fireplace.

I made a mental note of the shortage and then admiringly said that I didn't see how any man, even a count could help adoring a woman who held a cigarette to her lips as she did.

"Oh," said she coolly, "his friends were willing worshippers, all of them. There wasn't a man among them who failed to make violent love to me, and with the Count's permission at that. You must not look so shocked. I managed to keep them at a safe distance. My unreasonable attitude toward them used to annoy my husband intensely.

"Good Lord!"

"Pooh! He didn't care what became of me. There was one particular man whom he favoured the most. A dreadful man! We quarrelled bitterly when I declared that either he or I would have to leave the house—forever. I don't mind confessing to you that the man I speak of is your friend, the gentle Count Hohendahl, some time ogre of this castle."

I shuddered. A feeling of utter loathing for all these unprincipled scoundrels came over me, and I mildly took the name of the Lord in vain.

With an abrupt change of manner, she arose from her chair and began to pace the floor, distractedly beating her clinched hands against her bosom. Twice I heard her murmur: "Oh, God!"

This startling exposition of feeling gave me a most uncanny shock. It came out of a clear sky, so to say, at a moment when I was beginning to regard her as cold-blooded, callous, and utterly without the emotions supposed to exist in the breast of every high-minded woman. And now I was witness to the pain she suffered, now I heard her cry out against the thing that had hurt her so pitilessly. I turned my head away, vastly moved. Presently she moved over to the window. A covert glance revealed her standing there, looking not down at the Danube that seemed so far away but up at the blue sky that seemed so near.

I sat very still and repressed, trying to remember the harsh, unkind things I had said to her, and berating myself fiercely for all of them. What a stupid, vainglorious ass I was, not to have divined something of the inward fight she was making to conquer the emotions that filled her heart unto the bursting point.

The sound of dry, suppressed sobs came to my ears. It was too much for me. I stealthily quit my position by the mantel-piece and tip-toed toward the door, bent on leaving her alone. Half-way there I hesitated, stopped and then deliberately returned to the fireplace, where I noisily shuffled a fresh supply of coals into the grate. It would be heartless, even unmannerly, to leave her without letting her know that I was heartily ashamed of myself and completely in sympathy with her. Wisely, however, I resolved to let her have her cry out. Some one a great deal more far-seeing than I let the world into a most important secret when he advised man to take that course when in doubt.

For a long while I waited for her to regain control of herself, rather dreading the apology she would feel called upon to make for her abrupt reversion to the first principles of her sex. The sobs ceased entirely. I experienced the sharp joy of relaxation. Her dainty lace handkerchief found employment. First she would dab it cautiously in one eye, then the other, after which she would scrutinise its crumpled surface with most extraordinary interest. At least a dozen times she repeated this puzzling operation. What in the world was she looking for? To this day, that strange, sly peeking on her part remains a mystery to me.

She turned swiftly upon me and beckoned with her little forefinger. Greatly concerned, I sprang toward her. Was she preparing to swoon? What in heaven's name was I to do if she took it into her pretty head to do such a thing as that? Involuntarily I shot a quick look at her blouse. To my horror it was buttoned down the back. It would be a bachelor's luck to—But she was smiling radiantly. Saved!

"LOOK!" she cried, pointing upward through the window. "Isn't she lovely?"

I stopped short in my tracks and stared at her in blank amazement. What a stupefying creature she was!

She beckoned again, impatiently. I obeyed with alacrity. Obtaining a rather clear view of her eyes, I was considerably surprised to find no trace of departed tears. Her cheek was as smooth and creamy white as it had been before the deluge. Her eyelids were dry and orderly and her nose had not been blown once to my recollection. Truly, it was a marvellous recovery. I still wonder.

The cause of her excitement was visible at a glance. A trim nurse-maid stood in the small gallery which circled the top of the turret, just above and to the right of us. She held in her arms the pink-hooded, pink-coated Rosemary, made snug against the chill winds of her lofty parade ground. Her yellow curls peeped out from beneath the lace of the hood, and her round little cheeks were the colour of the peach's bloom.

"Now, *isn't* she lovely?" cried my eager companion. "Even a crusty bachelor can see that she is adorable."

"I am not a crusty bachelor, I protested indignantly, "and what's more, I am positive I should like to kiss those red little cheeks, which is saying a great deal for me. I've never voluntarily kissed a baby in my life."

"I do not approve of the baby-kissing custom," she said severely. "It is extremely unhealthy and—middle-class. Still," seeing my expression change, "I sha'n't mind your kissing her once."

"Thanks," said I humbly.

It was plain to be seen that she did not intend to refer to the recent outburst. Superb exposition of tact!

Catching the nurse's eye, she signalled for her to bring the child down to us. Rosemary took to me at once. A most embarrassing thing happened. On seeing me she held out her chubby arms and shouted "da-da!" at the top of her infantile lungs. *That* had never happened to me before.

I flushed and the Countess shrieked with laughter. It wouldn't have been so bad if the nurse had known her place. If there is one thing in this world that I hate with fervour, it is an ill-mannered, poorly-trained servant. A grinning nurse-maid is the worst of all. I may be super-sensitive and crotchety about such things, but I can see no excuse for keeping a servant—especially a nurse-maid—who laughs at everything that's said by her superiors, even though the quip may be no more side-splitting than a two syllabled "da-da."

"Ha, ha!" I laughed bravely. "She—she evidently thinks I look like the Count. He is very handsome, you say."

"Oh, that isn't it," cried the Countess, taking Rosemary in her arms and directing me to a spot on her rosy cheek. "Kiss right there, Mr. Smart. There! Wasn't it a nice kiss, honey-bunch? If you are a very, very nice little girl the kind gentleman will kiss you on the other cheek some day. She calls every man she meets da-da," explained the radiant young mother. "She's awfully European in her habits, you see. You need not feel flattered. She calls Conrad and Rudolph and Max da-da, and this morning in the back window she applied the same handsome compliment to your Mr. Poopendyke."

"Oh," said I, rather more crestfallen than relieved.

"Would, you like to hold her, Mr. Smart? She's such a darling to hold."

"No—no, thank you," I cried, backing off.

"Oh, you will come to it, never fear," she said gaily, as she restored Rosemary to the nurse's arms. "Won't he, Blake?"

"He will, my lady," said Blake with conviction. I noticed this time that Blake's smile wasn't half bad.

At that instant Jinko, the chow, pushed the door open with his black nose and strolled imposingly into the room. He proceeded to treat me in the most cavalier fashion by bristling and growling.

The Countess opened her eyes very wide.

"Dear me," she sighed, "you must be very like the Count, after all. Jinko never growls at any one but him."

At dinner that evening I asked Poopendyke point blank if he could call to mind a marriage in New York society that might fit the principals in this puzzling case.

He hemmed and hawed and appeared to be greatly confused.

"Really, sir I—I—really, I—"

"You make it a point to read all of the society news," I explained; "and you are a great hand for remembering names and faces. Think hard."

"As a matter of fact, Mr. Smart, I do remember this particular marriage very clearly," said he, looking down at his plate.

"You do?" I shouted eagerly. The new footman stared. "Splendid! Tell me, who is she—or was she?"

My secretary looked me steadily in the eye.

"I'm sorry, sir, but—but I can't do it. I promised her this morning I wouldn't let it be dragged out of me with red hot tongs."

CHAPTER VII

I RECEIVE VISITORS

SHE was indeed attended by faithful slaves.

The east wing of the castle was as still as a mouse on the day my house party arrived. Grim old doors took on new padlocks, keyholes were carefully stopped up; creaking floors were calked; windows were picketed by uncompromising articles of furniture deployed to keep my ruthless refugee from adventuring too close to the danger zone; and adamantine instructions were served out to all of my vassals. Everything appeared to be in tip-top shape for the experiment in stealth.

And yet I trembled. My secret seemed to be safely planted, but what would the harvest be? I knew I should watch those upper windows with hypnotic zeal, and listen with straining ears for the inevitable squall of a child or the bark of a dog. My brain ran riot with incipient subterfuges, excuses, apologies and lies with which my position was to be sustained.

There would not be a minute during the week to come when I would be perfectly free to call my soul my own, and as for nerves! well, with good luck they might endure the strain. Popping up in bed out of a sound sleep at the slightest disturbance, with ears wide open and nerves tingling, was to be a nightly occupation at uncertain intervals; that was plain to be seen. All day long I would be shivering with anxiety and praying for night to come so that I might lie awake and pray for the sun to rise, and in this way pass the time as quickly as possible. There would be difficulty in getting my visitors to bed early, another thing to test my power at conniving. They were bridge players, of course, and as such, would be up till all hours of the morning overdoing themselves in the effort to read each other's thoughts.

I thanked the Lord that my electric lighting system would not be installed until after they had departed. Ordinarily the Lord isn't thanked when an electric light company fails to perform its work on schedule time, but in this case delay was courted.

We were all somewhat surprised and not a little disorganised by the appearance of four unexpected servants in the train of my party. We hadn't counted on anything quite so elaborate. There were two lady's maids, not on friendly terms with each other; a French valet who had the air of one used to being served on a tray outside the servants' quarters; and a German attendant with hands constructed especially for the purpose of kneading and gouging the innermost muscles of his master, who it appears had to be kneaded and gouged three times a day by a masseur in order to stave off paralysis, locomotor ataxia or something equally unwelcome to a high liver.

We had ample room for all this physical increase, but no beds. I transferred the problem to Poopendyke. How he solved it I do not know, but from the woe-be-gone expression on his face the morning after the first night, and the fact that Britton was unnecessarily rough in shaving me, I gathered that the two of them had slept on a pile of rugs in the lower hall.

Elsie Hazzard presented me to her friends and, with lordly generosity, I presented the castle to them. Her husband, Dr. George, thanked me for saving all their lives and then, feeling a draft, turned up his coat collar and informed me that we'd all die if I didn't have the cracks stopped up. He seemed unnecessarily testy about it.

There was a Russian baron (the man who had to be kneaded) the last syllable of whose name was vitch, the first five evading me in a perpetual chase up and down the alphabet. For brevity's sake, I'll call him Umovitch. The French valet's master was a Viennese gentleman of twenty-six or eight (I heard), but who looked forty. I found myself wondering how dear, puritanic, little Elsie Hazzard could have fallen in with two such unamiable wrecks as these fellows appeared to be at first sight.

The Austrian's name was Pless. He was a plain mister. The more I saw of him the first afternoon the more I wondered at George Hazzard's carelessness. Then there were two very bright and charming Americans, the Billy Smiths. He was connected with the American Embassy at Vienna, and I liked him from the start. You could tell that he was the sort of a chap who is bound to get on in the world by simply looking at his wife. The man who could win the love and support of such an attractive creature must of necessity have qualifications to spare. She was very beautiful and very clever. Somehow the unforgetable resplendency of my erstwhile typist (who married the jeweller's clerk) faded into a pale, ineffective drab when opposed to the charms of Mrs. Betty Billy Smith. (They all called her Betty Billy.)

After luncheon I got Elsie off in a corner and plied her with questions concerning her friends. The Billy Smiths were easily accounted for. They belonged to the most exclusive set in New York and Newport. He had an incomprehensible lot of money and a taste for the diplomatic service. Some day he would be an Ambassador. The Baron was in the Russian Embassy and was really a very nice boy.

"Boy?" I exclaimed.

"He is not more than thirty," said she. "You wouldn't call that old." There was nothing I could say to that and still be a perfect host. But to you I declare that he wasn't a day under fifty. How blind women can be! Or is silly the word?

From where we sat the figure of Mr. Pless was plainly visible in the loggia. He was alone, leaning against the low wall and looking down upon the river. He puffed idly at a cigarette. His coal black hair grew very sleek on his smallish head and his shoulders were rather high, as if pinched upward by a tendency to defy a weak spine.

"And this Mr. Pless, who is he?"

Elsie was looking at the rakish young man with a pitying expression in her tender blue eyes.

"Poor fellow," she sighed. "He is in great trouble, John. We hoped that if we got him off here where it is quiet he might be able to forget—Oh, but I am not supposed to tell you a word of the story! We are all sworn to secrecy. It was only on that condition that he consented to come with us."

"Indeed!"

She hesitated, uncomfortably placed between two duties. She owed one to him and one to me.

"It is only fair, John, that you should know that Pless is not his real name," she said, lowering her voice. "But, of course, we stand sponsor for him, so it is all right."

"Your word is sufficient, Elsie."

She seemed to be debating some inward question. The next I knew she moved a little closer to me.

"His life is a—a tragedy," she whispered. "His heart is broken, I firmly believe. Oh!"

The Billy Smiths came up. Elsie proceeded to withdraw into herself.

"We were speaking of Mr. Pless," said I. "He has a broken heart."

The newcomers looked hard at poor Elsie.

"Broken fiddle-sticks," said Billy Smith, nudging Elsie until she made room for him beside her on the long couch. I promptly made room for Betty Billy.

"We ought to tell John just a little about him," said Elsie defensively. "It is due him, Billy."

"But don't tell him the fellow's heart is broken. That's rot."

"It isn't rot," said his wife. "Wouldn't your heart be broken?"

He crossed his legs comfortably.

"Wouldn't it?" repeated Betty Billy.

"Not if it were as porous as his. You can't break a sponge, my dear."

"What happened to it?" I inquired, mildly interested.

"Women," said Billy impressively.

"Then it's easily patched," said I. "Like cures like."

"You don't understand, John," said Elsie gravely. "He was married to a beauti-ful—"

"Now, Elsie, you're telling," cautioned Betty Billy.

"Well," said Elsie doggedly, "I'm determined to tell this much: his name isn't Pless, his wife got a divorce from him, and now she has taken their child and run off with it and they can't find—what's the matter?"

My eyes were almost popping from my head.

"Is—is he a count?" I cried, so loudly that they all said "sh!" and shot apprehensive glances toward the pseudo Mr. Pless.

"Goodness!" said Elsie in alarm. "Don't shout, John."

Billy Smith regarded me speculatively. "I daresay Mr. Smart has read all about the affair in the newspapers. They've had nothing else lately. I won't say he is a count, and I won't say he isn't. We're bound by a deep, dark, sinister oath, sealed with blood."

"I haven't seen anything about it in the papers," said I, trying to recover my self-possession which had sustained a most tremendous shock.

"Thank heaven!" cried Elsie devoutly.

"Do you mean to say you won't tell me his name?" I demanded.

Elsie eyed me suspiciously. "Why did you ask if he is a count?"

"I have a vague recollection of hearing some one speak of a count having trouble with his young American wife, divorce, or something of the sort. A very prominent New York girl, if I'm not mistaken. All very hazy, however. What is his name?"

"John," said Mrs. Hazzard firmly, "you must not ask us to tell you. Won't you please understand?"

"The poor fellow is almost distracted. Really, Mr. Smart, we planned this little visit here simply in order to—to take him out of himself for a while. It has been such a tragedy for him. He worshipped the child." It was Mrs. Billy who spoke.

"And the mother made way with him?" I queried, resorting to a suddenly acquired cunning.

"It is a girl," said Elsie in a loud whisper. "The *loveliest* girl. The mother appeared in Vienna about three weeks or a month ago and—whiff! Off goes the child. Abducted—kidnapped! And the court had granted him the custody of the child. That's what makes it so terrible. If she is caught anywhere in Europe—well, I don't know what may happen to her. It is just such silly acts as this that make American girls the laughing stocks of the whole world. I give you my word I am almost ashamed to have people point me out and say: 'There goes an American. Pooh!' "

By this time I had myself pretty well in hand.

"I daresay the mother loved the child, which ought to condone one among her multitude of sins. I take it, of course, that she was entirely to blame for everything that happened."

They at once proceeded to tear the poor little mother to shreds, delicately and with finesse, to be sure, but none the less completely. No doubt they meant to be charitable.

"This is what a silly American nobody gets for trying to be somebody over here just because her father has a trunkful of millions," said Elsie, concluding a rather peevish estimate of the conjugal effrontery laid at the door of Mr. Pless's late wife.

"Or just because one of these spendthrift foreigners has a title for sale," said Billy Smith sarcastically.

"He was deeply in love with her when they were married," said his wife. "I don't believe it was his fault that they didn't get along well together."

"The truth of the matter is," said Elsie with finality, "she couldn't live up to her estate. She was a drag, a stone about his neck. It was like putting one's waitress at the head of the table and expecting her to make good as a hostess."

"What was her social standing in New York?" I enquired.

"Oh, good enough," said Betty Billy. "She was in the smartest set, if that is a recommendation."

"Then you admit, both of you, that the best of our American girls fall short of being all that is required over here. In other words, they can't hold a candle to the Europeans."

"Not at all," they both said in a flash.

"That's the way it sounds to me."

Elsie seemed repentant. "I suppose we are a little hard on the poor thing. She was very young, you see."

"What you mean to say, then, is that she wasn't good enough for Mr. Pless and his coterie."

"No, not just precisely that," admitted Betty Billy Smith. "She made a bid for him and got him, and my contention is that she should have lived up to the bargain."

"Wasn't he paid in full?" I asked, with a slight sneer.

"What do you mean?"

"Didn't he get his money?"

"I am sure I don't see what, money has to do with the case," said Elsie, with dignity. "Mr. Pless is a poor man I've heard. There could not have been very much of a marriage settlement."

"A mere million to start with," remarked Billy Smith ironically. "It's all gone, my dear Elsie, and I gather that father-in-law locked the trunk you speak of and hid the key. You don't know women as well as I do, Mr. Smart. Both of these charming ladies professed to adore Mr. Pless's wife up to the time the trial for divorce came up. Now they've got their hammers and hat-pins out for her and—"

"That isn't true, Billy Smith," cried Elsie in a fierce whisper. "We stood by her until she disobeyed the mandate—or whatever you call it—of the court. She did steal the child, and you can't deny it."

"Poor little kiddie," said he, and from his tone I gathered that all was not rosy in the life of the infant in this game of battledore and shuttlecock.

To my disgust, the three of them refused to enlighten me further as to the history, identity or character of either Mr. or Mrs. Pless, but of course I knew that I was entertaining under my roof, by the most extraordinary coincidence, the Count and Countess of Something-or-other, who were at war, and the child they were fighting for with motives of an entirely opposite nature.

Right or wrong, my sympathies were with the refugee in the lonely east wing. I was all the more determined now to shield her as far as it lay in my power to do so, and to defend her if the worst were to happen.

Mr. Pless tossed his cigarette over the railing and sauntered over to join us.

"I suppose you've been discussing the view," he said as he came up. There was a mean smile on his—yes, it was a rather handsome face—and the two ladies started guiltily. The attack on his part was particularly direct when one stops to consider that there wasn't any view to be had from where we were sitting, unless one could call a three-decked plasterer's scaffolding a view.

"We've been discussing the recent improvements about the castle, Mr. Pless," said I with so much directness that I felt Mrs. Billy Smith's arm stiffen and suspected a general tension of nerves from head to foot.

"You shouldn't spoil the place, Mr. Smart," said he, with a careless glance about him.

"Don't ruin the ruins," added Billy Smith, of the diplomatic corps.

"What time do we dine?" asked Mr. Pless, with a suppressed yawn.

"At eight," said Elsie promptly.

We were in the habit of dining at seven-thirty, but I was growing accustomed to the over-riding process, so allowed my dinner hour to be changed without a word.

"I think I'll take a nap," said he. With a languid smile and a little flaunt of his hand as if dismissing us, he moved languidly off, but stopped after a few steps to say to me: "We'll explore the castle to-morrow, Mr. Smart, if it's just the same to you." He spoke with a very slight accent and in a peculiarly attractive manner. There was charm to the man, I was bound to admit. "I know Schloss Rothhoefen very well. It is an old stamping ground of mine."

"Indeed," said I, affecting surprise.

"I spent a very joyous season here not so many years ago. Hohendahl is a bosom friend."

When he was quite out of hearing, Billy Smith leaned over and said to me: "He spent his honeymoon here, old man. It was the girls' idea to bring him here to assuage the present with memories of the past. Quite a pretty sentiment, eh?"

"It depends on how he spent it," I said significantly. Smith grinned approvingly. Being a diplomat he sensed my meaning at once.

"It was a lot of money" he said.

At dinner the Russian baron, who examined every particle of food he ate with great care and discrimination, evidently looking for poison, embarrassed me in the usual fashion by asking how I write my books, where I get my plots, and all the rest of the questions that have become so hatefully unanswerable, ending up by blandly enquiring *what* I had written. This was made especially humiliating by the prefatory remark that he had lived in Washington for five years and had read everything that was worth reading.

If Elsie had been a man I should have kicked her for further confounding me by mentioning the titles of all my books and saying that he surely must have read them, as everybody did, thereby supplying mm with the chance to triumphantly say that he'd be hanged if he'd ever heard of any one of them. I shall always console myself with the joyful thought that I couldn't remember his infernal name and would now make it a point never to do so.

Mr. Pless openly made love to Elsie and the Baron openly made love to Betty Billy. Being a sort of noncommittal bachelor, I ranged myself with the two abandoned husbands and we had quite a reckless time of it, talking with uninterrupted devilishness about the growth of American dentistry in European capitals, the way one has his nails manicured in Germany, the upset price of hot-house strawberries, the relative merit of French and English bulls, the continued progress of the weather and sundry other topics of similar piquancy. Elsie invited all of us to a welsh rarebit party she was giving at eleven-thirty, and then they got to work at the bridge table, poor George Hazzard cutting in occasionally. This left Billy Smith and me free to make up a somewhat somnolent two-some.

I was eager to steal away to the east wing with the news, but how to dispose of Billy without appearing rude was more than I could work out. It was absolutely necessary for the Countess to know that her ex-husband was in the castle. I would have to manage in some way to see her before the evening was over. The least carelessness, the smallest slip might prove the undoing of both of us.

I wondered how she would take the dismal news. Would she become hysterical and go all to pieces? Would the prospect of a week of propinquity be too much for her, even though thick walls intervened to put them into separate worlds? Or, worst of all, would she reveal an uncomfortable spirit of bravado, rashly casting discretion to the winds in order to show him that she was not the timid, beaten coward he might suspect her of being? She had once said to me that she loathed a coward.

I have always wondered how it felt to be in a "pretty kettle of fish," or a "pickle," or any of the synonymous predicaments. Now I knew. Nothing could have been more synchronous than the plural howdy-do that confronted me.

My nervousness must have been outrageously pronounced. Pacing the floor, looking at one's watch, sighing profoundly, putting one's hands in the pockets and taking them out again almost immediately, letting questions go by unanswered, and all such, are actions or conditions that usually produce the impression that one is nervous. A discerning observer seldom fails to note the symptoms.

Mr. Smith said to me at nine-sixteen (I know it was exactly nine-sixteen to the second) with polite conviction in his smile: "You seem to have something on your mind, old chap."

Now no one but a true diplomat recognises the psychological moment for calling an almost total stranger "old chap."

"I have, old fellow," said I, immensely relieved by his perspicuity. "I ought to get off five or six very important letters to—"

He interrupted me with a genial wave of his hand. "Run along and get 'em off," he said. "Don't mind me. I'll look over the magazines."

Ten minutes later I was sneaking up the interminable stairways in the sepulchral east wing, lighting and relighting a tallow candle with grim patience at every other landing and luridly berating the drafts that swept the passages. Mr. Poopendyke stood guard below at the padlocked doors, holding the keys. He was to await my signal to reopen them, but he was not to release me under any circumstance if snoopers were abroad.

My secretary was vastly disturbed by the news I imparted. He was so startled that he forgot to tell me that he wouldn't spend another night on a pile of rugs with Britton as a bed-fellow, an omission which gave Britton the opportunity to anticipate him by *almost* giving notice that very night. (The upshot of it was the hasty acquisition of two brand new iron beds the next day, and the restoration of peace in my domestic realm.)

Somewhat timorously I knocked at the Countess's door. I realised that it was a most unseemly hour for calling on a young, beautiful and unprotected lady, but the exigencies of the moment lent moral support to my invasion.

After waiting five minutes and then knocking again so loudly that the sound reverberated through the empty halls with a sickening clatter, I heard some one fumbling with the bolts. The door opened an inch or two.

The Countess's French maid peered out at me.

"Tell your mistress that I must see her at once."

"Madame is not at home, m'sieur," said the young woman.

"Not at home?" I gasped. "Where is she?"

"Madame has gone to bed."

"Oh," I said, blinking. "Then she *is* at home. Present my compliments and ask her to get up. Something very exasperating has hap—"

"Madame has request me to inform m'sieur that she knows the Count is here, and will you be so good as to call to-morrow morning."

"What! She knows he's here? Who brought the information?"

"The bountiful Max, m'sieur. He bring it with *dejeuner,* again with *diner,* and but now with the hot water, m'sieur."

"Oh, I see," said I profoundly. "In that case, I—I sha'n't disturb her. How—er—how did she take it?"

She gave me a severely reproachful look.

"She took it as usual, m'sieur. In that dreadful little tin tub old Conrad—"

"Good heavens, girl! I mean the news—the news about the Count."

"Mon dieu! I thought m'sieur refer to——But yes! She take it beautifully. I too mean the news. Madame is not afraid. Has she not the good, brave m'sieur to—what you call it—to shoulder all the worry, no? She is not alarm. She reads m'sieur's latest book in bed, smoke the cigarette, and she say what the divil do she care."

"What!"

"Non, non! I, Helene Marie Louise Antoinette, say it for Madame. Pardon! Pardon, m'sieur! It is I who am wicked."

Very stiffly and ceremoniously I advised caution for the next twelve hours, and saying good night to Helene Marie Louise Antoinette in an unintentionally complimentary whisper, took myself off down the stairs, pursued by an equally subdued *bon soir* which made me feel like a soft-stepping Lothario.

Now it may occur to you that any self-respecting gentleman in possession of a castle and a grain of common sense would have set about to find out the true names of the guests beneath his roof. The task would have been a simple one, there is no doubt of that. A peremptory command with a rigid alternative would have brought out the truth in a jiffy.

But it so happens that I rather enjoyed the mystery. The situation was unique, the comedy most exhilarating. Of course, there was a tragic side to the whole matter, but now that I was in for it, why minimise the novelty by adopting arbitrary measures? Three minutes of stern conversation with Elsie Hazzard would enlighten me on all the essential points; perhaps half an hour would bring Poopendyke to terms; a half a day might be required in the brow-beating of the frail Countess. With the Schmicks, there was no hope. But why not allow myself the pleasure of enjoying the romantic feast that had been set before me by the gods of chance? Chance ordered the tangle; let chance unravel it. Somewhat gleefully I decided that it would be good fun to keep myself in the dark as long as possible!

"Mr. Poopendyke," said I, after that nervous factotum had let me into my side of the castle with gratifying stealthiness, "you will oblige me by not mentioning that fair lady's name in my presence."

"You did not stay very long, sir," said he in a sad whisper, and for the life of me I couldn't determine what construction to put upon the singularly unresponsive remark.

When I reached the room where my guests were assembled, I found Mr. Pless and the Baron Umovitch engaged in an acrimonious dispute over a question of bridge etiquette. The former had resented a sharp criticism coming from the latter, and they were waging a verbal battle in what I took to be five or six different tongues, none of which appeared to bear the slightest relationship to the English language. Suddenly Mr. Pless threw his cards down and left the table, without a word of apology to the two ladies, who looked more hurt than appalled.

He said he was going to bed, but I noticed that he took himself off in the direction of the moonlit loggia. We were still discussing his defection in subdued tones—with the exception of the irate baron—when he re-entered the room. I he expression on his face was mocking, even accusing. Directing his words to me, he uttered a lazy indictment.

"Are there real spirits in your castle, Mr. Smart, or have you flesh and blood mediums here who roam about in white night dresses to study the moods of the moon from the dizziest ramparts?"

I started. What indiscretion had the Countess been up to?

"I don't quite understand you, Mr. Pless," I said, with a politely blank stare.

Confound his insolence! He winked at me!

CHAPTER VIII

I RESORT TO DIPLOMACY

"MY dear Countess," said I, the next morning, "while I am willing to admit that all you say is true, there still remains the unhappy fact that you were very near to upsetting everything last night. Mr. Pless saw you quite plainly. The moon was very full, you'll remember. Fortunately he was too far away from your window to recognise you. Think how easy it might—"

But I've told you twice that I held my hand over Pinko's nose and he just couldn't bark, Mr. Smart. You are really most unreasonable about it. The dog had to have a breath of fresh air."

"Why not send him up to the top of the tower and let him run around on the—"

"Oh, there's no use talking about it any longer," she said wearily. "It is all over and no real harm was done. I am awfully sorry if they made it uncomfortable for you. It is just like him to suggest something—well, scandalous. And the rest of them are dreadful teases, especially Mrs. Smith. They love anything risque. But you haven't told me what they said that kept you awake all night."

My dignity was worth beholding.

"It was not what they said to me, Countess, but what they left unsaid. I sha'n't tell you what they said."

"I think I can make a pretty good guess—"

"Well, you needn't!" I cried hastily, but too late. She would out with it.

"They accuse you of being a sad, sad dog, a foxy bachelor, and a devil of a fellow. They all profess to be very much shocked, but they assure you that it's all right,—not to mind them. They didn't think you had it in you, and they're glad to see you behaving like a scamp. Oh, I know them!"

As a matter of fact, she was pretty near to being right. "All the more reason for you to be cautious and circumspect," said I boldly. "Pray think of my position, if not your own."

She gave me a queer little look and then smiled brightly. (She *is* lovely!)

"I'll promise to be good," she said.

"I only ask you to be careful," said I, blunderingly. She laughed aloud: her merriest, most distracting gurgle.

"And now will you be good enough to tell me who I am?" she asked, after a few minutes. "That is, who am I supposed to be?"

"Oh," said I uneasily, "you are really nobody. You are Britton's wife."

"What! Does Britton know it?"

"Yes," said I, with a wry smile. "He took a mean advantage of me in the presence of George Hazzard not an hour ago, and asked for a raise in wages on account of his wife's illness. It seems that you are an invalid."

"I hope he hasn't forgotten the baby in his calculations."

"He hasn't, you may be sure. He has named the baby after me."

"How original!"

"I thought it rather clever to change Rosemary's sex for a few days," said I. "Moreover, it will be necessary for Britton to take Max's place as your personal servant. He will fetch your meals and—"

"Oh, I can't agree to that, Mr. Smart," she cried with decision. "I must have Max. He is—"

"But Britton must have some sort of a pretext for—"

"Nonsense! No one cares about Britton and his sick wife. Let well enough alone."

"I—I'll think it over, Countess," said I weakly.

"And now tell me all about—Mr. Pless. How is he looking? Does he appear to be unhappy? "There was a curious note in her voice, as of anxiety or eagerness, it was hard to tell which. In any case, I found myself inwardly resenting her interest in the sneering Hungarian. (I had discovered that he was not an Austrian.) There was a queer sinking sensation in the region of my heart, and a slight chill. Could it be possible that she—But no! It was preposterous!

"He appears to be somewhat sentimental and preoccupied. He gazes at the moon and bites his nails."

"I—I wish I could have a peep at him some time without being—"

"For heaven's sake, don't even consider such a thing," I cried in alarm.

"Just a little peek, Mr. Smart," she pleaded.

"No!" said I firmly.

"Very well," she said resignedly, fixing me with hurt eyes. "I'm sorry to be such a bother to you."

"I believe you'll go back to him, after all," I said angrily. "Women are all alike. They—"

"Just because I want to see how unhappy he is, and enjoy myself a little, you say horrid things to me," she cried, almost pathetically. "You treat me very badly."

"There is a great deal at stake," said I. "The peril is—well, it's enormous. I am having the devil's own time heading off a scheme they've got for exploring the entire castle. Your hus—your ex-husband says he knows of a secret door opening into this part of the—"

She sprang to her feet with a sharp cry of alarm.

"Heavens! I—I forgot about *that!* There is a secret panel and—heaven save us!—it opens directly into my bedroom!" Her eyes were very wide and full of consternation. She gripped my arm. "Come! Be quick! We must pile something heavy against it, or nail it up, or—do something."

She fairly dragged me out into the corridor, and then, picking up her dainty skirts, pattered down the rickety stairs at so swift a pace that I had some difficulty in keeping her pink figure in sight. Why is it that a woman can go downstairs so much faster than a man? I've never been able to explain it. She didn't stumble once, or miss a step, while I did all manner of clumsy things, and once came near to pitching headlong to the bottom. We went down and down and round and round so endlessly that I was not only gasping but reeling.

At last we came to the broad hall at the top of the main staircase. Almost directly in front of us loomed the great padlocked doors leading to the other wing. Passing them like the wind she led the way to the farthermost end of the hall. Light from the big, paneless windows overlooking the river, came streaming into the vast corridor, and I could see doors ahead to the right and the left of us.

"Your bedroom?" I managed to gasp, uttering a belated question that should have been asked five or six flights higher up at a time when I was better qualified to voice it. "What the dickens is it doing down here?"

She did not reply, but, turning to the left, threw open a door and disappeared into the room beyond. I followed ruthlessly, but stopped just over the threshold to catch my breath in astonishment.

I was in "my lady's bed-chamber."

The immense Gothic bed stood on its dais, imposing in its isolation. Three or four very modern innovation trunks loomed like minarets against the opposite walls, half-open; one's imagination might have been excused if it conjured up sentries who stood ready to pop out of the trunks to scare one half to death. Some of my most precious rugs adorned the floor, but the windows were absolutely undraped. There were a few old chairs scattered about, but no other article of furniture except an improvised wash-stand, and a clumsy, portable tin bath-tub which leaned nonchalantly against the foot of the bed. There were great mirrors, in the wall at one end of the room, cracked and scaly it is true, but capable of reflecting one's presence.

"Don't stand there gaping," she cried in a shrill whisper, starting across the room only to turn aside with a sharp exclamation. "That stupid Helene!" she cried, flushing warmly. Catching up a heap of tumbled garments, mostly white, from a chair, she recklessly hurled them behind the bed. "This is the mirror—the middle one. It opens by means of a spring. There is a small hole in the wall behind it and then there is still another secret door beyond that, a thick iron one with the sixth Baron Rothhoefen's portrait on the outer side of it. The canvas swings open. We must—"

I was beginning to get my bearings.

"The sixth baron? Old Ludwig the Red?"

"The very one."

"Then, by Jove, he is in my study! You don't mean to say—"

"Please don't stop to talk," she cried impatiently, looking about in a distracted manner, "but for goodness sake get something to put against this mirror."

My mind worked rapidly. The only object in the room heavy enough to serve as a barricade was the bed, and it was too heavy for me to move, I feared. I suggested it, of course, involuntarily lowering my voice to a conspiratorial whisper.

"Pull it over, quick!" she commanded promptly.

"Perhaps I'd better run out and get Max and get Max and Ru—"

"If my hus—if Mr. Pless should open that secret door from the other side, Mr. Smart, it will be very embarrassing for you and me, let—"

I put my shoulder to the huge creaky bed and shoved. There were no castors. It did not budge. I he Countess assisted me by putting the tips of her small fingers against one end of it and pushing. It was not what one would call a frantic effort on her part, but it served to make me exert myself to the utmost. I, a big strong man, couldn't afford to have a slim countess pushing a bedstead about while I was there to do it for her.

"Don't do that," I protested. "I can manage it alone, thank you."

I secured a strong grip on the bottom of the thing and heaved manfully.

"You might let me help," she cried, firmly grasping a side piece with both hands.

The bed moved. The veins stood out on my neck and temples. My face must have been quite purple, find it is a hue that I detest. When I was a very small laddie my mother put me forward to be admired in purple velveteen. The horror of it still lingers.

By means of great straining I got the heavy bed over against the mirror, upsetting the tin bathtub with a crash that under ordinary circumstances would have made my heart stand still but now only tripled its pumping activities. One of the legs was hopelessly splintered in the drop from the raised platform.

"There," she said, standing off to survey our joint achievement, "we've stopped it up very nicely." She brushed the tips of her fingers daintily. "This afternoon you may fetch up a hammer and some nails and fasten the mirror permanently. Then you can move the bed back to its proper place. Goodness! What a narrow squeak!"

"Madam," said I, my hand on my heart but not through gallantry, "that bed stays where it is. Not all the king's horses nor all the king's men can put it back again."

"Was it so heavy, Mr. Smart?"

I swallowed very hard. A prophetic crick already had planted itself in my back. "Will you forgive me if I submit that you sleep quite a distance from home? "I remarked with justifiable irony. "Why the deuce don't you stay on the upper floors?"

"Because I am mortally afraid," she said, with a little shudder. You've no idea how lonely, how spooky it is up there at the dead hour of night. I couldn't sleep. After the third night I had my things moved down here, where I could at least feel that there were strong men within—you might say arm's length of me. I'm—I'm shockingly timid."

She smiled; a wavering, pleading little smile that conquered.

"Of course, I don't mind, Countess," I hastened to say. "Only I thought it would be cosier up there with Rosemary and the two maids for company."

She leaned a little closer to me. "We all sleep down here," she said confidentially. "We bring Rosemary's little mattress down every night and put it in the bathtub. It is a very good fit and makes quite a nice cradle for her. Helene and Blake sleep just across the hall and we leave the doors wide open. So, you see, we're not one bit at raid."

I sat down on the edge of the bed and laughed. "This is delicious," I cried, not without compunction for I was looking directly into her eager, wistful eyes. A shadow crossed them. "I beg your pardon. I—I can't help laughing."

"Pray do not stop laughing on my account," she said icily. "I am used to being laughed at since I left America. They laugh at all of us over here."

"I dare say they laugh at me, confound them," said I, lugubriously.

"They do," said she flatly. Before I could quite recover from this sentient dig, she was ordering me to put the bathtub where it belonged. This task completed, I looked up. She was standing near the head of the bed, with a revolver in her hand. I stared. "I keep it under my pillow, Mr. Smart," she said nervously. I said nothing, and she replaced it under the pillow, handling the deadly weapon as gingerly as if it were the frailest glass. "Of course I couldn't hit anything with it, and I know I should scream when it went off, but still—accidents will happen, you know."

"Um!" said I, judicially. "And so my study is just beyond this mirror, eh? May I enquire how you happen to know that I have my study there?"

"Oh, I peeked in the other day," she said, serene once more.

"The deuce you did!"

"I was quite sure that you were out," she explained.

"I opened Ludwig the Red an inch or two, that's all. You are quite cosy in there, aren't you? I envy you the grand old *chaise longe.*"

I wavered, but succeeded in subduing the impulse. "It is the only comfortable piece of furniture I have left in my apartments," said I, with convincing candour.

"You poor man," she said, with her rarest smile.

"How fortunate you are that I did not remember the *chaise longe.* You would have been deprived of it, I am quite sure. Of course I couldn't think of robbing you of it now."

"As a matter of fact, I never lie in it," I said, submitting to a once conquered impulse. "If you'd really like to have it, I'll see that it is taken up to your rooms at once."

"Thank you," she said, shaking her head. "It's kind of you, but I am not so selfish as all that, believe me."

"It is—quite in the way, Countess."

"Some one would be sure to miss it if you sent it up now," she said reflectively.

"We'll wait till they're all gone, said I.

She smiled and the bargain was settled without a word from her. You've heard of men being wrapped about little fingers, haven't you? Well, there you are.

We returned to the corridor. She closed the door softly, a mockery in view of the clatter I had made in shifting the bed and its impediments.

"We can't be too careful," she said in a whisper. She might have spoken through a megaphone and still been quite safe. We were tramping up the stairs. "Don't you think your guests will consider you rather inhospitable if you stay away from them all morning?"

I stopped short. "By Jove, now that you remind me of it, I promised to take them all out for a spin in the motor boat before luncheon. Hazzard has had his boat sent down."

She looked positively unhappy. "Oh, how I should love to get out for a spin on the river! I wonder if I'll ever be free to enjoy the things I like most of——"

"Listen! "I whispered suddenly, grasping her arm. "Did you hear footsteps in the—Sh!"

Some one was walking over the stone floor in the lower hall, brisk strides that rang out quite clearly as they drew nearer.

"It is—it is Mr. Pless," she whispered in a panic.

"I recognise his tread. As if I could ever forget it! Oh, how I hate him! He—"

"Don't stop here to tell me about it," I cut in sharply. "Make haste! Get up to your rooms and lock yourself in. I'll—I'll stop him. How the deuce did he get into this side of the—"

"Through the dungeons. There is a passage," she whispered, and then she was gone, flying noiselessly up the narrow stairway.

Assuming a nonchalance I certainly did not feel, I descended the stairs. We met in the broad hallway below. Mr. Pless approached slowly, evidently having checked his speed on hearing my footsteps on the stairs.

"Hello," I said agreeably. "How did you get in?"

He surveyed me coolly. "I know the castle from top to bottom, Mr. Smart. To be perfectly frank with you, I tried the secret panel in your study but found the opposite door blocked. You have no objection, I trust, to my looking over the castle? It is like home to me."

My plan was to detain him in conversation until she had time to secrete herself on the upper floor. Somehow I anticipated the banging of a door, and it came a moment later—not loud but very convicting, just the same. He glanced at me curiously.

"Then how *did* you get in?" I repeated, cringing perceptibly in response to the slam of the distant door.

"By the same means, I daresay, that you employ," said he.

For a moment I was confounded. Then my wits came to the rescue.

"I see. Through the dungeon. You *do* know the castle well, Mr. Pless."

"It is a cobwebby, unlovely passage," said he, brushing the dirt and cobwebs from his trousers. My own appearance was conspicuously immaculate, but I brushed in unison, just the same.

"Grewsome," said I.

He was regarding me with a curious smile in his eyes, a pleasantly bantering smile that had but one meaning. Casting an eye upwards, he allowed his smile to spread.

"Perhaps you'd rather I didn't disturb Mrs.—Mrs.—"

"Britton," said I. "My valet's wife. I don't believe you will disturb her. She's on the top floor, I think."

He still smiled. "A little remote from Britton isn't she?"

I think I glared. What right had he to meddle in Britton's affairs?

"I am afraid your fancy draws a rather long bow, Mr. Pless," said I, coldly.

He was at once apologetic. "If I offend, Mr. Smart, pray forgive me. You are quite justified in rebuking me. Shall we return to our own ladies?"

Nothing could have been more adroit than the way he accused me in that concluding sentence. It was the quintessence of irony.

"I'd like to have your opinion as to the best way of restoring or repairing those mural paintings in the dome of the east hall," I said, detaining him. It was necessary for me to have a good excuse for rummaging about in the unused part of the castle. "It seems too bad to let those wonderful paintings go to ruin. They are hanging down in some places, and are badly cracked in others. I've been worrying about them ever since I came into possession. For instance, that Murillo in the centre. It must be preserved."

He gave me another queer look, and I congratulated myself on the success of my strategy.

He took it all in. The mocking light died out in his eyes, and he at once became intensely interested in my heaven-sent project. For fifteen or twenty minutes we discussed the dilapidated frescoes and he gave me the soundest sort of advice, based on a knowledge and experience that surprised me more than a little. He was thoroughly up in matters of art. His own château near Buda Pesth, he informed me, had only recently undergone complete restoration in every particular. A great deal of money had been required, but the expenditures had been justified by the results.

Paintings like these had been restored to their original glory, and so on and so forth. He offered to give me the address of the men in Munich who had performed such wonders for him, and suggested rather timidly that he might be of considerable assistance to me in outlining a system of improvements. I could not help being impressed. His manner was most agreeable. When he smiled without malice, his dark eyes were very boyish. One could then forget the hard lines of dissipation in his face, and the domineering, discontented expression winch gave to him the aspect of a far greater age than he had yet attained. A note of eager enthusiasm in his voice proved beyond cavil that if this sprig of nobility had had half a chance in the beginning he might have been nobler than he was to-day. But underneath the fascinating charm of manner, back of the old world courtliness, there lurked the ever dominant signs of intolerance, selfishness and—even cruelty. He was mean to the core. He had never heard of the milk of human kindness, much less tasted of it.

There was no getting away from the fact that he despised me for no other reason than that I was an American. I could not help feeling the derision in which he held not only me but the Hazzards and the Smiths as well. He looked upon all of us as coming from an inferior race, to be tolerated only as passers by and by no means worthy of his august consideration. We were not of his world and never could be.

Ignoble to him, indeed, must have been the wife who came with the vulgar though welcome dollars and an ambition to be his equal and the sharer of his heaven born glory! He could not even pity her!

While he was discoursing so amiably upon the subjects he knew so well by means of an inherited intelligence that came down through generations, I allowed my thoughts to drift upstairs to that frightened, hunted little fellow-countrywoman of mine, as intolerant, as vain perhaps as he after a fashion, and cursed the infernal custom that lays our pride so low. Infinitely nobler than he and yet an object of scorn to him and all his people, great and small; a discredited interloper who could not deceive the lowliest menial in her own household into regarding her as anything but an imitation. Her loveliness counted for naught. Her wit, her charm, her purity of heart counted for even less than that. She was a thing that had been bartered for and could be cast aside without loss—a pawn. And she had committed the inconceivable sin of rebelling against the laws of commerce: she had defaulted! They would not forgive her for that.

My heart warmed toward her. She had been afraid of the dark! I can forgive a great deal in a person who is afraid of the dark.

I looked at my watch. Assuming a careless manner, I remarked:

"I am afraid we shall be late for the start. Are you going out with us in the boat or would you prefer to browse about a little longer? Will you excuse me? I must be off."

His cynical smile returned. "I shall forego the pleasure of browsing in another man's pasture, if you don't mind."

It was almost a direct accusation. He did not believe a word of the Britton story. I suddenly found myself wondering if he suspected the truth. Had he, by any chance, traced the fugitive countess to my doors? Were his spies hot upon the trail? Or had she betrayed herself by indiscreet acts during the past twenty-four hours? The latter was not unlikely; I knew her whims and her faults by this time. In either case, I had come to feel decidedly uncomfortable, so much so, in fact, that I was content to let the innuendo pass without a retort. It behooved me to keep my temper as well as my wits.

"Come along," said I, starting off in the direction of the lower regions. He followed. I manœuvred with such success that ultimately he took the lead. I hadn't the remotest idea how to get to the confounded dungeons!

It never rains but it pours. Just as we were descending the last flight of stairs before coming to the winding stone steps that led far down into the earth, who but Britton should come blithely up from the posterior regions devoted to servants and their ilk. He was carrying a long pasteboard box. I said something impressive under my breath. Britton, on seeing us, stopped short in his tracks. He put the box behind his back and gazed at me forlornly.

"Ah, Britton," said I, recovering myself most creditably; "going up to see little John Bellamy, I suppose."

I managed to shoot a covert look at Mr. Pless. He was gazing at the half-hidden box with a perfectly impassive face, and yet I knew that there was a smile about him somewhere.

The miserable box contained roses, I knew, because I had ordered them for Rosemary.

"Yes, sir," said my valet, quite rigid with uncertainty, "in a way, sir." A bright look flashed into his face. "I'm taking up the wash, Mr. Smart. From the laundry over in the town, sir. It is somethink dreadful the way they mangle things, sir. Especially lady's garments. Thank you, sir."

He stood aside to let us pass, the box pinned between him and the wall. Never in my life have I known roses with a more pungent and penetrating odour! Britton seemed to fairly reek with it.

"I like the perfumes the women are using nowadays," said Mr. Pless affably, as we felt our way down the steps.

"Attar of roses," said I, sniffing.

"Umph!" said he.

It was quite dark and very damp in the underground passages. I had the curious sensation of lizards wriggling all about me in the sinister shadows. Then and there I resolved that the doors of this pestilential prison should be locked and double locked and never opened again, while I was master of the place.

Moreover, old man Schmick was down for a bad half-hour with me. How came these doors to be unlocked when the whole place was supposed to be as tight as a drum? If nothing else sufficed, the two prodigious Schmicks would be required to stand guard, day and night, with bludgeons if needs be. I intended to keep snooping busybodies out of that side of the castle if I had to nail up every door in the place, even at the risk of starving those whom I would defend.

Especially was I firm in my resolve to keep the meddling ex-husband in his proper place. Granted that he suspected me of a secret amour, what right had he to concern himself about it? None whatever. I was not the first baron to hold a fair prisoner within these powerful walls, and I meant to stand upon my dignity and my rights, as every man should who—But, great heaven, what an imbecile view to take of the matter! Truly my brain was playing silly tricks for me as I stumbled through the murky corridors. I had my imagination in a pretty fair state of subjection by the time we emerged from the dungeons and started up the steps. Facts were facts, and I would have to stick to them. That is why I bethought myself to utter this sage observation:

"Britton is a faithful, obliging fellow, Mr. Pless. It isn't every Englishman who will gracefully submit to being chucked out of comfortable quarters to make room for others. We're a bit crowded, you know. He gave up his room like a gentleman and moved over temporarily into the other wing. He was afraid, don't you see, that the baby might disturb my guests. A very thoughtful, dependable fellow."

"Yes," said he, "a very dependable fellow, Mr. Smart. My own man is much the same sort of a chap. He also is married." Did I imagine that he chuckled?

Half an hour later when I rejoined my guests after a session with Conrad Schmick, I was somewhat annoyed by the dig George Hazzard planted in my devoted ribs, and the furtive wink he gave me. The two ladies were regarding me with expressions that seemed pretty well divided between disapproval and mirth. The baron, whose amicable relations with Mr. Pless evidently had been restored, was grinning broadly at me.

And the Countess imperiously had directed me to supply her with all the scandal of the hour!

CHAPTER IX

I AM INVITED OUT TO DINNER

I SOMETIMES wonder what would, happen if I really had a mind of my own. Would I be content to exercise it capably? Would I cease to be putty in the hands of other people? I doubt it. Even a strong, obdurate mind is liable to connect with conditions that render it weak and pliable for the simple reason that it is sometimes easier to put up with a thing than to try to put it down. An exacting, arbitrary mind perhaps might evolve a set of resolutions that even the most intolerant would hesitate to violate, but for an easygoing, trouble-dodging brain like my own there is no such thing as tenacity of purpose, unless it be in the direction of an obfuscated tendency to maintain its own pitiful equilibrium. I try to keep an even ballast in my dome of thought and to steer straight through the sea of circumstance, a very difficult undertaking and sometimes hazardous.

A man with a firm, resolute grip on himself would have checked Mr. Pless and Baron Umovitch at the outset of their campaign to acquire undisputed possession of *all* the comforts and conveniences that the castle afforded.

He would have said no to their demands that all work about the place should be regulated according to their own life-long habits, which, among other things, included lying in bed till noon, going back to bed at three for a quiet nap, and staying up all night so that they might be adequately worn out by the time they went to bed in the first place.

I mention this as a single instance of their power to over-ride me. It got to be so that when a carpenter wanted to drive a nail he had to substitute a screw and use a screw-driver, a noiseless process but an insufferable waste of time and money. Lathers worked four days on a job that should have been accomplished in as many hours. Can you imagine these expert, able-bodied men putting laths on a wall with screw-drivers?

When Elsie Hazzard, painfully aware of my annoyance, asked the two noblemen why on earth they couldn't get up for breakfast, they coldly informed her that they were civilised human beings and not larks.

They used my study for purposes of their own, and glared at me when I presumed to intrude upon their Mr. Pless took possession of this room, and here received all sorts of secret operatives engaged in the task of unearthing the former Mrs. Pless. Here he had as many as fifteen reports a day by messenger from all parts of the land and here he discussed every new feature of the chase as it presented itself, coolly barring me out of my sanctum sanctorum with the impassive command to knock before attempting to enter.

In spite of their acrimonious tilts over the card table, he and the baron were as thick as could be when it came to the question of the derelict countess. They maintained the strictest privacy and resented even the polite interest of their four American friends.

Finding Mr. Poopendyke at work over some typing one day, Mr. Pless peremptorily ordered him out of the study and subsequently complained to me about the infernal racket the fellow made with his typewriter. Just as I was on the point of telling him to go to the devil, he smilingly called my attention to a complete plan for the restoration of the two great halls as he had worked it out on paper. He had also written a personal letter, commanding the Munich firm to send their most competent expert to Schloss Rothhoefen without delay, to go over the plans with him. As I recall it, he merely referred to me as a rich American who needed advice.

They cursed my servants, drank my wines, complained of the food, and had everybody about the place doing errands for them. My butler and foot-man threatened to leave if they were compelled to continue to serve drinks until four in the morning; but were somewhat appeased when I raised their wages. Britton surreptitiously thrashed the French valet, and then had to serve Mr. Pless (to my despair) for two days while François took his time recovering.

The motor boat was operated as a ferry after the third day, hustling detectives, lawyers, messengers and newspaper correspondents back and forth across the much be-sung Danube. Time and again I shivered in my boots when these sly-faced detectives appeared and made their reports behind closed doors. When would they strike the trail?

To my surprise the Hazzards and the Smiths were as much in the dark as I concerning development in the great kidnapping case. The wily Mr. Pless suddenly ceased delivering his confidences to outsiders. Evidently he had been cautioned by those in charge of his affairs. He became as uncommunicative as the Sphinx.

I had the somewhat valueless satisfaction of knowing a blessed sight more about the matter than he and all of his bloodhounds put together. I could well afford to laugh, but under the extremely harassing conditions it was far from possible for me to get fat. As a matter of fact, it seemed to me that I was growing thinner. Mrs. Betty Billy Smith, toward the end of her visit, dolefully—almost tearfully— remarked upon my haggard appearance. She was very nice about it, too. I liked her immensely.

It did not require half an eye to see that she was thoroughly sick of the baron and Mr. Pless. She was really quite uncivil to them toward the end.

At last there came a day of deliverance. The guests were departing and I can truthfully say that I was speeding them.

Elsie Hazzard took me off to a remote corner, where a little later on Betty Billy and the two husbands found us.

"John, will you ever forgive me?" she said very soberly. "I swear to you I hadn't the faintest idea what it—"

"Please, please, Elsie," I broke in warmly; "don't abuse yourself in my presence. I fully understand everything. At least, *nearly* everything. What I can't understand, for the life of me, is this: how did you happen to pick up two such consummate bounders as these fellows are?"

"Alas, John," said she, shaking her head, "a woman never knows much about a man until she has lived a week in the same house with him. Now *you* are a perfect angel."

"You've always said that," said I. "You did not have to live in the same house with me to find it out, did you?"

She ignored the question. "I shall never, never forgive myself for this awful week, John. We've talked it all over among ourselves. We are ashamed—oh, so terribly ashamed. If you can ever like us again after—"

"Like you!" I cried, taking her by the shoulders. "Why, Elsie Hazzard, I have never liked you and George half so much as I like you now. You two and the Smiths stand out like Gibraltars in my esteem. I adore all of you. I sha'n't be happy again until I know that you four—and no more—are coming back to Schloss Rothhoefen for an indefinite stay. Good Lord, how happy we shall be!"

I said it with a great deal of feeling. The tears rushed into her eyes.

"You *are* a dear, John," she sighed.

"You'll come?"

"In a minute," said she with vehemence, a genuine American girl once more.

"Just as soon as these pesky workmen are out of the place, I'll drop you a line," said I, immeasurably exalted. "But I draw the line at noblemen."

"Don't worry," she said, setting her nice little white teeth. "I draw it too. Never again! *Never!*"

It occurred to me that here was an excellent opening for a bit of missionary work. Very pointedly I said to her: "I fancy you are willing to admit now that she wasn't such a simpleton for leaving him."

She went so far as to shudder, all the time regarding me with dilated eyes. "I can't imagine anything more dreadful than being that man's wife, John."

"Then why won't you admit that you are sorry for her? Why won't you be a little just to her?"

She looked at me sharply. "Do you know her?"

"Not by a long shot," I replied hastily, and with considerable truthfulness.

"Why are you so keen to have me take sides with her?"

"Because I did, the instant I saw that infernal cad."

She pursed her lips. It was hard for her to surrender.

"Out with it, Elsie," I commanded. "You know you've been wrong about that poor little girl. I can tell by the look in your eyes that you have switched over completely in the last four days, and so has Betty Billy."

"I can't forgive her for marrying him in the first place," she said stubbornly. "But I think she was justified in leaving him. As I know him now, I don't see how she endured it as long as she did. Yes, I am sorry for her. She is a dear girl and she has had a—a—"

"I'll say it, my dear: a hell of a time."

"Thank you."

"And I daresay you now think she did right in taking the child, too," I persisted.

"I—I hope she gets safely away with little Rosemary, back to God's country as we are prone to call it. Oh, by the way, John, I don't see why I should feel bound to keep that wretch's secret any longer. He has treated us like dogs. He doesn't deserve—"

"Hold on! You're not thinking of telling me his name, are you?"

"Don't you want to know it? Don't you care to hear that you've been entertaining the most talked of, the most interesting—"

"No, I don't!"

"Don't you care to hear who it was that he married and how many millions he got from—"

"No, I don't."

"And why not?"

"Well," said I, judicially, "in the first place I like the mystery of it all. In the second place, I don't want to know anything more about this fellow than I already know. He is enough of a horror to me, as it is, God knows, without giving a name to him. I prefer to think of him as Mr. Pleas. If you don't mind, Elsie, I'll try to eradicate him thoroughly from my system as Pless before I take him on in any other form of evil. No, I don't want to know his name at present, nor do I care a hang who it was he married. Silly notion, I suppose, but I mean what I say."

She looked at me in wonder for a moment and then shook her head as if considering me quite hopeless. "You are an odd thing, John. God left something out when He fashioned you. I'm just dying to tell you all about them, and you won't let me."

"Is she pretty?" I asked, yielding a little.

"She is lovely. We've been really quite hateful about her, Betty and I. Down in our hearts we like her. She was a spoiled child, of course, and all that sort of thing, but heaven knows she's been pretty thoroughly made over in a new crucible. We used to feel terribly sorry for her, even while we were deriding her for the fool she had made of herself in marrying him. I've seen her hundreds of times driving about alone in Vienna, where they spent two winters, a really pathetic figure, scorned not only by her husband but by every one else. He never was to be seen in public with her. He made it clear to his world that she was not to be inflicted upon it by any unnecessary act of his. She came to see Betty and me occasionally; always bright and proud and full of spirit, but we could see the wounds in her poor little heart no matter how hard she tried to hide them. I tell you, John, they like us as women but they despise us as wives. It will always be the same with them. They won't let us into their charmed circle. Thank God, I am married to an American. He *must* respect me whether he wants to or not."

"Poor little beggar," said I, without thinking of how it would sound to her; "she has had her fling, and she has paid well for it."

"If her stingy old father, who permitted her to get into the scrape, would come up like a man and pay what he ought to pay, there would be no more pother about this business. He hasn't lived up to his bargain. The—Mr. Pless has squandered the first million and now he wants the balance due him. A trade's a trade, John. The old man ought to pay up. He went into it with his eyes open, and I haven't an atom of sympathy for him. You have read that book of Mrs. Burnett's, haven't you?—'The Shuttle'? Well, there you are. This is but another example of what fools American parents can be when they get bees in their bonnets."

She seemed to be accusing me!

"I hope she gets away safely with the kiddie," said I, non-committally.

"Heaven knows where she is. Maybe she's as safe as a bug in a rug."

"I shouldn't be surprised," said I.

The Billy Smiths and George Hazzard came up at this juncture. Elsie at once proceeded to go into a long series of conjectures as to the probable whereabouts of Mr. Pless's former wife and their child. I was immensely gratified to find that they were now undivided in their estimate of Mr. Pless and firmly allied on the side of the missing countess.

I gathered from their remarks that the young woman's mother and brothers were still in Paris, where their every movement was being watched by secret agents. They were awaiting the arrival from New York of the father of the countess, after which they were to come to Vienna for the purpose of making a determined fight for the daughter's absolute freedom and the custody of the child.

Somehow this news gave me a strange feeling of apprehension, a sensation that later on was to be amply justified.

I daresay an historian less punctilious about the truth than I propose to be, would, at this stage of the narrative, insert a whopping lie for the sake of effect, or "action," or "heart interest," as such things are called in the present world of letters. He would enliven his tale by making Mr. Pless do something sensational while he was about it, such as yanking his erstwhile companion out of her place of hiding by the hair of her head, or kicking down all the barricades about the place, or fighting a duel with me, or—well, there is no end of things he might do for the sake of a "situation." But I am a person of veracity and the truth *is* in me. Mr. Pless did none of these interesting things, so why should I say that he did?

He went away with the others at half-past eleven, and that was the end of his first visit to my domain. For fear that you, kind reader, may be disappointed, I make haste to assure you that he was to come again.

Of course there was more or less turmoil and—I might say disaffection—attending his departure. He raised Cain with my servants because they did this and that when they shouldn't have done either; he (and the amiable baron) took me to task for having neglected to book compartments for them in the Orient Express; he insisted upon having a luncheon put up in a tea basket and taken to the railway station by Britton, and he saw to it personally that three or four bottles of my best wine were neatly packed in with the rest. He *said* three or four, but Britton is firm in his belief that there was nearer a dozen, judging by the weight.

He also contrived to have Mr. Poopendyke purchase first-class railway tickets for him and the baron, and then forgot to settle for them. It amounted to something like four hundred and fifty kronen, if I remember correctly. He took away eleven hundred and sixty-five dollars of my money, besides, genially acquired at roulette, and I dread to think of what he and the baron took out of my four friends at auction bridge.

I will say this for him: he was the smartest aristocrat I've ever known.

Need I add that the Hazzards and the Smiths travelled second-class?

"Well, thank the Lord!" said I, as the ferry put off with the party, leaving me alone on the little landing. The rotten timbers seemed to echo the sentiment. At the top of the steep all the Schmicks were saying it, too; in the butler's pantry it was also being said; a score of workmen were grunting it; and the windlass that drew me up the hill was screaming it in wild, discordant glee. I repeated it once more when Britton returned from town and assured me that they had not missed the train.

"That's what I'd like to say, sir," said he.

"Well, say it," said I. And he said it so vociferously that I know it must have been heard in the remotest corners of heaven.

The merry song of the hammer and the sweet rasp of the saw greeted my delighted ear as I entered the castle. Men were singing and whistling for all they were worth; the air was full of music. It was not unlike the grand transformation scene in the pantomime when all that has been gloom and despondency gives way in the flash of an eye to elysian splendour and dazzling gaiety. 'Pon my soul, I never felt so exuberant in all my life. The once nerve-racking clangour was like the soothing strains of an invisible orchestra to my delighted senses. Ha! Ha! What a merry old world it is, after all!

Nearing my study, I heard an almost forgotten noise: the blithe, incessant crackle of a typewriting machine. Never have I heard one rattle so rapidly or with such utter garrulousness.

I looked in at the door. Over in his corner by the window Poopendyke was at work, his lanky figure hunched over the key-board, his head enveloped in clouds from a busy pipe, for all the world like a tug-boat smothering in its own low-lying smoke. Sheets of paper were strewn about the floor. Even as I stood there hesitating, he came to the end of a sheet and jerked it out of the machine with such a resounding snap that the noise startled me. He was having the time of his life!

I stole away, unwilling to break in upon this joyful orgy.

Conrad, grinning from ear to ear, was waiting for me outside my bedroom door late in the day. He saluted me with unusual cordiality.

"A note, mein herr," said He, and handed me a dainty little pearl-grey envelope. He waited while I read the missive.

"I sha'n't be home for dinner, Conrad," said I, my eyes aglow. Tell Hawkes, will you?"

He bowed and scraped himself away; somehow he seemed to have grown younger by decades. It was in the air to be young and care-free. I read the note again and felt almost boyish. Then I went up to my room, got out my gayest raiment without shame or compunction, dressed with especial regard for lively effects and hied me forth to carry sunshine into the uttermost recesses of my castle.

The Countess welcomed me with a radiant smile. We shook hands.

"Well, he has gone," said I, drawing a deep breath.

"Thank the Lord," said she, and then I knew that the symphony was complete. We all had sung it.

It must not be supposed for an instant that I had been guilty of neglecting my lovely charge during that season of travail and despair. No, indeed! I had visited her every day as a matter of precaution. She required a certain amount of watching.

I do not hesitate to say at this time that she seemed to be growing lovelier every day. In a hundred little ways she was changing, not only in appearance but in manner.

Now, to be perfectly frank about it, I can't explain just what these little changes were—that is, not in so many words—but they were quite as pronounced as they were subtle. I may risk mentioning an improvement in her method of handling me. She was not taking quite so much for granted as she did at first. She was much more humble and considerate, I remarked; instead of bullying me into things she now cajoled me; instead of making demands upon my patience and generosity, she rather hesitated about putting me to the least trouble. She wasn't so arrogant, nor so hard to manage. In a nutshell, I may say with some satisfaction, she was beginning to show a surprising amount of respect for me and my opinions. Where once she had done as she pleased, she now did so only after asking my advice and permission, both of which I gave freely as a gentleman should. Fundamentally she was all right. It was only in a superficial sort of way that she fell short of being ideal. She really possessed a very sweet, lovely nature. I thought I could see the making of a very fine woman in her.

I do not say that she was perfect or ever could be, but she might come very close to it if she went on improving as she did every day. As a matter of fact, I found an immense amount of analytical pleasure in studying the changes that attended the metamorphosis. It seemed to my eager imagination that she was being translated before my eyes; developing into a serious, sensible, unselfish person with a soul preparing to mount higher than self. Her voice seemed to be softer, sweeter; the satirical note had disappeared almost entirely, and with it went the forced raillery that had been so pronounced at the beginning of our acquaintance.

Her devotion to Rosemary was wonderful to see. By the way, while I think of it, the child was quite adorable. She was learning to pronounce my name, and getting nearer and nearer to it every day. At the time of which I now write she was calling me (with great enthusiasm), by the name of "Go-go," which, reduced to aboriginal American, means "Man-with-the-Strong-Arm-Who-Carries-Baby."

"It is very nice of you to ask me up to dine with you," said I.

"Isn't it about time I was doing something for you in return for all that you have done for me?" she inquired gaily. "We are having a particularly nice dinner this evening, and I thought you'd enjoy a change."

"A change?" said I, with a laugh. "As if we haven't been eating out of the same kettle for days!"

"I was not referring to the food," she said, and I very properly squelched.

"Nevertheless, speaking of food," said, I, "it may interest you to know that I expected to have rather a sumptuous repast of my own to celebrate the deliverance. A fine plump pheasant, prepared a la Oscar, corn fritters like mother used to make, potatoes picard,—"

"And wonderful alligator pear salad," she interrupted, her eyes dancing.

I stared. "How in the world did you guess?"

She laughed in pure delight, and I began to understand. By the Lord Harry, the amazing creature was inviting me to eat my own dinner in her *salle manger!* "Well, may I be hanged! You do beat the Dutch!"

She was wearing a wonderful dinner gown of Irish lace, and she fairly sparkled with diamonds. There was no ornament in her brown hair, however, nor were her little pink ears made hideous by ear-rings. Her face was a jewel sufficient unto itself. I had never seen her in an evening gown before. The effect was really quite ravishing. As I looked at her standing there by the big oak table, I couldn't help thinking that the Count was not only a scoundrel but all kinds of a fool.

"It was necessary for me to bribe all of your servants, Mr. Smart," she said.

"You did not offer the rascals money, I hope," I said in a horrified tone.

"No, indeed!" She did not explain any farther than that, but somehow I knew that money isn't everything to a servant after all. "I hope you don't mind my borrowing your butler and footman for the evening," she went on. "Not that we really need two to serve two, but it seems so much more like a function, as the newspapers would call it."

It was my turn to say "No, indeed."

"And now you must come in and kiss Rosemary good night," she said, glancing at my great Amsterdam clock in the corner.

We went into the nursery. It was past Rosemary's bedtime by nearly an hour and the youngster was having great difficulty in keeping awake. She managed to put her arms around my neck when I took her up from the bed, all tucked away in her warm little nightie, and sleepily presented her own little throat for me to kiss, that particular spot being where the honey came from in her dispensation of sweets.

I was full of exuberance. An irresistible impulse to do a jig seized upon me. To my own intense amazement, and to Blake's horror, I began to dance about the room like a clumsy kangaroo. Rosemary shrieked delightedly into my ear and I danced the harder for that. The Countess, recovering from her surprise, cried out in laughter and began to clap time with her hands. Blake forgot herself and sat down rather heavily on the edge of the bed. I think the poor woman's knees gave way under her.

"Hurrah!" I shouted to Rosemary, but looking directly at the Countess. "We're celebrating!"

Whereupon the girl that was left in the Countess rose to the occasion and she pirouetted with graceful abandon before me, in amazing contrast to my jumping-jack efforts. Only Blake's reserved and somewhat dampening admonition brought me to my senses.

"Please don't drop the child, Mr. Smart." she said. I had the great satisfaction of hearing Rosemary cry when I delivered her up to Blake and started to slink out of the room in the wake of my warm-cheeked hostess.

"You would be a wonderful father, sir," said Blake, relenting a little.

I had the grace to say, "Oh, pshaw!" and then got out while the illusion was still alive. (As I've said before, I do not like a crying baby.)

It was the most wonderful dinner in the world, notwithstanding it was served on a kitchen table moved into the living room for the occasion. Imposing candelabra adorned the four corners of the table and the very best plate in the castle was put to use. There were roses in the centre of the board, a huge bowl of short-stemmed Marechal Niel beauties. The Countess's chair was pulled out by my stately butler, Hawkes; mine by the almost equally imposing footman, and we faced each other across the bowl of roses and lifted an American cocktail to the health of those who were about to sit down to the feast. I think it was one of the best cocktails I've ever tasted. The Countess admitted having made it herself, but wasn't quite sure whether she used the right ingredients or the correct proportions. She asked me what I thought of it.

"It is the best Manhattan I've ever tasted," said I, warmly.

Her eyes wavered. Also, I think, her faith in me. "It was meant to be a Martini," she said sorrowfully.

Then we both sat down. Was it possible that the corners of Hawkes' mouth twitched? I don't suppose I shall ever know.

My sherry was much better than I thought, too. It was deliciously oily. The champagne? But that came later, so why anticipate a joy with realisation staring one in the face?

We began with a marvellous hors-d'œuvres. Then a clear soup, a fish aspec, a—Why rhapsodise? Let it be sufficient if I say that in discussing the Aladdin-like feast I secretly and faithfully promised my chef a material increase in wages. I had never suspected him of being such a genius, nor myself of being such a Pantegru-elian disciple. I must mention the alligator pear salad. For three weeks I had been trying to buy alligator pears in the town hard by. These came from Pans. The chef had spoken to me about them that morning, asking me when I had ordered them. Inasmuch as I had not ordered them at all, I couldn't satisfy his curiosity. My first thought was that Elsie Hazzard, remembering my fondness for the vegetable—it is a vegetable, isn't it?—had sent off for them in order to surprise me. It seems, how-ever, that Elsie had nothing whatever to do with it. The Countess had ordered them for me through her mother, who was in Paris at the time. Also she had ordered a quantity of Parisian strawberries of the hot-house, one-franc-apiece variety, and a basket of peaches. At the risk of being called penurious, I confess that I was im-mensely relieved when I learned that these precious jewels in the shape of fruit had been paid for in advance by the opulent mother of the Countess.

"Have I told you, Mr. Smart, that I am expecting my mother here to visit me week after next?"

She tactfully put the question to me at a time when I was so full of contentment that nothing could have depressed me. I must confess, however, that I was guilty of gulping my champagne a little noisily. The question came with the salad course.

"You don't say so!" I exclaimed, quite cheerfully.

"That is to say, she is coming if you think you can manage it quite safely."

"I manage it? My dear Countess, why speak of managing a thing that is so obvi-ously to be desired?"

"You don't understand. Can you smuggle her into the castle without any one knowing a thing about it? You see, she is being watched every minute of the time by detectives, spies, secret agents, lawyers, and Heaven knows who else. The instant she leaves Paris, bang! It will be like the starter's shot in a race. They will be after her like a streak. And if you are not very, very clever they will play hob with everything."

"Then why run the risk?" I ventured.

"My two brothers are coming with her," she said reassuringly. "They are such big, strong fellows that—"

"My dear Countess, it isn't strength we'll need," I deplored.

"No, no, I quite understand. It is cunning, strategy, caution, and all that sort of thing. But I will let you know in ample time, so that you may be prepared."

"Do!" I said gallantly, trying to be enthusiastic.

"You are so wonderfully ingenious at working out plots and conspiracies in your books, Mr. Smart, that I am confident you can manage everything beautifully."

Blatchford was removing my salad plate. A spasm of alarm came over me. I had quite forgotten the two men. The look of warning I gave her brought forth a merry, amused smile.

"Don't hesitate to speak before Blatchford and Hawkes," she said, to my astonishment. "They are to be trusted implicitly. Isn't it true, Hawkes?"

"It is, Madam," said he.

"Do you mean to say, Countess, that—"

"It has all been quite satisfactorily attended to through Mr. Poopendyke," she said. "He consulted me before definitely engaging any one, Mr. Smart, and I referred him to my lawyers in Vienna. I *do* hope Hawkes and Blatchford and Henri, the chef, are quite satisfactory to you. They were recently employed by some one in the British embassy at—"

"Pray rest easy, Countess," I managed to say, interrupting out of consideration for Hawkes and Blatchford, who, I thought, might feel uncomfortable at hearing themselves discussed so impersonally. "Everything is most satisfactory. I did not realise that I had you to thank for my present mental and gastronomical comfort. You have surrounded me with diadems."

Hawkes and Blatchford very gravely and in unison said: "Thank you, sir."

"And now let us talk about something else," she said complacently, as if the project of getting the rest of her family into the castle were already off her mind. "I can't tell you how much I enjoyed your last book, Mr. Smart. It is so exciting. Why do you call it 'The Fairest of the Fair'?"

"Because my publisher insisted on substituting that title for the one I had chosen myself. I'll admit that it doesn't fit the story, my dear Countess, but what is an author to do when his publisher announces that he has a beautiful head of a girl he wants to put on the cover and that the title must fit the cover, so to speak?"

"But I don't consider it a beautiful head, Mr. Smart. A very flashy blonde with all the earmarks of having posed in the chorus between the days when she posed for your artist. And your heroine has very dark hair in the book. Why did they make her a blonde on the cover?"

"Because they didn't happen to have anything but blonde pictures in stock," said I, cheerfully. "A little thing like that doesn't matter, when it comes to my dear Countess. It isn't the hair that counts. It's the hat."

"But I should think it would confuse the reader," she insisted. "The last picture in the book has her with inky black hair, while in all the others she is quite blonde."

"A really intelligent reader doesn't have to be told that the artist changed his model before he got to the last picture," said I, and I am quite confident she didn't hear me grate my teeth.

"But the critics must have noticed the error and commented upon it."

"My dear Countess, the critics never see the last picture in a book. They are much too clever for that."

She pondered. "I suppose they must get horribly sick of all the books they have to read."

"And they never have a chance to experience the delicious period of convalescence that persons with less chronic afflictions have to look forward to," said I, very gently. "They go from one disease to another, poor chaps."

"I once knew an author at Newport who said he hated every critic on earth," she said.

"I should think he might," said I, without hesitation. It was not until the next afternoon that she got the full significance of the remark.

As I never encourage any one who seeks to discuss my stories with me, being a modest chap with a flaw in my vanity, she abandoned the subject after a few ineffectual attempts to find out how I get my plots, how I write my books, and how I keep from losing my mind.

"Would you be entertained by a real mystery?" she asked, leaning toward me with a gleam of excitement in her eyes. Very promptly I said I should be. We were having our coffee. Hawkes and Blatchford had left the room. "Well, tradition says that one of the old barons buried a vast treasure in the cellar of this—"

"Stop!" I commanded, shaking my head. "Haven't I just said that I don't want to talk about literature? Buried treasure is the very worst form of literature."

"Very well," she said indignantly. "You will be sorry when you hear I've dug it up and made off with it."

I pricked up my ears. This made a difference. "Are you going to hunt for it yourself?"

"I am," she said resolutely.

"In those dark, dank, grewsome cellars?"

"Certainly."

"Alone?"

"If necessary," she said, looking at me over the edge of the coffee cup.

"Tell me all about it," said I.

"Oh, we sha'n't find it, of course," said she calmly. I made note of the pronoun. "They've been searching for it for two centuries without success. My—that is, Mr. Pless has spent days down there. He is very hard-up, you know. It would come in very handy for

I glowered. "I'm glad he's gone. I don't like the idea, of his looking for treasures in my castle.

She gave me a smile for that.

CHAPTER X

I AGREE TO MEET THE ENEMY

THAT night I dreamed of going down, down, down into the bowels of the earth after buried treasure, and finding at the end of my hours of travel the countess's mother sitting in bleak splendour on a chest of gold with her feet drawn up and surrounded by an audience of spiders.

For an hour or more after leaving the enchanted rooms near the roof, I lounged in my study, persistently attentive to the portrait of Ludwig the Red, with my ears straining for sounds from the other side of the secret panels. Alas! those panels were many cubits thick and as staunch as the sides of a battleship. But there was a vast satisfaction in knowing that she was there, asleep perhaps, with her brown head pillowed close to, the wall but little more than an arm's length from the crimson waistcoat of Ludwig the Red,—for he sat rather low like a Chinese god and supported his waistcoat with his knees. A gross, forbidding chap was he! The story was told of him that he could quaff a flagon of ale at a single gulp. Looking at his portrait, one could not help thinking what a pitifully infinitesimal thing a flagon of ale is after all.

Morning came and with it a sullen determination to get down to work on my long neglected novel. I went down to breakfast. Everything about the place looked bleak and dreary and as grey as a granite tombstone. Hawkes, who but twelve hours before had seemed the embodiment of life in its most resilient form, now appeared as a drab nemesis with wooden legs and a frozen leer. My coffee was bitter, the peaches were like sponges, the bacon and rolls of uniform sogginess and the eggs of a strange liverish hue. I sat there alone, gloomy and depressed, contrasting the hateful sunshine with the soft, witching refulgence of twenty-four candles and the light that lies in a woman's eyes.

"A fine morning, sir," said Hawkes in a voice that seemed to come from the grave. It was the first time I had ever heard him speak so dolorously of the morning. Ordinarily he was a pleasant voiced fellow.

"Is it?" said I, and my voice sounded gloomier than his. I was not sure of it, but it seemed to me that he made a movement with his hand as if about to put it to his lips. Seeing that I was regarding him rather fixedly, he allowed it to remain suspended a little above his hip, quite on a line with the other one. His elbows were crooked at the proper angle I noticed, so I must have been doing him an injustice. He couldn't have had anything disrespectful in mind.

"Send Mr. Poopendyke to me, Hawkes, immediately after I've finished my breakfast."

"Very good, sir. Oh, I beg pardon, sir. I am forgetting, Mr. Poopendyke is out. He asked me to tell you he wouldn't return before eleven."

"Out? What business has he to be out?"

"Well, sir, I mean to say, he's not precisely out, and he isn't just what one would call in. He is up in the—ahem!—the east wing, sir, taking down some correspondence for the—for the lady, sir."

I arose to the occasion. "Quite so, quite so. I had forgotten the appointment."

"Yes, sir, I thought you had."

"Ahem! I daresay Britton will do quite as well. Tell him to—"

"Britton, sir, has gone over to the city for the newspapers. You forget that he goes every morning as soon as he has had his—"

"Yes, yes! Certainly," I said hastily. "The papers. Ha, ha! Quite right."

It was news to me, but it wouldn't do to let him know it. The countess read the papers, I did not. I steadfastly persisted in ignoring the Paris edition of the **New York Herald** for fear that the delightful mystery might disintegrate, so to speak, before my eyes, or become the commonplace scandal that all the world was enjoying. As it stood now, I had it all to myself—that is to say, the mystery. Mr. Poopendyke reads aloud the baseball scores to me, and nothing else.

It was nearly twelve when my secretary reported to me on this particular morning, and he seemed a trifle hazy as to the results of the games. After he had mumbled something about rain or wet grounds, I coldly enquired:

"Mr. Poopendyke, are you employed by me or by that woman upstairs?" I would never have spoken of her as "that woman," believe me, if I had not been in a state of irritation.

He looked positively stunned. "Sir?" he gasped.

I did not repeat the question, but managed to demand rather fiercely: "Are you?"

"The countess had got dreadfully behind with her work, sir, and I thought you wouldn't mind if I helped her out a bit," he explained nervously.

"Work? What work?"

"Her diary, sir. She is keeping a diary."

"Indeed!"

"It is very interesting, Mr. Smart. Rather beats any novel I've read lately. We— we've brought it quite up to date. I wrote at least three pages about the dinner last night. If I am to believe what she puts into her diary, it must have been a delightful occasion, as the newspapers would say."

I was somewhat mollified. "What did she have to say about it, Fred?" I asked. It always pleased him to be called Fred.

"That would be betraying a confidence," said he. "I will say this much, however: I think I wrote your name fifty times or more in connection with it."

"Rubbish!" said I.

"Not at all!" said he, with agreeable spirit.

A sudden chill came over me. "She isn't figuring on having it published, is she?"

"I can't say as to that," was his disquieting reply. "It wasn't any of my business, so I didn't ask."

"Oh," said I, "I see."

"I think it is safe to assume, however, that it is not meant for publication," said he. "It strikes me as being a bit too personal. There are parts of it that I don't believe she'd dare to put into print, although she reeled them off to me without so much as a blush. 'Pon my soul, Mr. Smart, I never was so embarrassed in my life. She—"

"Never mind," I interrupted hastily. "Don't tell tales out of school."

He was silent for a moment, fingering his big eyeglasses nervously. "It may please you to know that she thinks you are an exceedingly nice man."

"No, it doesn't!" I roared irascibly. "I'm damned if I like being called an exceedingly nice man."

"They were my words, sir, not hers," he explained desperately. "I was merely putting two and two together—forming an opinion from her manner not from her words. She is very particular to mention everything you do for her, and thanks me if I call her attention to anything she may have forgotten. She certainly appreciates your kindness to the baby."

"That is extremely gratifying," said I acidly.

He hesitated once more. "Of course, you understand that the divorce itself is absolute. It's only the matter of the child that remains unsettled. The—"

I fairly barked at him. "What the devil do you mean by that, sir? What has the divorce got to do with it?"

"A great deal, I should say," said he, with the rare, almost superhuman patience that has made him so valuable to me.

"Upon my soul!" was all that I could say.

Hawkes rapped, on the door luckily at that instant.

"The men from the telephone company are here, sir, and the electricians. Where are they to begin, sir?"

"Tell them to wait, said I. Then I hurried to the top of the east wing to ask if she had the least objection to an extension 'phone being placed in my study. She thought it would be very nice, so I returned with instructions for the men to put in three instruments: one in her room, one in mine, and one in the butler's pantry. It seemed a very jolly arrangement an 'round. As for the electric bell system, it would speak for itself.

Toward the middle of the afternoon when Mr. Poopendyke and I were hard at work on my synopsis we were startled by a dull, mysterious pounding on the wall hard by. We paused to listen. It was quite impossible to locate the sound, which ceased almost immediately. Our first thought was that the telephone men were drilling a hole through the wall into my study. Then came the sharp rat-a-ta-tat once more. Even as we looked about us in bewilderment, the portly façade of Ludwig the Red moved out of alignment with a heart-rending squeak and a long thin streak of black appeared at the inner edge of the frame, growing wider,—and blacker if anything,—before our startled eyes.

"Are you at home?" inquired a voice that couldn't by any means have emanated from the chest of Ludwig, even in his mellowest hours.

I leaped to my feet and started across the room with great strides. My secretary's eyes were glued to the magic portrait. His fingers, looking like claws, hung suspended over the keyboard of the typewriter.

"By the Lord Harry!" I cried. "Yes !"

The secret door swung quietly open, laying Ludwig's face to the wall, and in the aperture stood my amazing neighbour, as lovely a portrait as you'd see in a year's trip through all the galleries in the world. She was smiling down upon us from the slightly elevated position, a charming figure in the very latest Parisian hat and gown. Something grey and black and exceedingly chic, I remember saying to Poopendyke afterwards in response to a question of his.

"I am out making afternoon calls," said she. Her face was flushed with excitement and self-consciousness. "Will you please put a chair here so that I may hop down?"

For answer, I reached up a pair of valiant arms. She laughed, leaned forward and placed her hands on my shoulders. My hands found her waist and I lifted her gently, gracefully to the floor.

"How strong you are!" she said admiringly. "How do you do, Mr. Poopendyke!

Dear me! I am not a ghost, sir!"

His fingers dropped to the keyboard. "How do you do," he jerked out. Then he felt of his heart. "My God! I don't believe it's going."

Together we inspected the secret doors, going so far as to enter the room beyond, the Countess peering through after us from my study. To my amazement the room was absolutely bare. Bed, trunks, garments, chairs—everything in fact had vanished as if whisked away by an all-powerful genie.

"What does this mean?" I cried, turning to her.

"I don't mind sleeping upstairs, now that I have a telephone," she said serenely. "Max and Rudolph moved everything up this afternoon."

Poopendyke and I returned to the study. I, for one, was bitterly disappointed.

"I'm sorry that I had the 'phone put in," I said.

"Please don't call it a 'phone!" she objected. "I hate the word 'phone."

"So do I," said Poopendyke recklessly.

I glared at *him.* What right had he to criticise my manner of speech? He started to leave the room, after a perfunctory scramble to put his papers in order, but she broke off in the middle of a sentence to urge him to remain. She announced that she was calling on both of us.

"Please don't stop your work on my account," she said, and promptly sat down at his typewriter and began pecking at the keys. "You must teach me how to run a typewriter, Mr. Poopendyke. I shall be as poor as a church mouse before long, and I know father won't help me. I may have to become a stenographer."

He blushed abominably. I don't believe I've ever seen a more unattractive fellow than Poopendyke.

"Oh, every cloud has its silver lining," said he awkwardly.

"But I am used to gold," said she. The bell on the machine tinkled. "What do I do now?" He made the shift and the space for her.

"Go right ahead," said he. She scrambled the whole alphabet across his neat sheet but he didn't seem to mind.

"Isn't it jolly, Mr. Smart? If Mr. Poopendyke should ever leave you, I may be able to take his place as your secretary."

I bowed very low. "You may be quite sure, Countess, that I shall dismiss Mr. Poopendyke the instant you apply for his job."

"And I shall most cheerfully abdicate," said he. Silly ass!

I couldn't help thinking how infinitely more attractive and perilous she would be as a typist than the excellent young woman who had married the jeweller's clerk, and what an improvement on Poopendyke!

"I came down to inquire when you would like to go exploring for buried treasure, Mr. Smart," she said, after the cylinder had slipped back with a bang that almost startled her out of her pretty boots and caused her to give up typewriting then and there, forevermore.

"Never put off till to-morrow what you can do to-day," quoted I glibly.

She looked herself over. "If you knew how many times this gown had to be put off till to-morrow, you wouldn't ask me to ruin it the second time I've had it on my back."

"It is an uncommonly attractive gown," said I. "Shall we set to-morrow for the treasure quest?"

"To-morrow is Sunday."

"Can you think of a, better way to kill it?"

"Yes, you might have me down here for an old-fashioned midday dinner."

"Capital! Why not stay for supper, too?"

"It would be too much like spending a day with relatives," she said. "We'll go treasure hunting on Monday. I haven't the faintest notion where to look, but that shouldn't make any difference. No one else ever had. By the way, Mr. Smart, I have a bone to pick with you. Have you seen yesterday's papers? Well, in one of them, there is a long account of my—of Mr. Pless's visit to your castle, and a lengthy interview in which you are quoted as saying that he is one of your dearest friends and a much maligned man who deserves the sympathy of every law-abiding citizen in the land."

"An abominable lie!" I cried indignantly. "Confound the newspapers!"

"Another paper says that your fortune has been placed at his disposal in the fight he is making against the criminally rich Americans. In this particular article you are quoted as saying that I am a dreadful person and not fit to have the custody of a child."

"Good Lord!" I gasped helplessly.

"You also expect to do everything in your power to interest the administration at Washington in his behalf."

"Well, of all the—Oh, I say, Countess, you don't believe a word of all this, do you?"

She regarded me pensively. "You have said some very mean, uncivil things to me."

"If I thought you believed—" I began desperately, but her sudden smile relieved me of the necessity of jumping into the river. "By Jove, I shall write to these miserable sheets, denying every word they've printed. And what's more, I'll bring an action for damages against all of 'em. Why, it is positively atrocious! The whole world will think I despise you and—" I stopped very abruptly in great confusion.

"And—you don't? she queried, with real seriousness in her voice. "You don't despise me?"

"Certainly *not!*" I cried vehemently. Turning to Poopendyke, I said: "Mr. Poopendyke, will you at once prepare a complete and emphatic denial of every da—of every word they have printed about me, and I'll send it to all the American correspondents in Europe. We'll cable it ourselves to the United States. I sha'n't rest until I am set straight in the eyes of my fellow-countrymen. The whole world shall know, Countess, that I am for you first, last and all the time. It shall know—"

"But you don't know who I am, Mr. Smart," she broke in, her cheeks very warm and rosy. "How can you publicly espouse the cause of one whose name you refuse to have mentioned in your presence?"

I dismissed her question with a wave of the hand. "Poopendyke can supply the name after I have signed the statement. I give him carte blanche. The name has nothing to do with the case, so far as I am concerned. Write it, Fred, and make it strong.

She came up to me and held out her hand. "I knew you would do it," she said softly. "Thanks."

I bent low over the gloved little hand. "Don Quixote was a happy gentleman, Countess, with all his idiosyncrasies, and so am I."

She not only came for dinner with us on Sunday, but made the dressing for my alligator pear salad. We were besieged by the usual crowd of Sunday sight-seers, who came clamouring at our staunch, reinforced gates, and anathematised me soundly for refusing admission. One bourgeoise party of fifteen refused to leave the plaza until their return fares on the ferry barge were paid stoutly maintaining that they had come over in good faith and wouldn't leave until I had reimbursed them to the extent of fifty hellers apiece, ferry fare. I sent Britton out with the money. He returned with the rather disquieting news that he had recognised two of Mr. Pless's secret agents in the mob.

"I wonder if he suspects that I am here," said the Countess paling perceptibly when, I mentioned the presence of the two men.

"It doesn't matter," said I. "He can't get into the castle while the gates are locked, and, by Jove, I intend to keep them locked."

"What a delightful ogre you are, Mr. Smart," said she.

Nevertheless, I did not sleep well that night. The presence of the two detectives outside my gates was not to be taken too lightly. Unquestionably they had got wind of something that aroused suspicion in their minds. I confidently expected them to reappear in the morning, perhaps disguised as workmen. Nor were my fears wholly unjustified.

Shortly after nine o'clock a sly-faced man in overalls accosted, me in the hall.

"I beg your pardon, Mr. Smart," he said in fairly good English, "may I have a word with you? I have a message from Mr. Pless."

I don't believe he observed the look, of concern that flitted across my face.

"From Mr. Pless?" I inquired, simulating surprise. Then I looked him over so curiously that he laughed in a quiet, simple way.

"I am an agent of the secret service," he explained coolly. "Yesterday I failed to gain admission as a visitor, to-day I come as a labourer. We work in a mysterious way, sir."

"Is it necessary for Mr. Pless to resort to a subterfuge of this character in order to get a message to me? "I demanded indignantly.

He shrugged his shoulders.

"It was not necessary yesterday, but it is to-day," said he. He leaned closer and lowered his voice. "Our every movement is being watched by the Countess's detectives. We are obliged to resort to trickery to throw them off the scent. Mr. Pless has read what you had to say in the newspapers and he is too grateful, sir, to subject you to unnecessary annoyance at the hands of her agents. Your friendship is sacred to him. He realises that it means a great deal to have the support of one so powerful with the United States government. If we are to work together, Mr. Smart, in bringing this woman to justice, it must be managed with extreme skill or her family may—"

"What is this you are saying?" I broke in, scarcely able to believe my ears.

"I speak English so badly," he apologised. "Perhaps I should do no more than to give you his message. He would have you to meet him secretly to-night at the Rempf Hotel across the river. It is most important that you should do so, and that you should exercise great caution. I am to take your reply back to him."

For an instant I was fairly stupefied. Then I experienced a feeling of relief so vast that he must have seen the gleam of triumph in my eyes. The trick was mine, after all.

"Come into my study." I said. He followed me upstairs and into the room. Poopendyke was there. "This is my secretary, you may speak freely before him." Turning to Poopendyke, I said: "You have not sent that statement to the newspapers, have you? Well, let it rest for a day or two. Mr. Pless has sent a representative to see me." I scowled at my secretary, and he had the sense to hide his astonishment.

The fellow repeated what he had said before, and added a few instructions which I was to follow with care if I would do Mr. Pless the honour to wait upon him that evening at the Rempf Hotel.

"You may tell Mr. Pless that I shall be there at nine," said I. The agent departed. When he was safely out of the room, I explained the situation to Poopendyke, and then made my way through the secret panels to the Countess's rooms.

She was ready for the subterranean journey in quest of treasure, attired in a neat walking skirt, with her bonny hair encased in a swimming cap as a guard against cobwebs.

"Then you don't intend to send out the statements?" she cried in disappointment. "You are going to let every one think you are his friend and not mine?"

I was greatly elated. Her very unreasonableness was a prize that I could not fail to cherish.

"Only for the time being," I said eagerly. "Don't you see the advantage we gain by fooling him? Why, it is splendid—positively splendid!"

She pouted. "I don't feel at all sure of you now, Mr. Smart," she said, sitting down rather dejectedly in a chair near the fireplace. "I believe you are ready to turn against me. You want to be rid of me. I am a nuisance, a source of trouble to you. You will tell him that I am here—"

I stood over her, trying my best to scowl. "You know better than that. You know I—I am as loyal as—as can be. Hang it all," I burst out impulsively, "do you suppose for a minute that I want to hand you over to that infernal rascal, now that I've come to—that is to say, now that we're such ripping good friends?"

She looked up at me very pathetically at first. Then her expression changed swiftly to one of wonder and the most penetrating inquiry. Slowly a flush crept into her cheeks and her eyes wavered.

"I—I think I can trust you to——to do the right thing by me," she said, descending to a banality in her confusion.

I held out my hand. She laid hers in it rather timidly, almost as if she was afraid of me. "I shall not fail you," said I without the faintest intention to be heroic but immediately conscious of having used an expression so trite that my cheek flamed with humiliation.

For some unaccountable reason she arose hastily from the chair and walked to the window. A similar reason, no doubt, held me rooted rather safely to the spot on which I stood. I have a vague recollection of feeling dizzy and rather short of breath. My heart was acting queerly.

"Why do you suppose he wants to see you?" she asked, after a moment, turning toward me again. She was as calm as a summer breeze. All trace of nervousness had left her.

"I can't even supply a guess."

"You must be very, very tactful," she said uneasily. "I know him so well. He is very cunning."

"I am accustomed to dealing with villains," said I. "They always come to a bad end in my books, and virtue triumphs."

"But this isn't a book," she protested. "Besides virtue never triumphs in an international marriage. You must come—to see me to-night after you return from town. I won't sleep until I've heard everything."

"I may be very late," I said, contriving to hide my eagerness pretty well, I thought.

"I shall wait for you, Mr. Smart," she said, very distinctly. I took it as a command and bowed in submission. "There is no one here to gossip, so we may be as careless as we please about appearances. You will be hungry, too, when you come in. I shall have a nice supper ready for you." She frowned faintly. "You must not, under any circumstance, spoil everything by having supper with *him.*"

"Again I repeat, you may trust me implicitly to do the right thing," said I beamingly. "And now, what do you say to our trip to the bottom of the castle?"

She shook her head. "Not with the house full of spies, my dear friend. We'll save that for another day. A rainy day perhaps. I feel like having all the sunshine I can get to-day. To-night I shall be gloomy and very lonely. I shall take Rosemary and Jinko out upon the top of the tower and play all day in the sun."

I had an idea. "I am sure I should enjoy a little sunshine myself. May I come too?"

She looked me straight in the eye. There was a touch of dignity in her voice when she spoke.

"Not to-day, Mr. Smart."

A most unfathomable person!

CHAPTER XI

I AM INVITED TO SPEND MONEY

ANY one who has travelled in the Valley of the Donau knows the Rempf Hotel. It is an ancient hostelry, frequented quite as much in these days as it was in olden times by people who are by way of knowing the excellence of its cuisine and the character of its wines. Unless one possesses this intelligence, either through hearsay or experience, he will pass by the Rempf without so much as a glance at its rather forbidding exterior and make for the modern hotel on the platz, thereby missing one of the most interesting spots in this grim old town. Is it to the fashionable Bellevue that the nobility and the elect wend their way when they come to town? Not by any means. They affect the Rempf, and there you may see them in fat, inglorious plenty smugly execrating the plebeian rich of many lands who dismiss Rempf's with a sniff, and enjoying to their heart's content a privacy which the aforesaid rich would not consider at any price.

You may be quite sure that the rates are low at the historic Rempf, and that they would be much lower if the nobility had anything to say about it. One can get a very comfortable room, without bath, at the Rempf for a dollar a day, provided he gets in ahead of the native aristocracy. If he insists on having a room with bath he is guilty of *lese majeste* and is sent on his way.

But, bath or no bath, the food is the best in the entire valley and the cellar without a rival.

I found Mr. Pless at the Rempf at nine o'clock. He was in his room when I entered the quaint old place and approached the rotund manager with considerable uncertainty in my manner. For whom was I to inquire? Would he be known there as Pless?

The manager gave me a broad (I was about to say serviceable) smile and put my mind at rest by blandly inquiring if I was the gentleman who wished to see Mr. Pless. He directed me to the top floor of the hotel and I mounted two flights of stairs at the heels of a porter who exercised native thrift by carrying up a large trunk, thus saving time and steps after a fashion, although it may be hard to see wherein he really benefited when I say that after escorting me to a room on the third floor and knocking at the door while balancing the trunk on his back, he descended to the second and delivered his burden in triumph to the lady who had been calling for it since six o'clock in the evening. But even at that he displayed considerable cunning in not forgetting what room the luggage belonged in, thereby saving himself a trip all the way down to the office and back with the trunk.

Mr. Pless welcomed me with a great deal of warmth. He called me "dear old fellow" and shook hands with me with more heartiness than I had thought him capable of expressing. His dark, handsome face was aglow with pleasure. He was quite boyish. A smallish old gentleman was with him. My introduction to the stranger was a sort of afterthought, it seemed to me. I was informed that he was one of the greatest lawyers and advocates in Vienna and Mr. Pless's personal adviser in the "unfortunate controversy."

I accepted a cigar.

"So you knew who I was all the time I was at Schloss Rothhoefen," said Mr. Pless, smiling amiably. "I was trying to maintain my incognito so that you might not be distressed, Mr. Smart, by having in your home such a notorious character as I am supposed to be. I confess it was rather shabby in me, but I hold, your excellent friends responsible for the trick."

"It is rather difficult to keep a secret with women about," said I evasively.

"But never difficult to construct one," said Mr. Schymansky, winking rather too broadly. I think Schymansky was the name.

"By the way," said I, "I have had no word from our mutual friends. Have you seen them?"

Mr. Pless stiffened. His face grew perceptibly older.

"I regret to inform you, Mr. Smart, that our relations are not quite as friendly as they once were. I have reason to suspect that Mr. Smith has been working against me for the past two or three days, to such an extent, I may say, that the Ambassador now declines to advise your government to grant us certain privileges we had hoped to secure without trouble. In short, we have just heard that he will not ask the United States to consider anything in the shape of an extradition if the Countess is apprehended in her own country. Up to yesterday we felt confident that he would advise your State Department to turn the child over to our representatives in case she is to be found there. There has been underhand work going on, and Mr. Smith is at the bottom of it. He wantonly insulted me the day we left Rothhoefen. I have challenged him, but he—he committed the most diabolical breach of etiquette by threatening to kick my friend the Baron out of his rooms when he waited upon him yesterday morning."

With difficulty I restrained a desire to shout the single word: "Good!" I was proud of Billy Smith. Controlling my exultation, I merely said: "Perfectly diabolical! Perfectly!"

"I have no doubt, however, should our Minister make a formal demand upon your Secretary of State, the cause of justice would be sustained. It is a clear case of abduction, as you so forcibly declare in the interviews, Mr. Smart. I cannot adequately express my gratification for the stand you have taken. Will you be offended if I add that it was rather unexpected? I had the feeling that you were against me, that you did not like me."

I smiled deprecatingly. "As I seldom read the newspapers, I am not quite sure that they have done justice to my real feelings in the matter."

The lawyer sitting directly opposite to me, was watching my face intently. "They quoted you rather freely, sir," said he. Instinctively I felt that here was a wily person whom it would be difficult to deceive. "The Count is to be congratulated upon having the good will of so distinguished a gentleman as John Bellamy Smart. It will carry great weight, believe me."

"Oh, you will find to your sorrow that I cut a very small figure in national politics," said I. "Pray do not deceive yourselves."

"May I offer you a brandy and soda?" asked Mr. Pless, tapping sharply on the table top with his seal ring. Instantly his French valet, still bearing faint traces of the drubbing he had sustained at Britton's hands, appeared in the bedchamber door.

"Thank you, no," I made haste to say. "I am on the water wagon."

"I beg your pardon," said Mr. Pless in perplexity.

"I am not drinking, Mr. Pless," I explained.

"Sorry," said he, and curtly dismissed the man. I had a notion that the great lawyer looked, a trifle disappointed. "I fancy you are wondering why I sent for you, Mr. Smart."

"I am."

"Am I to assume that the newspapers were correct in stating that you mean to support my cause with—I may say, to the full extent of your powers?"

"It depends on circumstances, Mr. Pless."

"Circumstances?" He eyed me rather coldly, as if to say, "What right have you to suggest circumstances?"

"Perhaps I should have said that it depends somewhat on what my powers represent."

He crossed his slender legs comfortably and looked at me with a queer little tilt of his left eyebrow, but with an unsmiling visage. He was too cocksure of himself to grant me even so much as an ingratiating smile. Was not I a glory-seeking American and he one of the glorious? It would be doing me a favour to let me help him.

"I trust you will understand, Mr. Smart, that I do not ask a favour of you, but rather put myself under a certain obligation for the time being. You have become a land-owner in this country, and as such, you should any yourself with the representative people of our land. It is not an easy matter for a foreigner to plant himself in our midst, so to speak,—as a mushroom,—and expect to thrive on limited favours. I can be of assistance to you. My position, as you doubtless know, is rather a superior one in the capital. An unfortunate marriage has not lessened the power that I possess as a birthright nor the esteem in which I am held throughout Europe. The disgraceful methods employed by my former wife in securing a divorce are well known to you, I take it, and I am gratified to observe that you frown upon them. I suppose you know the whole story?"

"I think I do," said I, quietly. I have never known such consummate self-assurance as the fellow displayed.

"Then you are aware that her father has defaulted under the terms of an ante-nuptial agreement. There is still due me, under the contract, a round million of your exceedingly useful dollars."

"With the interest to be added," said the lawyer, thrumming on the chair-arm with his fingers something after the fashion my mother always employs in computing a simple sum in addition.

"Certainly," said Mr. Pless, sharply. "Mr. Smart understands that quite clearly,

Mr. Schymansky. It isn't necessary to enlighten him."

The lawyer cleared his throat. I knew him at once for a shyster. Mr. Pless continued, addressing me.

"Of course he will have to pay this money before his daughter may even hope to gain from me the right to share the custody of our little girl, who loves me devotedly. When the debt is fully liquidated, I may consent to an arrangement by which she shall have the child part of the time at least."

"It seems to me she has the upper hand of you at present, however," I said, not without secret satisfaction. "She may be in America by this time."

"I think not," said he. "Every steamship has been watched for days, and we are quite positive she has not sailed. There is the possibility, however, that she may have been taken by motor to some out-of-the-way place where she will await the chance to slip away by means of a specially chartered ship. It is this very thing that we are seeking to prevent. I do not hesitate to admit that if she once gets the child to New York, we may expect serious difficulty in obtaining our rights. I humbly confess that I have not the means to fight her in a land where her father's millions count for so much. I am a poor man. My estates are heavily involved through litigation started by my forbears. You understand my position?" He said it with a rather pathetic twist of his lips.

"I understand that you received a million in cash at the time of the wedding," said I. "What has become of all that?"

He shrugged his shoulders. "Can you expect me to indulge an extravagant wife, who seeks to become a social queen, and still save anything out of a paltry minion?"

"Oh, I see. This is a new phase of the matter that hasn't been revealed to me. It was she who spent the million?"

"After a fashion, yes," said he, without a spark of shame. "The château was in rather a dilapidated condition, and she insisted on its restoration. It was also necessary to spend a great deal of money in the effort to secure for herself a certain position in society. My own position was not sufficient for her. She wanted to improve upon it, I might say. We entertained a great deal, and lavishly. She was accustomed to gratifying every taste and whim that money could purchase. Naturally, it was not long before we were hard pressed for funds. I went to New York a year ago and put the matter clearly before her father. He met me with another proposition which rather disgusted me. I am a man who believes in fair dealing. If I have an obligation I meet it. Isn't that true, Mr. Schymansky?"

"It is," said the lawyer.

"Her father revoked his original plan and suggested an alternative. He proposed to put the million in trust for his granddaughter, our Rosemary,—a name, sir, that I abominate and which was given to her after my wife had sulked for weeks,—the interest to be paid to his daughter until the child reached the age of twenty-one. Of course, I could not accept such an arrangement. It—"

"Acting on my advice,—for I was present at the interview,—the Count emphatically declined to enterain—"

"Never mind, Schymansky," broke in the Count petulantly. "What is the use of going into all that?" He appeared to reflect for a moment. "Will you be good enough to leave the room for awhile, Mr. Schymansky? I think Mr. Smart and I can safely manage a friendly compact without your assistance. Eh, Mr. Smart?"

I couldn't feel sorry for Schymansky. He hadn't the backbone of an angleworm. If I were a lawyer and a client of mine were to speak to me as Pless spoke to him, I firmly believe I should have had at least a fair sprinkling of his blood upon my hands.

"I beg of you, Count, to observe caution and—"

"If you please, sir!" cut in the Count, with the austerity that makes the continental nobleman what he is.

"If you require my services, you will find me in the—"

"Not in the hall, I trust," said his client in a most insulting way.

Schymansky left the room without so much as a glance at me. He struck me as a man who knew his place better than any menial I've ever seen. I particularly noticed that not even his ears were red.

"Rather rough way to handle a lawyer, it strikes me," said I. "Isn't he any good?"

"He is as good as the best of them," said the Count, lighting his fourth or fifth cigarette. "I have no patience with the way they muddle matters by always talking law, law, law! If it were left to me, I should dismiss the whole lot of them and depend entirely upon my common-sense. If it hadn't been for the lawyers, I am convinced that all this trouble could have been avoided, or at least amicably adjusted out of court. But I am saddled with half a dozen of them, simply because two or three banks and as many private interests are inclined to be officious. They claim that my interests are theirs, but I doubt it, by Jove, I do. They're a blood-sucking lot, these bankers. But I sha'n't bore you with trivialities. Now here is the situation in a word. It is quite impossible for me to prosecute the search for my child without financial assistance from outside sources. My funds are practically exhausted and the banks refuse to extend my credit. You have publicly declared yourself to be my friend and well-wisher. I have asked you to come here to-night, Mr. Smart, to put you to the real test, so to speak. I want one hundred thousand dollars for six months."

While I was prepared in a sense for the request, the brazenness with which he put it up to me took my breath away. I am afraid that the degagé manner in which he paid compliment to my affluence was too much for me. I blinked my eyes rapidly for a second or two and then allowed them to settle into a stare of perplexity.

"Really, Mr. Pless," I mumbled in direct contrast to his sangfroid, "you—you surprise me."

He laughed quietly, almost reassuringly, as he leaned forward in his chair the better to study my face. "I hope you do not think that I expect you to produce so much ready money to-night, Mr. Smart. Oh, no! Any time within the next few days will be satisfactory. Take your time, sir. I appreciate that it requires time to arrange for the—"

I held up my hand with a rather lofty air. "Was it one hundred and fifty thousand that you mentioned, or—"

"That was the amount," said he, a sudden glitter in his eyes.

I studied the ceiling with a calculating squint, as if trying to approximate my balance in bank. He watched me closely, almost breathlessly. At last, unable to control his eagerness, he said:

"At the usual rate of interest, you understand"

"Certainly," I said, and resumed my calculations. He got the impression that I was annoyed by the interruption.

"I beg your pardon," he said.

"What security can you give, Mr. Pless?" I demanded in a very business-like way.

"Oh, you Americans!" he cried, his face beaming with premature relief. "You will pin us down, I see. I do not wonder that you are so rich. I shall give you my personal note, Mr. Smart, for the amount, secured by a mortgage—a supplementary mortgage—on the Château Tarnowsy."

Tarnowsy! Now I remembered everything. Tarnowsy! The name struck my memory like a blow. What a stupid dolt I had been ! The whole world had rung wedding bells for the marriage of the Count Maris Tarnowsy, scion of one of the greatest Hungarian houses, and Aline, the nineteen-year-old daughter of Gwendolen and Jasper Titus, of New York, Newport, Tuxedo, Hot Springs, Palm Beach and so forth. Jasper Titus, the banker and railway magnate, whose name as well as his hand was to be seen in every great financial movement of the last two decades!

What a fool I was not to recall a marriage that had been not only on the lips of every man, woman and child in the States but on mine in particular, for I had bitterly execrated the deliverance into bondage of this young girl of whose beauty and charm I had heard so much.

The whole spectacular travesty came back to me with a rush, as I sat there in the presence of the only man who had ever been known to get the better of Jasper Titus in a trade. I remembered with some vividness my scornful attitude toward the newspapers of the metropllis, all of which fairly sloshed over with the news of the great event weeks beforehand and weeks afterward. I was not the only man who said harsh things about Jasper Titus in those days. I was but one of the multitude.

I also recalled my scathing comments at the time of the divorce proceedings. They were too caustic to be repeated here. It is only necessary to state that the proceedings came near to putting two friendly nations into very bad temper. Statesmen and diplomats were drawn into the mess, and jingo congressmen on our side of the water introduced sensational bills bearing specifically upon the international marriage market. Newspaper humourists stood together as one man in advocating a revision of the tariff upward on all foreign purchases coming under the head of the sons of old masters. As I have said before I did not follow the course of the nasty squabble very closely, and was quite indifferent as to the result. I have a vague recollection of some one telling me that a divorce had been granted, but that is all.

There was also something said about a child.

My pleasant little mystery had come to a sharp and rather depressing end. The lovely countess about whom I had cast the veil of secrecy was no other than the much-discussed Aline Titus and Mr. Pless the expensive Count Tarnowsy. Cold, hard facts took the place of indulgent fancies. The dream was over. I was sorry to have it end. A joyous enthusiasm had attended me while I worked in the dark; now a dreary reality stared me in the face. The sparkle was gone. Is there anything so sad as a glass of champagne when it has gone flat and lifeless?

My cogitations were brief. The Count after waiting for a minute or two to let me grasp the full importance of the sacrifice he was ready to make in order to secure me against personal loss, blandly announced that there were but two mortgages on the château, whereas nearly every other place of the kind within his knowledge had thrice as many.

"You wish me to accept a third mortgage on the place?" I inquired, pursing my lips.

"The Château is worth at least a million," he said earnestly. "But why worry about that, Mr. Smart? My personal note is all that is necessary. The matter of a mortgage is merely incidental. I believe it is considered business-like by you Americans, so I stand quite ready to abide by your habits. I shall soon be in possession of a million in any event, so you are quite safe in advancing me any amount up to—"

"Just a moment, Count," I interrupted, leaning forward in my chair. "May I inquire where and from whom you received the impression that I am a rich man?"

He laughed easily. "One who indulges a whim, Mr. Smart, is always rich. Schloss Rothhoefen condemns you to the purgatory of Crœsus."

"Crœsus would be a poor man in these days," said I. "If he lived in New York he would be wondering where his next meal was to come from. You have made a very poor guess as to my wealth. I am not a rich man."

He eyed me coldly. "Have you suddenly discovered the fact, sir?"

"What do you mean?"

"I suggest a way in winch you can be of assistance to me, and you hesitate. How am I to take it, sir?"

His infernal air of superiority aggravated me. "You may take it just as you please, Mr. Pless."

"I beg you to remember that I am Count Tarnowsy. Mr.—"

I arose. "The gist of the matter is this: you want to borrow one hundred and fifty thousand dollars of me. That is—"

He hastened to correct me. "I do not call it borrowing when one gives ample security for the amount involved."

"What is your idea of borrowing, may I ask?"

"Borrowing is the same thing as asking a favour according to our conception of the transaction. I am not asking a favour of you, sir. Far from it. I am offering you an opportunity to put a certain amount of money out at a high rate of interest."

"Well, then, we'll look at it in that light. I am not in a position to invest so much money at this time. To be perfectly frank with you, I haven't the money lying loose."

"Suppose that I were to say that any day inside the next three or four weeks would be satisfactory to me," said he, as if he were granting me a favour. "Please be seated, Mr. Smart." He glanced at his watch. "I have ordered a light supper to be sent up at ten o'clock. We can—"

"Thank you. I fear it is impossible for me to remain."

"I shall be disappointed. However, another time if not to-night, I trust. And now to come to the point. May I depend upon you to help me at this trying period? A few thousand will be sufficient for present needs, and the balance may go over a few weeks without seriously inconveniencing me. If we can come to some sort of an understanding to-night, my attorney will be happy to meet you to-morrow at any time and place you may suggest."

I actually was staggered. Upon my word it was almost as if he were dunning me and magnanimously consenting to give me an extension of time if I could see my way clear to let him have something on account. My choler was rising.

"I may as well tell you first as last, Count Tarnowsy, that I cannot let you have the money. It is quite, impossible. In the first place, I haven't the amount to spare; in the second—"

"Enough, sir," he broke in angrily. "I have committed the common error of regarding one of you as a gentleman. Damn me, if I shall ever do so again. There isn't one in the whole of the United States. Will you be good enough, Mr. Smart, to overlook my mistake? I thank you for taking the trouble to rush into print in my defence. If you have gained anything by it, I do not begrudge you the satisfaction you must feel in being heralded as the host of Count Tarnowsy and his friend. You obtained the privilege very cheaply."

"You will do well, sir, to keep a civil tongue in your head," said I, paling with fury.

"I have nothing more said he contemptuously. "Good night. François! Conduct Mr. Smart to the corridor."

François—or "Franko" as Britton, whose French is very lame, had called him—preceded me to the door. In all my experience, nothing has surprised me so much as my ability to leave the room without first kicking François' master, or at least telling him what I thought of him. Strangely enough I did not recover my sense of speech until I was well out into the corridor. Then I deliberately took a gold coin out of my pocket and pressed it into the valet's hand.

"Kindly give that to your master with my compliments," said I, in a voice that was intended to reach Tarnowsy's ear.

"Bon soir, m'sieu," said François, with an amiable grin. He watched me descend the stairs and then softly closed the door.

In the office I came upon Mr. Schymansky.

"I trust everything is satisfactorily arranged, Mr.—" he began smiling and rubbing his hands. He was so utterly unprepared for the severity of the interruption that the smile was still in process of congealing as I stepped out into the narrow, illy-lighted street.

Max and Rudolph were waiting at the wharf for me. Their excellent arms and broad backs soon drove the light boat across the river. But once during the five or ten minutes of passage did I utter a word, and that word, while wholly involuntary and by no means addressed to my oarsmen, had the remarkable effect of making them row like fury for the remainder of the distance.

Mr. Poopendyke was waiting for me in the courtyard. He was carrying a lantern, which he held rather close to my face as if looking for something he dreaded to see.

"What the devil is the matter with you?" I demanded irascibly. "What's up? What are you doing out here with a lantern?"

"I was rather anxious," he said, a note of relief in his voice. "I feared that something unexpected might have befallen you. Five minutes ago the—Mr. Pless called up on the telephone and left a message for you. It rather upset me, sir."

"He did, eh? Well, what did he say?"

"He merely commanded me to give you his compliments and to tell you to go to the devil. I told him that you would doubtless be at home a little later on and it would sound very much better if it came from him instead of from me. Whereupon he told me to accompany you, giving rather explicit directions. He appeared to be in a tremendous rage."

I laughed heartily. "I must have got under his confounded skin after all."

"I was a little worried, so I came out with the lantern. One never can tell. Did you come to blows?"

"Blows? What puts that idea into your head?"

"The Countess was listening on the extension wire while he was speaking to me. She thought it was you calling up and was eager to hear what had happened. It was she who put it into my head. She said you must have given his nose a jolly good pulling or something of the sort. I am extremely sorry, but she heard every word he said, even to the mildest damn."

"It must have had a very familiar sound to her," I said sourly.

"So she informed me."

"Oh, you've seen her, eh?"

"She came down to the secret door a few minutes ago and urged me to set out to meet you. She says she can hardly wait for the news. I was to send you upstairs at once."

Confound him, he took that very instant to hold the lantern up to my face again, and caught me grinning like a Cheshire cat.

I hurried to my room and brushed myself up a bit. On my bureau, in a glass of water, there was a white boutonniere, rather clumsily constructed and all ready to be pinned in the lapel of my coat. I confess to a blush. I wish Britton would not be so infernally arduous in his efforts to please me.

The Countess gave a little sigh of relief when I dashed in upon her a few minutes later. She had it all out of me before I had quite recovered my breath after the climb upstairs.

"And so it was I who spent all the money," she mused, with a far-away look in her eyes.

"In trying to be a countess," said I boldly.

She smiled. "Are you hungry?"

"Delightfully," said I.

We sat down at the table. "Now tell me everything all over again," she said.

CHAPTER XII

I AM INFORMED THAT I AM IN LOVE

MR. POOPENDYKE began to develop a streak of romantic invention—in fact, tomfoolery—A day or two after my experience with Count Tarnowsy in the Rempf Hotel. He is the last person in the world of whom I—or any one else—would suspect silliness of a radical nature.

We were finding it rather difficult to get down to actual, serious work on the book. The plot and the synopsis, of course, were quite completely outlined; with ordinary intensity of purpose on my part the tale might have galloped through the introductory chapters with some clarity and decisiveness. But for some reason I lacked the power of concentration, or perhaps more properly speaking the power of initiative. I laid it to the hub-bub created by the final effort of the workmen to finish the job of repairing my castle before cold weather set in.

"That isn't it, Mr. Smart," said my secretary darkly. We were in the study and my pad of paper was lying idly on my knees. For half an hour I had been trying to think of a handy sentence with which to open the story; the kind of sentence that catches the unwary reader's attention at a glance and makes for interest.

"What is it, then?" I demanded, at once resenting an opinion.

He smiled mysteriously. "You were not thinking of the workmen just now, were you?"

"Certainly," said I, coldly. "What's that got to do with it?"

"Nothing. I suppose," said he resignedly.

I hesitated. "Of course it is the work that upsets me. What are you driving at?"

He stared for a long time at the portrait of Ludwig the Red. "Isn't it odd that the Countess, an American, should be descended from the old Rothhoefens? What a small world it is, after all!"

I became wary. "Nothing odd about it to me. We've all got to descend from somebody."

"I dare say. Still it *is* odd that she should be hiding in the castle of her ances—"

"Not at all, not at all. It just happens to be a handy place. Perfectly natural."

We lapsed into a prolonged spell of silence. I found myself watching him rather combatively, as who would anticipate the move of an adversary.

"Perfect rot," said I, at last, without rhyme or reason.

He grinned. "Nevertheless, it's the general opinion that you are," said he.

I sat up very straight. "What's that?"

"You're in love," said he succinctly. It was like a bomb, and a bomb is the very last thing in succinctness. It comes to the point without palaver or conjecture, and it reduces havoc to a single synonymous syllable.

"You're crazy!" I gasped.

"And the workmen haven't anything at all to do with it," he pronounced emphatically. It was a direct charge. I distinctly felt called upon to refute it. But while I was striving to collect my thoughts he went on, somewhat arbitrarily, I thought: "You don't think we're all blind, do you, Mr. Smart?"

"We?" I murmured, a curious dampness assailing me.

"That is to say, Britton, the Schmicks and myself."

"The Schmicks?" It was high time that I should laugh. "Ha! ha! The Schmicks! Good Lord, man,—the *Schmicks.*" It sounded mane even to me, but, on my soul, it was all I could think of to say.

"The Schmicks are tickled to death over it," said he. "And so is Britton."

Collecting all the sarcasm that I could command at me instant, I inquired: "And you, Mr. Poopendyke,—are you not ticklish?"

"Very" said he.

"Well, I'm not!" said I, savagely. "What does all this nonsense mean. Don't be an ass, Fred."

"Perhaps you don't know it, Mr. Smart, but you *are* in love," said he so convincingly that I was conscious of an abrupt sinking of the heart. Good heavens! Was he right? Was there anything in this silly twaddle? "You are quite mad about her."

"The deuce you say!" I exclaimed, rather blankly.

"Oh, I've seen it coming. For that matter, so has she. It's as plain as the nose—"

I leaped to my feet, startled. "She? You don't—Has she said anything that leads you to believe—Oh, the deuce! What rot!"

"No use getting angry over it," he said consolingly.

"Failing in love is the sort of thing a fellow can't help, you know. It happens without his assistance. It is so easy. Now I was once in love with a girl for two years without really knowing it."

"And how did you find it out? "I asked, weakly.

"I didn't find it out until she married another chap. Then I knew I'd been in love with, her all the time. But that's neither here nor there. You are heels over head in love with the Countess Tarnowsy and—"

"Shut up, Fred! You're going daffy from reading my books, or absorbing my manuscripts, or—"

"Heaven is my witness, I don't read your books and I merely correct your manuscripts. God knows there is no romance in that! You *are* in love. Now what are you going to do about it?"

"Do about it?" I demanded.

"You can't go on in this way, you know," he said relentlessly. "She won't—"

"Why, you blithering idiot," I roared, "do you know what you are saying? I'm not in love with anybody. My heart is—is—But never mind! Now, listen to me, Fred. This nonsense has got to cease. I won't have it. Why, she's already got a husband. She's had all she can stand in the way of husb—"

"Rubbish! She can stand a husband or two more, if you are going to look at it in a literal way. Besides, she hasn't a husband. She's chucked him. Good riddance, too. Now, do you imagine for a single instant that a beautiful, adorable young woman of twenty-three is going to spend the rest of her life without a man? Not much! She's free to marry again and she will."

"Admitting that to be true, why should she marry me?"

"I didn't say she was in love with you. I said you were in love with her."

"Oh," I said, and my face fell "I see."

He seemed to be considering something. After a few seconds, he nodded his head decisively. "Yes, I am sure of it. If the right man gets her, she'll make the finest, sweetest wife in the world. She's never had a chance to show what's really in her.

She would be adorable, wouldn't she?"

The sudden question caught me unawares.

"She would!" I said, with conviction.

"Well," said he, slowly and deliberately, "why don't you set about it, then?"

He was so ridiculous that I thought for the fun of it, I'd humour him.

"Assuming that you are right in regard to my feelings toward her, Fred, what leads you to believe that I would stand a chance of winning her?" It was a silly question, but I declare I hung on his answer with a tenseness that surprised me.

"Why not? You are good looking, a gentleman, a celebrity, and a man. Bless my soul, she *could* do worse."

"But you forget that I am—let me see—thirty-five and she is but twenty-three."

"To offset that, she has been married and unhappy. That brings her about up to your level, I should say. She's a mother, and that makes you seem a good bit younger. Moreover, she isn't a sod widow. She's a grass widow, and she's got a living example to use as a contrast. Regulation widows sometimes forget the past because it is dim and dead; but, by George, sir, the divorced wife doesn't forget the hard time she's had. She's mighty careful when she goes about it the second time. The other kind has lost her sense of comparison, her standard, so to speak. Her husband may have been a rotter and all that sort of thing, but he's dead and buried and she can't see anything but the good that was in him for the simple reason that it's on his tombstone. But when they're still alive and as bad as ever,—well, don't you see it's different?"

"It occurs to me she'd be more likely to see the evil in all men and steer clear of them."

"That isn't feminine nature. All women want to be loved. They want to be married. They want to make some man happy."

"I suppose all this is philosophy," I mused, somewhat pleased and mollified. "But we'll look at it from another point of view. The former Miss Titus set out for a title. She got it. Do you imagine she'll marry a man who has no position—By Jove! That reminds me of something. You are altogether wrong in your reasoning, Fred. With her own lips she declared to me one day that she'd never marry again. There you are!"

He rolled his eyes heavenward.

"They take delight in self-pity," said he. "You can't believe 'em under oath when they're in that mood."

"Well, granting that she will marry again," said I, rather insistently, "it doesn't follow that her parents will consent to a marriage with any one less than a duke the next time."

"They've had their lesson."

"And she is probably a mercenary creature, after all. She's had a taste of poverty, after a fashion. I imagine—"

If I know anything about women, the Countess Tarnowsy wants love more than anything else in the world, my friend. She was made to be loved and she knows it. And she hasn't had any of it, except from men who didn't happen to know how to combine love and respect. I'll give you my candid opinion, Mr. John Bellamy Smart. She's in a receptive mood. Strike while the iron is hot. You'll win or my name isn't—"

"Fred Poopendyke, you haven't a grain of sense," I broke in sharply. "Do you suppose, just to oblige you, I'll get myself mixed up in this wretched squabble? Why, she's not really clear of the fellow yet. She's got a good many months to wait before the matter of the child and the final decree—"

"Isn't she worth waiting a year for—or ten years? Besides, the whole squabble will come to an end the minute old man Titus puts up the back million. And the minute the Countess goes to him and says she's *willing* for him to pay it, you take my word for it, he'll settle like a flash. It rests with her."

"I don't quite get your meaning."

"She isn't going to let a stingy little million stand between her and happiness."

"Confound you, do you mean to say she'd ask her father to pay over that million in order to be free to marry—" I did not condescend to finish the sentence.

"Why not?" he demanded after a moment. "He owes it, doesn't he?"

I gasped. "But you wouldn't have him pay over a million to that damned brute of a Count!"

He grinned. "You've changed your song, my friend. A few weeks ago you were saying he ought to pay it, that it would serve him right, and—"

"Did I say that?"

"You did. You even said it to the Countess."

"But not with the view to making it possible for her to hurry off and marry again. Please understand that, Fred."

"He ought to pay what he owes. He gave a million to get one husband for her.

He ought to give a million to be rid of him, so that she could marry the next one without putting him to any expense whatsoever. It's only fair to her, I say. And now I'll tell you something else: the Countess, who has stood out stubbornly against the payment of this money, is now hallway inclined to advise the old gentleman to settle with Tarnowsy."

"She is?" I cried in astonishment. "How do you Know?"

"I told her I thought it was the cheapest and quickest way out of it, and she said: 'I wonder!'"

"Have you been discussing her most sacred affairs with her, you blithering—"

"No, sir," said he, with dignity. "She has been discussing them with *me.*"

I have no recollection of what I said as I stalked out of the room. He called out after me, somewhat pleadingly, I thought:

"Ask Britton what he has to say about it."

Things had come to a pretty pass! Couldn't a gentleman be polite and agreeable to a young and charming lady whom circumstances had thrown in his way without having his motives misconstrued by a lot of snooping, idiotic menials whose only zest in life sprung from a temperamental tendency to belittle the big things and enlarge upon the small ones? What rot! What utter rot! Ask Britton! The more I thought of Poopendyke's injunction the more furious I grew. What insufferable insolence! Ask Britton! The idea! Ask *my valet!* Ask him what? Ask him politely if he could oblige me by telling me whether I was in love? I suppose that is what Poopendyke meant.

It was the silliest idea in the world. In the first place I was *not* in love, and in the second place whose business was it but mine if I were? Certainly not Poopendyke's, certainly not Britton's, certainly not the Schmicks'! Absolute lack of any sense of proportion, that's what ailed the whole bally of them. What looked like love to them—benighted dolts!—was no more than a rather resolute effort on my part to be kind to and patient with a person who had invaded my home and set everybody—including myself by the ears.

But, even so, what right had my secretary to constitute himself adviser and mentor to the charming invader? What right had he to suggest what she should do, or what her father should do, or what *anybody* should do? He was getting to be disgustingly officious. What he needed was a smart jacking up, a little plain talk from me. Give a privileged and admittedly faithful secretary an inch and he'll have you up to your ears in trouble before you know what has happened. By the same token, what right had she to engage herself in confidential chats with—But just then I caught sight of Britton coming upstairs with my neatly polished tan shoes in one hand and a pair of number 3½A tan pumps in the other. Not expecting to meet me in the hall, he had neglected to remove his cap when he came in from the courtyard. In some confusion, he tried to take it off, first with one hand, then with the other, sustaining what one might designate as absent treatment kicks on either jaw from two distinct sexes in the shape of shoes. He managed to get all four of them into one hand, however, and then grabbed on his cap.

"Any think more, sir?" he asked, purely from habit.

I was regarding the shoes with interest. Never have I known anything so ludicrous as the contrast between my stupendous number tens and the dainty pumps that seemed almost babyish beside them.

Then I did the very thing I had excoriated Poopendyke for even suggesting. I asked Britton!

"Britton, what's all this gossip I hear going the rounds of the castle behind my back?"

Confound him, he looked pleased! "It's quite true, sir, quite true."

"Quite true!" I roared. "What's quite true, sir?"

"Isn't it, sir?" he asked, dismayed.

"Isn't what?"

"I mean to say, sir, isn't it true?"

"My God!" I cried, throwing up my hands in hopeless despair. "You—you—wait! I'm going to get to the bottom of this. I want the truth, Britton. Who put it into that confounded head of yours that I am—er—in love with the Countess? Speak! Who did it?"

He lowered his voice, presumably because I had dropped mine to a very loud whisper. I also had glanced over both shoulders.

"Begging your pardon, sir, but I must be honest, sir. It was you as first put it into my 'ead, sir."

"I?" My face went the colour of a cardinal's cap.

"You, sir. It's as plain as the nose on your—"

"That will do, Britton," I commanded. He remained discreetly silent. "That will do, I say," I repeated, somewhat testily. "Do you hear, sir?"

"Yes, sir," he responded. "That will do, you says."

"Ahem! I—ahem!" Somewhat clumsily I put on my nose-glasses and made a pretext of examining his burden rather closely. "What's this you have here."

"Shoes, sir."

"I see, I see. Let me have them."

He handed me my own. "The others, if you please," I said, disdaining the number tens. "May I inquire, sir, where you are taking ***these?***" I had the Countess's pumps in my hands. He explained that he was going to drop mine in my room and then take hers upstairs. "You may drop mine as you intended. I shall take care of these."

"Very good, sir," said he, with such positive relief in Jus voice that I glared at him. He left me standing there, a small pump in each hand.

Five minutes later I was at her door, a pump in each hand and my heart in my mouth. A sudden, inexplicable form of panic took possession of me. I stood there ready to tap resoundingly on the panel of the door with the heel of a slipper; I never raised my hand for the purpose.

Instead of carrying out my original design, I developed an overpowering desire to do nothing of the sort. Why go on making a fool of myself? Why add fuel to the already pernicious flame? Of course I was not in love with her, the idea was preposterous. But, just the same, the confounded servants were beginning to gossip, and back stair scandal is the very worst type. It was wrong for me to encourage it. Like a ninny, I had just given Britton something to support his contention, and he wouldn't be long in getting down to the servants' hall with the latest exhibit in the charge against me.

Moreover, if every one was talking about it, what was to prevent the silly gossip from reaching the sensitive ears of the Countess? A sickening thought struck me: could, it be possible that the Countess her-self suspected me of being in love with her? A woman's vanity goes a long way sometimes. The thought did not lessen the panic that afflicted me. I tip-toed away from the door to a less exposed, spot at the bend in the stairway.

There, after some deliberation, I came to a decision. The proper thing for me to do was to show all of them that their ridiculous suspicions were wrong. I owed it to the Countess, to say the least. She was my guest, as it were, and it was my duty to protect her while she was in my house. The only thing for me to do, therefore, was to stay away from her.

The thought of it distressed me, but it seemed to be the only way, and the fair one. No doubt she would expect some sort of an explanation for the sudden indifference on my part, but I could attribute everything to an overpowering desire to work on my story. (I have a habit of using my work as an excuse for not doing a great many things that I ought to do.)

All this time I was regarding the small tan pumps with something akin to pain in my eyes. I could not help thinking about the tiny feet they sometimes covered. By some sort of intuitive computation I arrived at the conclusion that they were adorably small, and pink, and warm. Suddenly it occurred to me that my present conduct was reprehensible, that no man of honour would be holding a lady's pumps in his hands and allowing his imagination to go too far. Resolutely I put them behind my back and marched down-stairs.

"Britton," said I, a few minutes later, "you may take these up to the Countess, after all."

He blinked his eyes. "Wasn't she at 'ome, sir?"

"Don't be insolent, Britton. Do as I tell you."

"Very good, sir." He held the pumps up to admire them. "They're very cute, ain't they, sir?"

"They are just like *all* pumps," said I, indifferently, and walked away. If I could have been quite sure that it was a chuckle I heard, I should have given Britton something to think about for the rest of his days. The impertinent rascal!

For some two long and extremely monotonous days I toiled. A chapter shaped itself—after a fashion. Even as I wrote, I knew that it wasn't satisfactory and that I should tear it up the instant it was 'finished. What irritated me more than anything else was the certain conviction that Poopendyke, who typed it as I progressed, also knew that it would go into the waste paper basket.

Both nights I went to bed early and to sleep late. I could not deny to myself that I was missing those pleasant hours with the Countess. I ***did*** miss them. I missed Rosemary and Jinko and Helen Mane Louise Antoinette and Blake.

An atmosphere of gloom settled around Poopendyke and Britton. They eyed me with a sort of pathetic wonder in their faces. As time went on they began to look positively forlorn and unhappy. Once or twice I caught them whispering in the hallway. On seeing me they assumed an air of nonchalance that brought a grim smile to my lips. I was beginning to hate them. Toward the end of the second day, the four Schmicks became so aggravatingly doleful that I ordered them, one and all, to keep out of my sight. Even the emotionless Hawkes and the perfect Blatchford were infected. I don't believe I've ever seen a human face as solemnly respectful as Hawkes' was that night at dinner. He seemed to be pitying me from the bottom of his heart. It was getting on my nerves.

I took a stroll in the courtyard after dinner, and I may be forgiven I hope for the few surreptitious glances I sent upwards in the direction of the rear-windows in the eastern wing. I wondered what she was doing, and what she was thinking of my extraordinary behaviour, and why the deuce she hadn't sent down to ask me to come up and tell her how busy I was. She had not made a single sign. The omission was not particularly gratifying, to say the least.

Approaching the servants' hall, I loitered. I heard, voices, a mixture of tongues. Britton appeared to be doing the most of the talking. Gradually I became aware of the fact that he was explaining to the four Schmicks the meaning of an expression in which must have been incorporated the words "turned him down."

Hawkes, the impeccable Hawkes, joined in. "If I know anything about it, I'd say she has threw the 'ooks into 'im."

Then they had to explain *that* to Conrad and Gretel, who repeated "Ach, Gott" and other simple expletives in such a state of misery that I could almost detect tears in their voices.

"It ain't that, Mr. 'Awkes," protested Britton loyally. "He's lost his nerve, that's wot it is. They allus do when they realise 'ow bad they're hit. Turn 'im down? Not much, Mr. 'Awkes. Take it from me, Mr. 'Awkes, he's not going to give 'er the *chawnce* to turn 'im down."

"Ach, Gott!" said Gretel. I will stake my head that she wrung her hands.

"Women is funny," said Hawkes. (I had no idea the wretch was so ungrammatical.) "You can't put your finger on 'em ever. While I 'aven't seen much of the Countess during my present engagement, I will say this: she has a lot more sense than people give 'er credit for. Now why should she throw the 'ooks into a fine, upstanding chap like 'im, even if he is an American? She made a rotten bad job the first time, mind you. If she has threw the 'ooks into 'im, as I am afeared, I can't see wot the deuce ails 'er."

My perfect footman, Blatchford, ventured an opinion, and I blessed him for it. "We may be off our nuts on the 'ole bloomink business," said he. "Maybe he as thrown the 'ooks into 'er. Who knows? It looks that w'y to me." (I remember distinctly that he used the word "thrown" and I was of half a mind to rush in and put him over Hawkes, there and then.)

"In any case," said Britton, gloom in his voice, "it's a most unhappy state of affairs. He's getting to be a perfect crank. Complines about everything I do. He won't 'ave 'is trousers pressed and he 'asn't been shaved since Monday."

I stole away, rage in my soul. Or was it mortification? In any event, I had come to an irrevocable decision: I would ship the whole lot of them, without notice, before another day was gone.

The more I thought of the way I was being treated by my own servants, and the longer I dwelt upon the ignominious figure I must have presented as the hero of their back-door romance, the angrier I got. I was an object of concern to them, an object of pity! Confound them, they were feeling sorry for me because I had received my congé, and they were actually finding fault with me for not taking it with a grin on my face!

Before going to bed I went into the loggia (for the first time in three days) and, keeping myself pretty well hidden behind a projection in the wall, tried to get a glimpse of the Countess's windows. Failing there, I turned my steps in another direction and soon stood upon my little balcony. There was no sign of her in the windows, although a faint light glowed against the curtains of a well-remembered room near the top of the tower.

Ah, what a cosy, jolly room! "What a delicious dinner I had had there! And what a supper! Somehow, I found myself thinking of those little tan pumps. As a matter of fact, they had been a source of annoyance to me for more than forty-eight hours. I had found myself thinking of them at most inopportune times, greatly to the detriment of my work as a realist.

It was cool on the balcony, and I was abnormally warm, as might be expected. It occurred to me that I might do worse than to sit out there in the cool of the evening and enjoy a cigar or two—three or four, if necessary.

But, though I sat there until nearly midnight and chattered my teeth almost out of my head with the cold, she did not appear at her window. The aggravating part of it was that while I was shivering out there in the beastly raw, miasmic air, she doubtless was lying on a luxurious couch before a warm fire in a dressing gown and slippers,—ah, slippers!—reading a novel and thinking of nothing in the world but her own comfort! And those rascally beggars presumed to think that I was in love with a selfish, self-centred, spoiled creature like that! Rubbish!

I am afraid that Poopendyke found me in a particularly irascible frame of mind the next morning. I know that Britton did. I thought better of my determination to discharge Britton. He was an exceptionally good servant and a loyal fellow, so why should I deprive myself of a treasure simply because the eastern wing of my abode was inhabited by an unfeeling creature who hadn't a thought beyond fine feathers and bonbons? I was not so charitably inclined toward Hawkes and Blatchford, who were in my service through an influence over which I did not appear to have any control. They would have to go.

"Mr. Poopendyke," said I, after Blatchford had left the breakfast room, "I want you to give notice to Hawkes and Blatchford to-day."

"Notice?" he exclaimed incredulously.

"Notice," said I, very distinctly.

He looked distressed. "I thought they were most satisfactory to you."

"I've changed my opinion."

"By Jove, Mr. Smart, I—I don't know how the Countess will take such high-handed—ahem! You see, sir, she—she was good enough to recommend them to me. It will be quite a shock to—"

"By the Lord Harry, Fred, am I to—"

"Don't misunderstand me," he made haste to say. "This is your house. You have a perfect right to hire and discharge, but—but—Don't you think you'd better consider very carefully—He seemed to be finding his collar rather tight.

I held up my hand. "Of course I do not care to offend the Countess Tarnowsy. It was very kind of her to recommend them. We—we will let the matter rest for a few days."

"She has informed me that you were especially pleased with the manner in which they served the dinner the other night. I think she said you regarded them as incomparable diadems, or something of the sort. It may have been the champagne."

My thoughts leaped backward to that wonderful dinner. "It wasn't the champagne," said I, very stiffly.

"Do you also contemplate giving notice to the chef and his wife, our only chambermaid?"

"No, I don't," I snapped. "I think they were in bed."

He looked at me as if he thought I had gone crazy. I wriggled uncomfortably in my chair for a second or two, and then abruptly announced that we'd better get to work. I have never ceased to wonder what construction he could have put on that stupid slip of the tongue.

I cannot explain why, but at the slightest unusual sound that morning I found myself shooting an involuntary glance at the imperturbable features of Ludwig the Red. Sometimes I stopped in the middle of a sentence, to look and to listen rather more intently than seemed absolutely necessary, and on each occasion I was obliged to begin the sentence all over again, because, for the life of me, I couldn't remember what it was I had set out to say in dictation. Poopendyke had an air of patient tolerance about him that irritated me intensely. More than once I thought I detected him in the act of suppressing a smile.

At eleven o'clock, Blatchford came to the door. His ordinarily stoical features bore signs of a great, though subdued excitement. I had a fleeting glimpse of Britton in the distance,—a sort of passing shadow, as it were.

"A note for you, sir, if you please," said he. He was holding the salver almost on a level with his nose. It seemed to me that lie was looking at it out of the corner of his eye.

My heart—my incomprehensible heart—gave a leap that sent the blood rushing to my face. He advanced, not with his usual imposing tread but with a sprightliness that pleased me vastly. I took the little pearl grey envelope from the salver, and carelessly glanced at the superscription. There was a curious ringing in my ears.

"Thank you, Blatchford; that will do."

"I beg pardon, sir, but there is to be an answer."

"Oh," said I. I had the feeling that at least fifty eyes were upon me, although I am bound to admit that both Poopendyke and the footman were actively engaged in looking in another direction.

I tore open the envelope.

"Have you deserted me entirely? Won't you please come and see me? Thanks for the violets, but I can't talk to violets, you know. Please come up for luncheon."

I managed to dash off a brief note in a fairly nonchalant manner. Blatchford almost committed the unpardonable crime of slamming the door behind him, he was in such a hurry to be on with the message.

Then I went over and stood above Mr. Poopendyke.

"Mr. Poopendyke," said I slowly, darkly, "what do you know about those violets?"

He quailed. "I hope you don't mind, Mr. Smart. It's all right. I put one of your cards in, so that there ***couldn't*** be any mistake."

CHAPTER XIII

I VISIT AND AM VISITED

HALFWAY up the winding stairways, I paused in some astonishment. It had just occurred to me that I was going up the steps two at a time and that my heart was beating like mad.

I reflected. Here was I racing along like a schoolboy, and wherefor? What occasion was there for such unseemly haste? In the first place, it was now but a few minutes after eleven, and she had asked me for luncheon; there was no getting around that. At best luncheon was two hours off. So why was I galloping like this? The series of self-inflicted questions found me utterly unprepared; I couldn't answer one of them. My brain somehow couldn't get at them intelligently; I was befuddled. I progressed more slowly, more deliberately, finally coming to a full stop in a sitting posture in one of the window casements, where I lighted a cigarette and proceeded to thresh the thing out in my mind before going any farther.

The fundamental problem was this: why was I breaking my neck to get to her before Blatchford had time to deliver my response to her appealing little note? It was something of a facer, and it set me to wondering. Why was I so eager? Could it be possible that there was anything in the speculation of my servants? I recalled the sensation of supreme delight that shot through me when I received her note, but after that a queer sort of oblivion seems to have surrounded me, from which I was but now emerging in a timely struggle for self-control. There was something really startling about it, after all.

I profess to be a steady, level-headed, prosaic sort of person, and this surprising reversion to extreme youthfulness rather staggered me. In fact it brought a cold chill of suspicion into existence. Grown-up men do not, as a rule, fly off the head unless confronted by some prodigious emotion, such as terror, grief or guilt. And yet here was I going into a perfect rampage of rapture over a simple, unconventional communication from a lady whom I had known for less than a month and for whom I had no real feeling of sympathy whatever. The chill of suspicion continued to increase.

If it had been a cigar that I was smoking it would have gone out through neglect. A cigarette goes on forever and smells.

After ten minutes of serious, undisturbed consideration of the matter, I came to the final conclusion that it was not love but pity that had driven me to such abnormal activity. It was nonsense to even argue the point.

Having thoroughly settled the matter to my own, satisfaction and relief, I acknowledged a feeling of shame for having been so precipitous. I shudder to think of the look she would have given me if I had burst in upon her while in the throes of that extraordinary seizure. Obviously I had lost my wits. Now I had them once more, I knew what to do with them. First of all, I would wait until one o'clock before presenting myself for luncheon. Clearly that was the thing to do. Secondly, I would wait on this side of the castle instead of returning to my own rooms, thereby avoiding a very unpleasant gauntlet. Luckily I had profited by the discussion in the servants' quarters and was not wearing a three days' growth of beard. Moreover, I had taken considerable pains in dressing that morning. Evidently a presentiment.

For an hour and a half by my watch, but five or six by my nerves, I paced the lonely, sequestered halls in the lower regions of the castle. Two or three times I was sure that my watch had stopped, the hands seemed so stationary. The third time I tried to wind it, I broke the mainspring, but as it was nearly one o'clock not much harm was done.

That one little sentence, ***"Have you deserted me?"*** grew to be a voluminous indictment. I could think of nothing else. There was something ineffably sad and pathetic about it. Had she been unhappy because of my beastly behaviour? Was her poor little heart sore over my incomprehensible conduct? Perhaps she had cried through sheer loneliness—But no! It would never do for me to even think of her in tears. I remembered having detected tears in her lovely eyes early in our acquaintance and the sight of them—or the sensation, if you please—quite unmanned me.

At last I approached her door. Upon my soul, my legs were trembling! I experienced a silly sensation of fear. A new problem confronted me: what was I to say to her? Following close upon this came another and even graver question: what would she say to me? Suppose she were to look at me with hurt, reproachful eyes and speak to me with a little quaver in her voice as she held out her hand to me timidly—what then? What would become of me? By Jove, the answer that flashed through my whole body almost deprived me of reason!

I hesitated, then, plucking up my courage and putting all silly questions behind me, I rapped resoundingly on the door.

The excellent Hawkes opened it! I started back in dismay. He stood aside impressively.

"Mr. Smart!" he announced. Damn it all!

I caught sight of the Countess. She was arranging some flowers on the table. Blatchford was placing the knives and forks. Helen Marie Louise Antoinette stood beside her mistress holding a box of flowers in her hands.

What was it that I had been thinking out there in those gloomy halls? That she would greet me with a pathetic, hurt look and . . .

"Good morning!" she cried gaily. Hurt? Pathetic? She was radiant! "So glad to see you again. Hawkes has told me how busy you've been." She dried her hands on the abbreviated apron of Helen Marie Louise Antoinette and then quite composedly extended one for me to shake.

I bowed low over it. "Awfully, awfully busy," I murmured. Was it relief at finding her so happy and unconcerned that swept through me? I am morally, but shamelessly certain it wasn't!

"Don't you think the roses are lovely in that old silver bowl?"

"Exquisite."

"Blatchford found it in the plate vault," she said, standing off to admire the effect. "Do you mind if I go on arranging them?" she asked, and without waiting for an answer resumed her employment.

"Bon jour, m'sieur," said Helen Marie Louise Antoinette over her mistress's shoulder. One never knows whether a French maid is polite or merely spiteful.

"It seems ages since I saw you last," said the Countess in a matter-of-fact tone, jiggling a rose into position and then standing off to study the effect, her head cocked prettily at an angle of inquiry.

It suddenly occurred to me that she had got on very well without me during the ages. The discovery irritated me. She was not behaving at all as I had expected. This cool, even casual reception certainly was not in keeping with my idea of what it ought to have been. "But Mr. Poopendyke has been awfully kind. He has given me all the news."

Poopendyke! Had he been visiting her without my knowledge or—was I about to say consent?

"There hasn't been a great deal of news," I said.

She dropped a long-stemmed rose and waited for me to pick it up.

"Thank you," she said. "Oh, did it prick you?"

"Yes," said I flatly. Then we both gave the closest attention to the end of my thumb while I triumphantly squeezed a tiny drop of blood out of it. I sucked it. The incident was closed. She was no longer interested in the laceration.

"Mr. Poopendyke knew how lonely I would be. He telephoned twice a day."

I thought I detected a slight note of pique in her voice. But it was so slight that it was hardly worth while to exult.

"So you thought I had deserted you," I said, and was a little surprised at the gruffness in my voice.

"The violets appeased me," she said, with a smile. For the first time I noticed that she was wearing a large bunch of them. "You will be bankrupt, Mr. Smart, if you keep on buying roses and violets and orchids for me."

So the roses were mine also! I shot a swift glance at the mantelpiece, irresistibly moved by some mysterious force. There were two bowls of orchids there. I couldn't help thinking of the meddling, over-zealous geni that served the hero of Anstey's "Brass Bottle" tale. He was being outdone by my efficacious secretary.

"But they are lovely," she cried, noting the expression in my face and misconstruing it. "You are an angel."

That was the last straw. "I am nothing of the sort," I exclaimed, very hot and uncomfortable.

"You *are,*" was her retort. "There! Isn't it a lovely centre-piece? Now, you must come and see Rosemary. She adores the new elephant you sent to her."

"Ele—"I began, blinking my eyes. "Oh—oh, yes, yes. Ha, ha! the elephant." Good Heavens, had that idiotic Poopendyke started a menagerie in my castle?

I was vastly relieved to find that the elephant was made of felt and not too large to keep Rosemary from wielding it skilfully in an assault upon the hapless Jinko. She had it firmly gripped by the proboscis, and she was shrieking with delight. Jinko was barking in vain-glorious defence. The racket was terrible.

The Countess succeeded in quelling the disturbance, and Rosemary ran up to kiss me. Jinko, who disliked me because I looked like the Count, also ran up but his object was to bite me. I made up my mind, there and then that if I should ever, by any chance, fall in love with his mistress I would inaugurate the courting period by slaying Jinko.

Rosemary gleefully permitted me to sip honey from that warm little spot on her neck, and I forgot many odious things. As I held her in my arms I experienced a vivid longing to have a child of my own, just like Rosemary.

Our luncheon was not as gay nor as unconventional as others that had preceded it. The Countess vainly tried to make it as sprightly as its predecessors, but gave over in despair in the face of my taciturnity. Her spirits drooped. She became strangely uneasy and, I thought, preoccupied.

"What is on your mind, Countess?" I asked rather gruffly, after a painful silence of some duration.

She regarded me fixedly for a moment. She seemed to be searching my thoughts. "You," she said very succinctly. "Why are you so quiet, so funereal?" I observed a faint tinge of red in her cheeks and an ominous steadiness in her gaze. Was there anger also?

I apologised for my manners, and assured her that my work was responsible. But her moodiness increased. At last, apparently at the end of her resources, she announced that she was tired: that after we had had a cigarette she would ask to be excused, as she wanted to lie down. Would I come to see her the next day?

"But don't think of coming, Mr. Smart," she declared, "if you feel you cannot spare the time away from your work."

I began to feel heartily ashamed of my boorishness. After all, why should I expend my unpleasant humour on her?

"My dear Countess," I exclaimed, displaying a livelier interest than at any time before, "I shall be delighted to come. Permit me to add that my work may go hang."

Her face brightened. "But men must work," she objected.

"Not when women are willing to play," I said.

"Splendid!" she cried. "You are reviving. I feel better. If you are going to be nice, I'll let you stay."

"Thanks. I'll do my best."

She seemed to be weighing something in her mind. Her chin was in her hands, her elbows resting on the edge of the table. She was regarding me with speculative eyes.

"If you don't mind what the servants are saying about us, Mr. Smart, I am quite sure I do not."

I caught my breath.

"Oh, I understand everything," she cried mischievously, before I could stammer anything in reply. "They are building a delightful romance around us. And why not? Why begrudge them the pleasure? No harm can come of it, you see."

"Certainly no harm," I floundered.

"The gossip is confined to the castle. It will not go any farther. We can afford to laugh in our sleeves, can't we?"

"Ha, ha!" I laughed in a strained effort, but not into my sleeve. "I rejoice to hear you say that you don't mind. No more do I. It's rather jolly."

"Fancy any one thinking we could possibly fall in love with each, other," she scoffed. Her eyes were very bright. There was a suggestion of cold water in that remark.

"Yes, just fancy," I agreed.

"Absurd!"

"But, of course, as you say, if they can get any pleasure out of it, why should we object? It's a difficult matter keeping a cook any way."

"Well, we are bosom friends once more, are we not? I am so relieved.

"I suppose Poopendyke told you the—the gossip?"

"Oh, no! I had it from my maid. She is perfectly terrible. All French maids are, Mr. Smart. Beware of French maids! She won't have it any other way than that I am desperately in love with you. Isn't she delicious?"

"Eh?" I gasped.

"And she confides the wonderful secret to every one in the castle, from Rosemary down to Jinko."

" 'Pon my soul!" I murmured.

"And so now they all are saying that I am in love with you," she laughed. "Isn't it perfectly ludicrous?"

"Perfectly," I said without enthusiasm. My heart sank like lead. Ludicrous? Was that the way it appeared to her? I had a little spirit left. "Quite as ludicrous as the fancy Britton has about me. He is obsessed by the idea that I am in love with you. What do you think of that?"

She started. I thought her eyes narrowed for a second. "Ridiculous," she said, very simply. Then she arose abruptly. "Please ring the bell for Hawkes."

I did so. Hawkes appeared. "Clear the table, Hawkes," she said. "I want you to read all these newspaper clippings, Mr. Smart," she went on, pointing to a bundle on a chair near the window. We crossed the room. "Now that you know who I am, I insist on your reading all that the papers have been saying about me during the past five or six weeks."

I protested but she was firm. "Every one else in the world has been reading about my affairs, so you must do likewise. No, it isn't necessary to read all of them. I will select the most lurid and the most glowing. You see there are two sides to the case. The papers that father can control are united in defending my action; the European press is just the other way. Sit down, please. I'll hand them to you."

For an hour I sat there in the window absorbing the astonishing history of the Tarnowsy abduction case. I felt rather than observed the intense scrutiny with which she favoured me.

At last she tossed the remainder of the bundle unread, into a corner. Her face was aglow with pleasure.

"You've read both sides, and I've watched you—oh, so closely. You don't be-lieve what the papers over here have to say. I saw the scowls when you read the translations that Mr. Poopendyke has typed for me. Now I know that you do not feel so bitterly toward me as you did at first."

I was resolved to make a last determined stand for my original convictions.

"But our own papers, the New York, Boston, Philadelphia, Chicago journals,—still voice, in a way, my principal contention in the matter, Countess. They deplore the wretched custom among the idle but ambitious rich that made possible this whole lamentable state of affairs. I mean the custom of getting a title into the fam-ily at any cost."

"My dear Mr. Smart," she said seriously, "do you really contend that all of the conjugal unhappiness and unrest of the world is confined to the American girls who marry noblemen? Has it escaped your notice that there are thousands of unhappy marriages and equally happy divorces in America every year in which noblemen do not figure at all? Have you not read of countless cases over there in which con-ditions are quite similar to those which make the Tarnowsy fiasco so notorious? Are not American women stealing their children from American husbands? Are all American husbands so perfect that Count Tarnowsy would appear black among them? Are there no American men who marry for money, and are there no Ameri-can girls given in marriage to wealthy suitors of all ages, creeds and habits? Why do you maintain that an unfortunate alliance with a foreign nobleman is any worse than an unhappy marriage with an ordinary American brute? Are there no bad husbands in America?"

"All husbands are bad," I said, "but some are more pre-eminently evil than others. I am not finding fault with Tarnowsy as a husband. He did just what was ex-pected of him. He did what he set out to do. He isn't to be blamed for living up to his creed. There are bad husbands in America, and bad wives. But they went into the game blindly, most of them. They didn't find out their mistake until after the mar-riage. The same statement applies to husbands and wives the world over. I hold a brief only against the marriage wherein the contracting parties, their families, their friends, their enemies, their bankers and their creditors know beforehand that it's a business proposition and not a sacred compact. But we've gone into all this before. Why rake it up again."

"But there are many happy marriages between American girls and foreign noblemen—dozens of them that I could mention."

"I grant you that. I know of a few myself. But I think if you will reflect for a moment you'll find that money had no place in the covenant. They married because they loved one another. The noblemen in such cases are *real* noblemen, and their American wives are *real* wives. There are no Count Tarnowsys among them. My blood curdles when I think of *you* being married to a man of the Tarnowsy type. It is that sort of a marriage that I execrate."

"The buy and sell kind?" she said, and her eyes fell. The colour had faded from her cheeks.

"Yes. The premeditated murder type."

She looked up after a moment. There was a bleak expression in her eyes.

"Will you believe me if I say to you that I went into it blindly?"

"God bless my soul, I am sure of it," I cried earnestly. "You had never been in love. You did not know."

"I have told you that I believed myself to be in love with Maris. Doesn't—doesn't that help matters a little bit?"

I looked away. The hurt, appealing look was in her eyes. It had come at last, and, upon my soul, I was as little prepared to repel it as when I entered the room hours ago after having lived in fear of it for hours before that. I looked away because

I knew that I should do something rash if I were to lose my head for an instant.

She was like an unhappy pleading child. I solemnly affirm that it was tender-heartedness that moved me in this crucial instant. What man could have felt otherwise?

I assumed a coldly impersonal tone. "Not a single editorial in any of these papers holds you responsible for what happened in New York," I said.

She began to collect the scattered newspaper clippings and the type-written transcriptions. I gathered up those in the corner and laid them in her lap. Her fingers trembled a little.

"Throw them in the fireplace, please," she said in a low voice. "I kept them only for the purpose of showing them to you. Oh, how I hate, how I loathe it all!"

When I came back from the fireplace, she was lying back in the big, comfortable chair, a careless, whimsical smile on her lips. She was as serene as if she had never known what it was to have a heart-pang or an instant of regret in all her life. I could not understand that side of her.

"And now I have some pleasant news for you," she said. "My mother will be here on Thursday. You will not like her, of course, because you are already prejudiced, but I know she will like you."

I knew I should hate her mother, but of course it would not do to say so.

"Next Thursday?" I inquired. She nodded her head. "I hope she will like me," I added feeling that it was necessary.

"She was a Colingraft, you know."

"Indeed?" The Colingraft family was one of the oldest and most exclusive in

New York. I had a vague recollection of hearing one of my fastidious friends at home say that it must have been a bitter blow to the Colingrafts when, as an expedient, she married the vulgarly rich Jasper Titus, then of St. Paul, Minnesota. It had been a clear case of marrying the money, not the man. Aline's marriage, therefore, was due to hereditary cold-bloodedness and not to covetousness. "A fine old name, Countess."

"Titus suggests titles, therefore it has come to be our family name," she said, with her satiric smile. "You will like my father. He loves me more than any one else in the world—more than all the world. He is making the great fight for me, Mr. Smart. He would buy off the Count to-morrow if I would permit him to do so. Of late I have been thinking very seriously of suggesting it to him. It would be the simplest way out of our troubles, wouldn't it? A million is nothing to my father."

"Nothing at all, I submit, in view of the fact that it may be the means of saving you from a term in prison for abducting Rosemary?"

She paled. "Do you really think they would put me in prison?"

"Unquestionably," I pronounced emphatically.

"Oh, dear!" she murmured.

"But they can't lock you up until they've caught you," said I reassuringly. "And I will see to it that they do not catch you."

"I—I am depending on you entirely, Mr. Smart," she said anxiously. "Some day I may be in a position to repay you for all the kindness—"

"Please, please!"

"—and all the risk you are taking for me," she completed. "You see, you haven't the excuse any longer that you don't know my name and story. You are liable to be arrested yourself for—"

There came a sharp rapping on the door at this instant—a rather imperative, sinister rapping, if one were to judge by the way we started and the way we looked at each other. We laughed nervously.

"Goodness! You'd thing Sherlock Holmes himself was at the door," she cried. "See who it is, please."

I went to the door. Poopendyke was there. He was visibly excited.

"Can you come down at once, Mr. Smart?" he said in a voice not meant to reach the ears of the Countess.

"What's up? I questioned sharply.

"The jig, I'm afraid," he whispered sententiously. Poopendyke, being a stenographer, never wasted words. He would have made a fine playwright.

"Good Lord! Detectives?"

"No. Count Tarnowsy and a stranger."

"Impossible!"

The Countess, alarmed by our manner, quickly crossed the room.

"What is it?" she demanded.

"The Count is downstairs," I said. "Don't be alarmed. Nothing can happen. You—"

She laughed. "Oh, is that all? My dear Mr. Smart, he has come to see you about the frescoes."

"But I have insulted him!"

"Not permanently," she said. "I know him too well. He is like a leech. He has given you time to reflect and therefore regret your action of the other night. Go down and see him."

Poopendyke volunteered further information. "There is also a man down there—a cheap looking person—who says he must see the Countess Tarnowsy at once."

"A middle-aged man with the upper button of his waistcoat off?" she asked sharply.

"I—I can't say as to the button."

"I am expecting one of my lawyers. It must be he. He was to have a button off."

"I'll look him over again," said Poopendyke.

"Do. And be careful not to let the Count catch a glimpse of him. That would be fatal."

"No danger of that. He went at once to old Conrad's room."

"Good! I had a note from him this morning, Mr. Smart. He is Mr. Bangs of London."

"May I inquire, Countess, how you manage to have letters delivered to you here? Isn't it extremely dangerous to have them go through the mails?"

"They are all directed to the Schmicks," she explained. "They are passed on to me. Now go and see the Count. Don't lend him any money."

"I shall probably kick him over the cliff," I said, with a scowl.

She laid her hand upon my arm. "Be careful," she said very earnestly, "for my sake."

Poopendyke had already started down the stairs. I raised her hand to my lips. Then I rushed away, cursing myself for a fool, an ingrate, a presumptuous bounder.

My uncalled-for act had brought a swift flush of anger to her cheek. I saw it quite plainly as she lowered her head and drew back into the shadow of the curtain. Bounder! That is what I was for taking advantage of her simple trust in me. Strange to say, she came to the head of the stairs and watched me until I was out of sight in the hall below.

The Count was waiting for me in the loggia. It was quite warm and he fanned himself lazily with his broad straw hat. As I approached, he tossed his cigarette over the wall and hastened to meet me. There was a quaint diffident smile on his lips.

"It is good to see you again, old fellow," he said, with an amiability that surprised me. "I was afraid you might hold a grievance against me. You Americans are queer chaps, you know. Our little tilt of the other evening, you understand. Stupid way for two grown-up men to behave, wasn't it? Of course, the explanation is simple. We had been drinking. Men do silly things in their cups."

Consummate assurance! I had not touched a drop of anything that night.

"I assure you, Count Tarnowsy, the little tilt, as you are pleased to call it, was of no consequence. I had quite forgotten that it occurred. Sorry you reminded me of it."

The irony was wasted. He beamed. "My dear fellow, shall we not shake hands?"

There **was** something irresistibly winning about him, as I've said before. Something boyish, ingenuous, charming,—what you will,—that went far toward accounting for many things that you who have never seen him may consider incomprehensible.

A certain wariness took possession of me. I could well afford to temporise. We shook hands with what seemed to be genuine fervour.

"I suppose you are wondering what brings me here," he said, as we started toward the entrance to the loggia, his arm through mine. "I do not forget a promise, Mr. Smart. You may remember that I agreed to fetch a man from Munchen to look over your fine old frescoes and to give you an estimate. Well, he is here, the very best man in Europe."

"I am sure I am greatly indebted to you, Count," I said, "but after thinking it over I've—"

"Don't say that you have already engaged some one to do the work," he cried, in horror. "My dear fellow, don't tell me **that!** You are certain to make a dreadful mistake if you listen to any one but Schwartzmuller. He is the last word in restorations. He is the best bet, as you would say in New York. Any one else will make a botch of the work. You will curse the day you—"

I checked him. "I have virtually decided to let the whole matter go over until next spring. However, I shall be happy to have Mr. Schwartzmuller's opinion. We may be able to plan ahead."

A look of disappointment flitted across his face. The suggestion of hard old age crept into his features for a second and then disappeared.

"Delays are dangerous," he said. "My judgment is that those gorgeous paintings will disintegrate more during the coming winter than in all the years gone by. They are at the critical stage. If not preserved now,—well, I cannot bear to think of the consequences. Ah, here is Herr Schwartzmuller."

Just inside the door, we came upon a pompous yet servile German who could not by any means have been mistaken for anything but the last word in restoration. I have never seen any one in my life whose appearance suggested a more complete state of rehabilitation. His frock coat was new, it had the unfailing smell of new wool freshly dyed; his shoes were painfully new; his gloves were new; his silk hat was resplendently new; his fat jowl was shaved to a luminous pink; his gorgeous moustache was twisted up at the ends to such a degree that when he smiled the points wavered in front of his eyes, causing him to blink with astonishment. He was undeniably dressed up for the occasion. My critical eye, however, discovered a pair of well-worn striped trousers badly stained, slightly frayed at the bottom and inclined to bag outward at the knee. Perhaps I should have said that he was dressed up from the knee.

"This is the great Herr Schwartzmuller, of the Imperial galleries in Munchen," said the Count introducing us.

The stranger bowed very profoundly and at the same time extracted a business card from the tail pocket of his coat. This he delivered to me with a smile which seemed to invite me to participate in a great and serious secret: the secret of irreproachable standing as an art expert and connoisseur. I confess to a mistaken impression concerning him up to the moment he handed me his clumsy business card. My suspicions had set him down as a confederate of Count Tarnowsy, a spy, a secret agent or whatever you choose to consider one who is employed in further-ing a secret purpose. But the business card removed my doubts and misgivings. It stamped him for what he really was: there is no mistaking a German who hands you his business card. He destroys all possible chance for discussion.

In three languages the card announced that he was "August Schwartzmuller, of the Imperial galleries, Munchen, Zumpe & Schwartzmuller, proprietors. Restorations a specialty." There was much more, but I did not have time to read all of it. Moreover, the card was a trine soiled, as if it had been used before. There could be no doubt as to his genuineness. He **was** an art expert.

For ten minutes I allowed them to expatiate on the perils of procrastination in the treatment of rare old canvases and pigments, and then, having formulated my plans, blandly inquired what the cost would be. It appears that Herr Schwartzmuller had examined the frescoes no longer than six months before in the interests of a New York gentleman to whom Count Hohendahl had tried to sell them for a lump sum. He was unable to recall the gentleman's name.

"I should say not more than one hundred and fifty thousand marks, perhaps less," said the expert, rolling his calculative eye upward and running it along the vast dome of the hall as if to figure it out in yards and inches.

The Count was watching me with an eager light in his eyes. He looked away as I shot a quick glance at his face. The whole matter became as clear as day to me. He was to receive a handsome commission if the contract was awarded. No doubt his share would be at least half of the amount stipulated. I had reason to believe that the work could be performed at a profit for less than half the figure mentioned by the German.

"Nearly forty thousand dollars, in other words," said I reflectively.

"They are worth ten times that amount, sir," said the expert gravely.

I smiled skeptically. The Count took instant alarm. He realised that I was not such a fool as I looked,

"Hohendahl was once offered two hundred and fifty thousand dollars, Mr. Smart," he said.

"Why didn't he accept it?" I asked bluntly. "He sold the whole place to me, contents included, for less than half that amount."

"It was years ago, before he was in such dire straits," he explained quickly.

A terrible suspicion entered my head. I felt myself turn cold. If the frescoes were genuine they were worth all that Schwartzmuller declared; that being the case why should Hohendahl have let them come to me for practically nothing when there were dozens of collectors who would have paid him the full price? I swallowed hard, but managed to control my voice.

"As a matter of fact, Count Tarnowsy," I said, resorting to unworthy means, "I have every reason to believe that Hohendahl sold the originals sometime ago, and had them replaced on the ceilings by clever imitations. They are not worth the canvas they are painted on."

He started. I intercepted the swift look of apprehension that passed from him to the stolid Schwartzmuller, whose face turned a shade redder.

"Impossible!" cried Tarnowsy sharply.

"By no means impossible," I said calmly, now sure of my ground. "To be perfectly frank with you, I've known from the beginning that they are fakes. Your friend, Count Hohendahl, is nobler than you give him credit for being. He confessed to me at the time our transaction took place that the frescoes were very recent reproductions. The originals, I think, are in London or New York." I saw guilt in the face of Herr Schwartzmuller. His moustaches drooped with the corners of his mouth; he did not seem to be filling out the frock coat quite so completely as when I first beheld him. A shrewd suspicion impelled me to take chances on a direct accusation. I looked straight into the German's eyes and said: "Now that I come to think of it, I am sure he mentioned the name of Schwartzmuller in connection with the—"

"It is not true! It is not true!" roared the expert, without waiting for me to finish. "He lied to you, we—the great firm of Zumpe & Schwartzmuller—we could not be tempted with millions to do such a thing."

I went a step farther in my deductions. Somehow I had grasped the truth: this pair deliberately hoped to swindle me out of forty thousand dollars. They knew the frescoes were imitations and yet they were urging me to spend a huge sum of money in restoring canvases that had been purposely made to look old and flimsy in order to deceive a more cautious purchaser than I. But, as I say, I went a step farther and deliberately accused Count Tarnowsy.

"Moreover, Count Tarnowsy, you are fully aware of all this."

"My dear fellow,—"

"I'll not waste words. You are a damned scoundrel!"

He measured the distance with his eye and then sprang swiftly forward, striking blindly at my face.

I knocked him down!

Schwartzmuller was near the door, looking over his shoulder as he felt for the great brass knob.

"Mein Gott!" he bellowed.

"Stop!" I shouted. "Come back here and take this fellow away with you!"

Tarnowsy was sitting up, looking about him in a dazed, bewildered manner.

At that moment, Poopendyke came running down the stairs, attracted by the loud voices. He was followed closely by three or four wide-eyed glaziers who were working on the second floor.

"In the name of heaven, sir!"

"I've bruised my knuckles horribly," was all that I said. I seemed to be in a sort of a daze myself. I had never knocked a man down before in my life. It was an amazingly easy thing to do. I could hardly believe that I had done it.

Tarnowsy struggled to his feet and faced me, quivering with rage. I was dumbfounded to see that he was not covered with blood. But he was of a light, yellowish green. I could scarcely believe my eyes.

"You shall pay for this!" he cried. The tears rushed to his eyes. "Coward! Beast! To strike a defenceless man!"

His hand went swiftly to his breast pocket, and an instant later a small revolver flashed into view. It was then that I did another strange and incomprehensible thing. With the utmost coolness I stepped forward and wrested it from his hand. I say strange and incomprehensible for the reason that he was pointing it directly at my breast and yet I had not the slightest sensation of fear. He could have shot me like a dog. I never even thought of that.

"None of that!" I cried sharply. "Now, will you be good enough to get out of this house—and stay out?"

"My seconds will call on you—"

"And they will receive just what you have received. If you or any of your friends presume to trespass on the privacy of these grounds of mine, I'll kick the whole lot of you into the Danube. Hawkes! Either show or lead Count Tarnowsy to the gates. As for you, Mr. Schwartzmuller, I shall expose—"

But the last word in restorations had departed.

CHAPTER XIV

I AM FORCED INTO BEING A HERO

MY humblest apologies, dear reader, if I have led you to suspect that I want to be looked upon as a hero. Far from patting myself on the back or holding my chin a little higher because of the set-to in my baronial halls, I confess to a feeling of shame. In my study, where the efficient Blatchford put arnica and bandages on my swollen knuckles, I solemnly declared in the presence of those who attended the clinic—(my entire establishment was there to see that I had the proper attention and to tell me how happy they were that it wasn't any worse)—I say, I declared to all of them that I was an unmitigated fool and undeserving of the slightest mead of praise.

They insisted upon making a hero of me, and might have succeeded, had not the incomparable Britton made the discovery that the Count's revolver was not loaded! Still, they vociferated, I could not have known that at the time of the encounter, nor was it at all likely that the Count knew it himself.

I confess to an inward and shameless glory, however, in the realisation that I had been able to punch the head of the man who had lived with and abused that lovely creature upstairs. He had struck her on more than one occasion, I had it from her own lips. Far worse than that, he had kissed her! But of course I had not knocked him down for that. I did it because it was simpler than being knocked down myself.

The worst feature of the whole unhappy business was the effect it was likely to have upon my commonly pacific nature. Heretofore I had avoided physical encounters, not because I was afraid of the result, but because I hate brutal, unscientific manifestations of strength. Now, to my surprise, I found that it was a ridiculously easy matter to knock a man down and end the squabble in short order, thereby es-

caping a great deal in the shape of disgusting recriminations, and coming off victorious with nothing more vital in the way of wounds than a couple of bruised knuckles. (No doubt, with practice, one could even avoid having his knuckles barked.)

Was it not probable, therefore, that my habitual tendency to turn away wrath
with a soft answer might suffer a more or less sanguinary shock? Now that I had
found out how simple it was, would I not be satisfied to let my good right hand
settle disputes for me—with uniform certainty and despatch? Heaven is my witness
that I have no desire to be regarded as a bruiser. I hope that it may never fall to my
lot to again knock a man down. But if it should be necessary, I also wish to record
the hope that the man may be a husband who has mistreated his wife.

In the course of Blatchford's ministrations I was regaled with eloquent descrip-
tions of the manner in which my late adversary took his departure from the castle.
He went forth vowing vengeance, calling down upon my head all the maledictions
he could lay his tongue to, and darkly threatening to have me driven out of the
country. I was not to expect a call from his seconds. He would not submit his friends
to the indignities they were sure to encounter at the hands of a barbarian of my
type. But, just the same, I would hear from him. I would regret the day, etc., etc.

I had forgotten Mr. Bangs, the lawyer. Sitting alone in my study, late in the
afternoon, smoking a solitary pipe of peace, I remembered him: the man with the
top button off. What had become of him? His presence (or, more accurately, his absence) suddenly loomed up before me as the forerunner of an unwelcome invasion
of my preserves. He was, no doubt, a sort of advance agent for the Titus family and
its immediate ramifications.

Just as I was on the point of starting out to make inquiries concerning him,
there came to my ears the sound of tapping on the back of Red Ludwig's portrait.
Not until then did it occur to me that I had been waiting for two hours for that
simple manifestation of interest and curiosity from the regions above.

I rushed over and rapped resoundingly upon Ludwig's pudgy knee. The next instant there was a click and then the secret door swung open, revealing the eager, concerned face of my neighbour.

"What has happened?" she cried.

I lifted her out of the frame. Her gaze fell upon the bandaged fist.

"Mr. Bangs spoke of a pistol. Don't tell me that he—he shot you!"

I held up my swollen hand rather proudly. It smelled vilely of arnica.

"This wound was self-inflicted, my dear Countess," I said, thrilled by her expression of concern. "I had the exquisite pleasure—and pain—of knocking your former husband down."

"Oh, splendid!" she cried, her eyes gleaming with excitement. "Mr. Bangs was rather hazy about it, and he would not let me risk telephoning. You knocked Maris down?"

"Emphatically," said I.

She mused. "I think it is the first time it has ever happened to him. How—how did he like it?"

"It appeared to prostrate him."

She smiled understandingly. "I am glad you did it, Mr. Smart."

"If I remember correctly, you once said that he had struck you, Countess."

Her face flushed. "Yes. On three separate occasions he struck me in the face with his open hand. I—I testified to that effect at the trial. Every one seemed to look upon it as a joke. He swore that they were—were love pats."

"I hope his lack of discrimination will not lead him to believe that I was delivering a love pat," said I, grimly.

"Now, tell me everything that happened," she said, seating herself in my big armchair. Her feet failed to touch the floor. She was wearing the little tan pumps.

When I came to that part of the story where I accused Tarnowsy of duplicity in connection with the frescoes, she betrayed intense excitement.

"Of course it was all a bluff on my part," I explained.

"But you were nearer the truth than you thought," she said, compressing her lips. After a moment she went on: "Count Hohendahl sold the originals over three years ago. I was here with Maris at the time of the transaction and when the paintings were removed. Maris acted as an intermediary in the deal. Hohendahl received two hundred thousand dollars for the paintings, but they were worth it. I have reason to believe that Maris had a fourth of the amount for his commission. So, you see, you were right in your surmise."

"The infernal rascal! Where are the originals, Countess?"

"They are in my father's villa at Newport," she said. "I intended speaking of this to you before, but I was afraid your pride would be hurt. Of course, I should have spoken if it came to the point where you really considered having those forgeries restored."

"Your father bought them?"

"Yes. While we were spending our honeymoon here in Schloss Rothhoefen, Mr. Smart," she said. Her face was very pale.

I could see that the dark associations filled her mind, and abruptly finished my tale without further reference to the paintings.

"He will challenge you," she said nervously. "I am so sorry to have placed you in this dreadful position, Mr. Smart. I shall never forgive myself for—"

"You are in no way concerned in what happened to-day," I interrupted. "It was a purely personal affair. Moreover, he will not challenge me."

"He has fought three duels," she said. "He is not a physical coward." Her dark eyes were full of dread.

I hesitated. "Would you be vitally interested in the outcome of such an affair?" I asked. My voice was strangely husky.

"Oh, how can you ask?"

"I mean, on Rosemary's account," I stammered. "He—he is her father, you see. It would mean—"

"I was not thinking of the danger to him, Mr. Smart," she said simply.

"But can't you see how dreadful it would be if I were to kill Rosemary's father?" I cried, completely forgetting myself. "Can't you see?"

A slow flush mounted to her brow. "That is precisely what I was thinking, Mr. Smart. It would be—unspeakably dreadful."

I stood over her. My heart was pounding heavily. She must have seen the peril that lay in my eyes, for she suddenly slipped out of the chair and faced me, the flush dying in her cheek, leaving it as pale as ivory.

"You must not say anything more, Mr. Smart," she said gently.

A bitter smile came to my lips, and I drew back with a sickening sense of realisation. There *was* nothing more to be said. But I now thoroughly understood one thing: I was in love with her! . . .

I am something of a philosopher. I submit that my attitude at the time of my defeat at the hands of the jeweller's clerk proves the point conclusively. If I failed at that time to inspire feelings of love in the breast of a giddy stenographer, what right had I to expect anything better from the beautiful Countess Tarnowsy, whose aspirations left nothing to the imagination? While she was prone to chat without visible restraint at this significantly trying moment, I, being a philosopher, remained silent and thoughtful. Quite before I knew it, I was myself again: a steady, self-reliant person who could make the best of a situation, who could take his medicine like a man. Luckily, the medicine was not so bitter as it might have been if I had made a vulgar, impassioned display of my emotions. Thank heaven, I had *that* to be thankful for.

She was speaking of the buttonless lawyer, Mr. Bangs. "He is waiting to see you this evening, Mr. Smart, to discuss ways and means of getting my mother and brothers into the castle without discovery by the spies who are undoubtedly watching their every move."

I drew in another long, deep breath. "It seems to me that the thing cannot be done. The risk is tremendous. Why not head her off?"

"Head her off? You do not know my mother, Mr. Smart. She has made up her mind that her place is here with me, and there isn't anything in the world that can—head her off, as you say."

"But surely *you* see the danger?"

"I do. I have tried to stop her. Mr. Bangs has tried to stop her. So has father. But she is coming. We must arrange something."

I was pacing the floor in front of her. She had resumed her place in the chair.

"My deepest regret, Countess, lies in the fact that our little visits will be—well, at an end. Our delightful little suppers and—"

"Oh, but think of the comfort it will be to you, not having me on your mind all of the time. I shall not be lonesome, I shall not be afraid, I shall not be forever annoying you with selfish demands upon your good nature. You will have time to write without interruption. It will be for the best."

"No," said I, positively. "They were jolly parties, and I shall miss them."

She looked away quickly. "And, if all goes well, I shall soon be safely on my way to America. Then you will be rid of me completely."

I was startled. "You mean that there is a plan afoot to—to smuggle you out of the country?"

"Yes. And I fear I shall have to trouble you again when it comes to that. You must help me, Mr. Smart."

I nodded slowly. Help her to get away? I hadn't thought of that lately. The prospect left me rather cold and sick.

"I'll do all that I can, Countess."

She smiled faintly, but I was certain that I detected a challenge,—a rather unkind challenge,—in her eyes. "You will come to see me in New York, of course."

I shook my head. "I am afraid we are counting our chickens before they're hatched. One or the other of us may be in jail for the next few years."

"Heavens!"

"But I'll come to see you in New York, if you'll let me," I cried, trying to repair the damage I had done. "I was jesting when I spoke of jail."

Her brow was puckered in thought. "It has just occurred to me, my dear friend, that even if I do get safely away, you will be left here to face the consequences. When it becomes known that you sheltered me, the authorities may make it extremely uncomfortable for you."

"I'm not worrying about that."

"Just the same, it is something to worry about," she said, seriously. "Now, here is what I have had in mind for a long, long time. Why don't you come with me when I leave? That will be the safest plan."

"You are not in earnest!"

"Assuredly. The plan is something like this: I am to be taken by slow stages, overland, to a small Mediterranean port. One of a half-dozen American yachts now cruising the sea will be ready to pick me up. Doesn't it seem simple?"

"It *seems* simple enough," said I. "But there are a lot of 'ifs' between here and the little port you hope to reach. It will not be an easy matter to manage the successful flight of a party as large as yours will be."

"Oh," she cried, "I shall be quite alone, except for Rosemary and Blake,—and Mr. Bangs."

"But your mother? You can't leave her here."

"You will have to smuggle her out of the castle a day or two in advance. It is all thought out, Mr. Smart."

"By Jove!" I exclaimed, with more irascibility than I intended to show. "If I succeed in doing all that is expected of me, I certainly will be entitled to more than an invitation to come and see you in New York."

She arose and laid her fingers upon my bandaged hand. The reckless light had died out of her eyes.

"I have thought that out, too, Mr. Smart," she said, quietly. "And now, good-bye. You will come up to see Mr. Bangs to-night?"

Considerably mystified by her remark, I said I would come, and then assisted her through the opening in the wall. She smiled back at me as the portrait swung into place.

What did she mean? Was it possible that she meant to have old man Titus reward me in a pecuniary way? The very thought of such a thing caused me to double up my fist—my recently discovered fist!—and to swear softly under my breath. After a few moments I was conscious of a fierce pain in the back of my hand.

Bangs was a shrewd little Englishman. As I shook hands with him—using my left hand with a superfluous apology—I glanced at the top of his waistcoat. There was no button missing.

"The Countess sewed it on for me," he said drily, reading my thoughts.

I stayed late with them, discussing plans. He had strongly advised against any attempt on Mrs. Titus's part to enter her daughter's hiding-place, but had been overruled. I conceived the notion, too, that he was a very strong-minded man. What then must have been the strength of Mrs. Titus's resolution to overcome the objections he put in her way?

He, too, had thought it all out. Everybody seems to have thought everything out with a single exception,—myself. His plan was not a bad one. Mrs. Titus and her sons were to enter the castle under cover of night, and I was to meet them in an automobile at a town some fifteen kilometers away, where they would leave the train while their watchers were asleep, and bring them overland to Schloss Roth-hoefen. They would be accompanied by a single lady's maid and no luggage. A char-tered motor boat would meet us up the river a few miles, and—well, it looked very simple! All that was required of me was a willingness to address her as "Mother" and her sons as "brothers" in case there were any questions asked.

This was Tuesday. They were coming on Thursday, and the train reached the station mentioned at half-past twelve at night. So you will see it was a jolly arrange-ment.

I put Mr. Bangs up in my best guest-chamber, and, be it said to my credit, the Countess did not have to suggest it to me. As we said good night to her on the little landing at the top of the stairs, she took my bandaged paw between her two little hands and said:

"You will soon be rid of me forever, Mr. Smart. Will you bear with me pa-tiently for a little while longer?" There was a plaintive, appealing note in her voice. She seemed strangely subdued.

"I can bear with you much easier than I can bear the thought of being rid of you," I said in a very low voice. She pressed my clumsy hand fiercely, and I felt no pain.

"You have been too good to me," she said in a very small voice. "Some day, when I am out of all this trouble, I may be able to tell you how much I appreciate all you have done for me."

An almost irresistible—I was about to say ungovernable—impulse to seize her in my arms came over me, but I conquered it and rushed after Mr. Bangs, as blind as a bat and reeling for a dozen steps or more. It was a most extraordinary feeling.

I found myself wondering if passion had that effect on all men. If this was an illustration of what a real passionate love could do to a sensible, level-headed person, then what, in heaven's name, was the emotion I had characterised as love during my placid courtship of the faintly remembered typewriter? There had been no such blinding, staggering sensation as this. No thoughts of physical contact with my former inamorata had left me weak and trembling and dazed as I was at this historic moment.

Bangs was chattering in his glib English fashion as we descended to my study, but I did not hear half that he said. He looked surprised at two or three of the answers I made to his questions, and I am sure there were several of them that I didn't respond to at all. He must have thought me an unmannerly person.

One remark of his brought me rather sharply to my senses. I seemed capable of grasping its awful significance when all the others had gone by without notice.

"If all goes well," he was saying, "she should be safely away from here on the fourteenth. That leaves less than ten days more, sir, under your hospitable roof."

"Less than ten days," I repeated. This was the fifth of the month. "If all goes well. Less than ten days."

Again I passed a sleepless night. A feeling of the utmost loneliness and desolation grew up within me. Less than ten days! And then she would be "safely away" from me. She and Rosemary! There was a single ray of brightness in the gloom that shrouded my thoughts: she had urged me to fly away with her. She did not want to leave me behind to face the perils after she was safely out of them. God bless her for thinking of that!

But of course what little common sense and judgment I had left within me told me that such a course was entirely out of the question. I could not go away with her. I could do no more than to see her safely on her way to the queer little port on the east coast of Italy. Then I should return to my bleak, joyless castle,—to my sepulchre,—and suffer all the torments of the damned for days and weeks until word came that she was actually safe on the other side of the Atlantic.

What courage, what pluck she had! Criminal? No, a thousand times, no! She was claiming her own, her dearest own. The devil must have been in the people who set themselves up as judges to condemn her for fighting so bravely for that which God had given her. Curse them all!. . . . I fear that my thoughts became more and more maudlin as the interminable night went on.

Always they came back to the sickening realisation that I was to lose her in ten days, and that my castle would be like a tomb.

Of course the Hazzards and the Billy Smiths were possible panaceas, but what could they bring to ease the pangs of a secret nostalgia? Nothing but their own blissful contentment, their own happiness to make my loneliness seem all the more horrible by contrast. Would it not be better for me to face it alone? Would it not be better to live the life of a hermit?

She came to visit me at twelve o'clock the next day. I was alone in the study. Poopendyke was showing Mr. Bangs over the castle.

She was dressed in a gown of some soft grey material, and there was a bunch of violets at her girdle.

"I came to dress your hand for you," she said as I helped her down from Red Ludwig's frame.

Now I have neglected to mention that the back of my hand was swollen to enormous proportions, an unlovely thing.

"Thank you," I said, shaking my head; "but it is quite all right. Britton attended to it this morning. It is good of you to think about it, Countess. It isn't—"

"I thought about it all night," she said, and I could believe her after the light from the windows had fallen upon her face. There were dark circles under her eyes and she was quite pale. Her eyes seemed abnormally large and brilliant. "I am so sorry not to be able to do one little thing for you. Will you not let me dress it after this?"

I coloured. "Really, it—it is a most trifling bruise," I explained, "just a little black and blue, that's all. Pray do not think of it again."

"You will never let me do anything for you," she said. Her eyes were velvety. "It isn't fair. I have exacted so much from you, and—"

"And I have been most brutal and unfeeling in many of the things I have said to you," said I, despairingly. "I am ashamed of the nasty wounds I have given you. My state of repentance allows you to exact whatsoever you will of me, and, when all is said and done, I shall still be your debtor. Can you—will you pardon the coarse opinions of a conceited ass? I assure you I am not the man I was when you first encountered me."

She smiled. "For that matter, I am not the same woman I was, Mr. Smart. You have taught me three things, one of which I may mention: the subjection of self. That, with the other two, has made a new Aline Titus of me. I hope you may be pleased with the—transfiguration."

"I wish you were Aline Titus," I said, struck by the idea.

"You may at least be sure that I shall not remain the Countess Tarnowsy long, Mr. Smart," she said, with a very puzzling expression in her eyes.

My heart sank. "But I remember hearing you say not so very long ago that you would never marry again," I railed.

She regarded me rather oddly for a moment. "I am very, very glad that you are such a steady, sensible, practical man. A vapid, impressionable youth, during this season of propinquity, might have been so foolish as to fall in love with me, and that would have been too bad."

I think I glared at her. "Then,—then, you *are* going to marry some one?"

She waited a moment, looking straight into my eyes. "Yes," she said, and a delicate pink stole into her cheek, "I *am* going to marry some one."

I muttered something about congratulating a lucky dog, but it was all very hazy to me.

"Don't congratulate him yet," she cried, the flush deepening. "I may be a very, very great disappointment to him, and a never-ending nuisance."

"I'm sure you will—will be all right," I floundered. Then I resorted to gaiety. "You see, I've spent a lot of time trying to—to make another woman of you, and so I'm confident he'll find you quite satisfactory."

She laughed gaily. "What a goose you are!" she cried.

I flushed painfully, for, I give you my word, it hurt to have her laugh at me. She sobered at once.

"Forgive me," she said very prettily, and I forgave her. "Do you know we've never given the buried treasure another thought?" she went on, abruptly changing the subject. "Are we not to go searching for it?"

"But it isn't there," said I, steeling my heart against the longing that tried to creep into it. "It's all balderdash."

She pouted her warm red lips. "Have you lost interest in it so soon?"

"Of course, I'll go any time you say," said I, lifelessly. "It will be a lark, at all events."

"Then we will go this very afternoon," she said, with enthusiasm.

My ridiculous heart gave a great leap. "This very afternoon," I said, managing my voice very well.

She arose. "Now I must scurry away. It would not do for Mr. Bangs to find me here with you. He would be shocked."

I walked beside her to the chair that stood below the portrait of Ludwig the Red, and took her hand to assist her in stepping upon it.

"I sincerely hope this chap you're going to marry, Countess, may be the best fellow in the world," said I, still clasping her hand.

She had one foot on the chair as she half-turned to face me.

"He is the best fellow in the world," she said.

I gulped. "I can't tell you how happy I shall be if you—if you find real happiness. You deserve happiness—and love."

She gripped my hand fiercely. "I want to be happy! I want to be loved! Oh, I want to be loved!" she cried, so passionately that I turned away, unwilling to be a witness to this outburst of feeling on her part. She slipped her hand out of mine and a second later was through the frame. I had a fleeting glimpse of a slim, adorable ankle. "Good-bye," she called back in a voice that seemed strangely choked. The spring in the gold mirror clicked. A draft of air struck me in the face. She was gone.

"What an infernal fool you've been," I said to myself as I stood there staring at the black hole in the wall. Then, I gently, even caressingly swung old Ludwig the

Red into place. There was another click. The incident was closed.

A very few words are sufficient to cover the expedition in quest of the legendary treasures of the long dead Barons. Mr. Bangs accompanied us. Britton carried a lantern and the three Schmicks went along as guides. We found nothing but cobwebs.

"Conrad," said I, as we emerged from the last of the underground chambers, "tell me the truth: was there ever such a thing as buried treasure in this abominable hole?"

"Yes, mein herr," he replied, with an apologetic grin; "but I think it was discovered three years ago by Count Hohendahl and Count Tarnowsy."

We stared at him. "The deuce you say!" cried I, with a quick glance at the Countess. She appeared to be as much surprised as I.

"They searched for a month," explained the old man, guiltily. "They found something in the walls of the second tier. I cannot say what it was, but they were very, very happy, my lady." He now addressed her. "It was at the time they went away and did not return for three weeks, if you remember the time."

"Remember it!" she cried bitterly. "Too well, Conrad." She turned to me. "We had been married less than two months, Mr. Smart."

I smiled rather grimly. "Count Tarnowsy appears to have had a great run of luck in those days." It was a mean remark and I regretted it instantly. To my surprise she smiled—perhaps patiently—and immediately afterward invited Mr. Bangs and me to dine with her that evening. She also asked Mr. Poopendyke later on.

Poopendyke! An amazing, improbable idea entered my head. ***Poopendyke!***

The next day I was very busy, preparing for the journey by motor to the small station down the line where I was to meet Mrs. Titus and her sons. It seemed to me that every one who knew anything whatever about the arrangements went out of his way to fill my already rattle-brained head with advice. I was advised to be careful at least one hundred times; first in regard to the running of the car, then as to road directions, then as to the police, then as to the identity of the party I was to pick up; but more often than anything else, I was urged to be as expeditious as possible and to look out for my tires.

In order to avoid suspicion, I rented a big German touring car for a whole month, paying down a lump sum of twelve hundred marks in advance. On Thursday morning I took it out for a spin, driving it myself part of the time, giving the wheel to Britton the remainder.

(The year before I had toured Europe pretty extensively in a car of the same make, driving alternately with Britton, who besides being an excellent valet was a chauffeur of no mean ability, having served a London actress for two years or more, which naturally meant that he had been required to do a little of everything.)

We were to keep the car in a garage across the river, drive it ourselves, and pay for the up-keep. We were therefore quite free to come and go as we pleased, without the remotest chance of being questioned. In fact, I intimated that I might indulge in a good bit of joy-riding if the fine weather kept up.

Just before leaving the castle for the ferry trip across the river that evening, I was considerably surprised to have at least a dozen brand new trunks delivered at my landing stage. It is needless to say that they turned out to be the property of Mrs. Titus, expressed by **grande vitesse** from some vague city in the north of Germany. They all bore the name "Smart, U. S. A.," painted in large white letters on each end, and I was given to understand that they belonged to my own dear mother, who at that moment, I am convinced, was sitting down to luncheon in the Adirondacks, provided her habits were as regular as I remembered them to be.

I set forth with Britton at nine o'clock, in a drizzling rain. There had been no rain for a month. The farmers, the fruit-raisers, the growers of grapes and all the birds and beasts of the field had been begging for rain for weeks. No doubt they rejoiced in the steady downpour that came at half-past nine, but what must have been their joy at ten when the very floodgates of heaven opened wide and let loose all the dammed waters of July and August (and perhaps some that was being saved up for the approaching September!) I have never known it to rain so hard as it did on that Thursday night in August, nor have I ever ceased reviling the fate that instituted, on the very next day, a second season of drought that lasted for nearly six weeks.

But we went bravely through that terrible storm, Britton and I, and the vehement Mercedes, up hill and down, over ruts and rocks, across bridges and under them, sozzling and swishing and splashing in the path of great white lights that rushed ahead of us through the gloom. At half-past eleven o'clock we were skidding over the cobblestones of the darkest streets I have ever known, careening like a drunken sailor but not half as surely, headed for the Staatsbahnhof, to which we had been directed by an object in a raincoat who must have been a policeman but who looked more like a hydrant.

"Britton," said I, wearily, "have you ever seen anything like it?"

"Once before, sir," said he. "Niagara Falls, sir."

CHAPTER XV

I TRAVERSE THE NIGHT

We were drenched to the skin and bespattered with mud, cold and cheerless but full of a grim excitement. Across the street from the small, poorly lighted railway station there was an eating-house. Leaving the car in the shelter of a freight shed, we sloshed through the shiny rivulet that raced between the curbs and entered the clean, unpretentious little restaurant.

There was a rousing smell of roasted coffee pervading the place. A sleepy German waiter first came up and glanced sullenly at the mud-tracks we left upon the floor; then he allowed his insulting gaze to trail our progress to the lunch counter by means of a perfect torrent of rain-water drippings. He went out of the room grumbling, to return a moment later with a huge mop. Thereupon he ordered us out of the place, standing ready with the mop to begin the cleansing process the instant we vacated the stools. It was quite clear to both of us that he wanted to begin operations at the exact spot where we were standing.

"Coffee for two," said I, in German. To me anything uttered in the German language sounds gruff and belligerent, no matter how gentle its meaning. That amiable sentence: "Ich liebe dich" is no exception; to me it sounds relentless. I am confident that I asked for coffee in a very mild and ingratiating tone, in direct contrast to his command to get out, and was somewhat ruffled by his stare of speechless rage.

"Zwei," said Britton, pointing to the big coffee urn.

The fellow began mopping around my feet—in fact, he went so far as to mop the tops of them and a little way up my left leg in his efforts to make a good, clean job of it.

"Stop that!" I growled, kicking at the mop. Before I could get my foot back on the floor he skilfully swabbed the spot where it had been resting, a feat of celerity that I have never seen surpassed. "Damn it, don't!" I roared, backing away. The resolute mop followed me like the spectre of want. Fascinated, I found myself retreating to the doorway.

Britton, resourceful fellow, put an end to his endeavours by jumping upon the mop and pinning it to the floor very much as he would have stamped upon a wounded rat.

The fellow called out lustily to some one in the kitchen, at the same time giving the mop handle a mighty jerk. If you are expecting me to say that Britton came to woe, you are doomed to disappointment. It was just the other way about. Just as the prodigious yank took place, my valet hopped nimbly from the mop, and the waiter sat down with a stunning thud.

I do not know what might have ensued had not the proprietress of the place appeared at that instant, coming from the kitchen. She was the cook as well, and she was large enough to occupy the space of at least three Brittons. She was huge beyond description.

"Wass iss?" she demanded, pausing aghast. Her voice was a high, belying treble.

I shall not attempt to describe in detail all that followed. It is only necessary to state that she removed the mop from the hands of the quaking menial and fairly swabbed him out into the thick of the rainstorm.

While we were drinking our hot, steaming coffee and gorging ourselves with frankfurters, the poor wretch stood under the eaves with his face glued to the window, looking in at us with mournful eyes while the drippings from the tiles poured upon his shoulders and ran in rivulets down his neck. I felt so sorry for him that I prevailed upon the muttering, apologetic hostess to take him in again. She called him in as she might have called a dog, and he edged his way past her with the same scared, alert look in his eyes that one always sees in those of an animal that has its tail between its legs.

She explained that he was her nephew, just off the farm. Her sister's son, she said, and naturally not as intelligent as he ought to be.

While we were sitting there at the counter, a train roared past the little station. We rushed to the door in alarm. But it shot through at the rate of fifty miles an hour. I looked at my watch. It still wanted half-an-hour of train time, according to the schedule.

"It was the express, mein herr," explained the woman. "It never stops. We are too small yet. Some time we may be big enough." I noticed that her eyes were fixed in some perplexity on the old clock above the pie shelves. "Ach! But it has never been so far ahead of time as to-night. It is not due for fifteen minutes yet, and here it is gone yet."

"Perhaps your clock is slow," I said. "My watch says four minutes to twelve."

Whereupon she heaped a tirade of abuse upon the shrinking Hans for letting the clock lose ten minutes of her valuable time. To make sure, Hans set it forward nearly half an hour while she was looking the other way. Then he began mopping the floor again.

At half-past twelve the train from Munich drew up at the station, panted awhile in evident disdain, and then moved on.

A single passenger alighted: a man with a bass viol. There was no sign of the Tituses!

We made a careful and extensive search of the station, the platform and even the surrounding neighbourhood, but it was quite evident that they had not left the train. Here was a pretty pass! Britton, however, had the rather preposterous idea that there might be another train a little later on. It did not seem at all likely, but we made inquiries of the station agent. To my surprise—and to Britton's infernal British delight—there was a fast train, with connections from the north, arriving in half an hour. It was, however, an hour late, owing to the storm.

"Do you mean that it will arrive at two o'clock?" I demanded in dismay.

"No, no," said the guard; "it will arrive at one but not until two. It is late, mein herr."

We dozed in the little waiting-room for what I consider to be the longest hour

I've ever known, and then hunted up the guard once more. He blandly informed me that it was still an hour late.

"An hour from *now*?" I asked.

"An hour from two," said he, pityingly. What ignorant lummixes we were!

Just ten minutes before three the obliging guard came in and roused us from a mild sleep.

"The train is coming, mein herr."

"Thank God!"

"But I neglected to mention that it is an express and never stops here."

My right hand was still in a bandage, but it was so nearly healed that I could have used it without discomfort—(note my ability to drive a motor car)—and it was with the greatest difficulty that I restrained a mad, devilish impulse to strike that guard full upon the nose, from which the raindrops coursed in an interrupted descent from the visor of his cap.

The shrill, childish whistle of the locomotive reached us at that instant. A look of wonder sprang into the eyes of the guard.

"It—it is going to stop, mein herr," he cried. "Gott in himmel! It has never stopped before." He rushed out upon the platform in a great state of agitation, and we trailed along behind him, even more excited than he.

It was still raining, but not so hard. The glare of the headlight was upon us for an instant and then, passing, left us in blinding darkness. The brakes creaked, the wheels grated and at last the train came to a standstill. For one horrible moment I thought it was going on through in spite of its promissory signal. Britton went one way and I the other, with our umbrellas ready. Up and down the line of *wagon lits* we raced. A conductor stepped down from the last coach but one, and prepared to assist a passenger to alight. I hastened up to him.

"Permit me," I said, elbowing him aside.

A portly lady squeezed through the vestibule and felt her way carefully down the steps. Behind her was a smallish, bewhiskered man, trying to raise an umbrella inside the narrow corridor, a perfectly impossible feat.

She came down into my arms with the limpness of one who is accustomed to such attentions, and then wheeled instantly upon the futile individual on the steps above.

"Quick! My hat! Heaven preserve us, how it rains!" she cried, in a deep, wheezy voice and—in German!

"Moth—" I began insinuatingly, but the sacred word died unfinished on my lips. The next instant I was scurrying down the platform to where I saw Britton standing.

"Have you seen them?" I shouted wildly.

"No, sir. Not a sign, sir. Ah! See!"

He pointed excitedly down the platform.

"No!" I rasped out. "By no possible stretch of the imagination can *that* be Mrs. Titus. Come! We must ask the conductor. *That* woman? Good Lord, Britton, she *waddles!*"

The large lady and the smallish man passed us on the way to shelter, the latter holding an umbrella over her hat with one hand and lugging a heavy hamper in the other. They were both exclaiming in German. The station guard and the conductor were bowing and scraping in their wake, both carrying boxes and bundles.

No one else had descended from the train. I grabbed the conductor by the arm.

"Any one else getting off here?" I demanded in English and at once repeated it in German.

He shook himself loose, dropped the bags in the shelter of the station house, doffed his cap to the imperious backs of his late passengers, and scuttled back to the car. A moment later the train was under way.

"Can you not see for yourself?" he shouted from the steps as he passed me by.

Once more I swooped down upon the guard. He was stuffing the large German lady into a small, lopsided carriage, the driver of which was taking off his cap and putting it on again after the manner of a mechanical toy.

"Go away," hissed the guard angrily. "This is the Mayor and the Mayoress. Stand aside! Can't you see?"

Presently the Mayor and the Mayoress were snugly stowed away in the creaking hack, and it rattled away over the cobblestones.

"When does the next train get in?" I asked for the third time. He was still bowing after the departing hack.

"Eh? The next? Oh, mein herr, is it you?"

"Yes, it is still I. Is there another train soon?"

"That was Mayor Berg and his wife," he said, taking off his cap again in a sort of ecstasy. "The express stops for him, eh? Ha! It stops for no one else but our good Mayor. When he commands it to stop it stops—"

"Answer my question," I thundered, "or I shall report you to the Mayor!"

"Ach, Gott!" he gasped. Collecting his thoughts, he said: "There is no train until nine o'clock in the morning. Nine, mein herr."

"Ach, Gott!" groaned I. "Are you sure?"

"Jah! You can go home now and go to bed, sir. There will be no train until nine and I will not be on duty then. Good night!"

Britton led me into the waiting-room, where I sat down and glared at him as if he were to blame for everything connected with our present plight.

"I daresay we'd better be starting 'ome, sir," said he timidly. "Something 'as gone wrong with the plans, I fear. They did not come, sir."

"Do you think I am blind?" I roared.

"Not at all, sir," he said in haste, taking a step or two backward.

Inquiries at the little eating-house only served to verify the report of the station-guard. There would be no train before nine o'clock, and that was a very slow one; what we would call a "local" in the States. Sometimes, according to the proprietress, it was so slow that it didn't get in at all. It had been known to amble in as late as one in the afternoon, but when it happened to be later than that it ceased to have an identity of its own and came in as a part of the two o'clock train. Moreover, it carried nothing but third-class carriages and more often than not it had as many as a dozen freight cars attached.

There was not the slightest probability that the fastidious Mrs. Titus would travel by such a train, so we were forced to the conclusion that something had gone wrong with the plans. Very dismally we prepared for the long drive home.

What could have happened to upset the well-arranged plan? Were Tarnowsy's spies so hot upon the trail that it was necessary for her to abandon the attempt to enter my castle? In that case, she must have sent some sort of a message to her daughter, apprising her of the unexpected change; a message which, unhappily for me, arrived after my departure. It was not likely that she would have altered her plans without letting us know, and yet I could not shake off an exasperating sense of doubt. If I were to believe all that Bangs said about the excellent lady, it would not be unlike her to do quite as she pleased in the premises without pausing to consider the comfort or the convenience of any one else interested in the undertaking. A selfish desire to spend the day in Lucerne might have overtaken her *en passant*, and the rest of us could go hang for all that she cared about consequences!

I am ashamed to confess that the longer I considered the matter, the more plausible this view of the situation appeared to me. By the time we succeeded in starting the engine, after cranking for nearly half an hour, I was so consumed by wrath over the scurvy trick she had played upon us that I swore she should not enter my castle if I could prevent it; moreover, I would take fiendish delight in dumping her confounded luggage into the Danube.

I confided my views to Britton who was laboriously cranking the machine and telling me between grunts that the "bloody water 'ad got into it," and we both resorted to painful but profound excoriations without in the least departing from our relative positions as master and man: he swore about one abomination and I another, but the gender was undeviatingly the same.

We also had trouble with the lamps.

At last we were off, Britton at the wheel. I shall not describe that diabolical trip home. It is only necessary to say that we first lost our way and went ten or twelve kilometers in the wrong direction; then we had a blow-out and no quick-detachable rim; subsequently something went wrong with the mud-caked machinery and my unfortunate valet had to lie on his back in a puddle for half an hour; eventually we sneaked into the garage with our trembling Mercedes, and quarrelled manfully with the men who had to wash her.

"Great heaven, Britton!" I groaned, stopping short in my sloshy progress down the narrow street that led to the ferry.

He looked at me in astonishment. I admit that the ejaculation must have sounded weak and effeminate to him after what had gone before.

"What is it, sir?" he asked, at once resuming his status as a servant after a splendid hiatus of five hours or more in which he had enjoyed all of the by-products of equality.

"Poopendyke!" I exclaimed, aghast. "I have just thought of him. The poor devil has been waiting for us three miles up the river since midnight! What do you think of that!"

"No such luck, sir," said he, grumpily.

"Luck! You heartless rascal! What do you mean by that?"

"I beg pardon, sir. I mean to say, he could sit in the boat 'ouse and twiddle 'is thumbs at the elements, sir. Trust Mr. Poopendyke to keep out of the rain."

"In any event, he is still waiting there for us, wet or dry. He and the two big Schmicks." I took a moment for thought. "We must telephone to the castle and have Hawkes send Conrad out with word to them." I looked at my watch. It was twenty minutes past seven. "I suppose no one in the castle went to bed last night. Good Lord, what a scene for a farce!"

We retraced our steps to the garage, where Britton went to the telephone. I stood in the doorway of the building, staring gloomily, hollow-eyed at the—well, at nothing, now that I stop to think of it. The manager of the place, an amiable, jocund descendant of Lazarus, approached me.

"Quite a storm last night, Mr. Schmarck," he said, rubbing his hands on an oil-rag. I gruffly agreed with him in a monosyllable. "But it is lovely to-day, sir. Heavenly, sir."

"Heavenly?" I gasped.

"Ah, but look at the glorious sun," he cried, waving the oil-rag in all directions at once.

The sun! Upon my word, the sun *was* shining fiercely. I hadn't noticed it before. The tops of the little red-tiled houses down the street glistened in the glare of sunshine that met my gaze as I looked up at them. Suddenly I remembered that I had witnessed the sunrise, a most doleful, dreary phenomenon that overtook us ten miles down the valley. I had seen it but it had made no impression on my tortured mind. The great god of day had sprung up out of the earth to smile upon me—or at me—and I had let him go unnoticed, so black and desolate was the memory of the night he destroyed! I had only a vague recollection of the dawn. The thing that caused me the most concern was the discovery that we had run the last half of our journey in broad daylight with our acetylene lamps going full blast. I stared at the tiles, blinking and unbelieving.

"Well, I'm—dashed," I said, with a silly grin.

"The moon will shine to-night, Mr. Schmarck—" he began insinuatingly.

"*Smart*, if you please," I snapped.

"Ah," he sighed, rolling his eyes, "it is fine to be in love."

A full minute passed before I grasped the meaning of that soft answer, and then it was too late. He had gone about his business without waiting to see whether my wrath had been turned away. I had been joy-riding!

The excitement in Britton's usually imperturbable countenance as he came running up to me from the telephone closet prepared me in a way for the startling news that was to come.

"Has anything serious happened?" I cried, my heart sinking a little lower.

"I had Mr. Poopendyke himself on the wire, sir. What do you think, sir?"

A premonition! "She—she has arrived?" I demanded dully.

He nodded. "She 'as, sir. Mrs.—your mother, sir, is in your midst." The proximity of the inquisitive manager explains this extraordinary remark on the part of my valet. We both glared at the manager and he had the delicacy to move away. "She arrived by a special train at twelve lawst night, sir."

I was speechless. The brilliant sunshine seemed to be turning into sombre night before my eyes; everything was going black.

"She's asleep, he says, and doesn't want to be disturbed till noon, so he says he can't say anything more just now over the telephone because he's afraid of waking 'er." (Britton drops them when excited.)

"He doesn't have to shout so loud that he can be heard on the top floor," said I, still a trifle dazed.

"She 'appens to be sleeping in your bed, sir, he says."

"In *my* bed? Good heavens, Britton! What's to become of *me*?"

"Don't take it so 'ard, sir," he made haste to say. "Blatchford 'as fixed a place for you on the couch in your study, sir. It's all very snug, sir."

"But, Britton," I said in horror, "suppose that I should have come home last night. Don't you see?"

"I daresay she 'ad the door locked, sir," he said.

"By special train," I mumbled. A light broke in upon my reviving intellect. "Why, it was the train that went through at a mile a minute while we were in the coffee-house. No wonder we didn't meet her!"

"I shudder to think of wot would 'ave 'appened if we had, sir," said he, meaning no doubt to placate me. "Mr. Poopendyke says the Countess 'as been up all night worrying about you, sir. She has been distracted. She wanted 'im to go out and search for you at four o'clock this morning, but he says he assured 'er you'd turn up all right. He says Mrs.—the elderly lady, begging your pardon, sir,—thought she was doing for the best when she took a special. She wanted to save us all the trouble she could. He says she was very much distressed by our failure to 'ave some one meet her with a launch when she got here last night, sir. As it was, she didn't reach the castle until nearly one, and she looked like a drowned rat when she got there, being hex—exposed to a beastly rainstorm. See wot I mean? She went to bed in a dreadful state, he says, but he thinks she'll be more pleasant before the day is over."

I burst into a fit of laughter. "Hurray!" I shouted, exultantly. "So she was out in it too, eh? Well, by Jove, I don't feel half as badly as I did five minutes ago. Come! Let us be off."

We started briskly down the street. My spirits were beginning to rebound. Poopendyke had said that she worried all night about me! She had been distracted! Poor little woman! Still I was glad to know that she had the grace to sit up and worry instead of going to sleep as she might have done. I was just mean enough to be happy over it.

Poopendyke met us on the town side of the river. He seemed a trifle haggard, I thought. He was not slow, on the other hand, to announce in horror-struck tones that I looked like a ghost.

"You must get those wet clothes off at once, Mr. Smart, and go to bed with a hot water bottle and ten grains of quinine. You'll be very ill if you don't. Put a lot more elbow grease into those oars, Max. Get a move on you. Do you want Mr. Smart to die of pneumonia?"

While we were crossing the muddy river, my secretary, his teeth chattering with cold and excitement combined, related the story of the night.

"We were just starting off for the boat-house up the river, according to plans, Max and Rudolph and I with the two boats, when the Countess came down in a mackintosh and a pair of gum boots and insisted upon going along with us. She said it wasn't fair to make you do all the work, and all that sort of thing, and I was having the devil's own time to induce her to go back to the castle with Mr. Bangs. While we were arguing with her,—and it was getting so late that I feared we wouldn't be in time to meet you,—we heard some one shouting on the opposite side of the river. The voice sounded something like Britton's, and the Countess insisted that there had been an accident and that you were hurt, Mr. Smart, and nothing would do but we must send Max and Rudolph over to see what the trouble was. It was raining cats and dogs, and I realised that it would be impossible for you to get a boatman on that side at that hour of the night,—it was nearly one,—so I sent the two Schmicks across. I've never seen a night as dark as it was. The two little lanterns bobbing in the boat could hardly be seen through the torrents of rain, and it was next to impossible to see the lights on the opposite landing stage—just a dull, misty glow.

"To make the story short, Mrs. Titus and her sons were over there, with absolutely no means of crossing the river. There were no boatmen, the ferry had stopped, and they were huddled under the eaves of the wharf building. Everything was closed and locked up for the night. The night-watchman and a policeman lit the pier lamps for them, but that's as far as they'd go. It took two trips over to fetch the whole party across. Raining pitchforks all the time, you understand. Mrs. Titus was foaming at the mouth because you don't own a yacht or at least a launch with a canopy top, or a limousine body, or something of the sort.

"I didn't have much of a chance to converse with her. The Countess tried to get her upstairs in the east wing but she wouldn't climb another step. I forgot to mention that the windlass was out of order and she had to climb the hill in mud six inches deep. The Schmicks carried her the last half of the distance. She insisted on sleeping in the hall or the study,—anywhere but upstairs. I assumed the responsibility of putting her in your bed, sir. It was either that or—"

I broke in sarcastically "You couldn't have put her into your bed, I suppose."

"Not very handily, Mr. Smart," he said in an injured voice. "One of her sons occupied my bed. Of course, it was all right, because I didn't intend to go to bed, as it happened. The older son went upstairs with the Countess. She gave up her bed to him, and then she and I sat up all night in the study waiting for a telephone message from you. The younger son explained a good many things to us that his mother absolutely refused to discuss, she was so mad when she got here. It seems she took it into her head at the last minute to charter a special train, but forgot to notify us of the switch in the plans. She traveled by the regular train from Paris to some place along the line, where she got out and waited for the special which was following along behind, straight through from Paris, too. A woeful waste of money, it seemed to me. Her idea was to throw a couple of plain-clothes men off the track, and, by George, sir, she succeeded. They thought she was changing from a train to some place in Switzerland, and went off to watch the other station. Then she sneaked aboard the special, which was chartered clear through to Vienna. See how clever she is? If they followed on the next train, or telegraphed, it would naturally be to Vienna. She got off at this place and—well, we have her with us, sir, as snug as a bug in a rug."

"What is she like, Fred?" I inquired. I confess that I hung on his reply.

"I have never seen a wet hen, but I should say, on a guess, that she's a good bit like one. Perhaps when she's thoroughly dried out she may not be so bad, but—" He drew a long, deep breath. "But, upon my word of honour, she was the limit last night. Of course one couldn't expect her to be exactly gracious, with her hair plastered over her face and her hat spoiled and her clothes soaked, but there was really no excuse for some of the things she said to me. I shall overlook them for your sake and for the Countess's." He was painfully red in the face.

"The conditions, Fred," I said, "were scarcely conducive to polite persiflage."

"But, hang it all, I was as wet as she was," he exploded, so violently that I knew his soul must have been tried to the utmost.

"We must try to make the best of it," I said. "It will not be for long." The thought of it somehow sent my heart back to its lowest level.

He was glum and silent for a few minutes. Then he said, as if the thought had been on his mind for some hours: "She isn't a day over forty-five. It doesn't seem possible, with a six-foot son twenty-six years old."

Grimly I explained. "They marry quite young when it's for money, Fred."

"I suppose that's it," he sighed. "I fancy she's handsome, too, when she hasn't been rained upon."

We were half way up the slope when he announced nervously that all of my dry clothing was in the closet off my bedroom and could not be got at under any circumstance.

"But," he said, "I have laid out my best frock coat and trousers for you, and a complete change of linen. You are quite welcome to anything I possess, Mr. Smart.

I think if you take a couple of rolls at the bottom of the trousers, they'll be present-able. The coat may be a little long for you, but—"

My loud laughter cut him short.

"It's the best I could do," he said in an aggrieved voice.

I had a secret hope that the Countess would be in the courtyard to welcome me, but I was disappointed. Old Gretel met me and wept over me, as if I was not already sufficiently moist. The chef came running out to say that breakfast would be ready for me when I desired it; Blatchford felt of my coat sleeve and told me that I was quite wet; Hawkes had two large, steaming toddies waiting for us in the vesti-bule, apparently fearing that we could get no farther without the aid of a stimulant. But there was no sign of a single Titus.

Later I ventured forth in Poopendyke's best suit of clothes—the one he uses when he passes the plate on Sundays in far-away Yonkers. It smelled of moth-balls, but it was gloriously dry, so why carp! We sneaked down the corridor past my own bedroom door and stole into the study.

Just inside the door, I stopped in amazement. The Countess was sound asleep in my big armchair, a forlorn but lovely thing in a pink peignoir. Her rumpled brown hair nestled in the angle of the chair; her hands drooped listlessly at her sides; dark lashes lay upon the soft white cheeks; her lips were parted ever so slightly, and her bosom rose and fell in the long swell of perfect repose.

Poopendyke clutched me by the arm and drew me toward the door, or I might have stood there transfixed for heaven knows how long.

"She's asleep," he whispered.

It was the second time in twelve hours that some one had intimated that I was blind.

CHAPTER XVI

I INDULGE IN PLAIN LANGUAGE

THE door creaked villainously. The gaunt, ecclesiastical tails of my borrowed frock coat were on the verge of being safely outside with me when she cried out. Whereupon I swiftly transposed myself, and stuck my head through the half-open door.

"Oh, it's you!" she cried, in a quavery voice. She was leaning forward in the chair, her eyes wide open and eager.

I advanced into the room. A look of doubt sprang into her face. She stared for a moment and then rather piteously rubbed her eyes.

"Yes, it is I," said I, spreading my arms in such a way that my hands emerged from the confines of Poopendyke's sleeves. (Upon my word, I had no idea that he was so much longer than I!) "It is still I, Countess, despite the shrinkage."

"The shrinkage?" she murmured, slowly sliding out of the chair. As she unbent her cramped leg, she made a little grimace of pain, but smiled as she limped toward me, her hand extended.

"Yes, I always shrink when I get wet," I explained, resorting to facetiousness.

Then I bent over her hand and kissed it. As I neglected to release it at once, the cuff of Poopendyke's best coat slid down over our two hands, completely enveloping them. It was too much for me to stand. I squeezed her hand with painful fervour, and then released it in trepidation.

"Poopendyke goes to church in it," I said vaguely, leaving her to guess what it was that Poopendyke went to church in, or, perhaps, knowing what I meant, how I happened to be in it for the time being. "You've been crying!"

Her eyes were red and suspiciously moist.

As she met my concerned gaze, a wavering, whimsical smile crept into her face.

"It has been a disgustingly wet night," she said. "Oh, you don't know how happy I am to see you standing here once more, safe and sound, and—and amiable. I expected you to glower and growl and—"

"On a bright, glorious, sunshiny morning like this?" I cried. "Never! I prefer to be graciously refulgent. Our troubles are behind us."

"How good you are." After a moment's careful, scrutiny of my face: "I can see the traces of very black thoughts, Mr. Smart,—and recent ones."

"They were black until I came into this room," I confessed. "Now they are rose-tinted."

She bent her slender body a little toward me and the red seemed to leap back into her lips as if propelled by magic. Resolutely I put my awkward, ungainly arms behind my back, and straightened my figure. I was curiously impressed by the discovery that I was very, very tall and she very much smaller than my memory recorded. Of course, I had no means of knowing that she was in bedroom slippers and not in the customary high-heeled boots that gave her an inch and a half of false stature.

"Your mother is here," I remarked hurriedly.

She glanced toward my bedroom door.

"Oh, what a night!" she sighed. "I did all that I could to keep her out of your bed. It was useless. I *did* cry, Mr. Smart. I know you must hate all of us."

I laughed. " 'Love thy neighbour as thyself,' " I quoted. "You *are* my neighbour, Countess; don't forget that. And it so happens that your mother is also my neighbour at present, and your brothers too. Have you any cousins and aunts?"

"I can't understand how any one can be so good-natured as you," she sighed.

The crown of her head was on a level with my shoulder. Her eyes were lowered; a faint line of distress grew between them. For a minute I stared down at the brown crest of her head, an almost ungovernable impulse pounding away at my sense of discretion. I do take credit unto myself for being strong enough to resist that opportunity to make an everlasting idiot of myself. I knew, even then, that if a similar attack ever came upon me again I should not be able to withstand it. It was too much to expect of mortal man. Angels might survive the test, but not wingless man.

All this time she was staring rather pensively at the second button from the top of Poopendyke's coat, and so prolonged and earnest was her gaze that I looked down in some concern, at the same time permitting myself to make a nervous, jerky and quite involuntary digital examination of the aforesaid button. She looked up with a nervous little laugh.

"I shall have to sew one on right there for poor Mr. Poopendyke," she said, poking her finger into the empty buttonhole. "You dear bachelors!"

Then she turned swiftly away from me, and glided over to the big armchair, from the depths of which she fished a small velvet bag. Looking over her shoulder, she smiled at me.

"Please look the other way," she said. Without waiting for me to do so, she took out a little gold box, a powder puff, and a stick of lip rouge. Crossing to the small

Florentine mirror that hung near my desk, she proceeded, before my startled eyes, to repair the slight—and to me unnoticeable—damage that had been done to her complexion before the sun came up.

"Woman works in a mysterious way, my friend, her wonders to perform," she paraphrased calmly.

"No matter how transcendently beautiful woman may be, she always does that sort of thing to herself, I take it," said I.

"She does," said the Countess with conviction. She surveyed herself critically. "There! And now I am ready to accept an invitation to breakfast. I am disgustingly hungry."

"And so am I!" I cried with enthusiasm. "Hurray! You shall eat Poopendyke's breakfast, just to penalise him for failing in his duties as host during my unavoidable—"

"Quite impossible," she said. "He has already eaten it."

"He has?"

"At half-past six, I believe. He announced at that ungodly hour that if he couldn't have his coffee the first thing in the morning he would be in for a headache all day. He suggested that I take a little nap and have breakfast with you—if you succeeded in surviving the night."

"Oh, I see," said I slowly. "He knew all the time that you were napping in that chair, eh?"

"You shall not scold him!"

"I shall do even worse than that. I shall pension him for life."

She appeared thoughtful. A little frown of annoyance clouded her brow.

"He promised faithfully to arouse me the instant you were sighted on the opposite side of the river. I made him stand in the window with a field glass. No, on second thought, *I* shall scold him. If he had come to the door and shouted, you wouldn't have caught me in this odious dressing-gown. Helene—"

"It is most fascinating," I cried. "Adorable! I love flimsy, pink things. They're so intimate. And Poopendyke knows it, bless his ingenuous old soul."

I surprised a queer little gleam of inquiry in her eyes. It flickered for a second and died out.

"Do you really consider him an ingenuous old soul?" she asked. And I thought there was something rather metallic in her voice. I might have replied with intelligence if she had given me a chance, but for some reason she chose to drop the subject. "You *must* be famished, and I am dying to hear about your experiences. You must not omit a single detail. I—"

There came a gentle, discreet knocking on the half-open door. I started, somewhat guiltily.

"Come!"

Blatchford poked his irreproachable visage through the aperture and then gravely swung the door wide open.

"Breakfast is served, sir,—your ladyship. I beg pardon."

I have never seen him stand so faultlessly rigid. As we passed him on the way out a mean desire came over me to tread on his toes, just as an experiment. I wondered if he would change expression. But somehow I felt that he would say "Thank you, sir," and there would be no satisfaction in knowing that he had had all his pains for nothing.

I shall never forget that enchanted breakfast—never! Not that I can recall even vaguely what we had to eat, or who served it, or how much of the naked truth I related to her in describing the events of the night; I can only declare that it was a singularly light-hearted affair.

At half-past one o'clock I was received by Mrs. Titus in my own study. The Countess came down from her eerie abode to officiate at the ceremonious function—if it may be so styled—and I was agreeably surprised to find my new guest in a most amiable frame of mind. True, she looked me over with what seemed to me an unnecessarily and perfectly frank stare of curiosity, but, on sober reflection, I did not hold it against her. I was still draped in Poopendyke's garments.

At first sight I suppose she couldn't quite help putting me down as one of those literary freaks who typify intellect without intelligence.

As for her two sons, they made no effort to disguise their amazement. (I have a shocking notion that the vowel *u* might be substituted for the *a* in that word without loss of integrity!)

The elder of the two young men, Colingraft Titus, who being in the business with his father in New York was permitted to travel most of the time so that he couldn't interfere with it, was taller than I, and an extremely handsome chap to boot. He was twenty-six. The younger, Jasper, Jr., was nineteen, short and slight of build, with the merriest eyes I've ever seen. I didn't in the least mind the grin he bestowed upon me—and preserved with staunch fidelity throughout the whole interview,—but I resented the supercilious, lordly scorn of his elder brother.

Jasper, I learned, was enduring a protracted leave of absence from Yale; the hiatus between his freshman and sophomore years already covered a period of sixteen months, and he had a tutor who appreciated the buttery side of his crust.

Mrs. Titus, after thanking me warmly—and I think sincerely—for all that I had done for Aline, apologised in a perfunctory sort of way for having kept me out of my bed all night, and hoped that I wouldn't catch cold or have an attack of rheumatism.

I soon awoke to the fact that she was in the habit of centralising attention. The usually volatile Countess became subdued and repressed in her presence; the big son and the little one were respectfully quiescent; I confess to a certain embarrassment myself.

She was a handsome woman with a young figure, a good complexion, clear eyes, wavy brown hair, and a rich, low voice perfectly modulated. No doubt she was nearing fifty but thirty-five would have been your guess, provided you were a bachelor. A bachelor learns something about women every day of his life, but not so much that he cannot be surprised the day after.

I endeavoured to set her mind at rest by politely reminding her that I couldn't have slept in the bed any way, having been out all night, and she smilingly assured me that it was a relief to find a literary man who wasn't forever saying flat stupid things.

I took them over the castle—that is, a ***part*** of the castle. Mrs. Titus wouldn't climb stairs. She confessed to banting, but drew the line at anything more exhausting. I fear I was too palpably relieved when she declined to go higher than the second story.

"It isn't necessary, Mr. Smart," she said sweetly, "to go into the history of the wretched Rothhoefens, as a Cook's interpreter might do. You see, I know the castle quite well—and I have had all the *late* news from my daughter."

"Of course!" I agreed. "Stupid of me not to remember that you are descended from—"

"Mother isn't half as stuck up about it as you might think, Mr. Smart," interrupted Jasper, Jr., glibly. "She prefers to let people think her ancestors were Dutch instead of merely German. Dutch ancestors are the proper thing in Jew York."

"Jappie," said his mother severely, "how often must I caution you not to speak of New York as Jew York? Some day you will say it to a Jew. One can't be too careful. Heaven alone knows when one is in the presence of a Jew in these days."

"Oh, I'm not Hebraic," said I quickly. "My ancestors *were* Dutch. They came over with the original skin grafters."

She looked puzzled for a moment. The Countess laughed. Then Jasper saw the point. Colingraft was the last to see it, and then it was too late for him to smile.

We had tea in the loggia and I dined with the family in the Countess's apartment at eight that night. I think Mrs. Titus was rather favourably impressed when she beheld me in my own raiment. Britton had smoothed out my evening clothes until they almost shone, and I managed to carry myself with unusual buoyancy.

Everything went very well that evening. We were all in fine humour and the dinner was an excellent one. I perpetrated but one unhappy blunder. I asked Mrs. Titus if she knew the Riley-Werkheimers and the Rocksworths in New York.

"Visually," she said succinctly, and I made haste to change the subject. The Countess looked amused, and Colingraft said something about it being more than likely that we did not have any mutual acquaintances in New York. His sister came to my rescue with a very amusing and exaggerated account of my experience with the Riley-Werkheimers and Rocksworths. Jasper was enthusiastic. Something told me that I was going to like him.

My real troubles began the next day—and at the rather unseemly hour of eight o'clock in the morning. Colingraft came down the hall in a bath-gown and slippers, banged on my bedroom door, and wanted to know why the devil he couldn't have hot water for his bath. He was too full-blooded, and all that sort of thing, he said, to take a cold plunge. Moreover, he wasn't used to taking his tub in a tin-cup. (That was his sarcastic way of referring to my portable, handy bath-tub.) I asked him why he didn't ring for Britton, and he said he did but that Britton was assisting Jasper in a wild chase for a bat which had got into the lad's room during the night.

"Thank your lucky stars it didn't get into Mother's room," he said surlily. I silently thanked them.

He made such a row about his tub that I had to give him the pail of hot water Britton had placed in my bedroom, preparatory to my own bath.

At breakfast Jasper complained about the bats. He couldn't for the life of him see why I didn't have screens in the windows.

Later on Mrs. Titus, who had coffee and toast in her room, joined us in the loggia and announced that the coffee was stone cold. Moreover, she did not like the guest-chamber into which she had been moved by order of the Countess. It was too huge for a bed-chamber, and the iron window shutters creaked all night long.

"But don't you love the view you have of the Danube?" I queried, rather mournfully.

"I don't sit in the window all night, Mr. Smart," she said tartly.

I at once insisted on her resuming possession of my bedroom, and promptly had all of my things moved into the one she had occupied during the night. When the Countess heard of this arrangement she was most indignant. She got me off in a corner and cruelly informed me that I hadn't the vestige of a backbone. She must have said something to her mother, too, for when evening came around I had to move back into my own room, Mrs. Titus sweetly assuring me that under no consideration would she consent to impose upon my good nature and hospitality to such an extent, etc., etc.

During the day, at odd times, Colingraft made lofty suggestions in regard to what ***could*** be done with the place to make it more or less inhabitable, and Jasper,—who, by the way, I was beginning to fear I should not like after all,—said he'd just like to have a whack at the thing himself. First thing he'd do would be to turn some of those old, unused rooms into squash and racquet courts, and he'd also put in a swimming-pool and a hot-water plant.

Late in the afternoon, I stole far up into the eastern tower to visit my adorable friend Rosemary. We played house together on the nursery floor and I soon got over my feeling of depression. But even in play I was made to realise that I was not the master of the house. She ruled me with the utmost despotism, but I didn't mind. She permitted me to sip honey from that cunning place in her little neck and managed to call me Unko. My heart grew warm and soft again under the spell of her.

The Countess watched us at play from her seat by the window. She was strangely still and pensive. I had the feeling that she was watching me all the time, and that there was a shadow of anxiety in her lovely eyes. She smiled at our pranks, and yet there was something sad in the smile.

I was young again with Rosemary, and full of glee. She took me out of myself. I forgot the three Tituses and with them many of my woes. Here was a cure for the blues: this gay little kiddie of the unspeakable Tarnowsy!

I lay awake for hours that night, but when I finally went to sleep and heaven knows I needed it!—it was with the soporific resolution to put my house rigidly in order the very next day. I would be polite about it, but very firm. The Titus family (omitting the Countess and Rosemary) was to be favoured with an ultimatum from which there could be no appeal. John Bellamy Smart had decided—with Morpheus smoothing out the wrinkles of perplexity—that he would be master in his own house.

My high resolve flattened itself out a little after the sound sleep I had, and I make no doubt I should have wavered sadly in my purpose had not a crisis arisen to shape my courage for me in a rather emphatic way.

Shortly after breakfast Mrs. Titus came downstairs very smartly gowned for the street. She announced that she was going into the town for an hour or two and asked me to have one of the Schmicks ferry her across the river. There was a famous antique shop there—memory of other days—and she wanted to browse a while in search of brasses and bronzes.

I looked at her, aghast. I recognised the crisis, but for a moment was unable to marshal my powers of resistance. Noting my consternation, she calmly assured me that there wouldn't be the least danger of detection, as she was going to be heavily veiled and *very* cautious.

"My dear Mrs. Titus," I murmured in my dismay, "it isn't to be considered. I am sure you won't persist in this when I tell you that Tarnowsy's agents are sure to see you and—"

She laughed. "Tarnowsy's agents! Why should they be here?"

"They seem to be everywhere."

"I can assure you there is none within fifty miles of Schloss Rothhoefen. Our men are in the city. Four of them preceded me. This morning I had Mr. Bangs telephone to the hotel where the chief operative is staying—in the guise of an American tourist, and he does it very cleverly for an Englishman, too,—and he assures me that there is absolutely no danger. Even Mr. Bangs is satisfied."

"I am forced to say that I am by no means satisfied that it is a safe or wise thing to do, Mrs. Titus," I said, with more firmness than I thought I possessed.

She raised her delicate eyebrows in a most exasperating well-bred, admonitory way.

"I am quite sure, Mr. Smart, that Dillingham is a perfectly trustworthy detective, and—"

"But why take the slightest risk?"

"It is necessary for me to see Dillingham, that is the long and short of it," she said coldly. "One can't discuss things over a telephone, you know. Mr. Bangs understands. And, by the way, Mr. Smart, I have taken the liberty of calling up the central office of the telephone company to ask if they can run an extension wire to my dressing-room.

I hope you do not mind."

"Not in the least. I should have thought of it myself."

"You have so much to think of, poor man. And now will you be good enough to have Hawkes order the man to row me across the—"

"I am very sorry, Mrs. Titus," said I firmly, "but I fear I must declare myself. I cannot permit you to go into the town to-day."

She was thunderstruck. "Are you in earnest?" she cried, after searching my face rather intently for a moment.

"Unhappily, yes. Will you let me explain—"

"The *idea!*" she exclaimed as she drew herself to her full height and withered me with a look of surpassing scorn. "Am I to regard myself as a prisoner, Mr. Smart?"

"Oh, I beg of you, Mrs. Titus—" I began miserably.

"Please answer my question."

Her tone cut me like the lash of a whip. My choler rose.

"I do not choose to regard myself as a jailer. My only object in opposing this—"

"I have never known anything so absurd." Two bright red spots appeared in her cheeks. "Your attitude is most extraordinary. However, I shall go to the city this morning, Mr. Smart. Pray give me the credit of having sense enough to—Ah, Colingraft."

The two sons approached from the breakfast-room, where they had been enjoying a ten o'clock chop. Colingraft, noting his mother's attire, accelerated his speed and was soon beside us.

"Going out, Mother?" he enquired, flicking the ash from his cigarette.

"If Mr. Smart will be good enough to withdraw his opposition," she said icily.

He gave me a sharp look. "What's up?"

"Mrs. Titus doesn't seem to realise the risk she runs in—"

"Risk? Do you suppose, Mr. Smart, I would jeopardise my daughter's—"

"What's up?" repeated Colingraft insistently.

"Mr. Smart calmly informs me that I am not to go into the city."

"I don't see that Mr. Smart has anything to say about it," said her son coolly. "If he—" He paused, glaring.

I looked him squarely in the eye. If he had possessed the acumen of a pollywog he would have seen that my Dutch was up.

"One moment, Mr. Titus," I said, setting my jaw. "I have this to say about it. You are guests in my house. We are jointly interested in the effort to protect the Countess Tarnowsy. I consider it to be the height of imprudence for any member of your family to venture into the city, now or at any time during her stay in this castle. I happen to know that Tarnowsy is having me watched for some purpose or other. I don't think he suspects that the Countess is here, but I greatly fear that he believes I am interested in her cause. He suspects *me*. You have heard of our recent encounter. He knows my position pretty well by this time. Mrs. Titus says that the man Dillingham assures her there is no danger. Well, I can only say that Dillingham is a fool, and I don't purpose having my own safety threatened by—"

"Your safety?" exclaimed he. "I like that! What have you got to be afraid of?"

"You seem to forget that I am harbouring a fugitive from justice," I said flatly.

Mrs. Titus gasped. "How dare you—" "The Countess Tarnowsy is wanted by the authorities for kidnapping, and I think you know the facts quite as well as I do," I went on harshly. "God knows I am doing my best to protect her. I am risking more than you seem to appreciate. If she is found here, my position isn't likely to be an enviable one. I am not thinking solely of myself, believe me, but after all I contend that I have a right to assert myself in a crisis that may affect me vitally. I trust you will see my position and act accordingly,—with consideration, if nothing else."

Mrs. Titus did not take her eyes off mine while I was speaking. There was an expression of utter amazement in them. No one had ever opposed her before in just this way, I gathered. She didn't know what to make of it.

"I fear you exaggerate the extent of your peril, Mr. Smart," she said drily. "Of course, I have no desire to put you in jeopardy, but it seems to me—"

"Leaving me out of the case altogether, don't you think it is a bit unfair to the Countess?" I asked in some heat. "She doesn't want to go to jail."

"Jail?" she cried angrily.

"That's no way to speak about—" began Colingraft furiously.

I broke in rashly. "If you please, Mr. Titus, be good enough to keep your temper. I have no desire to appear harsh and arbitrary, but I can see that it is necessary to speak plainly. There isn't anything in the world I will not do to help you and the Countess in this unfortunate business, Mrs. Titus. I hope you believe me when I say as much. I am her friend; I want to be yours if you will let me. But I reserve the right to say what shall be and what shall not be done as long as you are under my roof. Just a moment, Mr. Titus! I think we are quite agreed that your sister is to depart from here on the fourteenth of the month. I am to be her escort, so to speak, for a considerable distance, in company with Mr. Bangs. Well, it must be clearly understood that not one of you is to show his or her face outside these walls until after that journey is over. That's plain-speaking, isn't it?"

"I shall go where I please, and I'll go to the town to-day—" roared Colingraft, getting no farther for the reason that his mother, seeing that I was desperately in earnest, gave vent to a little cry of alarm and clutched her big son by the shoulder. She begged him to listen to reason!

"Reason!" he gasped.

"If you—or any of you—put a foot outside these walls," I declared, "you will not be allowed to re-enter. That's flat!"

"By cricky!" fell in fervent admiration from the lips of Jasper, Jr. I glanced at his beaming, astonished face. He positively was grinning! "Good for you! You're a wonder, Mr. Smart! By cricky! And you're ***dead right***. We're darn fools!"

"Jasper!" gasped Mrs. Titus.

"Good for you, Jasper!" I cried warmly, and took the hand he proffered.

"Colingraft, please take me to my room," murmured the mother. "I—I feel faint. Send for Aline. Ask Mr. Bangs to come to me at once."

I bowed stiffly. "I am sorry, Mrs. Titus, to have been so harsh, so assertive—"

She held up both hands. "I never was so spoken to in all my life, Mr. Smart. I shall not forget it to my dying day."

She walked away from me, her pretty head held high and her chin suspiciously aquiver. Colingraft hastened after her, but not without giving me a stare in which rage and wonder struggled for the mastery.

I ran my hand over my moist brow.

"Gee!" said Jasper, Jr. "You've corked her all right, all right." He followed me into the study and I couldn't get rid of him for hours.

Later in the forenoon the Countess, with a queer little smile on her lips, told me that her mother considered me the most wonderful, the most forceful character she had ever encountered. I brightened up at that.

But Colingraft was not yet through with me.

CHAPTER XVII

I SEE TO THE BOTTOM OF THINGS

He sought me out just before luncheon. I was in the courtyard, listening patiently to Jasper Jr.'s theories and suggestions concerning the restoration of the entire facade of the castle, and what he'd do if he were in my place. Strange to say, I was considerably entertained; he was not at all offensive; on the contrary, he offered his ideas in a pleasantly ingenuous way, always supplementing them with some such salve as: "Don't you think so, Mr. Smart?" or "I'm sure you have thought of it yourself," or "Isn't that your idea, too?" or "You've done wonders with the joint, old man."

Colingraft came directly up to where we were standing. There was trouble in his eye.

"See here, Mr. Smart," he began austerely. "I've got something to say to you, and I'm not the sort to put it off. I appreciate what you've done for Aline and all that sort of thing, but your manner to-day has been intolerable, and we've got to come to an understanding."

I eyed him closely. "I suppose you're about to suggest that one or the other of us must—evacuate—get out, so to speak," said I.

"Don't talk rubbish. You've got my mother bawling her eyes out upstairs, and wishing she were dead. You've got to come off this high horse of yours. You've got to apologise to her, and damned quick, at that. Understand?"

"Nothing will give me greater joy than to offer her my most abject apology, Mr. Titus, unless it would be her unqualified forgiveness."

"You'll have to withdraw everything you said."

"I'll withdraw everything except my ultimatum in respect to her putting a foot outside these walls. That still stands."

"I beg to differ with you."

"You may beg till you're black in the face," said I coolly.

He swallowed hard. His face twitched, and his hands were clenched.

"You are pretty much of a mucker, Mr. Smart," he said, between his teeth. "I'm sorry my sister has fallen into your hands. The worst of it is, she seems satisfied with everything you do. Good Lord! What she can see in you is beyond my comprehension. Protection! Why you couldn't protect her from the assault of a chicken."

"Are you trying to insult me, Mr. Titus?"

"You couldn't resent it if I were. There never was an author with enough moral backbone to—"

"Wait! You are her brother. I don't want to have trouble with you. But if you keep on in this strain, Mr. Titus, I shall be compelled to thresh you soundly."

He fairly gasped. "Th—thresh me!" he choked out. Then he advanced.

Much to his surprise—and, strangely enough, not to my own—I failed to retreat. Instead, I extended my left fist with considerable abruptness and precision and he landed on his back.

I experienced a sensation of unholy joy. Up to that moment I had wondered whether I could do it with my left hand.

I looked at Jasper, Jr. He was staring at me in utter bewilderment.

"Good Lord! You—you've knocked him down!"

"I didn't think I could do it," said I hazily.

He sprang to his brother's side, and assisted him to a sitting posture.

"Right to the jaw," shouted Jasper, with a strange enthusiasm.

"Left," I corrected him.

Colingraft gazed about him in a stupid, vacant fashion for a moment, and then allowed his glazed eyes to rest upon me. He sat rather limply, I thought.

"Are you hurt, Colly?" cried Jasper, Jr.

A sickly grin, more of surprise than shame, stole over Colingraft's face. He put his hand to his jaw; then to the back of his head.

"By Jove!" he murmured. "I—I didn't think he had it in him. Let me get up!"

Jasper, Jr. was discreet. "Better let well enough alone, old—"

"I intend to," said Colingraft, as he struggled to his feet.

For a moment he faced me, uncertainly.

"I'm sorry, Mr. Titus," said I calmly.

"You—you are a wonder!" fell from his lips. "I'm not a coward, Mr. Smart. I've boxed a good deal in my time, but—by Jove, I never had a jolt like that."

He turned abruptly and left us. We followed him slowly toward the steps. At the bottom he stopped and faced me again.

"You're a better man than I thought," he said. "If you'll bury the hatchet, so will I. I take back what I said to you, not because I'm afraid of you, but because I respect you. What say? Will you shake hands?"

The surly, arrogant expression was gone from his face. In its place was a puzzled, somewhat inquiring look.

"No hard feeling on my part," I cried gladly. We shook hands. Jasper, Jr. slapped me on the back. "It's a most distressing, atavistic habit I'm getting into, knocking people down without rhyme or reason."

"I daresay you had reason," muttered Colingraft. "I got what was coming to me." An eager light crept into his handsome eyes. "By Jove, we can get in some corking work with the gloves while I'm here. I box quite a bit at home, and I miss it travelling about like this. What say to a half-hour or so every day? I have the gloves in one of my trunks. I'm getting horribly seedy. I need stirring up."

"Charmed, I'm sure," I said, assuming an enthusiasm I did not feel. Put on the gloves with this strapping, skillful boxer? Not I! I was firmly resolved to stop while my record was good. In a scientific clash with the gloves he would soon find out what a miserable duffer I was.

"And Jappy, here, is no slouch. He's as shifty as the dickens."

"The shiftier the better," said I, with great aplomb. Jasper, Jr., stuck out his chest modestly, and said: "Oh, piffle, Colly." But just the same I hadn't the least doubt in my mind that Jasper could "put it all over me." It was a rather sickening admission, though strictly private.

We made our way to my study, where I mildly suggested that we refrain from mentioning our little encounter to Mrs. Titus or the Countess. I thought Colingraft was especially pleased with the idea. We swore secrecy.

"I've always been regarded as a peaceful, harmless grub," I explained, still somewhat bewildered by the feat I had performed, and considerably shaken by the fear that I was degenerating into a positive ruffian. "You will believe me, I hope, when I declare that I was merely acting in self-defence when I—"

He actually laughed. "Don't apologise." He could not resist the impulse to blurt out once more: "By Jove, I didn't think you could do it."

"With my left hand, too," I said wonderingly. Catching myself up, I hastily changed the subject.

A little later on, as Colingraft left the room, slyly feeling of his jaw, Jasper, Jr. whispered to me excitedly: "You've got him eating out of your hand, old top."

Things were coming to a pretty pass, said I to myself when I was all alone. It certainly is a pretty pass when one knocks down the ex-husband and the brother of the woman he loves, and quite without the least suspicion of an inherited pugnacity.

I had a little note from the Countess that afternoon, ceremoniously delivered by Helene Marie Louise Antoinette. It read as follows:

"You did Colingraft a very good turn when you laid him low this morning. He is tiresomely interested in his prowess as a box-maker, or a boxster, or whatever it is in athletic parlance. He has been like a lamb all afternoon and he really can't get over the way you whacked him. (Is whack the word?) At first he was as mum as could be about it, but I think he really felt relieved when I told him I had seen the whole affair from a window in my hall. You see it gave him a chance to explain how you got in the whack, and I have been obliged to listen to intermittent lectures on the manly art of self-defence all afternoon, first from him, then from Jappy. I have a headache, and no means of defence. He admits that he deserved it, but I am not surprised. Colly is a sporting chap. He hasn't a mean drop of blood in his body. You have made a friend of him. So please don't feel that I hold a grudge against you for what you did. The funny part of it all is that mamma quite agrees with him. She says he deserved it! Mamma is wonderful, really, when it comes to a pinch. She has given up all thought of 'putting a foot outside the castle.' Can you have luncheon with us to-morrow? Would it be too much trouble if we were to have it in the loggia? I am just mad to get out-of-doors if only for an hour or two in that walled-in spot. Mr. Poopendyke has been perfectly lovely. He came up this morning to tell me that you haven't sneezed at all and there isn't the remotest chance now that you will have a cold. It seems he was afraid you might. You must have a very rugged constitution. Britton told Blake that most men would have died from exposure if they had been put in your place. How good you are to me.

"ALINE T."
"P. S.—I may come down to see you this evening."

I shall skip over the rather uninteresting events of the next two or three days. Nothing of consequence happened, unless you are willing to consider important two perfectly blissful nights of sleep on my part. Also, I had the pleasure of taking the Countess "out walking" in my courtyard, to use a colloquialism: once in the warm, sweet sunshine, again 'neath the glow of a radiant moon. She had not been outside the castle walls, literally, in more than five weeks, and the colour leaped back into her cheeks with a rush that delighted me. I may mention in passing that I paid particular attention to her suggestion concerning my dilapidated, gone-to-seed garden, although I had been bored to extinction by Jasper, Jr. when he undertook to enlighten me horticulturally. She agreed to come forth every day and assist me in building the poor thing up; propping it, so to speak.

As for Mrs. Titus, that really engaging lady made life so easy for me that I wondered why I had ever been apprehensive. She *was* quite wonderful when "it came to a pinch." I began to understand a good many things about her, chief among them being her unvoiced theories on matrimony. While she did not actually commit herself, I had no difficulty in ascertaining that, from her point of view, marriages are not made in heaven, and that a properly arranged divorce is a great deal less terrestrial than it is commonly supposed to be. She believed in matrimony as a trial and divorce as a reward, or something to that effect.

My opinion seemed to carry considerable weight with her. For a day or two after our somewhat sanguinary encounter, she was prone to start—even to jump slightly—when I addressed myself to her with unintentional directness. She soon got over that, however.

We were discussing Aline's unfortunate venture into the state of matrimony and I, feeling temporarily august and superior, managed to say the wrong thing and in doing so put myself in a position from which I could not recede without loss of dignity. If my memory serves me correctly I remarked, with some asperity, that marriages of that kind never turned out well for any one except the bridegroom.

She looked at me coldly. "I am afraid, Mr. Smart, that you have been putting some very bad notions into my daughter's head," she said.

"Bad notions?" I murmured.

"She has developed certain pronounced and rather extraordinary views concerning the nobility as the result of your—ah—argument, I may say."

"I'm very sorry. I know one or two exceedingly nice noblemen, and I've no doubt there are a great many more. She must have misunderstood me. I wasn't running down the nobility, Mrs. Titus. I was merely questioning the advisability of elevating it in the way we Americans sometimes do."

"You did not put it so adroitly in discussing the practice with Aline," she said quickly. "Granted that her own marriage was a mistake,—a dreadful mistake,—it does not follow that all international matches are failures. I would just as soon be unhappily married to a duke as to a dry-goods merchant, Mr. Smart."

"But not at the same price, Mrs. Titus," I remarked.

She smiled. "A husband is dear at any price."

"I shouldn't put it just that way," I protested. "A good American husband is a necessity, not a luxury."

"Well, to go back to what I started to say, Aline is very bitter about matrimony as viewed from my point of view. I am sorry to say I attribute her attitude to your excellent counselling."

"You flatter me. I was under the impression she took her lessons of Tarnowsy."

"Granted. But Tarnowsy was unfit. Why tar all of them with the same stick? There are good noblemen, you'll admit."

"But they don't need rehabilitation."

"Aline, I fear, will never risk another experiment. It's rather calamitous, isn't it? When one stops to consider her youth, beauty and all the happiness there may be—"

"I beg your pardon, Mrs. Titus, but I think your fears are groundless."

"What do you mean?"

"The Countess will marry again. I am not betraying a secret, because she has intimated as much to my secretary as well as to me. I take it that as soon as this unhappy affair is settled, she will be free to reveal the true state of her feelings toward—" I stopped, somewhat dismayed by my garrulous turn.

"Toward whom?" she fairly snapped.

"I don't know," I replied truthfully—and, I fear, lugubriously.

"Good heaven!" she cried, starting up from the bench on which we were sitting in the loggia. There was a queer expression in her eyes. "Hasn't—hasn't she ever hinted at—hasn't she mentioned any one at all?"

"Not to me."

Mrs. Titus was agitated, I could see that very plainly. A thoughtful frown appeared on her smooth brow, and a gleam of anxiety sprang into her eyes.

"I am sure that she has had no opportunity to—" She did not complete the sentence, in which there was a primary note of perplexity and wonder.

It grilled me to discover that she did not even so much as take me into consideration.

"You mean since the—er—divorce?" I inquired.

"She has been in seclusion all of the time. She has seen no man,—that is to say, no man for whom she could possibly entertain a—But, of course, you are mistaken in your impression, Mr. Smart. There is absolutely nothing in what you say."

"A former sweetheart, antedating her marriage," I suggested hopelessly.

"She has no sweetheart. Of that I am positive," said she with conviction.

"She must have had an army of admirers. They were legion after her marriage, I may be pardoned for reminding you."

She started. "Has she never mentioned Lord Amberdale to you?" she asked.

"Amberdale?" I repeated, with a queer sinking of the heart. "No, Mrs. Titus. An Englishman?"

She was mistress of herself once more. In a very degage manner she informed me that his lordship, a most attractive and honourable young Englishman, had been one of Aline's warmest friends at the time of the divorce proceedings. But, of course, there was nothing in that! They had been good friends for years, nothing more, and he was a perfect dear.

But she couldn't fool me. I could see that there was something working at the back of her mind, but whether she was distressed or gratified I was not by way of knowing.

"I've never heard her mention Lord Amberdale," said I.

Her eyes narrowed slightly. Had I but known, the mere fact that the Countess had *not* spoken of his lordship provided her experienced mother with an excellent reason for believing that there was something between them. She abruptly brought the conversation to a close and left me, saying that she was off for her beauty nap.

Alone, I soon became a prey to certain disquieting thoughts. Summed up, they resolved themselves into a condition of certainty which admitted of but one aspect: the charming Countess was in love with Amberdale. And the shocking part of it all was that she was in love with him prior to her separation from Tarnowsy! I felt a cold perspiration start out all over my body as this condition forced itself upon me. *He* was the man; *he* had been the man from the beginning. My heart was like lead for the rest of the day, and, very curiously, for a leaden thing it was subject to pain.

Just before dinner, Britton, after inspecting me out of the corner of his eye for some time, advised me to try a little brandy.

"You look seedy, sir," he said with concern in his voice. "A cold setting in perhaps, sir."

I tried the brandy, but not because I thought I was taking a cold. Somehow it warmed me up. There is virtue in good spirits.

The Countess was abroad very early the next morning. I discovered her in the courtyard, giving directions to Max and Rudolph who were doing some spading in the garden. She looked very bright and fresh and enticing in the light of an early moon, and I was not only pleased but astonished, having been led to believe all my life that a woman, no matter how pretty she may be, appears at her worst when the day is young.

I joined her at once. She gave me a gay, accusing smile.

"What have you been saying to mother?" she demanded, as she shook hands with me. "I thought you were to be trusted."

I flushed uncomfortably. "I'm sorry, Countess. I—I didn't know it was a secret."

She looked at me somewhat quizzically for a moment. Then she laughed softly. "It is a secret."

"I hope I haven't got you into bad odour with your—"

"Oh, dear me, no! I'm not in the least worried over what mother may think. I shall do as I please, so there's the end of it."

I swallowed something that seemed to be sticking in my throat. "Then it is true that you are going to marry?"

"Quite," she said succinctly.

I was silent for a moment. "Well, I'm—I'm glad to know it in time," I said, rather more gruffly than was necessary.

She smiled too merrily, I thought. "You must not tell any one else about it, however."

"I can promise that," I said, a sullen rage in my soul. "Devils could not drag it out of me. Rest easy."

It occurred to me afterwards that she laughed rather jerkily, you might say uneasily. At any rate, she turned away and began speaking to Max.

"Have you had your breakfast?" I asked stupidly.

"No."

"Neither have I. Will you join me?"

"Isn't it getting to be a habit?"

"Breakfast or—you?"

"Breakfast *and* me."

"I confess, my dear Countess, that I like you for breakfast," I said gallantly.

"That is a real tribute," she said demurely, and took her place beside me. Together we crossed the courtyard.

On the steps Colingraft Titus was standing. I uttered an audible groan and winced as if in dire pain.

"What is it?" she cried quickly.

"Rheumatism," I announced, carefully raising my right arm and affecting an expression of torture. I am not a physical coward, kind reader. The fact that young Mr. Titus carried in his hands a set of formidable looking boxing-gloves did not frighten me. Heaven knows, if it would give him any pleasure to slam me about with a pair of gloves, I am not without manliness and pluck enough to endure physical pain and mental humiliation. It was diplomacy, cunning, astuteness,—whatever you may choose to call it,—that stood between me and a friendly encounter with him. Two minutes' time would serve to convince him that he was my master, and then where would I be? Where would be the prestige I had gained? Where my record as a conqueror? "I must have caught cold in my arms and shoulders," I went on, making worse faces than before as I moved the afflicted parts experimentally.

"There!" she exclaimed ruefully. "I *knew* you would catch cold. Men always do. I'm so sorry."

"It's nothing," I made haste to explain:—"that is, nothing serious. I'll get rid of it in no time at all." I calculated for a minute. "A week or ten days at the most. Good morning, Colingraft."

"Morning. Hello, sis. Well?" He dangled the gloves before my eyes.

My disappointment was quite pathetic. "Tell him," I said to the Countess.

"He's all crippled up with rheumatism, Colly," she said. "Put those ugly things away. We're going in to breakfast."

He tossed the gloves into a corner of the vestibule. I felt a little ashamed of my subterfuge in the face of his earnest expression of concern.

"Tell you what I'll do," he said warmly. "I know how to rub a fellow's muscles—"

"Oh, I have a treasure in Britten," said I, hastily. "Thanks, old man. He will work it out of me. Sorry we can't have a go this morning."

The worst of it all was that he insisted, as a matter of personal education, on coming to my room after breakfast to watch the expert manœuvres of Britton in kneading the stiffness out of my muscles. He was looking for new ideas, he explained. I first consulted Britton and then resignedly consented to the demonstration.

To my surprise, Britton was something of an expert. I confess that he almost killed me with those strong, iron-like hands of his; if I was not sore when he began with me, I certainly was when he finished. Colingraft was most enthusiastic. He said he'd never seen any one manipulate the muscles so scientifically as Britton, and ventured the opinion that he would not have to repeat the operation often. To myself I said that he wouldn't have to repeat it at all.

We began laying our plans for the fourteenth. Communications arrived from Italy, addressed to me but intended for either the Countess or the rather remote Mr. Bangs, who seemed better qualified to efface himself than any human being I've ever seen. These letters informed us that a yacht—one of three now cruising in the-Mediterranean—would call at an appointed port on such and such a day to take her out to sea. Everything was being arranged on the outside for her escape from the continent, and precision seamed to be the watchword.

Of course I couldn't do a stroke of work on my novel. How could I be expected to devote myself to fiction when fact was staring me in the face so engagingly? We led an idle, **dolce far niente** life in these days, with an underlying touch of anxiety and excitement that increased as the day for her departure drew near. I confess to a sickening sense of depression that could not be shaken off.

Half of my time was spent in playing with Rosemary. She became dearer to me with each succeeding day. I knew I should miss her tremendously. I should even miss Jinko, who didn't like me but who no longer growled at me. The castle would be a very gloomy, drear place after they were out of it. I found myself wondering how long I would be able to endure the loneliness. Secretly I cherished the idea of selling the place if I could find a lunatic in the market.

An unexpected diversion came one day when, without warning and figuratively out of a clear sky, the Hazzards and the Billy Smiths swooped down upon me. They had come up the river in the power boat for a final September run, and planned to stop over night with me!

They were the last people in the world whom I could turn away from my door. There might have been a chance to put them up for the night and still avoid disclosures, had not circumstance ordered that the Countess and I should be working in the garden at the very moment that brought them pounding at the postern gates. Old Conrad opened the gate in complete ignorance of our presence in the garden. (We happened to be in a somewhat obscure nook and seated upon a stone bench— so he must be held blameless.) The quartette brushed past the old man and I, hearing their chatter, foolishly exposed myself.

I shall not attempt to describe the scene that followed their discovery of the Countess Tarnowsy. Be it said, however, to the credit of Elsie and Betty Billy, the startled refugee was fairly smothered in kisses and tears and almost deafened by the shrill, delighted exclamations that fell from their eager lips. I doubt if there ever was such a sensation before!

They brought rather interesting news concerning the Count. It appears that he and the baron had quarrelled and at the time of my friends' departure from Vienna it was pretty generally understood that there would be a duel.

"I never liked the baron," I said, with a grim smile that could not have been misinterpreted, "but I hope to heavens *he* isn't killed."

Mrs. Titus sighed. "Tarnowsy is regarded as a wonderful marksman."

"Worse luck!" growled Colingraft, gloomily twiddling his thumbs.

"What kind of a shot is the baron?" asked Jasper Jr., hopefully.

No one was able to enlighten him, but Billy Smith shook his head dolefully.

"Maris Tarnowsy is a dead shot. He'll pot the baron sure."

"Hang it all," said I, and then lapsed into a horrified silence.

When the Hazzards and Smiths departed the next morning they were in full possession of all of our plans, hopes and secrets, but they were bound by promises that would have haunted them throughout all eternity if they allowed them to be violated. I do not recall having seen two more intensely excited, radiant women in my life than Elsie and Betty Billy. They were in an ecstatic state of mind. Their husbands, but little less excited, offered to help us in every way possible, and, to prove their earnest, turned the prow of the motor-boat down-stream, abandoning the trip up the river in order to be in Vienna in case I should need them for any purpose whatsoever.

"You may rest easy so far as I am concerned, Mrs. Titus," said the young diplomat. "As a representative of the United States government I can't become publicly involved in this international muddle. I've just *got* to keep my lips sealed. If it were discovered that I knew of all this, my head would be under the snickersnee in no time at all. Swish! Officially suicided!"

At ten o'clock the next morning I was called to the telephone. Smith had startling news to impart. Count Tarnowsy and Baron Umovitch had engaged in a duel with pistols at sunrise and the latter had gone down with a bullet through his lungs! He died an hour later. Tarnowsy, according to the rumours flying about official Vienna, was already on his way to Berlin, where he would probably remain in seclusion until the affair blew over or imperial forgiveness was extended to him.

There was cause for satisfaction among us, even though the baron had fallen instead of the count. The sensational affair would serve to keep Tarnowsy under cover for some weeks at least and minimise the dangers attending the Countess's flight from the castle. Still, I could not help feeling disappointed over the outcome of the meeting. Why couldn't Count Tarnowsy have been the one to fall?

The Countess, very pale and distrait, gave utterance to her feelings in a most remarkable speech. She said: "This is one of the few fine things that Maris has ever done. I am glad that he killed that man. He should have done so long ago,—the beast! He was—ugh!—the most despicable creature I've ever known."

She said no more than this, but one could readily grasp all that she left unuttered.

Colingraft rather sententiously remarked to little Rosemary, who could not have comprehended the words, of course: "Well, little Rosebud, your papa may be a spendthrift but he never wastes bullets."

Which was entirely uncalled for, I contend. I was struck by the swift look of dread that leaped into Aline's eyes and her pallor.

On top of all this came the astonishing news, by cipher despatch from old Jasper Titus's principal adviser in London, that his offer of one million dollars had been declined by Tarnowsy two days before, the Count having replied through his lawyers that nothing short of two millions would induce him to relinquish all claims to his child.

I had been ignorant of this move in the case, and expressed my surprise.

"I asked father to do it, Mr. Smart," said the Countess dejectedly. "It seemed the easiest way out of our difficulties—and the cheapest. He will never give in to this new demand, though. We must make the best of it."

"But why did you suggest such a thing to him?" I demanded with heat.

She looked hurt. "Because *you* seemed to think it was the right and honourable thing to do," she said patiently. "I do not forget what you said to me, days and days ago, even though it may have slipped your mind. You said that a bargain is a bargain and—well, I had Mr. Bangs write father just what you thought about it."

There was a suspicion of tears in her voice as she turned away and left me without another word. She was quite out of sight around the bend in the staircase, and her little boots were clattering swiftly upwards, before I fully grasped the significance of her explanation—or, I might better say, her reproach. It slowly dawned upon me that I had said a great many things to her that it would pay me to remember before questioning her motives in any particular.

As the day for her departure drew nearer,—it was now but forty-eight hours away,—her manner seemed to undergo a complete change. She became moody, nervous, depressed. Of course, all this was attributable to the dread of discovery and capture when she was once outside the great walls of Schloss Rothhoefen. I could understand her feelings, and rather lamely attempted to bolster up her courage by making light of the supposed perils.

She looked at me with a certain pathetic sombreness in her eyes that caused my heart to ache. All of her joyous raillery was gone, all of her gentle arrogance. Her sole interest in life in these last days seemed to be of a sacrificial nature. She was sweet and gentle with every one,—with me in particular, I may say,—and there was something positively humble in her attitude of self-abnegation. Where she had once been wilful and ironic, she was now gentle and considerate. Nor was I the only one to note these subtle changes in her. I doubt, however, if the others were less puzzled than I. In fact, Mrs. Titus was palpably perplexed, and there were times when I caught her eyeing me with distinct disapproval, as if she were seeking in me the cause of her daughter's weaknesses; as much as to say: "What other nonsense have you been putting into the poor child's head, you wretch?"

I went up to have a parting romp with Rosemary on the last night of her stay with me, to have my last sip of honey from her delectable neck. The Countess paid but little attention to us. She sat over in the window and stared out into the dusky shadows of the falling night. My heart was sore. I was miserable. The last romp!

Blake finally snatched Rosemary off to bed. It was then that the Countess aroused herself and came over to me with a sad little smile on her lips.

"Good night," she said, rather wistfully, holding out her hand to me.

I deliberately glanced at my watch. "It's only ten minutes past eight," I said, reproachfully.

"I know," she said, quietly. "Good night."

CHAPTER XVIII

I SPEED THE PARTING GUEST

FOUR o'clock in the morning is a graceless hour. Graveyards may yawn at twelve but even they are content to slumber at four. I don't believe there is anything so desolate in this world as the mental perspective one obtains at four o'clock. Tombstones are bright beacons of cheer as compared to the monumental regret one experiences on getting up to greet the alleged and vastly over-rated glories of a budding day. The sunrise is a pall! It is a deadly, dour thing. It may be pink and red and golden and full of all the splendours of the east, but it is a resurrection and you can't make anything else out of it. Staying up till four and then going to bed gives one an idea of the sunrise that is not supported by the facts; there is but one way to appreciate the real nature of the hateful thing called dawn, and that is to get up with it instead of taking it to bed with you.

Still, I suppose the sun *has* to come up and perhaps it is just as well that it does so at an hour when people are least likely to suspect it of anything so shabby.

Four o'clock is more than a graceless, sodden hour when it ushers in a day that you know is to be the unhappiest in your life; when you know that you are to say farewell forever to the hopes begot and nurtured in other days; when the one you love smiles and goes away to smile again but not for you. And that is just what four o'clock on the morning of the fourteenth of September meant to me.

Britton and I set forth in the automobile just at the break of dawn, crossing the river a few miles below the castle, and running back to a point on the right hand bank where we were to await the arrival of the boat conveying the Countess and her escort. Her luggage, carefully disguised as crated merchandise, had gone to Trieste by fast express a couple of days before, sent in my name and consigned to a gentleman whose name I do not now recall, but who in reality served as a sort of middleman in transferring the shipment to the custody of a certain yacht's commander.

It was required of me—and of my machine, which is more to the point—that the distance of one hundred and twenty miles through the foothills of the Austrian Alps should be covered and the passengers delivered at a certain railway station fifty miles or more south of Vienna before ten o'clock that night. There they were to catch a train for the little seaport on the upper Adriatic, the name of which I was sworn never to reveal, and, as I have not considered it worth while to be released from that oath, I am of necessity compelled to omit the mention of it here.

Mr. Bangs went on to Vienna the night before our departure, taking with him Helene Marie Louise Antoinette, a rather shocking arrangement you would say unless you had come to know the British lawyer as well as we knew him. They were to proceed by the early morning train to this obscure seaport. Colingraft Titus elected to accompany his sister the entire length of the journey, with the faithful Blake and Rosemary.

Billy Smith was to meet us a few miles outside the town for which we were bound, with a word of warning if there was anything sinister in the wind.

I heard afterwards from Poopendyke that the departure of the Countess and Rosemary from the castle in the grey; forlorn dawn of that historic fourteenth was attended by a demonstration of grief on the part of the four Schmicks that was far beyond his powers of description, and he possesses a wonderful ability to describe lachrymose situations, rather running to that style of incident, I may say. The elder Schmicks wailed and boo-hooed and proclaimed to the topmost turrets that the sun would never shine again for either of them, and, to prove that she was quite in earnest about the matter, Gretel fell off the dock into the river and was nearly drowned before Jasper, Jr., could dive in and get her. Their sons, both of whom cherished amorous feelings for Blake, sighed so prodigiously all the way down the river that the boat rocked. Incidentally, during the excitement, Jinko, who was to remain behind and journey westward later on with Mrs. Titus and Jasper, Jr., succeeded after weeks of vain endeavour in smartly nipping the calf of Hawkes' left leg, a feat of which he no doubt was proud but which sentenced my impressive butler to an everlasting dread of hydrophobia and a temporary limp.

It was nearing five o'clock when the boat slipped into view around the tree-covered point of land and headed straight for our hiding place on the bank.

I shall not stop here to describe the first stage of our journey through the narrow, rocky by-roads that ended eventually in the broad, alpine highway south and west of Vienna. Let it be sufficient to say that we jostled along for twelve or fifteen miles without special incident, although we were nervously anxious and apprehensive. Our guide book pointed, or rather twiddled, a route from the river flats into the hills, where we came up with the main road about eight o'clock.

We were wrapped and goggled to the verge of ludicrousness. It would have been quite impossible to penetrate our motor-masks and armour, even for one possessed of a keen and practiced eye. The Countess was heavily veiled; great goggles bulged beneath the green, gauzy thing that protected her lovely face from sun, wind and man. A motor coat, two or three sizes too large, enveloped her slender, graceful figure, and gauntlets covered her hands. Even Rosemary's tiny face was wrapped in a silken veil of white. As for the rest of us, we could not have been mistaken for anything on earth but American automobilists, ruthlessly inspired to see Europe with the sole view to comparing her roads with our own at home. You would have said, on seeing us, that we knew a great deal about roads and very little about home.

Colingraft and Britton,—the latter at the wheel,—sat in the front seat, while I shared the broad cushions of the tonneau with the Countess, part of the time holding Rosemary, who was clamouring for food, and the rest of the time holding my breath in the fear that we might slip over a precipice. I am always nervous when not driving the car myself.

We stopped for breakfast at a small mountain inn, fifteen miles from our starting place. The Countess, a faint red spot in each cheek and a curiously bright, feverish glow in her dark eyes, revealed a tendency to monopolise the conversation, a condition properly attributed to nervous excitement. I could see that she was vastly thrilled by the experiences of the hour; her quick, alert brain was keeping pace with the rush of blood that stimulated every fibre in her body to new activities. She talked almost incessantly, and chiefly about matters entirely foreign to the enterprise in hand. The more I see of women, the less I know about them. Why she should have spent the whole half hour devoted to breakfast to a surprisingly innocuous dissertation on Schopenhauer and Nietzsche is—or was—beyond me.

How was I to know that tears lay close to the surface of those shimmering, vivacious eyes? How was I to know that sobs took refuge behind a simulated interest in philosophy?

We had luncheon picnic fashion half-way to our journey's end, diverging from the main road to find a secluded spot where we could spread our cloth and open our hampers without fear of interruption or, to use a more sinister word, detection. It was rather a jolly affair, that first and last al fresco banquet of ours under the spreading branches of mighty trees and beside the trickling waters of a gay little mountain brook that hurried like mad down to the broad channel of the Danube, now many miles away. The strain of the first few hours had slackened. Success seemed assured. We had encountered no difficulties, no dangers in town or country. No one appeared to be interested in us except through idle curiosity; villagers and peasants stared at us and grinned; policemen and soldiers stood aside to let us pass, or gave directions politely when requested to do so. There were no signs of pursuit, no indications of trouble ahead. And so we could afford to be gay and confident at our midday meal in the hills bordering the broad highway.

We even went so far as to arrange for a jolly reunion in New York City at no distant day! I remember distinctly that we were to dine at Sherry's. To me, the day seemed a long way off.

I suppose, being a writer of fiction, I should be able to supply at this point in the narrative, a series of thrilling, perhaps hair-raising encounters with the enemy, in the form of spies, cut-throats, imperial mercenaries or whatever came handiest to the imagination. It would be a very simple matter to transform this veracious history into the most lurid of melodramas by the introduction of the false and bizarre, but it is not my purpose to do so. I mean to adhere strictly to the truth and stand by the consequences. Were I inclined to sensationalism it would be no trouble at all for me to have Tarnowsy's agents shooting at our tires or gasoline tank from every crag and cranny; or to have Rosemary kidnapped by aeroplanists supplied with drag-hooks; or to have the Countess lodged in a village prison from which I should be obliged to liberate her with battle-axe and six-shooter, my compensation being a joyous rest in a hospital with the fair Aline nursing me back to health and strength and cooing fond words in my rapacious ear the while I reflected on the noble endowments of a nature that heretofore had been commonplace and meek. But, no! None of these things happened and I decline to perjure myself for the privilege of getting into the list of "six best sellers."

So far as I am able to judge, there was absolutely no heroism displayed during our flight through the hills and valleys, unless you are willing to accept as such a single dash of sixty miles an hour which Britton made in order to avoid a rain-shower that threatened to flank us if we observed the speed laws.

But wait! There was an example of bravado on my part that shall not go unrecorded. I hesitated at first to put it down in writing, but my sense of honour urges me to confess everything. It happened just after that memorable picnic luncheon in the shady dell. The Countess, I maintain, was somewhat to blame for the incident.

She suggested that we,—that is to say, the two of us,—explore the upper recesses of this picturesque spot while the others were making ready for the resumption of our journey.

Shame, contrition, humiliation or whatever you may elect to call it, forbids a lengthy or even apologetic explanation of what followed her unfortunate suggestion. I shall get over with it in as few words as possible.

In the most obscure spot in all those ancient hills, I succumbed to an execrable impulse to take her forcibly in my arms and kiss her! I don't know why I did it, or how, but that is just what happened. My shame, my horror over the transcendental folly was made almost unbearable by the way in which she took it. At first I thought she had swooned, she lay so limp and unresisting in my arms. My only excuse, whispered penitently in her ear, was that I couldn't help doing what I had done, and that I deserved to be drawn and quartered for taking advantage of my superior strength and her gentle forbearance. Strange to say, she merely looked at me in a sort of dumb wonder and quietly released herself, still staring at me as if I were the most inexplicable puzzle in the world. Her cheeks, her throat, her brow grew warm and pink with a just indignation; her lips parted but she uttered no word. Then I followed her dejectedly, cravenly back to the roadside and executed an inward curse that would hang over my miserable head so long as it was on my shoulders.

Her vivacity was gone. She shrank down into the corner of the seat, and, with her back half turned toward me, gazed steadfastly at the panoramic valley which we were skirting. From time to time I glanced, at her out of the corners of my eyes, and eventually was somewhat relieved to see that she had closed her own and was dozing. My soul was in despair. She loathed, despised me. I could not blame her. I despised myself.

And yet my heart quickened every time I allowed myself to think of the crime I had committed.

The day was a glorious one and the road more than passably good. We bowled along at a steady rate of speed and sundown found us about twenty-five miles from our destination. Not caring to run the risk of a prolonged stay in the town, we drew up at a roadside inn and had our dinner in the quaint little garden, afterwards proceeding leisurely by moonlight down the sloping highway.

Billy Smith met us six or eight miles out and we stopped to parley. He examined the Countess's skilfully prepared passports, pronounced them genuine (!), and then gave us the cheerful news that "everything was lovely and the goose hung high." The train for the coast was due to leave the Staats-bahn-hof at 10.05, and we had an hour to spare. He proposed that we spend it quite comfortably at the roadside while Britton went through the pretence of repairing our tires. This seemed an agreeable arrangement for every one but Britton, who looked so glum that I, glad of the excuse, offered to help him.

No sooner was I out of the car and Billy Smith in my place beside the Countess than she became quite gay and vivacious once more. She laughed and chatted with him in a manner that promptly convinced me that propinquity so far as I was concerned had had a most depressing effect upon her, and that she revelled in the change of companions.

I was so disturbed by the discovery that Britton had to caution me several times to handle the inner tubes less roughly or I **would** damage them and we might suffer a blow-out after all.

Every one appeared to be gay and frivolous, even Blake, who chattered *sotto voce* with Britton, that excellent rascal spending most of his time leaning against the spare tires in order to catch what she was saying for his benefit. All efforts to draw me into the general conversation were unavailing. I was as morose and unresponsive as an Egyptian mummy, and for a very excellent reason, I submit. The Countess deliberately refused to address a single remark to me. Indeed, when I seemed perilously near to being drawn into the conversation she relapsed into a silence that was most forbidding. My cup of misery was overflowing.

I wondered if she would feel called upon, at some distant confessional, to tell the fortunate Lord Amberdale that I had brutally kissed her. And Lord Amberdale would grin in his beastly supercilious English way and say: "What else could you have expected from a bally American bounder?" She would no doubt smile indulgently.

Heigh-ho!

All things come to an end, however. We found ourselves at last uttering our good-byes in the railway station, surrounded by hurrying travelers and attended by eager porters.

The Countess did not lift her veil. I deliberately drew her aside. My hot hand clasped hers, and found it as cold as ice and trembling.

"For God's sake," I whispered hoarsely in my humbleness, "say that you forgive me?"

She did not speak for many seconds. Then her voice was very low and tremulous. I felt that her sombre eyes were accusing me even as they tried to meet my own with a steadiness that was meant to be reassuring.

"Of course I forgive you," she said. "You have been so good to me."

"Good!" I cried bitterly. "I've been harsh, unreasoning, super-critical from the day I met—"

"Hush!" she said, laying her free hand upon my arm. "I shall never forget all that you have done for me. I—I can say no more."

I gulped. "I pray to heaven that you may be happy, Aline,—happier than any one else in the world."

She lowered her head suddenly, and I was made more miserable than before by hearing a quick, half-suppressed sob. Then she withdrew her cold little hand and turned away to follow Colingraft who had called out to her.

I saw them board the train. In my heart there was the memory of a dozen kisses I had bestowed in repentant horror upon the half-asleep Rosemary, who, God bless her little soul, cried bitterly on being torn away from my embrace.

"Well," said Billy Smith, taking me by the arm a few minutes later, "let's have a bite to eat and a cold bottle before we go to bed, old chap. I hope to heaven she gets through all right. Damme, I am strong for her, aren't you?"

"I am," said I, with conviction, coming out of a daze.

He led me off to a café where he seemed to be more or less at home, and where it was bright and gay for him but gloomier than the grave to me.

I drove the car home the next day. When we got down at the garage, Britton shivered and drew a prodigious breath. It was as if he had not breathed for hours. We had gone the distance in little more than half the time taken on the trip down.

"My word, sir," was all he said, but there was a significant tremor in his voice. It smacked of pride.

Mrs. Titus placidly inquired how we had got along, and appeared quite relieved when I told her we had caught the train at K——. Jasper, Jr., revealed a genuine interest in the enterprise, but spoiled it all by saying that Aline, now prematurely safe, was most likely to leap out of the frying-pan into the fire by marrying some blithering foreigner and having the whole beastly business to do over again.

"How soon do they go?" asked Poopendyke late that afternoon, after listening to Mrs. Titus's amiable prophecies concerning Aline's future activities, and getting my harassed ear in a moment of least resistance.

"I don't know," said I, hopelessly. I had heard about all I could endure concerning his lordship's magnificent estates in England, and the sort of a lord he was besides. "There's nothing to do but wait, Fred."

"She is a remarkably fine woman but—" He completed the estimate by shaking his head, trusting to my intelligence, I suppose.

We waited two days for word from the fugitives. Late in the afternoon of the second day, Britton returned from town with a telegram for me. It said:

"Cargo safely aboard *Pendennis*, Captain Pardee commanding. Clear at two to-day. Everything satisfactory.
(Signed) "C. G. RAFT."

No sooner was this reassuring news received than Mrs. Titus complacently set about having her trunks packed. The entire household was in a stew of activity, for she had suddenly decided to catch the eight o'clock train for Paris. I telephoned to reserve accommodation on the Orient Express from Vienna, and also to have it stopped at the town across the river, a concession secured at a no inconsiderable cost.

She was to travel once more as my mother.

"You will not fail to look us up when you come to New York, will you, Mr. Smart? Mr. Titus will not be happy until he has expressed to you in person his endless gratitude. You have been splendid. We shall never forget your kindness, your thoughtfulness, your—your forbearance. I—I—"

Upon my word, there were real tears in the dear lady's eyes! I forgot and forgave much in recognition of this instant of genuine feeling on her part. It was not necessary for her to complete the sentence so humbly begun.

Their departure was made with some degree of caution, Mrs. Titus rather considerately reminding herself that my interests were at stake. I saw them aboard the train; she played her part admirably, I will say that for her. She lifted her veil so that I could bestow a farewell filial kiss upon her cheek. Jasper, Jr.'s, eyes popped very wide open at this, and, as he shook my hand warmly at parting, he said:

"You are a wonder, John,—a sure enough wonder. Why, hang it all, she doesn't even let dad do that."

But Jasper, Jr., was very young and he couldn't understand.

At last we were to ourselves, my extensive household and I. Late that night I sat in my study considering the best means of reducing my staff of servants and in computing, with dismay, the cost of being a princely host to people who had not the least notion what it meant to do sums in economic subtraction. It was soon apparent to me that retrenchment, stern and relentless, would have to follow upon my wild though brief season of profligacy. I decided to dismiss the scullery-maid.

I was indescribably lonely. Poopendyke was worried about my pallor, my lassitude. At the end of a week, he took it upon himself to drop a line to the Hazzards, urging them to run out for a visit in the hope that company might take me out of myself. All attempts to renew my work on the ill-fated novel met with utter failure. The power of mental concentration was gone. I spent most of my time in the garden.

The Hazzards came and with them the joyously beautiful Betty Billy. Poopendyke must have prepared them for the task in hand, for they proceeded at once to transform the bleak, dreary old castle into a sort of hilarious merry-go-round, with me in the very vortex of it all. They succeeded in taking me "out of myself," I will say that for them. My spirits took an upward bound and, wonderful to relate, retained their altitude in spite of all I could do to lower them. I did not want to be happy; I figured that I owed it to my recently aroused temperament to be permanently unhappy. But the wind blew another way and I drifted amiably with it, as a derelict drifts with the currents of the ocean but preferably with the warm gulf stream.

We had word from Mrs. Titus, in London, that negotiations had been reopened with the Count, and that a compromise might be expected. The obdurate nobleman had agreed, it seemed, to meet Jasper Titus's lawyers in Paris at no distant date. My chief concern however was for the Countess herself. That she had successfully reached the high seas was apparent; if not, the newspapers, which I read with eagerness, would have been filled with accounts of her seizure. We eagerly awaited the promised cablegram from New York, announcing her safe arrival there.

Smith joined us at the end of the week. I nerved myself to question him about the Englishman.

"Splendid fellow," said he, with discouraging fervour. "One of the finest chaps I know, eh, George?"

"For an Englishman," admitted Hazzard.

"He's a gentleman, and that's more than you can say for the rag-tag of nobility that paid court to Aline Tarnowsy. He was in love with her, but he was a gentleman about it. A thoroughbred, I say."

"Good looking?" I enquired.

"Well, rather! The sort of chap women rave about. Ask Betty. She was mad about him. But he couldn't see anything in her. I think she hates him now. He had eyes for no one but the fair Countess. An awful grind on Betty. She's used to something different."

Hazzard studied the clouds that drifted over our heads. "I wonder if Aline cared anything for him."

"I've always believed that she liked him better than she cared to admit, even to herself."

"I fancy he'll not let any grass grow under his feet, now that she's free," said Dr. Hazzard.

"Think she'll have him?"

"Why not? He has a much better position in England than Tarnowsy has here, and he's not after her money. I hate to say it, but Aline is a seeker after titles. She wouldn't be averse to adding 'your ladyship' to her collection."

"Oh, come!" I protested. "That is a nasty thing to say, George."

"She may have been regenerated," he said obligingly. "You know her better than I do, old chap. What say?"

"I didn't say anything," I muttered.

"I thought you did."

I hesitated a moment and then purged myself of the truth. "As a matter of fact, I have reason to believe she's in love with Amberdale and has been for a long time. I'm not saying it in disparagement, believe me. God knows she's entitled to something decent and fine in the shape of love. I hope he's good enough for her."

They looked at me with interest, and Smith broke the momentary silence.

"Oh, he's good enough for her," he said, with a queer smile.

"I'm glad of that," I said gruffly.

"The old la—I mean Mrs. Titus will be tickled to death if the match is pulled off," said Hazzard.

"She was tickled the first time," said I sententiously, and changed the subject. There was no sense in prolonging the agony.

Toward the close of their visit, a message arrived from the Countess herself, signed with the fictitious name we had agreed upon. The news she gave caused us to celebrate that night. We had a bonfire in the courtyard and drank to the god of Good Luck.

"Cargo safely landed in New York and forwarded to the Adirondacks for storage and to await the appearance of a claimant. Former owner has agreed to accept million and a half and release all claims. When are you coming over? (Signed) Alrose."

By the most extraordinary coincidence, a curt, business-like letter arrived in the evening post from Maris Tarnowsy, post-marked Paris. Its contents staggered me.

"*John Bellamy Smart, Esquire.*

"DEAR MR. SMART: Will you put a price on Schloss Rothhoefen? I am desirous of purchasing the castle if you care to sell and we can agree upon a fair price for the property. Sentiment moves me in this matter and I earnestly hope that you may be induced to part with your white elephant. If you will be so kind as to wire your decision, you will find me deeply grateful, and at the Ritz for the ensuing fortnight.

"Faithfully yours,
"MARIS TARNOWSY."

My "white elephant!" I was so eager to get rid of it that I would have wired at once, naming a figure proportionately low had it not been for the united protests of my four friends and the canny advice of Mr. Poopendyke.

"Soak him," said he, and I arose to the occasion.

I waited for three days and then telegraphed him that I would not take a heller less than two hundred and fifty thousand dollars, more than doubling the price I had paid for the property. I was prepared, however, to come down a paltry hundred thousand or so if he revealed signs of reluctance.

We built another bonfire that night and danced around it like so many savages.

"Terms acceptable. Will come to Schloss Rothhoefen at once to complete the transfer.

"TARNOWSY."

CHAPTER XIX

I BURN A FEW BRIDGES

Accompanied by Hazzard and Smith, I went over the castle from top to bottom, in quest of the reason for Tarnowsy's prompt acceptance of my demand. We made no doubt that he had a good and sufficient reason for wanting the place, and but one thing suggested itself to our imagination: his absolute certainty that treasure was hidden somewhere about the venerable pile, treasure of considerable magnitude, you may be sure, or he would not have revealed such alacrity in accepting my terms. Sentiment had nothing to do with this surprising move on his part. That was all bosh. He had an ulterior motive, and it was for me to get the better of him at his own game if I could. While I was eager to get rid of the castle at any price, I did not relish the thought of being laughed at for a fool by Maris Tarnowsy after he had laid his greedy hands upon treasure that had been mine without my knowledge.

He was no fool. The castle meant nothing to him as a home or as an investment. No doubt he would blow it to pieces in order to unearth the thing he knew its walls secreted.

We spent two unprofitable days in going over the place, and in the end sank down tired, defeated and without the slightest evidence in our possession that so much as a half crown lay hidden there as treasure-trove. I gave in and announced that if Tarnowsy could find anything worth having he was entitled to it so far as I was concerned, and I wouldn't begrudge him a farthing's worth.

He telegraphed that he would arrive on the morning of the third day, accompanied by his lawyer, a notary and an architect. My four guests departed in haste by the late night train, after extracting a promise from me to join them in Vienna when I was no longer the master of Schloss Rothhoefen. I rather relished the thought of a brief vacation!

Then, like the spider, I crept back into my web and waited for the foolish fly, knowing all the time that he would have the better of me in the long run.

I confess to a feeling of sadness in parting with the place, after all, elephantine though it was in every sense of the word. Within its grey and ancient walls that beautiful thing called love had come to me, to live with me forever. It had come unbidden, against my will, against my better judgment, and in spite of my prejudices, but still it was a thing to cherish and to hold in its virgin youth all through the long years to come. It would always be young and sweet and rose-coloured, this unrequited love of mine. Walking through the empty, dismantled rooms that had once been hers, I grew sick with longing, and, in something like fear, fled downward, absurd tears blinding my eyes. Verily, I was a fool,—a monstrous, silly fool!

Tarnowsy was as bland and smiling as a May morning as he came jauntily down the great hall to where I awaited him.

"I am here incognito, my dear Smart," he said, extending his gloved hand, which I took perforce. "Sub rosa, you might say," he went on with a wry smile. "A stupid, unchivalric empire has designs upon me, perfunctorily perhaps, but it's just as well not to stir up the monkeys, as you Americans would put it."

"Our late friend, the baron, was not totally without friends, I take it," said I drily.

He made a grimace. "Nor enemies," he declared. "Brave men usually have more enemies than friends, and he was a brave man, a truly brave man. Because he was a brave man I have no feeling of regret over the outcome of our—er—meeting. It is no honour to kill a coward, Mr. Smart."

He introduced his three companions. I was surprised to see that the lawyer was not the fawning Schymansky, and later on inquired for him. Tarnowsy laughed. "Poor old Schymansky! He is in prison."

"Aha! I am not surprised," said I.

"He was my second, poor chap. It did not occur to him to run away after the— er—duel. They had to make an example of some one. His trial comes up next week. I am afraid he may be dealt with rather harshly. I miss him dreadfully. But let us come to the matter in hand, Mr. Smart. I daresay your time is valuable. You have no objection to my going over the place with Mr. Saks, I am sure. He is the architect who is to rebuild the castle for me. My attorney and Mr. Pooly,—the notary,—will, with your assistance, draw up the proper contracts preliminary to the formal trans- fer, and I will sign them with you upon my return."

"Would it not be better to discuss the question of payments before we go any further, Count Tarnowsy?"

"You will be paid in cash, Mr. Smart, the instant the deed is transferred," he said coldly.

I followed him to the top of the stairs which descended to the basement of the castle. It was rather significant that he elected to explore the lower regions first of all.

"I shall accompany you," said I deliberately.

A faint scowl came into his face. He eyed me fixedly for a moment, then shrugged his shoulders and said that his only desire was to avoid putting me to any unnecessary trouble. If I cared to come, he would be more than grateful.

"It isn't necessary to visit the cellars, Saks," he said to the architect. "Ample time for that sort of rummaging. I particularly want your opinion on the condition of the intersecting walls on this floor and above. My scheme of improvements, Mr. Smart, contemplates the enlargement of these halls by throwing them into one."

"A very simple process," said I, "if the whole structure doesn't topple down upon your heads while you're about it."

"I shall contrive to save my scalp, Mr. Smart, no matter what happens. It is very precious to me."

We went over the castle rather hurriedly, I thought, but he explained that Saks merely wanted a general idea of the structure; he would return another day to make a careful inspection.

"I daresay you are surprised that I should be willing to pay double your original price for Schloss Rothhoefen," he ventured, pausing in the corridor to light a cigarette. We were on our way to the top of the east wing.

"Oh, no," I said calmly. "I am aware that treasure is buried here. As a matter of fact, I've tried to unearth it myself, but without success. I wish you better luck."

"Thanks," said he laconically, after the first swift glance of inquiry. "It is doubt-less a fairy tale, handed down by tradition. I take no stock in it. My principal object in acquiring Rothhoefen is to satisfy a certain vanity which besets me. I have it on excellent authority that my ex-father-in-law,—the man Titus, you know,—talks of buying the property and performing the stupendous, characteristic American feat of removing it, stone and timber, just as it is, to his estate north of New York City. No one but a vulgar, purse-proud American would think of doing such a thing."

The news staggered me. Could there be anything in what he said? If it was true that Jasper Titus contemplated such a quixotic move, there could be but one com-pelling force behind the whim: sentiment. But not sentiment on the part of Jasper Titus.

"I cannot believe that he considers doing such a thing," I said rather blankly. "You see, if any one should know, I am that one. He has not approached me, of that you may be sure."

He did not appear to be interested.

"My information is not authoritative, Mr. Smart," said he. "It came to me through my representatives who conferred with his lawyers a fortnight ago in re-gard to certain difficulties that had existed between us. From what they were able to gather, the idea has taken root in the old man's head. Now, I want to buy this place for no other reason than to tell him that he hasn't enough money in his possession to purchase it from me. D'you see? Vanity, you may call it, as I do, but it pleases me to coddle it."

Very thoughtfully I strode along beside him. Would I be serving the Countess ill or well by selling the place to Tarnowsy? It was *her* whim, of course, and it was a foolish one.

"Suppose that he offered you twice what you are to pay me for the place," said

I, struck by a sudden thought.

He laughed easily. "You will not, it seems, acquit me of cupidity, Mr. Smart. I should not sell to him under any consideration. That is final. Take it or leave it."

By this time we were in the rooms once occupied by the Countess. He glanced about the apartment carelessly.

"Deserted, I observe," he remarked with a queer smile.

My heart almost stood still. "Eh? What do you mean?"

"If I am not mistaken, these are the rooms once occupied by your valet's wife. Am I right?"

I steadied myself. "She has gone away," I said. "Couldn't stand the climate."

"I see," said he, but he was still smiling. "How does your valet stand it?"

"Nicely," said I, with a conscious blush.

"I mean the separation, of course."

"Certainly. He is used to it."

"Isn't it rather odd that he should still think she is here, in the castle?"

"Does he?" I murmured.

"I inquired for her when I encountered him downstairs. He said she was quite well this morning, except for a headache."

"She is subject to headaches, I believe," said I, with the utmost nonchalance. He lifted his right eyebrow slightly, but said no more on the subject.

A pile of rubbish lay heaped in one corner of the room, swept up and left there by the big Schmicks to await the spring house cleaning season I presume. Tarnowsy at first eyed the heap curiously, then rather intently. Suddenly he strode across the room and gingerly rooted among the odds and ends with the toe of his highly polished boot.

To my horror a dilapidated doll detached itself and rolled out upon the floor,—a well-remembered treasure of Rosemary's and so unique in appearance that I doubt if there was another in the world like it. Indeed, I have a distinct recollection of being told that the child's father had painted in the extraordinary features and had himself decorated the original flaxen locks with singular stripes of red and white and blue, a sardonic tribute to the home land of her mother.

I turned away as he stooped and picked up the soiled, discarded effigy. When next I looked at him, out of the corner of my eye, he was holding the doll at arm's length and staring at it with a fixed gaze. I knew that he recognised it. There could be no doubt in his mind as to the identity of that tell-tale object. My heart was thumping fiercely.

An instant later he rejoined me, but not a word did he utter concerning the strange discovery he had made. His face was set and pallid, and his eyes were misty. Involuntarily I looked to see if he had the doll in his hand, and in that glance observed the bulging surface of his coat pocket.

In silence we stood there awaiting the reappearance of Saks, who had gone into one of the adjoining rooms. I confess that my hand trembled as I lighted a fresh cigarette. He was staring moodily at the floor, his hands clasped behind his back. Something smacking of real intelligence ordered me to hold my tongue. I smoked placidly, yet waited for the outburst. It did not come. It never came. He kept his thoughts, his emotions to himself, and for that single display of restraint on his part I shall always remember him as a true descendant of the nobility.

We tramped down the long flights of stairs side by side, followed by the superfluous Mr. Saks, who did all of the talking. He was, I think, discoursing on the extraordinary ability of ancient builders, but I am not absolutely certain. I am confident Tarnowsy did not hear a word the fellow said.

In my study we found Poopendyke and the two strangers.

"Have you made out the papers?" demanded the Count harshly. An ugly gleam had come to his eyes, but he did not direct it toward me. Indeed, he seemed to avoid looking at me at all.

"Yes, Count Tarnowsy," said the lawyer. "They are ready for the signatures."

"Perhaps Mr. Smart may have reconsidered his offer to sell," said Tarnowsy. "Let him see the contracts."

"I have not reconsidered," I said quietly.

"You may sign here, Mr. Smart," said the notary, as he gave me the document, a simple contract, I found.

"Jasper Titus will offer more than I can afford to pay," said the Count. "Please do not feel that I am taking an unfair advantage of you. I am absolutely certain that he wants to buy this place for—his granddaughter, a descendant of barons."

The significance of this remark was obvious, and it was the nearest he ever came to uttering the conviction that had been formed in that illuminating five minutes upstairs. If he suspected,—and I think he did,—he preferred not to ask the questions that must have been searing his curious brain. It was a truly wonderful demonstration of self-restraint. I would have given much to have been able to read his innermost thoughts, to watch the perplexed movements of his mind.

"Schloss Rothhoefen is yours, Count Tarnowsy," said I. "It is for you to say whether his whim shall be gratified."

His lips twitched. I saw his hand touch the bulging coat-pocket with a swift, passing movement.

"Will you be good enough to sign, Mr. Smart?" he said coldly. He glanced at his watch. "My time is valuable. When can you give possession?"

"The day the deed is transferred."

"That will be in less than three days. I have satisfied myself that the title is clear. There need be no delay."

We signed the contract after I had requested Poopendyke to read it aloud to me. It called for the payment of fifty thousand kronen, or a little over two thousand pounds sterling, at the time of signing. His lawyer handed me a package of crisp banknotes and asked me to count them. I did so deliberately, the purchaser looking on with a sardonic smile.

"Correct," said I, laying the package on the table. He bowed very deeply.

"Are you satisfied, Mr. Smart, that there are no counterfeits among them?" he inquired with polite irony. Then to his lawyer: "Take the gentleman's receipt for the amount in the presence of witnesses. This is a business transaction, not a game of chance." It was the insult perfect.

As he prepared to take his departure, he assumed an insinuating air of apology, and remarked to me:

"I owe you an apology, Mr. Smart. There was a time when I did you an injustice. I suspected you of keeping your mistress here. Pray forgive my error."

Five days later I was snugly ensconced in the ducal suite at the Bristol, overlooking the Kartnerring-strasse, bereft of my baronial possessions but not at all sorry. My romance had been short-lived. It is one thing to write novels about mediaeval castles and quite another thing to try to write a novel in one of them. I trust I may never again be guilty of such arrant stupidity as to think that an American-born citizen can become a feudal baron by virtue of his dollars and cents, any more than an American-born girl can hope to be a real, dyed-in-the-wool countess or duchess because some one needs the money more than she does. It would be quite as impossible, contrariwise, to transform a noble duke into a plain American citizen, so there you are, even up.

My plans were made. After a fortnight in Vienna, I expected to go west to London for the autumn, and then back to New York. Strange to relate, I was homesick. Never before had my thoughts turned so restlessly, so wistfully to the haunts of my boyhood days. I began to long for the lights of Broadway (which I had scornfully despised in other days), and the gay peacockery of Fifth Avenue at four in the afternoon. It seemed to me that nowhere in all the world was life so joyous and blithe and worth while as in "old New York"; nowhere were the theatres so attractive, nowhere such restaurants. Even, in retrospect, the subway looked alluring, and as for the Fifth Avenue stages they were too beautiful for words. Ah, what a builder of unreal things a spell of homesickness may become if one gives it half a chance!

As for Schloss Rothhoefen, I had it on excellent authority (no less a person than Conrad Schmick himself) that barely had I shaken the dust of the place from myself before the new master put into execution a most extraordinary and incomprehensible plan of reconstruction. In the first place, he gave all the servants two weeks' notice, and then began to raze the castle from the bottom upward instead of the other way round, as a sensible person might have been expected to do. He was knocking out the walls in the cellars and digging up the stone floors with splendid disregard for that ominous thing known as a cataclysm. The grave question in the minds of the servants was whether the usual and somewhat mandatory two weeks' notice wouldn't prove a trifle too long after all. In fact, Hawkes, with an inspiration worthy of an office boy, managed to produce a sick grand-mother and got away from the place at the end of one week, although having been paid in full for two.

The day on which I left for Pans still saw Tarnowsy at work with his masons, heroically battering down the walls of the grim old stronghold, and I chuckled to myself. It was quite evident that he hadn't found the hiding place up to that time.

After several days in Paris, I took myself off to London. I was expecting letters at Claridge's, where I always take rooms, not because I think it is the best hotel in London but because I am, to some extent, a creature of habit. My mother took me to Claridge's when I was a boy and I saw a wonderful personage at the door whom I was pleased to call the King. Ever since then I have been going to Claridge's and while my first king is dead there is one in his place who bids fair to live long, albeit no one shouts encouragement to him. He wears the most gorgeous buttons I've ever seen, and I doubt if King Solomon himself could have been more regal. Certainly not Nebuchadnezzar. He works from seven in the morning until seven at night, and he has an imperial scorn for anything smaller than half a sovereign.

There were many letters waiting there for me, but not one from the Countess Aline. I had encouraged the hope that she might write to me; it was the least she could do in return for all that I had done for her, notwithstanding my wretched behaviour on the last day of our association. While I had undoubtedly offended in the most flagrant manner, still my act was not unpardonable. There was tribute, not outrage in my behaviour.

Poopendyke fidgeted a good deal with the scanty results of my literary labours, rattling the typed pages in a most insinuating way. He oiled his machine with accusative frequency, but I failed to respond. I was in no mood for writing. He said to me one day:

"I don't see why you keep a secretary, Mr. Smart. I don't begin to earn my salt."

"Salt, Mr. Poopendyke," said I, "is the cheapest thing I know of. Now if you had said pepper I might pause to reflect. But I am absolutely, inexorably opposed to rating anything on a salt basis. If you—"

"You know what I mean," he said stiffly. "I am of no use to you."

"Ah," said I triumphantly, "but you forget! Who is it that draws the salary checks for yourself and Britton, and who keeps the accounts straight? Who, I repeat? Why, you, Mr. Poopendyke. You draw the checks. Isn't that something?"

"If—if I didn't know you so well, I wouldn't hesitate to call you a blooming fool, Mr. Smart," said he, but he grinned as he said it.

"But he who hesitates is lost," said I. "This is your chance, don't let it slip." He looked at me so steadily for a moment that I was in some fear he would not let it slip.

Before I had been in London a week it became perfectly clear to me that I could not stretch my stay out to anything like a period of two months. Indeed, I began to think about booking my passage home inside of two weeks. I was restless, dissatisfied, homesick. On the ninth day I sent Poopendyke to the booking office of the steamship company with instructions to secure passage for the next sailing of the *Mauretania,* and then lived in a state of positive dread for fear the confounded American tourists might have gobbled up all of the cabins. They are always going home it seems to me, and they are always trying to get on a single unfortunate ship. In all my experience abroad, I've never known a time when Americans were not tumbling over each other trying to get back to New York in time to catch a certain train for home, wherever that may be. But Poopendyke managed it somehow. He must have resorted to bribery.

I awoke one morning to find a long and—I was about to say interesting—letter from the Countess! It was a very commonplace communication I found on the third or fourth reading. The sum and substance of its contents was the information that she was going to Virginia Hot Springs with the family for a month or two and that

Lord Amberdale was to join them there.

It appeared mat her father, being greatly overworked, was in need of a rest, and as the golf links at Hot Springs are especially designed to make it easy for rich men, his doctor had ordered him to that delightful resort. She hoped the rest would put him on his feet again. There was a page or so of drivel about Amberdale and what he expected to do at the New York Horse Show, a few lines concerning Rosemary; and a brief, almost curt intimation that a glimpse or two of me would not be altogether displeasing to her if I happened to be coming mat way.

It may be regarded as a strange coincidence that I instructed Britton that very evening to see that my golf clubs were cleaned up and put into good shape for a little practice on a course near London, where I had been put up by an English author, and who was forever ding-donging at me to come out and let him "put it all over me." I went out and bought a new brassie to replace the one destroyed by the experimenting Rocksworth youth, and before I got through with it had a new putter, a niblick and a spoon, neither of which I needed for the excellent reason that I already possessed a half dozen of each.

Keyed up to a high pitch of enthusiasm, I played golf for ten days, and found my friend to be a fine sportsman. Like all Englishmen, he took a beating gracefully, but gave me to understand that he had been having a good deal of trouble with rheumatism or neuritis in his right elbow. On the last day we played he succeeded in bringing me in two down and I've never seen neuritis dispersed so quickly as it was in his case. I remember distinctly that he complained bitterly of the pain in his elbow when we started out, and that he was as fit as a fiddle at the eighteenth hole. He even went so far as to implore me to stay over till the next sailing of the *Mauretania.*

But I took to the high seas. Mr. Poopendyke cabled to the Homestead at Hot Springs for suitable accommodations. I cannot remember when I had been so forehanded as all that, and I wonder what my secretary thought of me. My habit is to procrastinate.

I almost forgot to mention a trifling bit of news that came to me the day before sailing. Elsie Hazzard wrote in great perturbation and at almost unfeeling length to tell me that Count Tarnowsy had unearthed the supposedly mythical Rothhoefen treasure chests and was reputed to have found gold and precious jewels worth at least a million dollars. The accumulated products of a century's thievery! The hoard of all the robber barons! Tarnowsy's!

Strange to say I did not writhe nor snarl with disappointment and rage. I took the news with a *sang froid* that almost killed poor Poopendyke. He never quite got over it.

Nor was I especially disturbed or irritated by the telegram of condolence I received on board ship from Tarnowsy himself. He could not resist the temptation to gloat. I shall not repeat the message for the simple reason that I do not wish to dignify it by putting it into permanent form.

We were two days out when I succeeded in setting my mind at rest in respect to Aline, Countess Tarnowsy. I had not thought of it before, but I remembered all of a sudden that I held decided scruples against marrying a divorced woman. Of course, that simplified matters. When one has preconceived notions about such matters they afford excellent material to fall back upon, even though he may have disregarded them after a fashion while unselfishly thinking of some one else. As I say, the recollection of this well-defined though somewhat remorseless principle of mine had the effect of putting my mind at rest in regard to the Countess. Feeling as strongly as I did about marriage with divorcees, she became an absolutely undesirable person so far as matrimony was concerned. I experienced a rather doubtful feeling of relief. It was not so hard to say to myself that Lord Amberdale was welcome to her, but it was very, *very* difficult to refrain from adding the unamiable words: "damn him."

This rigid, puritanical principle of mine, however, did not declare against the unrighteousness of falling in love with a divorcee.

CHAPTER XX

I CHANGE GARDEN SPOTS

IF I have, by any chance, announced earlier in this narrative that the valley of the Donau is the garden spot of the world, I must now ask you to excuse the ebullience of spirit that prompted the declaration. The Warm Springs Valley of Virginia is infinitely more attractive to me, and I make haste to rectify any erroneous impression I may have given, while under the spell of something my natural modesty forbids me to describe.

If you happen not to know the Warm Springs Valley, permit me to say that you are missing a great deal. It is a garden spot and—but why discourse upon a subject that is so aptly handled by the gentlemen who supply railway folders with descriptive material and who will tell you in so many words that God's noblest work was done in the green hills and vales of fair Virginia? Any railway folder will acquaint you with all this and save me a great deal of time and trouble, besides giving you a sensible and adequate idea of how to get there and where to stop when you reach your journey's end, together with the price of Pullman tickets and the nature of the ailments you are supposed to have if you take the waters. It is only necessary for me to say that it is a garden spot and that you don't have to change cars if you take the right train out of New York City, a condition which does not obtain if you happen to approach from the opposite direction.

I arrived there early one bright November morning, three days after landing in New York. You will be rendered unhappy, I fear, by the announcement that I left Mr. Poopendyke behind. He preferred to visit an aunt at New Rochelle and I felt that he deserved a vacation. Britton, of course, accompanied me. He is indispensable, and, so far as I know, hasn't the faintest notion of what a vacation means unless he considers employment with me in some such light. At any rate he has never mentioned a relation in need of a visit from him.

Before leaving New York I had a rather unpleasant encounter with my publishers. It was in the nature of a luncheon at which I was led to believe that they still expected me to supply them with the manuscript of a novel at a very early date. They seemed considerably put out when I blandly informed them that I had got no farther along than the second chapter.

"We have been counting on this book of yours for January publication," said they.

I tried to explain that the muse had abandoned me in a most heartless fashion.

"But the public demands a story from you," said they. "What have you been doing all summer?"

"Romancing," said I.

I don't know just how it came about, but the suggestion was made that I put into narrative form the lively history of my sojourn on the banks of the Danube, trusting implicitly to me imagination yet leaving nothing to it.

"But it's all such blithering rot," said I.

"So much the better," said they triumphantly—even eagerly.

"I do not suppose that you, as publishers, can appreciate the fact that an author may have a soul above skittles," said I indignantly. "I cannot, I will not write a line about myself, gentlemen. Not that I consider the subject sacred but—"

"Wait!" cried the junior member, his face aglow. "We appreciate the delicacy of—er—your feelings, Mr. Smart, but I have an idea,—a splendid idea. It solves the whole question. Your secretary is a most competent, capable young man and a genius after a fashion. I propose that he write the story. We'll pay him a lump sum for the work, put your name on the cover, and there you are. All you will have to do is to edit his material. How's that?"

And so it came to pass that I took myself off that evening for Hot Springs, secure in the thought that Poopendyke would attend to my literary estate far more capably than I could do it myself, and that my labours later on would be pleasantly devoted to the lazy task of editing, revising and deleting a tale already told. . . .

If you are lucky enough to obtain rooms in the Homestead, looking out over the golf course, with the wonderful November colourings in the hills and gaps beyond; over the casino, the tennis courts and the lower levels of the fashionable playground, you may well say to yourself that all the world is bright and sweet and full of hope. From my windows I could see far down the historic valley in the direction of Warm Springs, a hazy blue panorama wrapped in the air of an Indian summer and redolent with the incense of autumn.

Britton reminded me that it was a grand morning for golf, and I was at once reminded that Britton is an excellent chap whose opinions are always worth considering. So I started for the links, stopping first at the office on my way out, ostensibly to complain about the absence of window-screens but in reality to glance over the register in quest of certain signatures.

A brisk, oldish little man came up beside me and rather testily inquired why the deuce there were no matches in his room; also why the hot water was cold so much longer than usual that morning. He was not much of a man to look at, but I could not fail to note the obsequious manner in which the two clerks behind the desk looked at him. You couldn't possibly have discovered anything in their manner to remind you of hotel clerks you may have come to know in your travels. A half dozen boxes of matches were passed out to him in the twinkling of an eye, and I shudder to think what might have happened if there had been a hot water faucet handy, they were so eager to please.

"Mr. Brewster gone out yet?" demanded this important guest, pocketing all of the matches. (I could see at once that he was a very rich man.) "Did he leave any message for me? He didn't? He was to let me know whether he could play golf with—eh? Playing with Logan, eh? Well, of all the—He knows I will **not** play with Logan. See if Mr. Scott is in his room. Tell him I'd like to take him on for eighteen holes this morning."

He crossed to the news-counter and glanced over the papers while a dusky bell-boy shot off in quest of Mr. Scott.

"They all hate to play with the old geezer," said one of the clerics,—a young one, you may be sure,—lowering his voice and his eyebrows at the same time.

"He's the rottenest player in the world."

"Who is he?" I inquired, mildly interested.

"Jasper Titus," was the reply. "The real old Jasper himself."

Before I could recover from my surprise, the object of my curiosity approached the desk, his watch in his hand.

"Well, what does he say?" he demanded.

"The—the boy isn't back yet, Mr. Titus," said one of the clerks, involuntarily pounding the call-bell in his nervousness.

"Lazy, shiftless niggers, the whole tribe of them," was Mr. Titus's caustic comment.

At that instant the boy, quite out of breath, came thumping down the stairs.

"Mr. Scott's got rheumatiz, Mr. Titus. He begs to be excused—"

"Buncombe!" snapped Mr. Titus. "He's afraid to play me. Well, this means no game for me. A beautiful day like this and—"

"I beg your pardon, Mr. Titus," said I, stepping forward. "If you don't mind taking on a stranger, I will be happy to go around with you. My name is Smart. I think you must have heard of me through the Countess and your—"

"Great Scott! Smart? Are—are you the author, James Byron Smart? The—the man who—" He checked himself suddenly, but seized me by the hand and, as he wrung it vigorously, dragged me out of hearing of the men behind the desk.

"I am John Bellamy Smart," said I, a little miffed.

His shrewd, hard old face underwent a marvellous change. The crustiness left it as if by magic. His countenance radiated joy.

"I owe you a debt of gratitude, Mr. Smart, that can never be lifted. My daughter has told me everything. You must have put up with a fearful lot of nonsense during the weeks she was with you. I know her well. She's spoiled and she's got a temper, although, upon my soul, she seems different nowadays. There *is* a change in her, by George."

"She's had her lesson," said I. "Besides I didn't find she had a bad temper."

"And say, I want to tell you something else before I forget it: I fully appreciate your views on international marriage. Allie told me everything you had to say about it. You must have rubbed it in! But I think it did her good. She'll never marry another foreigner if I can help it, if she **never** marries. Well, well, I **am** glad to see you, and to shake your hand. I—I wish I could really tell you how I feel toward you, my boy, but I—I don't seem to have the power to express myself. If I—"

I tried to convince him that the pleasure had been all mine, and then inquired for Mrs. Titus and the Countess.

"They're both here, but the good Lord only knows where. Mrs. Titus goes driving every morning. Roads are fine if you can stick to them. Aline said something last night about riding over to Fassifern this forenoon with Amberdale and young Skelly. Let's see, it's half-past ten. Yes, they've gone by this time. Why didn't you write or telegraph Aline? She'll be as mad as a wet hen when she finds you've come within out letting her know."

"I thought I should like to take her by surprise," I mumbled uncomfortably.

"And my son Jasper—why, he will explode when he hears you're here. He's gone over to Covington to see a girl off on the train for Louisville. You've never seen such a boy. He is always going to Covington with some girl to see that she gets the right train home. But why are we wasting time here when we might be doing a few holes before lunch? I'll take you on. Of course, you understand. I'm a wretched player, but I've got one virtue: I never talk about my game and I never tell funny stories while my opponent is addressing the ball. I'm an old duffer at the game, but I've got more sense than most duffers."

We sauntered down to the club house where he insisted on buying me a dozen golf balls and engaging a caddy for me by the week. Up to the moment we stepped up to the first tee he talked incessantly of Aline and Rosemary, but the instant the game was on he settled, into the grim reserve that characterises the man who takes any enterprise seriously, be it work or play.

I shall not discuss our game, further than to say that he played in atrociously bad form but with a purpose that let me, to some degree, into the secret of his success in life. If I do say it myself, I am a fairly good player. My driving is consistently long. It may not be difficult for even you who do not go in for golf to appreciate the superior patience of a man whose tee shots are rarely short of two hundred and twenty yards when he is obliged to amble along doing nothing while his opponent is striving to cover the same distance in three or four shots, not counting the misses. But I was patient, agreeably patient, not to say tolerant. I don't believe I was ever in a better humour than on this gay November morn. I even apologised for Mr. Titus's execrable foozles; I amiably suggested that he was a little off his game and that he'd soon strike his gait and give me a sound beating after the turn. His smile was polite but ironic, and it was not long before I realised that he knew his own game too well to be affected by cajolery. He just pegged away, always playing the odd or worse, uncomplaining, unresentful, as even-tempered as the May wind, and never by any chance winning a hole from me. He was the rarest "duffer" it has ever been my good fortune to meet. As a rule, the poorer the player the louder his execrations. Jasper Titus was one of the worst players I've ever seen, but he was the personification of gentility, even under the most provoking circumstances. For instance, at the famous "Crater," it was my good fortune to pitch a ball fairly on the green from the tee. His mashie shot landed his ball about twenty feet up the steep hill which guards the green. It rolled halfway back. Without a word of disgust, or so much as a scowl, he climbed up and blazed away at it again, not once but fourteen times by actual count. On the seventeenth stroke he triumphantly laid his ball on the green. Most men would have lifted and conceded the hole to me. He played it out.

"A man never gets anywhere, Mr. Smart," said he, unruffled by his miserable exhibition, "unless he keeps plugging away at a thing. That's my principle in life. Keep at it. There is satisfaction in putting the damned ball in the hole, even if it does require twenty strokes. You did it in three, but you'll soon forget the feat. I'm not likely to forget the troubles I had going down in twenty, and there lies the secret of success. If success comes easy, we pass it off with a laugh, if it comes hard we grit our teeth and remember the ways and means. You may not believe it, but I took thirty-three strokes for that hole one day last week. Day before yesterday I did it in four. Perhaps it wouldn't occur to you to think that it's a darned sight easier to do it in four than it is in thirty-three. Get the idea?"

"I think I do, Mr. Titus," said I. "The things that 'come easy' are never appreciated."

"Right, my boy. It's what we have to work for like nailers that we lie awake thinking about."

We came out upon the eminence overlooking the next hole, which lay far below us. As I stooped to tee-up my ball, a gleeful shout came up the hillside.

"Hello, John Bellamy!"

Glancing down, I saw Jasper, Jr., at the edge of the wagon road. He was waving his cap and, even at that distance, I could see the radiance in his good-looking young face. A young and attractively dressed woman stood beside him. I waved my hand and shouted a greeting.

"I thought you said he'd gone to Covington to see her off," I said, turning to the young man's father with a grin.

"Not the same girl," said he succinctly, squinting his eyes. "That's the little Parsons girl from Richmond. He was to *meet* her at Covington. Jasper is a scientific butterfly. He makes both ends meet,—nearly always. Now no one but a genius could have fixed it up to see one girl off and meet another on the same train."

Later on, Jasper, Jr., and I strolled over to the casino verandah, the chatty Miss Parsons between us, but leaning a shade nearer to young Titus than to me, although she appeared to be somewhat overwhelmed at meeting a real live author. Mr. Titus, as was his habit, hurried on ahead of us. I afterwards discovered he had a dread of pneumonia.

"Aline never said a word about your coming, John," said Jasper, Jr. He called me John with considerable gusto. "She's learning how to hold her tongue."

"It happens that she didn't know I was coming," said I drily. He whistled.

"She's off somewhere with Amberdale. Ever meet him? He's one of the finest chaps I know. You'll like him, Miss Parsons. He's not at all like a Britisher."

"But I like the British," said she.

"Then I'll tell him to spread it on a bit," said Jappy obligingly. "Great horseman, he is. Got some ripping nags in the New York show next week, and he rides like a dream. Watch him pull down a few ribbons and rosettes. Sure thing."

"Your father told me that the Countess was off riding with him and another chap,—off to Fassifern, I believe."

"For luncheon. They do it three or four times a week. Not for me. I like waiters with shirt fronts and nickle tags."

Alone with me in the casino half an hour later, he announced that it really looked serious, this affair between Aline and his lordship.

I tried to appear indifferent,—a rather pale effort, I fear.

"I think I am in on the secret, Jappy," said I soberly.

He stared. "Has she ever said anything to you, old chap, that would lead you to believe she's keen about him?"

I temporised. "She's keen about somebody, my son; that's as far as I will go."

"Then it must be Amberdale. I'm on to her all right, all right. I know women. She's in love, hang it all. If you know a thing about 'em, you can spot the symptoms without the x-rays. I've been hoping against hope, old man. I don't want her to marry again. She's had all the hell she's entitled to. What's the matter with women, anyhow? They no sooner get out of one muddle than they begin looking around for another. Can't be satisfied with good luck."

"But every one speaks very highly of Lord Amberdale. I'm sure she can't be making a mistake in marrying him."

"I wish she'd pick out a good, steady, simplified American, just as an experiment. We're not so darned bad, you know. Women can do worse than to marry Americans."

"It is a matter of opinion, I fancy. At any rate we can't go about picking out husbands for people who have minds of their own."

"Well, some one in our family picked out a lemon for Aline the first time, let me tell you that," said he, scowling.

"And she's doing the picking for herself this time, I gather."

"I suppose so," said he gloomily.

I have visited the popular and almost historic Fassifern farm a great many times in my short career, but for the life of me I cannot understand what attraction it possesses that could induce people to go there for luncheon and then spend a whole afternoon lolling about the place. But that seems to have been precisely what the Countess and his lordship did on the day of my arrival at the Homestead. The "other chap," Skerry, came riding home alone at three o'clock. She did not return until nearly six. By that time I was in a state of suppressed fury that almost drove me to the railway station with a single and you might say childish object in view.

I had a pleasant visit with Mrs. Titus, who seemed overjoyed to see me. In fact, I had luncheon with her. Mr. Titus, it appeared, never ate luncheon. He had a dread of typhoid, I believe, and as he already possessed gout and insomnia and an intermittent tendency to pain in his abdomen, and couldn't drink anything alcoholic or eat anything starchy, I found myself wondering what he really did for a living.

Mrs. Titus talked a great deal about Lord Amberdale. She was most tiresome after the first half hour, but I must say that the luncheon was admirable. I happened to be hungry. Having quite made up my mind that Aline was going to marry

Amberdale, I proceeded to upset the theory that a man in love is a creature without gastronomical aspirations by vulgarly stuffing myself with half a lamb chop, a slice of buttered bread and nine pickles.

"Aline will be glad to see you again, Mr. Smart," said she amiably. "She was speaking of you only a day or two ago."

"Was she?" I inquired, with sudden interest which I contrived to conceal.

"Yes. She was wondering why you have never thought of marrying."

I closed my eyes for a second, and the piece of bread finally found the right channel.

"And what did you say to that?" I asked quietly.

She was disconcerted. "I? Oh, I think I said you didn't approve of marrying except for love, Mr. Smart."

"Um!" said I. "Love on both sides is the better way to put it."

"Am I to infer that you may have experienced a one-sided leaning toward matrimony?"

"So far as I know, I have been singularly unsupported, Mrs. Titus."

"You really ought to marry."

"Perhaps I may. Who knows?"

"Aline said you would make an excellent husband."

"By that she means a stupid one, I suppose. Excellent husbands are invariably stupid. They always want to stay at home."

She appeared thoughtful. "And expect their wives to stay at home too."

"On the contrary, an excellent husband lets his wife go where she likes—without him."

"I am afraid you do not understand matrimony, Mr. Smart," she said, and changed the subject.

I am afraid that my mind wandered a little at this juncture, for I missed fire on one or two direct questions. Mrs. Titus was annoyed; it would not be just to her to say that she was offended. If she could but have known that my thoughts were of the day and minute when I so brutally caressed the Countess Tarnowsy, I fancy she would have changed her good opinion of me. To tell the truth, I was wondering just how the Countess would behave toward me, with the memory of that unforgettable incident standing between us. I had been trying to convince myself for a very long time that my fault was not as great in her eyes as it was in mine.

Along about five o'clock, I went to my room. I daresay I was sulking. A polite bell-boy tapped on my door at half-past six. He presented a small envelope to me, thanked me three or four times, and, as an afterthought, announced that there was to be an answer. Whereupon I read the Countess's note with a magnificently unreadable face.

I cleared my throat, and (I think) squared my shoulders somewhat as a soldier does when he is being commended for valour, and said:

"Present my compliments to the Countess, and say that Mr. Smart will be down in five minutes."

The boy stared. "The—the what, sir?"

"The *what?*" I demanded.

"I mean the *who,* sir."

"The Countess. The lady who sent you up with this note."

"Wasn't no Countess sent me up hyer, boss. It was Miss Tarsney."

Somehow staggered, I managed to wave my hand comprehensively.

"Never mind. Just say that I'll be down in two minutes."

He grinned. "I reckon I'd better hustle, or you'll beat me down, boss."

CHAPTER XXI

SHE PROPOSES

She was still in her riding habit when I found her alone in the parlour of the Titus suite.

I give you my word my heart almost stopped beating. I've never seen any one so lovely as she was at that moment. *Never,* I repeat. Her hair, blown by the kind November winds, strayed--but no! I cannot begin to define the loveliness of her. There was a warm, rich glow in her cheeks and a light in her eyes that actually bewildered me, and more than that I am not competent to utter.

"You have come at last," she said, and her voice sounded very far off; although I was lifting her ungloved hand to my lips. She clenched my fingers tightly, I remember that; and also that my hand shook violently and that my face *felt* pale.

I think I said that I had come at last. She took my other hand in hers and drawing dangerously close to me said:

"I do not expect to be married for at least a year, John."

"I—I congratulate you," I stammered foolishly.

"I have a feeling that it isn't decent for one to marry inside of two years after one has been divorced."

"How is Rosemary?" I murmured.

"You *are* in love with me, aren't you, John, dear?"

"Goo—good heaven!" I gasped.

"I *know* you are. That's why I am so sure of myself. Is it asking too much of you to marry me in a year from—"

I haven't the faintest notion how long afterward it was that I asked her what was to become of that poor, unlucky devil, Lord Amberdale.

"He isn't a devil. He's a dear, and he is going to marry a bred-in-the-bone countess next January. You will like him, because he is every bit as much in love with his real countess are you are with a sham one. He is a bird of your feather. And now don't you want to come with me to see Rosemary?"

"Rosemary," I murmured, as in a dream—a luxurious lotus-born dream.

She took my arm and advanced with me into a room adjoining the parlour. As we passed through the door, she suddenly squeezed my arm very tightly and laid her head against my shoulder.

We were in a small sitting-room, confronting Jasper Titus, his wife and his tiny grand-daughter, who was ready for bed.

"You won't have to worry about me any longer, daddy dear," said Aline, her voice suddenly breaking.

"Well, I'll be—well, well, well!" cried my late victim of the links. "Is **this** the way the wind blows?"

I was perfectly dumb. My face was scarlet. My dazzled eyes saw nothing but the fine, aristocratic features of Aline's mother. She was leaning slightly forward in her chair, and a slow but unmistakable joyous smile was creeping into her face.

"Aline!" she cried, and Aline went to her.

Jasper Titus led Rosemary up to me.

"Kiss the gentleman, kiddie," said he huskily, lifting the little one up to me.

She gave a sudden shriek of recognition, and I took her in my arms.

"Ha! ha! ha!" laughed I, without the slightest idea of what I was doing or why I did it. Sometimes I wonder if there has ever been any insanity in our family. I know there have been fools, for I have my Uncle Rilas's word for it.

Mr. Titus picked up the newspaper he had been reading.

"Listen to this, Allie. It will interest you. It says here that our friend Tarnowsy is going to marry that fool of a Cincinnati girl we were talking about the other day. I know her father, but I've never met her mother. Old Bob Thackery has got millions but he's only got one daughter. What a blamed shame!"

It must be perfectly obvious to you, kind reader, that I am going to marry Aline Tarnowsy, in spite of all my professed opposition to marrying a divorcee. I argued the whole matter out with myself, but not until after I was irrevocably committed. She says she needs me. Well, isn't that enough? In fact, I am now trying my best to get her to shorten the probationary period. She has taken off three months, God bless her, but I still hope for a further and more generous reduction—for good behaviour!

THE END

The Codes Of Hammurabi And Moses
W. W. Davies

QTY

The discovery of the Hammurabi Code is one of the greatest achievements of archaeology, and is of paramount interest, not only to the student of the Bible, but also to all those interested in ancient history...

Religion   **ISBN:** *1-59462-338-4*

Pages:132
MSRP $12.95

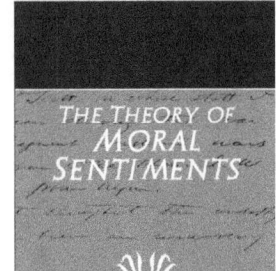

The Theory of Moral Sentiments
Adam Smith

QTY

This work from 1749. contains original theories of conscience amd moral judgment and it is the foundation for systemof morals.

Philosophy **ISBN:** *1-59462-777-0*

Pages:536
MSRP $19.95

Jessica's First Prayer
Hesba Stretton

QTY

In a screened and secluded corner of one of the many railway-bridges which span the streets of London there could be seen a few years ago, from five o'clock every morning until half past eight, a tidily set-out coffee-stall, consisting of a trestle and board, upon which stood two large tin cans, with a small fire of charcoal burning under each so as to keep the coffee boiling during the early hours of the morning when the work-people were thronging into the city on their way to their daily toil...

Childrens   **ISBN:** *1-59462-373-2*

Pages:84
MSRP $9.95

My Life and Work
Henry Ford

QTY

Henry Ford revolutionized the world with his implementation of mass production for the Model T automobile. Gain valuable business insight into his life and work with his own auto-biography... "We have only started on our development of our country we have not as yet, with all our talk of wonderful progress, done more than scratch the surface. The progress has been wonderful enough but..."

Biographies/   **ISBN:** *1-59462-198-5*

Pages:300
MSRP $21.95

The Art of Cross-Examination
Francis Wellman

QTY

I presume it is the experience of every author, after his first book is published upon an important subject, to be almost overwhelmed with a wealth of ideas and illustrations which could readily have been included in his book, and which to his own mind, at least, seem to make a second edition inevitable. Such certainly was the case with me; and when the first edition had reached its sixth impression in five months, I rejoiced to learn that it seemed to my publishers that the book had met with a sufficiently favorable reception to justify a second and considerably enlarged edition. ..

Pages:412

Reference   **ISBN: *1-59462-647-2***   *MSRP $19.95*

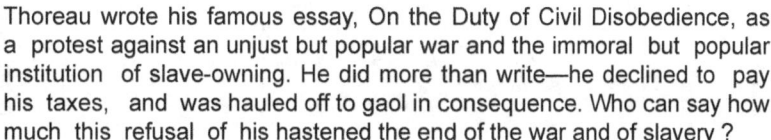

On the Duty of Civil Disobedience
Henry David Thoreau

QTY

Thoreau wrote his famous essay, On the Duty of Civil Disobedience, as a protest against an unjust but popular war and the immoral but popular institution of slave-owning. He did more than write—he declined to pay his taxes, and was hauled off to gaol in consequence. Who can say how much this refusal of his hastened the end of the war and of slavery ?

Law   **ISBN: *1-59462-747-9***   **Pages:48**

MSRP $7.45

Dream Psychology Psychoanalysis for Beginners
Sigmund Freud

QTY

Sigmund Freud, born Sigismund Schlomo Freud (May 6, 1856 - September 23, 1939), was a Jewish-Austrian neurologist and psychiatrist who co-founded the psychoanalytic school of psychology. Freud is best known for his theories of the unconscious mind, especially involving the mechanism of repression; his redefinition of sexual desire as mobile and directed towards a wide variety of objects; and his therapeutic techniques, especially his understanding of transference in the therapeutic relationship and the presumed value of dreams as sources of insight into unconscious desires.

Pages:196

Psychology   **ISBN: *1-59462-905-6***   *MSRP $15.45*

The Miracle of Right Thought
Orison Swett Marden

QTY

Believe with all of your heart that you will do what you were made to do. When the mind has once formed the habit of holding cheerful, happy, prosperous pictures, it will not be easy to form the opposite habit. It does not matter how improbable or how far away this realization may see, or how dark the prospects may be, if we visualize them as best we can, as vividly as possible, hold tenaciously to them and vigorously struggle to attain them, they will gradually become actualized, realized in the life. But a desire, a longing without endeavor, a yearning abandoned or held indifferently will vanish without realization.

Pages:360

Self Help   **ISBN: *1-59462-644-8***   *MSRP $25.45*

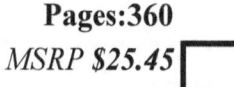

www.bookjungle.com *email: sales@bookjungle.com fax: 630-214-0564 mail: Book Jungle PO Box 2226 Champaign, IL 61825*

QTY

The Rosicrucian Cosmo-Conception Mystic Christianity *by Max Heindel* ISBN: *1-59462-188-8* **$38.95**
The Rosicrucian Cosmo-conception is not dogmatic, neither does it appeal to any other authority than the reason of the student. It is: not controversial, but is: sent forth in the, hope that it may help to clear... New Age/Religion Pages 646

Abandonment To Divine Providence *by Jean-Pierre de Caussade* ISBN: *1-59462-228-0* **$25.95**
"The Rev. Jean Pierre de Caussade was one of the most remarkable spiritual writers of the Society of Jesus in France in the 18th Century. His death took place at Toulouse in 1751. His works have gone through many editions and have been republished... Inspirational/Religion Pages 400

Mental Chemistry *by Charles Haanel* ISBN: *1-59462-192-6* **$23.95**
Mental Chemistry allows the change of material conditions by combining and appropriately utilizing the power of the mind. Much like applied chemistry creates something new and unique out of careful combinations of chemicals the mastery of mental chemistry... New Age Pages 354

The Letters of Robert Browning and Elizabeth Barret Barrett 1845-1846 vol II ISBN: *1-59462-193-4* **$35.95**
by Robert Browning and Elizabeth Barrett Biographies Pages 596

Gleanings In Genesis (volume I) *by Arthur W. Pink* ISBN: *1-59462-130-6* **$27.45**
Appropriately has Genesis been termed "the seed plot of the Bible" for in it we have, in germ form, almost all of the great doctrines which are afterwards fully developed in the books of Scripture which follow... Religion/Inspirational Pages 420

The Master Key *by L. W. de Laurence* ISBN: *1-59462-001-6* **$30.95**
In no branch of human knowledge has there been a more lively increase of the spirit of research during the past few years than in the study of Psychology, Concentration and Mental Discipline. The requests for authentic lessons in Thought Control, Mental Discipline and... New Age/Business Pages 422

The Lesser Key Of Solomon Goetia *by L. W. de Laurence* ISBN: *1-59462-092-X* **$9.95**
This translation of the first book of the "Lemegton" which is now for the first time made accessible to students of Talismanic Magic was done, after careful collation and edition, from numerous Ancient Manuscripts in Hebrew, Latin, and French... New Age/Occult Pages 92

Rubaiyat Of Omar Khayyam *by Edward Fitzgerald* ISBN: *1-59462-332-5* **$13.95**
Edward Fitzgerald, whom the world has already learned, in spite of his own efforts to remain within the shadow of anonymity, to look upon as one of the rarest poets of the century, was born at Bredfield, in Suffolk, on the 31st of March, 1809. He was the third son of John Purcell... Music Pages 172

Ancient Law *by Henry Maine* ISBN: *1-59462-128-4* **$29.95**
The chief object of the following pages is to indicate some of the earliest ideas of mankind, as they are reflected in Ancient Law, and to point out the relation of those ideas to modern thought. Religion/History Pages 452

Far-Away Stories *by William J. Locke* ISBN: *1-59462-129-2* **$19.45**
"Good wine needs no bush, but a collection of mixed vintages does. And this book is just such a collection. Some of the stories I do not want to remain buried for ever in the museum files of dead magazine-numbers an author's not unpardonable vanity..." Fiction Pages 272

Life of David Crockett *by David Crockett* ISBN: *1-59462-250-7* **$27.45**
"Colonel David Crockett was one of the most remarkable men of the times in which he lived. Born in humble life, but gifted with a strong will, an indomitable courage, and unremitting perseverance... Biographies/New Age Pages 424

Lip-Reading *by Edward Nitchie* ISBN: *1-59462-206-X* **$25.95**
Edward B. Nitchie, founder of the New York School for the Hard of Hearing, now the Nitchie School of Lip-Reading, Inc, wrote "LIP-READING Principles and Practice". The development and perfecting of this meritorious work on lip-reading was an undertaking... How-to Pages 400

A Handbook of Suggestive Therapeutics, Applied Hypnotism, Psychic Science ISBN: *1-59462-214-0* **$24.95**
by Henry Munro Health/New Age/Health/Self-help Pages 376

A Doll's House: and Two Other Plays *by Henrik Ibsen* ISBN: *1-59462-112-8* **$19.95**
Henrik Ibsen created this classic when in revolutionary 1848 Rome. Introducing some striking concepts in playwriting for the realist genre, this play has been studied the world over. Fiction/Classics/Plays 308

The Light of Asia *by sir Edwin Arnold* ISBN: *1-59462-204-3* **$13.95**
In this poetic masterpiece, Edwin Arnold describes the life and teachings of Buddha. The man who was to become known as Buddha to the world was born as Prince Gautama of India but he rejected the worldly riches and abandoned the reigns of power when... Religion/History/Biographies Pages 170

The Complete Works of Guy de Maupassant *by Guy de Maupassant* ISBN: *1-59462-157-8* **$16.95**
"For days and days, nights and nights, I had dreamed of that first kiss which was to consecrate our engagement, and I knew not on what spot I should put my lips..." Fiction/Classics Pages 240

The Art of Cross-Examination *by Francis L. Wellman* ISBN: *1-59462-309-0* **$26.95**
Written by a renowned trial lawyer, Wellman imparts his experience and uses case studies to explain how to use psychology to extract desired information through questioning. How-to/Science/Reference Pages 408

Answered or Unanswered? *by Louisa Vaughan* ISBN: *1-59462-248-5* **$10.95**
Miracles of Faith in China Religion Pages 112

The Edinburgh Lectures on Mental Science (1909) *by Thomas* ISBN: *1-59462-008-3* **$11.95**
This book contains the substance of a course of lectures recently given by the writer in the Queen Street Hall, Edinburgh. Its purpose is to indicate the Natural Principles governing the relation between Mental Action and Material Conditions... New Age/Psychology Pages 148

Ayesha *by H. Rider Haggard* ISBN: *1-59462-301-5* **$24.95**
Verily and indeed it is the unexpected that happens! Probably if there was one person upon the earth from whom the Editor of this, and of a certain previous history, did not expect to hear again... Classics Pages 380

Ayala's Angel *by Anthony Trollope* ISBN: *1-59462-352-X* **$29.95**
The two girls were both pretty, but Lucy who was twenty-one who supposed to be simple and comparatively unattractive, whereas Ayala was credited, as her Bombwhat romantic name might show, with poetic charm and a taste for romance. Ayala when her father died was nineteen... Fiction Pages 484

The American Commonwealth *by James Bryce* ISBN: *1-59462-286-8* **$34.45**
An interpretation of American democratic political theory. It examines political mechanics and society from the perspective of Scotsman James Bryce Politics Pages 572

Stories of the Pilgrims *by Margaret P. Pumphrey* ISBN: *1-59462-116-0* **$17.95**
This book explores pilgrims religious oppression in England as well as their escape to Holland and eventual crossing to America on the Mayflower, and their early days in New England... History Pages 268

QTY

The Fasting Cure *by Sinclair Upton*   ISBN: *1-59462-222-1*   **$13.95**

In the Cosmopolitan Magazine for May, 1910, and in the Contemporary Review (London) for April, 1910, I published an article dealing with my experiences in fasting. I have written a great many magazine articles, but never one which attracted so much attention... New Age/Self Help/Health Pages 164

Hebrew Astrology *by Sepharial*   ISBN: *1-59462-308-2*   **$13.45**

In these days of advanced thinking it is a matter of common observation that we have left many of the old landmarks behind and that we are now pressing forward to greater heights and to a wider horizon than that which represented the mind-content of our progenitors...   Astrology Pages 144

Thought Vibration or The Law of Attraction in the Thought World   ISBN: *1-59462-127-6*   **$12.95**

by William Walker Atkinson   *Psychology/Religion Pages 144*

Optimism *by Helen Keller*   ISBN: *1-59462-108-X*   **$15.95**

Helen Keller was blind, deaf, and mute since 19 months old, yet famously learned how to overcome these handicaps, communicate with the world, and spread her lectures promoting optimism. An inspiring read for everyone...   Biographies/Inspirational Pages 84

Sara Crewe *by Frances Burnett*   ISBN: *1-59462-360-0*   **$9.45**

In the first place, Miss Minchin lived in London. Her home was a large, dull, tall one, in a large, dull square, where all the houses were alike, and all the sparrows were alike, and where all the door-knockers made the same heavy sound...   Childrens/Classic Pages 88

The Autobiography of Benjamin Franklin *by Benjamin Franklin*   ISBN: *1-59462-135-7*   **$24.95**

The Autobiography of Benjamin Franklin has probably been more extensively read than any other American historical work, and no other book of its kind has had such ups and downs of fortune. Franklin lived for many years in England, where he was agent...   Biographies/History Pages 332

Name	
Email	
Telephone	
Address	
City, State ZIP	

☐ **Credit Card**   ☐ **Check / Money Order**

Credit Card Number	
Expiration Date	
Signature	

Please Mail to: Book Jungle
PO Box 2226
Champaign, IL 61825
or Fax to: 630-214-0564

ORDERING INFORMATION

web*: www.bookjungle.com*
email*: sales@bookjungle.com*
fax*: 630-214-0564*
mail*: Book Jungle PO Box 2226 Champaign, IL 61825*
or PayPal *to sales@bookjungle.com*

Please contact us for bulk discounts

DIRECT-ORDER TERMS

**20% Discount if You Order
Two or More Books**
Free Domestic Shipping!
Accepted: Master Card, Visa,
Discover, American Express

www.ingramcontent.com/pod-product-compliance
Lightning Source LLC
Chambersburg PA
CBHW081353050726

47504CB00015B/1974